The

DEVIL'S FEAST

ALSO BY M. J. CARTER

FICTION

The Infidel Stain

The Strangler Vine

NONFICTION (AS MIRANDA CARTER)

Anthony Blunt: His Lives

George, Nicholas and Wilhelm: Three Royal Cousins and the Road to World War I

The
DEVIL'S FEAST

M. J. CARTER

G. P. PUTNAM'S SONS
New York

PUTNAM

G. P. PUTNAM'S SONS
Publishers Since 1838
An imprint of Penguin Random House LLC
375 Hudson Street
New York, New York 10014

Originally published in the United Kingdom by Fig Tree 2016
First U.S. edition published by G. P. Putnam's Sons in 2017

Library of Congress Cataloging-in-Publication Data

Names: Carter, Miranda, author.
Title: The Devil's feast / M. J. Carter.
Description: New York : G. P. Putnam's Sons, 2017.
Identifiers: LCCN 2016040951| ISBN 9780399171697 (hardcover) |
ISBN 9780698168756 (epub) Subjects: LCSH: Private investigators—
England—London—19th-Century—Fiction. | Murder—Investigation—Fiction. |
Celebrity Chefs—Fiction. | Private clubs—England—London—Fiction. |
BISAC: FICTION / Mystery & Detective / Historical. | FICTION /
Mystery & Detective / General. | GSAFD: Mystery fiction.
Classification: LCC PR6103.A7735 D48 2017 | DDC 823/.92—dc23
LC record available at https://lccn.loc.gov/2016040951
p. cm.

Printed in the United States of America
1 3 5 7 9 10 8 6 4 2

BOOK DESIGN BY MEIGHAN CAVANAUGH

The

DEVIL'S FEAST

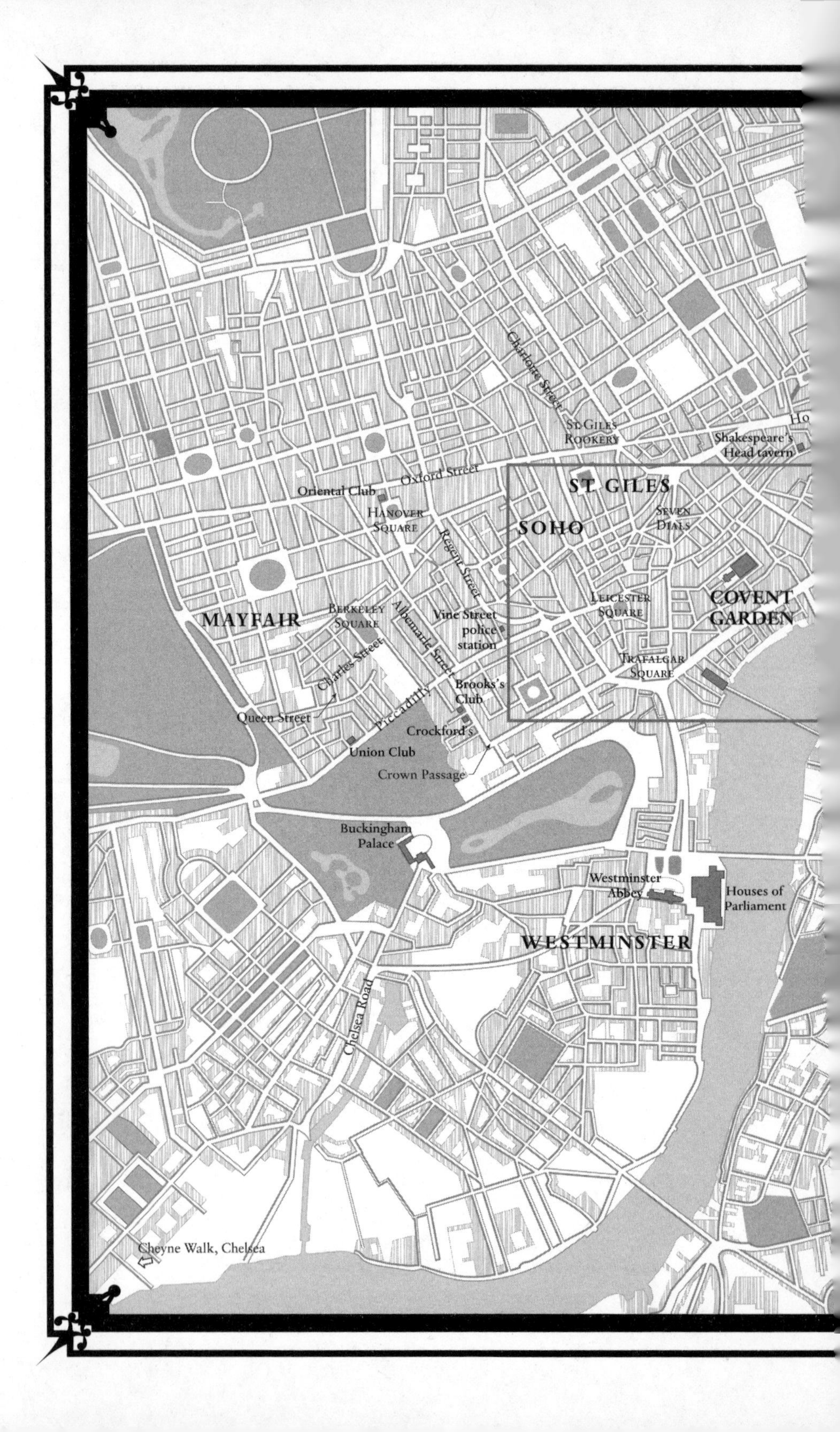
Charlotte Street
St Giles Rookery
Shakespeare's Head tavern
Oxford Street
Oriental Club
Hanover Square
ST GILES
SOHO
Seven Dials
Regent Street
MAYFAIR
Berkeley Square
Albemarle Street
Vine Street police station
Leicester Square
COVENT GARDEN
Charles Street
Trafalgar Square
Brooks's Club
Piccadilly
Queen Street
Crockford's
Union Club
Crown Passage
Buckingham Palace
Westminster Abbey
Houses of Parliament
WESTMINSTER
Chelsea Road
Cheyne Walk, Chelsea

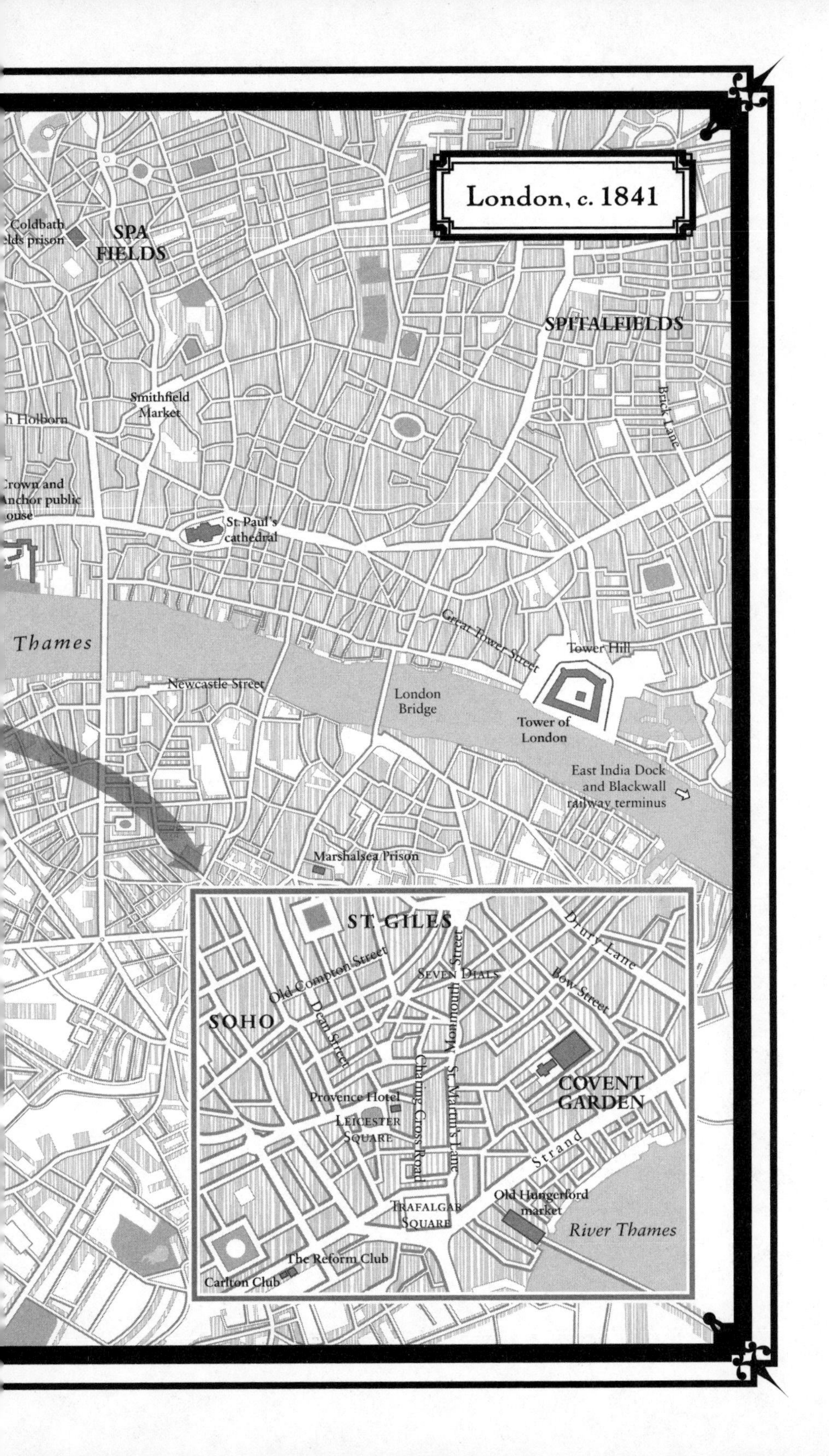

London, c. 1841
Coldbath
elds prison
SPA
FIELDS
SPITALFIELDS
Smithfield
Market
h Holborn
Brick Lane
Crown and
Anchor public
ouse
St. Paul's
cathedral
Thames
Great Tower Street
Tower Hill
Newcastle Street
London
Bridge
Tower of
London
East India Dock
and Blackwall
railway terminus
Marshalsea Prison
ST. GILES
Drury Lane
Old Compton Street
SEVEN DIALS
Monmouth Street
Bow Street
SOHO
Dean Street
Charing Cross Road
St. Martin's Lane
COVENT
GARDEN
Provence Hotel
LEICESTER
SQUARE
Strand
Old Hungerford
market
TRAFALGAR
SQUARE
River Thames
The Reform Club
Carlton Club

Prologue

The fire in the grate had burned itself down to a series of glimmering embers in among the drifts of ash, and the room was now dark, save for the candle. The one small window high in the wall brought in the evening's cold, for the nights were still sharp.

He shivered.

The room was mean and ill-kempt and well below his station. The floor was covered in dust and debris and the walls bloomed with mildew, but it served his purpose well enough. For furniture, there was a worn cane chair, a deal table and on one wall two stained and dusty shelves. On the table, carefully arranged in a line and neatly labeled, were several bottles and boxes. In front of these were four bowls and four teaspoons—too fine for their surroundings—two sets of metal tongs, a plate on which lay part of a stale loaf of bread and a bottle of beer, opened.

On the shelves behind, there were two long, well-used leather cases. One contained a hacksaw with several spare blades; in the other, upon old but beautiful watered silk, were two knives with bone handles and long, thin, well-polished blades, sharp on the side and blunt at the tip.

He bent over the table, squinting in the half-light, the candle flickering in the draft, as he sought the correct bottle, ignoring the scratchings and whimpers. Finding it, he pulled off the top and poured out a heaped spoonful of white powder and tipped it into a clean bowl. He again perused the bottles and boxes. Hovering between two, he finally took up a slim blue bottle, and with a fresh spoon scooped out more powder and decanted this into another bowl. Into both bowls he then poured a generous helping of beer.

He sat and watched.

The two dogs were hard-tethered against the bare brick on either side of the hearth. The one on the right sat complacently, maw open, tongue lolling, expectant, its thick coat and rolls of fat cushioning it against the rough floor. The other was a sorry beast, crazed with hunger, frantic at one moment, listless the next. Now it was dashing its head from side to side and issuing a low growl. Its eyes were bloodshot and its hair was mangy across its hollow haunches. Had it been shaken, its ribs would have rattled. It was only the short leash and the muzzle tight round its jaw that kept it in check. He imagined the animal loose, falling upon him, its foul breath in his face, its fangs meeting in his neck.

On the other side of the room, the two rats lay in their cages: one lazy, fat and well-fed, the other ugly, starved and desperate.

"Not long now," he said to the room.

The mixtures had sat long enough; it was time. He took up the stale bread and broke it into four pieces, placing two in each bowl to soak up the liquid. Then he seized one pair of tongs, picked up a piece of dripping bread and set it down before the fat dog; the other he dropped before the hungry dog, taking care to evade its snapping jaws. The first idly nosed the offering, while the starving one had snapped it up almost before he had snatched back the tongs. The first dog continued to sniff its portion quizzically for some time, before slurping it up with its tongue.

Now the rats. He unhooked the top of each pen, placing the morsel before each one. The starved rat leaped up, its claws and teeth scrabbling for bare flesh. But when the bread landed, the famished creature gobbled the whole thing in one gulp. Meanwhile, the fat one sniffed its portion fastidiously, then turned away from it. He considered for a moment, then took the honey he had brought and spooned a little over the bread. The rat returned, sniffed consideringly, then started upon the bread with small, precise bites.

He took to his chair. He waited.

The starving rat was first. Within a few minutes it began to twitch and squeak piteously. When he held the candle above it, its little jaws bared involuntarily. A few moments later its whole body spasmed as if it were being stretched on an invisible rack. When this passed, it thrashed about and clawed, first at its belly, then at its face, until it was taken by another violent seizure. This brought back the rictus grin but also caused the rat's head and spine to bend backward into a hideous, trembling arch. It gasped for air, producing a pathetic, breathless hawking. He watched, fascinated, as despite its weakness and hunger, it fought vainly against its fate.

By now, the cadaverous dog was in distress. It forced itself up, pulling against its leash, and coughed up a thin spew of yellow liquid. Within two or three minutes it was unsteady on its feet and had begun to froth about the mouth, choking and gasping. It staggered a few steps and fell, lying on its side, one front paw clawing at its neck and chest, the other scratching uselessly at the wall. The well-fed hound began perhaps ten or fifteen minutes later, whimpering and barking as the burning began in its stomach.

To his surprise and satisfaction, the fat rat's symptoms came last of all. It, too, began to writhe, its little body rolling around and convulsing in its cage. He watched them all silently, as their struggles waxed and waned. The starving rat succumbed first, falling upon its back, as a series of final spasms finished it off. The dogs continued to writhe and bark and whine.

He looked up at the small window, his concern that they might be heard outside getting the better of him. He tiptoed up the broken steps. Outside, the street was filled with night sounds and traffic: he need not have worried. He descended again, listening out for barking, but the creatures were now quiet. When he re-entered the room, the hungry dog was in its last struggles, surrounded by a pool of filth; the fat one had quite given up.

The smell was unpleasant, to say the least. But the result was just as he had hoped. Hungry or well fed, they had all succumbed more or less at the same time, and in the same way.

"A step closer," he whispered to himself, and gave himself up to a moment of exultation.

PART ONE

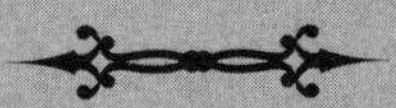

Chapter One

I stood on the south side of the Thames—"over the water," the locals call it—by London Bridge, looking at the north bank. They say it is one of the great sights of the world. It was certainly one of the most congested. Lining the shore, wharves and warehouses crushed against each other, and below them the sides of the slick, viscous river were crowded so deeply with ships and barges that only a narrow channel in the middle remained, through which, nose to tail, skiffs and steamships all passed. In India, I had seen wider rivers and bigger vistas, but nothing compared with the scale of human activity upon and around the banks of the Thames. Only the view upward at the high panorama of the city, the dozen needle spires and the dome of St. Paul's reaching up out of the smut, gave any sense of tranquility.

I turned away from the river and jostled my way down Borough High Street for some few hundred yards, then turned right into the streets west of the coaching inns, into that place that had once been the haunt of fugitives and criminals, of Dick Turpin and Jack Sheppard, and was known picturesquely as the Liberty of the Mint. Little about it was picturesque now. The broken-down dens and sewers stank and were crowded with wretched, beggarly men and thin, dirty children who would steal from you as soon as look at you—as I had already discovered to my cost.

It was almost with relief that I reached the old brick wall of the prison and followed it round to the entrance. The gatekeeper smiled obsequiously and shook his keys; I dropped a penny into his hand as I went in but did not look at him. The long yard—bare and chilled by a bitter spring wind—was peopled with the usual seedy rabble. New arrivals wandered about gloomily, clutching their worn coats and scarves about them, as they waited for a third or fourth day to be apportioned a room. The regular inmates, driven out of their cramped and unventilated lodgings, watched them. Wives and daughters, some resigned, some tearful, sat with husbands and fathers, while, indecently near, the prison whores touted for trade.

There were three houses in that first yard. The first was occupied by those who could afford their own quarters; the second housed the taproom and the female prisoners. I made for the third, mounted the staircase to the first floor and took the rackety walkway to the last door.

It was a dismal room, narrow and dark. The walls were gray and the day overcast, and the small, dirty window contributed little light.

Wrapped in his old Indian banyan, he sat at a small table with a flickering taper. There was, of course, a pile of books before him, but he was not reading. His chin was propped upon his palm, his eyes were in shadow—the half-light cast the scar on his eyebrow into dark relief and made the stumps of his missing fingers strange—as he listened to the nervous whisperings of a small, inconspicuous man with a threadbare mustache who sat next to him.

On the only mattress lay the grizzled shipping clerk with whom he shared the room. Seeing me, this man looked up blearily and without a word rose, felt around for his comforter and departed. The other man glanced up anxiously and said, "You've a visitor, Mr. Blake. I'll take my leave."

Blake said, "If one of your creditors will not agree to your release, you will have to stay here, though you'll get a little money from the county and from charity, but only just enough to get by, and like as not you'll be stuck. It's up to you."

"Thank you, Mr. Blake. Thank you. They all says you is a fine, kind gentleman, and that you is."

"I'm no gentleman," he said.

The little man darted out of the room, as if fearful of catching too much of my attention.

"You should charge a fee, Jeremiah," I said. I deposited my prizes on the table—three large oranges, a covered bowl of cooling but tasty stew and another weighty tome—and sat down. "At least it would pay for your dinner."

He lifted a pewter mug of beer and took a sip. "Oh, he sees to it I'm fed."

He took another mouthful. Cautiously, I made my next move.

"People have been asking after you."

"Who?" he said suspiciously.

"Friends. Mayhew, for one. Miss Jenkins, your devoted neighbor, for another. She saw me coming from your lodgings. She was worried. And while I was speaking to her, a man I did not know asked after you."

He grimaced. "And you answered—"

"—that I had no idea where you were," I said, unable to hide my exasperation. "Do not fear, I keep your little secret."

"What were you doing with Mayhew?" he asked.

"If you recall, I like him," I said. "Besides, he has arranged for Mr. Jerrold to take me to the Reform Club—since you cannot—so I may see Matty Horner before I return to Devon."

"So you are going home." This more a statement than a question.

"I would stay, were there a reason. But there is no point, is there? I depart tomorrow."

He nodded, staring at the mildewed wall before him. I searched his face for any sign that he might have relented.

I made my play. "You will not change your mind?"

"No."

Irritation—anxiety mixed with it—rose in me.

"Please. Reconsider. Do not leave yourself like this. Do not let Collinson do this to you."

"And yet you are here on his behalf."

"I am here because he told me you were here. Please, Jeremiah. Surely, accepting Collinson's task cannot be worse than being confined in this foul place."

"To me it is."

"That is madness. No, not madness. Typical perversity. Stubbornness." I could hear myself, and I was not persuasive: an unfortunate combination of pleading and anger. "For God's sake, Jeremiah, take the commission! It would not be so bad. I would stay, assist you in any way you needed. It would be done in a couple of days."

I had no great hopes of my speech. I had already made it at much greater length several times.

"It would be done, and then Collinson would have another job for me. And another. I have told you, I would rather be here than in bondage to him."

"But, Jeremiah, you are in bondage *here*. Fire and fury! Everyone is in thrall to someone. From the top to the bottom. It is how the world works.

Every man to his master, every smallholder to his landowner, every clerk to his chief. I am bound to the calls of my father, my second cousin whose tenant I am, even my—" I stopped. "This is your work. What you are good at. Is the task really so terrible?"

"He trades my labor for favors from men I despise. I will not work at his whim." He coughed, a horrid, wracking sound, and his body shook. When he had recovered, he asked, "What news of my namesake? Is he any better?"

I grinned. He knew that any mention of Fred—Frederick Jeremiah—my son of four months, would distract me. "He is indeed. My sister Louisa wrote to say his fever is down and his cough is much improved. He is back to gurgling and smiling. His hands and feet are a matter of utter fascination to him. He is almost sitting up."

"That's a good thing," he said, and gave me his rare smile. "And Mrs. Avery?"

"Helen. She is . . . relieved. Matters are better, I think," I said, nodding my head vigorously, though I did not really think this was true. "We are doing our best."

He nodded back.

"Oh, Jeremiah! There must be another way. You cannot stay in this place."

"Stop clucking over me, William," he said. "I shall get along. I managed well enough before I knew you. Did you bring me what I asked for?"

This, I had dreaded. From inside my coat I drew out what looked like a filleting knife but shorter and very sharp. I handed it to him. "If you are managing so very well, why do you need this?

He did not answer.

"Oh, eat one of your oranges," I said, pushing them at him. He picked one up and began carefully to peel it. "Do we even know how great the debt is?" I asked.

"I do."

"Well?"

"It is between me and Collinson. I'm not telling you. You'd do something foolish and get yourself into trouble."

"It must be registered somewhere. I shall find out myself."

For the first time, Blake was roused. "I forbid you to."

"Do you?!"

Thus it was that my friend, my associate, my burden, Jeremiah Blake, had fetched up in the Marshalsea Prison, imprisoned for debt by his sometime patron Theophilus Collinson. Collinson was quietly influential in London's highest political and social circles. Blake was a private inquiry agent, Collinson sent him to investigate and resolve matters which his rich and powerful acquaintances did not want to leak into the public domain. Blake was paid for his work, and Collinson built up a bank of favors. But Collinson had come to feel he had a justified hold over Blake, and Blake was not—and as far as I could tell never had been—good at taking orders. He had a wholly prejudiced dislike of the aristocracy and what I had once heard him call "the undeserving rich." He hated doing Collinson's bidding and despised many of the people for whom he was forced to work. And though a skilled dissembler when he cared to be, when it came to Collinson and his friends, he did not try. Matters had reached such a pass that when Blake had refused his most recent commission, Collinson, a man used to having his own way, had had him arrested and imprisoned for debt. He had sharpened the punishment by enforcing a special rule that Blake, unlike all the other Marshalsea debtors, could not leave the prison during daylight. The debt appeared legitimate, but I was in no doubt that the whole thing had been got up to punish Blake. Collinson had papers which apparently showed that he had paid Blake a figure in excess of his usual fee as an advance for services he had subsequently refused to render, and had passed this off as a debt.

He had assumed the shock would subdue Blake's rebelliousness: he had made it clear that he would withdraw the claim if Blake accepted his commission. Collinson had, however, underestimated his adversary's stubbornness. Blake had refused, choosing to remain in prison. They were at a standoff: Blake stuck in the noxious Marshalsea; Collinson gnashing his teeth and desperate to have Blake out and working.

Collinson's next move had been to write to me, knowing I would be horrified to hear of Blake's situation and that I would rush from my home in Devon to try to have him freed. This was exactly what I had done. I had met with Collinson and was in no doubt of his intentions, but I had been unable to see any way of having Blake freed other than him agreeing to his patron's terms. And of course he would not, and so this was my fourth visit. All to no avail.

The only thing upon which the two men were agreed was that Blake's situation should remain secret. And so, to my further frustration, I had to undertake not to speak of it. I had once before broken a promise to Blake; the consequences had been disastrous. He knew I would keep this one. However, while polite society knew nothing of Blake's whereabouts, London's criminal community had found out about it. A blackguard with a grudge against Blake had deputed a particularly unsavory inmate of the Marshalsea, who gloried in the name of Nathaniel Gore, to do him as much harm as he could. Thus the knife.

Blake seemed remarkably sanguine about this. As the days passed, I, however, had grown increasingly desperate to free him. I was sure that there were more than a few wealthy men in the capital who owed him a good deal and would be happy to pay the debt, but he refused to countenance the thought, as well as flatly forbidding me to pay off the debt myself (not, I confess, that I would necessarily have been able to do so).

"Lord, you are perverse!" I said. "When I depart, what then? You will stew here with no visitors, wasting away from boredom and sickness, until that demon Gore gets you! Collinson will let you rot here, you know, and your friends will know nothing of it."

Blake shrugged in his most annoying manner and ate a piece of orange. I almost stamped my foot. We did not speak for some minutes.

"So you have made all your calls?" he said.

"Just Matty left to see."

On my last visit to London a bare few months before, we had rescued Matty Horner from a life on the streets. Blake had found her and her brother, Pen, work in the kitchen of the Reform Club, which, under the direction of Alexis Soyer, was said to be the Eighth Wonder of the World. Soyer was the most famous chef in London—perhaps in the world; even I had heard of him. The Reform Club was a political club, an alliance of Whigs and radicals—or "liberals," as some of them now called themselves—which had been founded to counter the Tory party. Opened for not quite a year in grand new premises in Pall Mall, it had quickly become the most desirable dining room in London.

"As a Tory born and bred," I said, "I won't be entering the club itself, but Mr. Jerrold has arranged for me to visit the kitchens. Shall I send Monsieur Soyer your regards?"

Blake snorted. He thought little of my political affiliations. "You keep me out of it." Then he moved his head so his eyes were again in shadow and his expression unreadable.

I could not resist further needling. "Why you should be so keen to keep your achievements a secret, I do not understand." My voice was thick with sarcasm. "Why hide the fact that you have gone to such trouble to put yourself in the Marshalsea, resisting all efforts to release you, apparently determined to get yourself killed?"

"Enough." He suddenly looked utterly fatigued, and I was anxious again. "Truly, William, I am glad you came. I am. I just—I can't do otherwise."

I gave a small, defeated nod.

"Besides, I may not be here much longer." He looked suddenly mischievous.

"What do you mean?" I said, taken aback but hopeful.

"The Marshalsea's closing in a month or so. Likely they'll move me to King's Bench instead."

I scowled, my concern seesawing to infuriation, then back again to concern.

"I saw Matty about a month ago," he said. "She's doing well. Kitchen's impressive. Introduce yourself to Soyer. He'll like you."

"Jeremiah, I hate to leave you in this place."

He looked pained.

"Tell me you have a plan. That there is some rhyme and reason to this."

He looked away.

I stood up abruptly. "I cannot help you, Blake, and I do not know when I shall see you next. I would ask you to take care of yourself, but it seems you are determined not to."

"Do not fret for me, William. Please."

He returned to his former pose, head propped upon his hand. I strode out of the room onto the walkway, scattering inmates in my wake.

Chapter Two

I thought the worst of the day was done when I met Henry Mayhew and Douglas Jerrold on the southwest corner of Trafalgar Square. How utterly wrong I was.

Mayhew was his usual amiably disorderly self. His coat was misbuttoned and his fingers stained with ink; tufts of hair stood out from his head, and his satchel bulged alarmingly, as if it might at any moment explode, shooting numerous notes and scraps of paper into the air. He seemed to be a little drunk. His older companion, Douglas Jerrold, the journalist and playwright, cut no less of an odd figure. He was short and almost humpbacked, with straggling salt-and-pepper hair and bristling eyebrows, and wielding a walking stick, his features lent a certain dignity by a heroically hawk-like nose. I liked them both, almost more than anyone in London, though I found Jerrold's acerbic tongue disconcerting.

"My dear friends!" I said, with an enthusiasm I truly felt. "Henry, did you have a late night? You look jiggered."

"More like twenty late nights," Jerrold muttered.

Mayhew tugged at his hair and grinned anxiously. "I was a bit up to the knocker last night."

"Enough!" said Jerrold. "Now, we must congratulate you, Avery, on being a father! A healthy young son, I hear. And in flight from him, you have returned to London."

"I had a number of obligations, a great-uncle . . ." I mumbled unconvincingly.

"Well," said Jerrold, "I'm sure we'll have the truth of it eventually. And news of Mr. Blake, about whom young Henry says you have been ostentatiously reticent."

Mayhew and I both looked stricken and spoke over each other:

"Oh, Douglas!" Mayhew said—and I, lamely: "He has a habit of disappearing from time to time."

"Well, well, never mind that," said Jerrold. "How is the son and heir?"

"Oh! Naturally the most handsome, hairless little sporting fellow the world has ever seen!" I said.

"Excellent! My only advice on the subject of fatherhood is not to take after Henry's father, who had seventeen children and has disinherited them all."

"Not all," said Henry, "and in his defense, I did almost get him arrested for negligence."

"And how are you, Mr. Jerrold?" I asked.

"Oh, I stumble along. *Punch*, Henry's paper, for which I am now writing, is, as usual, in dire financial straits, and we are both scratching about for pennies. I am at present writing a play. If I remember rightly, Henry, you are at present *not* engaged to my daughter?"

Mayhew, wincing, shook his head.

"Well, let us to the Reform," said Jerrold. "I have arranged for you to visit the kitchens where young Matty works, which is no hardship, since they are quite remarkable and females are, of course, not permitted in the club itself. You may even have a sighting of the famous Monsieur Soyer."

"Along here," said Jerrold, turning into a very wide thoroughfare on which all the buildings on the left-hand side appeared to be palaces. "Do you know Pall Mall?"

I shook my head. "Barely."

"I shall instruct you." He stretched out his arms theatrically. "Behold, the splendors and miseries of St. James's. On our side, the right, a hotch-potch of battered, elderly buildings which one wouldn't look at twice. On the left, however, we have a series of edifices that would not have disgraced the Roman Forum, temples to the interests and pursuits of the English gentleman. Of course, as the son of an actor, I am barely a gentleman, but the Reform takes pity upon me and my ilk. First"—he pointed to a massive square building, gray and austere—"we have the United Service Club. Full of majors and brigadiers, dull dogs indeed, who bought their commissions and are happy to pay the highest fees in London for the pleasure of each other's company . . . If only you'd held on a little longer, Captain Avery, you might have secured yourself the right to be bored rigid by them."

"I was an East India Company man, Mr. Jerrold. I couldn't afford a commission in the British Army."

"Avery's a member of the Oriental, aren't you, Avery?" said Mayhew. I was, in fact, an honorary member—I could not have afforded the fees else. It was where I stayed in London. They served a good curry.

"The Athenaeum next," said Jerrold. In form, this building was the twin of the first, but it was covered in gleaming white stucco with a handsome blue frieze. "The members like to give themselves intellectual and philosophical airs: the frieze was copied in its entirety from the Parthenon in Athens. The club is invariably full of slumbering bishops. Far less interesting than it thinks it is.

"Now, we have the Travellers." A smaller building this, an elegantly proportioned stone town house. "Members are supposed to have visited at least four foreign lands. The members are diplomats and would-be spies, or so I'm told. And here we are. The palace of the marriage of Whigs, liberals and radicals, united at last to fight the Tories.

"The Reform Club is modeled on the Palazzo Farnese in Rome," continued Jerrold with a flourish, "but given an admirable, if slightly gloomy, English accent—and a little bit of Greece in the frieze, copied from the top of the Acropolis."

It was much larger than the Travellers, built of pale gray stone and, to my mind, very severe. An elaborate balustrade ran the length of the front, behind which were three stories of heavy casement windows and a basement. The building was grand, imperious, very sure of itself.

Jerrold lowered his voice theatrically. "It cost three times more than any other club on this street. No small part of that was the kitchen, whose fame has quite eclipsed the rest of it. It now provides the best dinner in London, so good that the members forget about politics in their fondness for lamb cutlets *à la* Reform. Obviously, it was worth every penny." I could not tell if he was joking. "And see, dear Captain, just next door is the Carlton Club, home of the Tories, designed by the aptly named Mr. Smirke. Rather florid, in my opinion. Your natural habitat, I think? Let us hope none of them see you lurking over here. You may be run out of town."

I was a Tory by birth and by upbringing. Jerrold was insistently anti and liked to tease me, though in truth I had little involvement in politics and was hardly known in London. Even so, I was discomfited at the thought of being spotted by someone I knew. Almost involuntarily, I tucked my head into my collar and wedged my beaver hat down over my nose.

"Here endeth the geography lesson," announced Jerrold. He hobbled up the steep front steps to the tall, dark green, double-leafed doors, and a porter, solemn in a blue dress coat and buff waistcoat—the colors of the Whig party—opened it.

"Good afternoon, Mr. Jerrold," he said.

We stepped into a high lobby with a black-and-white marble floor and the porter's cubbyhole on the right.

"My friend Captain Avery has an appointment in the kitchen. I've arranged it. Mr. Mayhew and I shall take a restorative in the smoking room," said Jerrold.

"Very good, sir," said the porter, and waved, whereupon a footman opened the glass-paneled door that led into the club. I caught a waft of warm air and a glimpse of marble and gilt.

"*Bon appétit,*" said Jerrold, and they disappeared.

"Take your coat, sir?" said the porter. "The kitchen can be very hot."

I was led through a small side door, and down an unadorned flight of stairs to a bare corridor and a pair of sturdy baize doors which swung open to reveal another set behind them, and through these we now went.

I found myself at one end of a series of interconnecting chambers, one opening onto the next, all together the length of a large ballroom. My first sensation was of great noise—the loud and ceaseless sound of steam whistling, a gurgling and the crash of pans. It was exceedingly hot. The overwhelming impression—apart from the noise—was of great openness, whiteness and cleanliness. The ceilings were white barrel vaults, supported by tall, slim iron columns. Light was provided by dozens of white, gas-lit globes mounted on the walls. It was the brightest subterranean place I had ever seen. Through the wide doorways I could see glimpses of an array of cupboards and tables and shelves and rows of dishes and lines of hung birds, and spits and stoves and vast stew pans. All about, an army in starched white—many of them, I noted, women—

moved purposefully, carrying boxes and plates, or buckets and mops, stirring the contents of pans, wiping tables, prodding meat, as if part of some remarkable, orderly dance. A kitchen boy ushered me through the first two chambers and, without a word of explanation, deposited me next to a man of middle height and in early middle age. He had a pleasant, competent look about him and was extremely well turned out, in a plain dark suit and waistcoat, his shirt and necktie perfectly pressed and snowy white.

He turned to me with the slightly jaded look of the professional once the performance is over and the magic is done.

"May I help you, sir?"

"I am here to visit one of your kitchen maids, Matty Horner. I believe I am expected?"

I saw a hint of distaste in his eyes, that he attributed some grubby purpose to me.

"My name is Captain William Avery. You may not know the girl—I believe she is a scullery maid. Monsieur Soyer took her and her brother in last year at the request of my associate, Jeremiah Blake, after they had been cruelly mistreated. I have not been in London since then and I am here to see how she does."

"Of course! Of course!" He shook his head apologetically and smoothed down his jacket. "Captain Avery. It had slipped my mind. Quite inexcusable."

"Not at all," I said coolly.

"Please forgive me! I am Mr. Percy, steward of the Reform Club. If I may say so, I am delighted to make your acquaintance. We have heard of your exploits with Mr. Blake and how you saved Matilda's life. You are indeed expected. Follow me. I will inform Monsieur Soyer. He will certainly wish to meet you. Is Mr. Blake with you?" he added hopefully.

"I am afraid not. He is . . . detained."

"Such a shame. I have never had the pleasure. He sounds like a most fascinating gentleman."

Not a gentleman, I thought.

MATTY WAS in the pastry kitchen, furiously beating cream with a birch whisk. When last I saw her, she had been clutching the shreds of her girlhood, pinched and underfed and passing for twelve years old. Now there was no mistaking that she was a young woman. In four months she seemed to have grown as many inches and, though there were dark smudges under her eyes, she had filled out. She wore a neat, close-fitting black dress with a high white collar and a white apron. Her hair was secured under a white cap. She was laughingly fending off the attentions of three young men who were addressing her in the most familiar terms.

"Matilda! Your gentleman is here."

"Matilda, your gentleman is here," one of the young men echoed mockingly.

"Monsieur Blanche! If you have nothing better to do than chase the kitchen maids, you and your very small talent may return to the street. *Vous avez été prévenu!*"

These words, pronounced in a thick French accent, issued from a slight man in the white uniform of the kitchen. He wore a tall, starched chef's hat, crowned with a pouched cap. The young culprit instantly sprang back, reddened and mumbled a groveling apology; the other young men also jumped to attention and scattered.

"Monsieur Morel," said Percy to the slight man, "this is Captain Avery, who saved young Matilda's life." The cooks and kitchen maids glanced at me covertly. Percy went on: "Monsieur Soyer's second-in-command, our *sous-chef,* Monsieur Morel."

"*Enchanté,*" said the chef, somewhat distractedly, and continued on his way.

"Matilda, ask Herr Schmidt for his permission," said Percy, "and you may take twenty minutes with your visitor." Matty made a small bob and turned to an older man who was overseeing an elaborate confection behind her. He waved her away, barely looking up.

"Thank you, Mr. Percy," she said. She did not look at me. Her voice at least had not changed; it retained its old huskiness.

We followed Percy into the corridor. Matty kept her eyes on the floor. He led us to the other end of the kitchen and, opening a side door, he said, "You may have the butler's room, Matty. I have had a fire laid. And take half an hour."

"Thank you, sir."

He gave a quick, indulgent smile. "I have no need of it, and I am sure it would be pleasant to have a few moments' quiet talk with your rescuer. Besides, you may be working late tonight, Matilda. The secretary, Mr. Grove, has left, and Chef is likely to be in need of your services."

It was a comfortable parlor, with two well-worn armchairs set before a little grate of glowing logs. We stood for a moment. Then she looked up at me and began a smile that became broader and broader.

"Oh my *lawd*, Captain!" she said, pulling off her cap and grasping my hands, her voice thick with excitement but hardly above a whisper. "Can you *believe* this!"

There was a knock; another kitchen maid, older, pretty, stood with a tray. Matty dropped my hands abruptly and we both sat down. A large brown teapot, two cups, a plate of soft white bread and butter, another with slices of seed cake, and a saucer on which there were four tiny pairs of slightly crushed meringues pressed together with purple jam and a lick of whipped cream. As she laid down the tray, the kitchen maid gave Matty a look of such pure scowling dislike that I was quite disturbed. As she straightened, she gave me a look of bald, almost suggestive, insolence.

"Thank you, Margaret," said Matty, not looking at her. The girl retired, with a toss of her shoulders.

Matty turned back to me. "Oh, Captain! Do you remember: when first we met, you bought me a sandwich? It tasted like sawdust, but I was glad for it. The food here. Even the bread and butter's like—what's it called?—ambrosia! Taste it!"

I took a piece. "It is a remarkable place," I said, relieved to see the Matty I knew.

"Isn't it?" She leaned back luxuriously in her chair. "I can't believe Mr. Percy let me see you here. Even the first kitchen maids don't get that."

"So it has gone well?"

She nodded vigorously. "How we live! I have two good dresses. Boots that fit. A clean apron each day that someone else washes! I eat two meals every day, meat three times a week! And every so often, a little taste of what they get upstairs. They had these last night." She pointed at the meringues. "I begged Herr Schmidt for any that were left. Chef says we must all understand what the kitchen aims for: perfection. Here."

She watched as I placed a meringue in my mouth. It crumbled and vanished like a sugar cloud.

"Chef calls them 'a little piece of the divine.'"

"He is right," I said, unable not to return her smile. "I could not be more delighted, Matty. It seems you have conquered all before you."

"Not nearly. When I first came I was in the scullery, heaving the slops, scraping grease, scrubbing crocks and stew pans, washing aprons, arms in water up to me elbows all day, six in the morning till late at night. But even in the scullery, the water comes in from a faucet, and you don't have to pump, you just turn it and the water's hot. First off, I had to learn to stop talking and do what I was told. I got beaten a few times for chattering and disobedience. It's still a job to hold my tongue. Maybe that's why I'm so full of words today. Oh, it's good to see you, Captain!

"I got my head down, worked hard. After a few weeks of mopping and scrubbing, one of the kitchen boys found I could write a good hand and asked me to write to his ma. So I did. Then a porter asked, will I scribe him a letter? I started writing letters for the kitchen boys and porters, then one of the kitchen maids—a nice one, 'cos most of them won't give a scullery girl the time of day—and a couple of the chefs. Most of them can't hardly write, and not in English—well, they are foreign. I charge a ha'penny a time."

She handed me a cup, and as she did so I saw her hands were red and chapped and covered in dozens of small burns and sores.

"Good God! What are these?"

She laughed. "These are nothing. All the girls' hands are like these. There's no kitchen work without them: if you're not scrubbing with carbolic half the day, you're burning yourself the rest. Anyway, one day, Mr. Percy comes into the scullery—that's a shock, because no one comes into the scullery. He's discovered I'm writing letters. He asks to see my scribing. I swear I thought I was for the sack; I was to go to Chef's office. I was proper—I mean very—scared. I go in, all dripping from the sinks. And Chef looks hard at me and says he has no time for those who are distracted by other tasks and do not put their heart and soul into the kitchen.

"Well, I was sure I was for it and I thought my heart would break. Then he asks me where I learned to write. I told him about my pa being a printer and that I could write before I spoke. He says, 'You're the girl Blake brought.' He tells me to take a piece of paper and write what he says. He starts on at a terrible old rate on a recipe for salmon with a shrimp sauce, all scrambled around with French words I didn't know. I copied it down as best as I could, though my copy was awful. Full of crossings-out like a cat's catechism. He held it up in the air with his finger and thumb like it was a dead mouse and dropped it on the floor. 'Excuse me, Chef,' I said, 'but I can make you a fair copy in four minutes flat.' Not my best hand, but I did it.

"Well, he looked it over, then Mr. Percy looked it over. Turns out his secretary had left in a fury, the kitchen clerks were off sick, and his wife was off in the country, and all the chefs are foreign, so there's no one left to do his correspondence. For five days, I wrote his letters until he got a new secretary. I went to the kitchen clerk and I got him to give me a list of dishes so as to see how they were spelled. I studied the menus and learned the words, and I sat up all night with a candle to work out the spellings.

"Then I went back to the scullery. But then Chef calls me back a few days later. He says he'll promote me to kitchen maid. Six weeks, and I'm out of the scullery! It's usually a year or more till you get the chance, and some never do, but suddenly I'm in the kitchen.

"So then Chef calls me in a few weeks ago and says I've worked hard and he's going to put me on pastry and sweets. That means I'm practically a first kitchen maid! In four months! I get to warm the milk and yeast for the bread, start the sorbets, whip the egg whites and the cream. And you know, one of the pastry cooks is a woman, Mrs. Relph, and she looks out for me. She says I'm as good as any of the apprentices, and she's going to teach me.

"Oh, I'm going on, but it's just, well, I've kept my mouth shut so long, and stored it all up inside me, and there's not many I can glory in my good fortune with—Blake's hardly one for prattle. And I wanted you to know, I'm so grateful." Her whole face was alight with gladness.

"And now and again I clerk for Chef. The secretaries are always leaving. See, Mr. Grove has just thrown in his hand. That's why I might be needed."

"Why do they leave?"

"He just can't keep them. He wants them at all hours, and they mind, or they don't get along with the kitchen. Or they get along too well, if you know what I mean." She mimed drinking a glass to the dregs. "So then I'm up for a few days. He says I turn his French *orotundities*—whatever they are—into good plain English.

"But you know," she said, entirely serious, "he's a genius. He thinks of every detail." She jumped up. Behind her was a little china basin set in a sideboard. "Look." She lifted up a small, shining copper cup like a tiny colander which was attached to a rod and chain. "He invented this. It fits into the plughole and stops all the bits of food and grease from sliding into the drain. It's a small thing, but when you're a scullery maid all you think of is drains and grease! Every basin has one. Captain, it's so clean here. There's a boy whose whole job is getting rid of the vermin and catching cockroaches. And I swear there's no bedbugs! Well, almost. And here." She pulled open the drawer under the basin. "See? It's for ice, and it's lined with lead to keep the ice from melting, and then as it does melt, there's a little hole in the corner to drain away the water. Chef thinks of everything. But"—and she leaned forward and said in a near-whisper—"he can't hardly write. But he can't help that. Anyway," she said, finally drawing breath, "a gentleman doesn't want to hear about drains and pastry."

"I do," I said. "I can see Monsieur Soyer is a remarkable man."

"He is. Oh, Captain, I never thought anything such as this could happen!" She rocked with pleasure.

"Matty, you are so grown, and it suits you."

"I was seventeen last week," she said, with a queenly tilt of her head. "Blake was supposed to come, but he didn't. You must have seen him. What's become of him?"

"I have barely seen him," I said, taking a gulp of my tea. "He is buried in a very mysterious case. You are taking care of yourself?" I thought of the look the other kitchen maid had given her. "Do those young men tease you often?"

"Now, don't you start! You sound like Mrs. Relph. She says I should never smile because men will take advantage."

"Well, they might. Men are rough things. You must be on your guard."

"Do you not recall where I'm from?" she said sharply, then relented. "And you, you've a son, Blake says. What's he like?"

"He is a soft, fat little fellow who laughs a good deal." I could not restrain a smile as I thought of him.

Mr. Percy appeared at the doorway. "A visitor," he said, and stepped back to reveal a short man whose attire would have stood out anywhere. A dark blue velvet jacket hung open to reveal a blue silk cravat tied with a puffed knot, tucked into a most extravagant red waistcoat patterned with dashes of blue and gold; a pair of exceedingly baggy trousers with a gold stripe down the sides; and flat leather evening pumps buffed to an almost metallic sheen. His fingers were adorned with a number of gaudy rings, and upon his head he wore a soft red velvet cap tilted at a rakish, if not actively precarious, angle.

"Mathilde!" he said, rushing forward. "This must be Captain Avery, who so bravely rescued you, come to visit you, and I hear nothing! I expressly wish to meet him, to thank him for delivering you to us!" He turned to me and executed a little bow. "Alexis Soyer, *chef de cuisine* of the Reform Club, at your service! You must forgive me, I am French, and though I have endeavored to master your most marvelous tongue, there are moments when I fall short." It seemed to me Monsieur Soyer mangled his words rather more than was entirely necessary: "club" became *cloob*, "tongue" emerged as *terrng*. "Captain Avery, your fame precedes you. You are most welcome! No Monsieur Blake?" he added, pronouncing it *Bleck*.

"Alas, he is otherwise engaged," I said.

"A shame."

"Your kitchen is a marvel, Monsieur."

"We labor to impress. I should very much like to make your better acquaintance, Captain Avery. Please, you must attend one of our dinners."

"I should be delighted, but I return to Devon tomorrow."

"Then the answer is obvious. You must come tonight! Have you an engagement? Cancel it! I am having a few *amis* to dinner in my private room. A lord, an artist or two. A simple meal."

"Well, I . . ." Monsieur Soyer seemed to me rather preposterous, and I had plans to dine with Mayhew. But I was very tempted.

"I insist! Do not think of refusing!"

"Then I suppose I must accept." Curiosity won out over good manners.

"Excellent! Ten o'clock. Come to the kitchen. Mathilde, say your goodbyes. I need you, I have recipes to dictate. Sir, I bid you"—he gave another exaggerated bow, his precarious cap remaining miraculously attached to his head—"*au revoir.*"

"You are going home tomorrow?" Matty said.

"Yes. I came to see that you were happy and settled. And you are."

"I've hardly seen you."

"I shall call next time I am in London."

She nodded, disappointed. And I, ill wretch, took pleasure in her disappointment. But her new life absorbed her, and I knew that soon I should be little in it.

I took her hand. "Miss Horner, it has been an absolute pleasure."

Soyer put his head round the door.

"Captain Avery, it will be, I promise you, a meal to remember."

I had no idea how right he would be.

I HAD ONE LAST VISIT to make before my departure. It did not promise to be pleasant, nor was it.

"You have failed me, Avery," said Sir Theophilus Collinson, former head of the East India Company's Secret Department, and Blake's patron turned jailer. "I expected more of you."

The room, a library, Collinson's own, smelled of tobacco and leather. It was ill-lit and the corners sat in shadow, which, given its owner, seemed entirely appropriate.

"He does not listen to anyone, sir, and you of all people should know that."

"Do not be surly with me, sir!"

"I am not being surly, merely truthful. You once called him pigheaded. He is. You have pushed him into a corner with no way out. So he will not move."

"There is a perfectly good way out!" Collinson barked. "He does as I say. He takes up the task I have given him!"

I sighed. Collinson was, as a rule, the personification of equanimity. I had never seen him so angry.

"What of this fellow in the prison who means him harm? What is his name—Nathaniel Gore?"

"Blake says he is violent, a murderer, and may have accomplices and, as you know, he is not given to overstatement. Can you not at least write to the prison governor about it?"

Sir Theo stroked his several chins and allowed his sharp little teeth to show. The effect was alarmingly vulpine. "It may do him good to sit in harm's way for a few days. I am sure he can take care of himself. After all, he is so very resourceful. Then he may come to his senses."

"He will not."

"I will be the judge, Avery. And you will be in Devon."

"Sir, ignore me if you wish but, I assure you, you will not prize him out with threats. You must offer him a compromise."

"Do not lecture me, young man. May I remind you who I am? Blake refuses a perfectly simple task, and I am professionally embarrassed. My reputation depends on providing such expertise when it is required. Now, since you cannot help me, you may as well leave. I am told you are to be on the train tomorrow morning."

I did not ask how he knew. "Yes, sir."

"Dining at the Oriental?" It was said as an afterthought, a bored semi-courtesy.

"No, sir. At the Reform."

"The Reform?" The teeth reappeared. He was curious. "But you are a Tory. Do they know they have an interloper among them?"

No, I thought, *but I am sure you would not scruple to tell them.*

"I have been invited to dine with the chef in his private room, so I am not precisely dining in the club itself."

"A nice distinction, but a most tantalizing invitation. Dinner with the legendary Monsieur Soyer. How very fortunate of you. And how is that? Of course, he took that girl on as a scullery maid." He spoke half to himself and half to remind me that he knew all my business. "I myself shall be attending a very grand banquet at the Reform Club next week. Lord Palmerston is entertaining the Prince of Egypt, Ibrahim Pasha. It will be the most august event the club has ever held. So we are both fortunate."

"Will they know they have an interloper among them?"

"Do not sauce me, young man. I always win."

"I apologize. I considered you a Tory."

He assumed a world-weary expression and waved his hand. "Tory, Whig or radical, landowner, mill owner or manufacturer, they all come to me in the end. Who am I to refuse them?"

"I was simply surprised you would bother with Lord Palmerston and the Whigs when the Tories are in government."

He had beady little eyes of an indeterminate color. He fixed them upon me. "Lord Palmerston is a very able man, with an unrivaled understanding of foreign affairs. He may not be in power now, but he will be again. Besides, the Reform serves the best dinner in London. Now. You may go."

I rose, but could not resist a final attempt.

"Sir Theo, if Blake were to die in the Marshalsea, he would be of no further use to you."

"Blake be damned."

Chapter Three

It was a quarter to ten when I presented myself at the Reform's kitchens in my evening clothes.

Past the larders and crockery cupboards and rows of copper saucepans I went, full of anticipation. Through the brightly gas-lit kitchens and then through a handsome, polished mahogany door into Soyer's private room.

It was a finely proportioned room, almost twenty feet long, with a roaring fire, a Turkey carpet and a dining table laid for eleven, glittering with silver, candles and crystal and two vases of mauve, hothoused hyacinths. There were four other gentleman guests in the room, whom I did not know, so I took a glass of champagne and set myself to examining the paintings over the sideboard. One was a portrait of our host, Monsieur Soyer, with a fork in his hand and a velvet cap askew on his head, grinning over a plate of chicken like some greedy schoolboy.

"You admire the paintings of the divine Emma." An elderly fellow, tall and stringy in an old-fashioned tailcoat frayed at the cuffs and a pair of knee breeches with baggy gray stockings.

"Emma?"

"Monsieur Soyer's delightful wife," said he.

"Monsieur Soyer is married?"

"Why, yes, indeed. He is wonderfully proud of her. A most talented painter." He tapped his pockets as if he had forgotten something, then thrust out his right hand. "Where are my manners? Alvanley. I lodge with Monsieur Ude," he said, as if that were all the explanation I should require.

"Pleased to make your acquaintance, sir. I am Captain Avery. I am afraid I do not know Monsieur Oood."

"Not know Ude?" He glanced over his shoulder at an older man, small and well-padded, with close-cropped white hair and saucerlike hangdog eyes, to whom two younger men were paying court. One, I now recognized as Morel, Soyer's *sous-chef*, whom I had met earlier in the kitchen. Alvanley lowered his voice.

"But you must know Ude. He was the chef at Crockford's. He was—is—the greatest French cook in England. He worked for Louis XVI and Napoleon! He escaped the guillotine by a whisker! A chef among chefs, a king among men."

Crockford's was the most fashionable gambling club in London, well above my means and connections. "I fear I am but a provincial gentleman, sir, and do not inhabit such elevated circles," I said.

"Oh, I, too," Alvanley said. "Which is why I lodge with Ude! I was a dreadful spendthrift in my youth; lost everything. What's left I spend on rent and dinner. Splendid solution!" He sipped his champagne and whispered, "Of course, he bleeds me dry, but it is worth it!"

The door opened and the room fell silent. Soyer paused in the doorway. He did not disappoint. His black frock coat was embroidered with exotic flowers in scarlet and purple thread; beneath it he wore a purple and gold waistcoat from which no less than two gold watch chains dangled, and a purple silk cravat tied into a lavish bow. He completed his attire with a pair of tight silk trousers, a dark purple velvet hat worn at the usual precarious angle and a fistful of large rings over his white gloves.

He came over at once to greet my companion and myself. "So good to see you, Lord Alvanley," he said. I was surprised to discover the jolly old fossil had a title.

"We were admiring your wife's paintings."

"Ah, Emma, my dearest one, she is a great, great talent." He smiled at the pictures. "She is traveling in Europe."

"Alone?" I said. "I mean, how unusual."

"She is a most unusual woman," he said. "A genius. The King of Hanover, no less, has commissioned her to paint a portrait, and who am I to curtail the exercise of her talents? My work keeps me here, and her stepfather—her father in all but name—chaperones her."

"And while the wife is away . . . eh, Alexis?" said the man who was not Morel, winking. There was an awkward pause.

"I adore the ladies, as do we all," said Soyer cheerfully, "but for me the summit of female perfection is Emma," and he raised his glass as if to toast her. The young man who had spoken raised his glass, and his eyebrows, too. Soyer ignored him. "But though a dinner without ladies is like a garden without flowers, tonight we dine among only trees and shrubs—though most distinguished ones."

The company laughed. "You have met Lord Alvanley, epicurean and devotee of haute cuisine," said Soyer. "And this is Monsieur Louis Eustache Ude, the great chef at whose feet we all kneel." He made a small bob before the white-haired man, who gave a small, imperious nod back.

The rude young man was another chef, one Giovanni Francobaldi, not French but Italian, formerly in the employ of some duke but now, Soyer informed us, running the dining room of the Union Club. Something about Soyer's introduction annoyed Francobaldi, and he gave him a surly look. On Ude's other side was Monsieur Morel. Two more guests now appeared in the doorway. Soyer introduced one as Thomas Blackwell, proprietor of Crosse & Blackwell, according to Soyer, "makers of the finest relishes and pickles by appointment to the Queen." Blackwell had brought a splendid jar of vivid green peas, which he deposited on Soyer's sideboard. The other was John Joseph Prestage, co-owner of the engineering firm of Bramah and Prestage, which had manufactured some of the novelties in Soyer's kitchens. Another man rushed into the room, looking rather harried and bent in an ill-fitting black frock coat.

"Mr. Douglas Jerrold, our friend from the worlds of theater and journalism! Our wit and conscience for the evening. Welcome!" said Soyer.

"Jerrold!" I cried.

Jerrold gave a small wave and made his way over to me. "Avery! You must have made a very good impression," he muttered. "I have been hoping for an invitation to one of these for months. They are said to be extraordinary."

Behind him came two peacock-like figures dressed in brilliant colors with exaggeratedly cinched waists and rings on every finger.

"Do you know this man?" Jerrold muttered, gesturing at the first, older man. "Tommy Duncombe MP, 'the dandy demagogue' himself. Interesting specimen: universally acknowledged to be the best-dressed man in the House of Commons, incorrigible gambler, ladies' man and spendthrift, said to be at least forty thousand pounds in debt—not, of course, that this prevents him from living extravagantly: his credit apparently stretches on forever, unlike the rest of us. At the same time, he is a famous radical, and the Chartists' most active supporter in Parliament. Behind him is Mr. Charles Rowlands MP, a rich young Whig. They are fast friends, divided by politics, united by a love of gambling, I'm told. But then, Tommy is famous for getting on with everyone."

Rowlands's long hair had been curled into ringlets; he wore a burgundy velvet coat lined with purple satin, a blue silk cravat in a pigeon's-egg knot, a veritable jewelry box of watch chains and rings, and carried a cream-colored top hat. Duncombe, however, surpassed him. A little heavier and a good deal older than his friend, he wore a tight-waisted gray velvet frock coat with black silk lapels and gilt buttons, perfectly cut, inside which one glimpsed a red velvet waistcoat with gold thread, adorned with two gold watch chains. Beneath this was a French cambric shirt with ruffled cuffs which extended just beyond the sleeves of his coat onto his knuckles. He also wore a pair of tight yellow trousers and carried a gold-tipped cane and a pair of canary-yellow gloves.

As a junior officer in Calcutta, I had fancied myself a dandy, poring over five-month-old issues of the society journals for details of the latest London fashions. I still appreciated a well-cut waistcoat, but there was little call for red velvet in rural Devon, and my own black frock coat, discreetly checked trousers, Indian paisley waistcoat and cream silk cravat, ordered in London the autumn before, seemed perfectly drab by comparison.

"Now, my dear friends"—Monsieur Soyer tapped his glass—"introductions! May I present Captain William Avery. You will recall that he fought with the sainted Mountstuart in India at the hour of his death at the hands of the nefarious Thugs! And that he also saved a maharajah from a tiger!" There was a murmur of recognition. "More recently, he saved from certain death a poor young girl, whom I am glad to say is now one of our kitchen maids."

I smiled as gracefully as I could, but I increasingly found such introductions embarrassing.

"I am afraid you exaggerate, Monsieur Soyer, I was merely aiding Mr. Blake."

"The mysterious Mr. Blake. Does he really exist?" said the rude Francobaldi.

"I assure you he does," I said.

To my surprise, Mr. Duncombe wafted up to me, Mr. Rowlands trotting along behind him.

"Captain Avery," said Duncombe, making a deep bow and smiling charmingly, "I am delighted to have the opportunity to meet you. It is rare to meet a real man of action in London, and I was a great admirer of Xavier Mountstuart." He had a small, almost feminine mouth, a thin, prominent nose and full and luxuriant dark hair which grew down to long, neat sideburns.

"The pleasure is mine," I said, a little awkwardly.

"I have heard about your exploits. Captain Avery helped to solve the Holywell Street murders last year, Rowlands."

"And sent Lord Allington round the twist," said Mr. Rowlands, raising his glass to me. He had a lazy, drawling voice which rather belied his pink, milky complexion and innocent blue eyes.

"I am the chief supporter in Parliament of the Chartists and their demands for the universal vote," said Duncombe. "We are few, but we are active. Of course, I entirely abjure physical force. Rowlands, meanwhile, is a dyed-in-the-wool Whig. He has no time for radicals like me, though I hope, eventually, to bring him round. After all, we are all part of the liberal party now."

"Never," said Rowlands, laughing into his drink. "We've had quite enough progress for one decade."

"Are we to meet Mr. Blake?" Mr. Duncombe said hopefully.

"I am afraid he is not at liberty—" I said, "—I mean, to be here."

"Too bad, I should very much like to make his acquaintance."

"Gentlemen," Soyer called, "pray be seated. I have an *amuse-bouche* upon which I would like your opinion and a fine white burgundy which will complement it perfectly." He unlocked a small cabinet and extricated a bottle chilling in a bucket of ice.

Mr. Percy, the steward, whom I had met earlier, arrived and poured the wine—a deep, transparent gold—into eleven small glasses. A waiter served each of us with a morsel of lobster in a buttery sauce flavored very gently with Indian spices laid inside a small, crisp, layered pastry case or *vol-au-vent*. It was so light, one almost inhaled it. The wine, scented with butter and honey, was gone all too soon.

"Gentlemen, what do you think?" Soyer asked. "I am planning to serve it, along with a number of other dishes we shall eat tonight, at our banquet for the Prince of Egypt next week. I wish my dishes to be perfect, so I rely on your opinions." He bowed low. "Is the spicing correct? Is the sauce too heavy?"

The chef Francobaldi laughed. "Another of your butter sauces, eh, Alexis? A mite safe, I'd say." But there was ice in his laugh, and I should have said he was envious.

Soyer's colleague, Monsieur Morel, stiffened, but Soyer waved it off. "Giovanni likes to tease."

"It is a masterful combination, Alexis," Ude, the elderly chef, pronounced imperiously. "Quite classical."

"Quite heavenly," said Mr. Jerrold.

"Of course, I am not the first to produce a lobster *vol-au-vent*," said Soyer, "but I am pleased with the spicing and the delicacy of the dish. I think no one can rival me there. And, may I say, several distinguished persons have commented upon its refinement. The Duke of Leinster said so only last week, and the Marquess of Ailsa, too."

Francobaldi rolled his eyes.

"Now for our simple supper." The door opened, and Mr. Percy ushered a troop of footmen into the room, carrying dozens of plates.

How shall I describe it? Vivid, surprising, complicated, delicious. I had never tasted the like. We began with a soup of early asparagus, light yet intensely flavorful, then turbot in a delicate pink sauce of lobster roe, then a whole salmon trout, remarkably suspended in aspic as if at the moment just before it took the hook.

Then the first of the "removes," or *relevés,* arrived: braised pigeons with asparagus and peas, and an extraordinary construction made of pastry in the shape of a crown, stuffed with small poached chickens, which had in turn been stuffed with mushrooms, ox tongues and sweetbreads. Into the pastry crown's sides had been stuck little golden skewers on which were strung slices of truffle and pink crayfish tails. We applauded wildly. Soyer described it as his little *trompe l'œil,* and said again that he was confident no one had ever seen anything like it and it would astonish the guests at the banquet.

There was a short pause while we were entertained with *hors d'œuvres*—among them a fresh salad of celery, young onions and sliced radish, another of *haricots verts,* early green beans dressed in a warm brown butter, and tiny crab rissoles.

It was at this moment that Francobaldi suddenly looked across Monsieur Ude at Morel and said with an anger that took us all by surprise, "What the *fuck* did you say?"

There was a collective gasp.

"Jo! That is no word for this company!" said Monsieur Ude.

Morel frowned. "Nothing, Jo, it was nothing. Calm yourself."

Francobaldi threw down his napkin furiously and stood up. He seemed so angry that I thought he might strike Morel. "No. I wish to know what you meant by it."

Ude placed his hand on Francobaldi's arm. "Jo, *tais-toi*, we want no disagreements here. You will apologize to the company."

With some difficulty, Francobaldi mastered himself, grunted an apology and sat down, pointedly ignoring Morel.

"Francobaldi is said to be the up-and-coming chef," Jerrold murmured to me. "More worked up than coming up, I should say."

Soyer said, "Messieurs, I give you: the roasts and the entrées."

Under Percy's supervision, the napery was removed to reveal a new, fresh white tablecloth, then the footmen brought the dishes. First came a plate of crisp white duckling with a sauce of sour oranges, a capon stuffed with black truffles and dressed with watercress, and a ham in a Madeira sauce.

"No one carves as skillfully as Mr. Percy," said Soyer. "I yield to him the floor." Percy set about his work. Soyer was right: he carved with great skill, every perfect slice finding its way faultless onto our plates.

After this there was a warm terrine of quail and chicken; peas stewed with lettuces; small, buttery omelets flavored with herbs; and a delicious dish of tripe between unctuous layers of leeks, onions and carrots, which I would have thought would be far too rustic for the Reform's table.

From Soyer's special cupboard, bottle after exquisite bottle emerged.

The man himself was in perpetual motion: if not leaping up to oversee the arrival of a particular dish or to supervise the completion of another, then talking constantly. He told stories about his past. He boasted tirelessly of the dukes and countesses who admired his food. He showed off his latest invention, a "tendon separator" manufactured by Mr. Prestage, for dissecting meat and poultry that would "soon be available to purchase from reputable grocers."

We applauded. We tasted, we were transported, we asked for more.

Monsieur Ude ate sparingly, nodding from time to time, his expression revealing nothing—and Soyer watched him constantly out of the corner of his eye. Lord Alvanley stuck his fork into dish after dish like a happy child surrounded by his favorite toys. Morel, Soyer's deputy, watched us eat with a melancholy look upon his face and spoke only to mutter to his chef or to Ude. As for Francobaldi, within ten minutes of his outburst, he had completely regained his spirits and was making loud and occasionally boorish comments about the dishes. Mr. Blackwell asked questions about the ingredients between eager mouthfuls. Mr. Jerrold ate and smiled, teased Soyer and made passing references to Monsieur Ude's apparently vast wealth. As for myself, whenever anyone addressed me I seemed to be in the midst of a glorious mouthful.

"It's not so much that the cat's got your tongue, Avery," said Jerrold, "as that Monsieur Soyer has taken it prisoner for the evening."

Everyone laughed, and I coughed and turned scarlet. Mr. Duncombe passed me a glass of a first-rate claret.

He ate with great fastidiousness; not a drop seemed to have spattered his ensemble. Not so young Mr. Rowlands MP, who ate with remarkable greediness: dribbles of Madeira sauce flecked his cravat and waistcoat, and he asked for more glasses of the claret. By the time the *entremets* arrived, he was looking a little blotchy, and perspiring freely, too, though by then we were all beginning to glow. At one point, he extracted a small bottle from his waistcoat and took a discreet swig.

I lost count of the *entremets*, but recall particularly tartlets filled with crystallized pineapple and an airy mousse that seemed to vanish as you tasted it. Once or twice, the vision of Blake sitting in the Marshalsea rose before me, but I forced the thought away, reminding myself he had chosen his fate.

"Now," said Soyer, "for another new invention, my *pagodatique* entrée platter, upon which we have been working for many months. The platter has a false bottom in which there is silver sand, which we heat up in order to keep the dish warm."

Once again under the supervision of Mr. Percy, a large silver platter with its silver dome was brought in, held by two footmen.

"Behold, a joint of British beef, turnips, apples and peas, and my special sauce Victoria!"

Off came the dome. In silence we inspected the dish: it seemed to shine almost luridly. For the first time, my stomach lurched a little; I suspected my fellow guests felt the same. Suddenly, the room erupted in cries.

"I see!" cried Mr. Blackwell. "It is a cake! Monsieur Soyer—quite extraordinary. Bravo!"

It was true: the whole dish was a dessert, got up to resemble an entrée.

"Another little illusion of mine to stimulate the eyes as well as the tongue," said Soyer. "The beef is in truth a light sponge, carved and iced. Inside, there is fruit and whipped cream. The turnips and apples are frangipane, the peas are early green currants, the sauce is a *crème aux fruits*."

We cheered and set to, each with a little plate of dessert. To be honest, I was not at all certain my stomach would manage it.

The young dandy Mr. Rowlands, who had eaten and drunk as much, if not more, than anyone, emitted a belch, apologized profusely and excused himself. Francobaldi laughed. "The first to succumb," he said.

Just in time, the footmen came round with a tiny spoon of refreshing rosewater ice, and Soyer announced that coffee and cigars would be served. I sat back—perhaps "slumped" would be a better word—inhaled my cigar and fell into an agreeably hazy state as I listened idly to Jerrold and Duncombe gossiping and Mr. Percy filled my glass.

After a while I, too, succumbed—there is no more delicate way to put it—to the call of nature. Mr. Rowlands had not returned to the table. A footman ushered me upstairs into the club.

. . .

I HEARD HIM BEFORE I saw him: a long, awful moan. He had fallen to the floor outside the water closets and was clutching his stomach. I knelt to help him to his feet, but one look told me that it was not drunkenness or dyspepsia that ailed him. His face was gray, his skin was clammy and he could not move.

"I thirst," he croaked. He cried out again and vomited suddenly upon himself. The next moment, he was visited by a terrible convulsion which caused his knees to jerk up to his head. I told the footman to bring help.

"No," Rowlands gasped. "I cannot be seen like this."

Ignoring him, I told the footman to be quick. After some minutes, Mr. Percy arrived with a jug of water, the footman in tow.

"He cannot stand. I think you must call a doctor as soon as possible."

"I imagine he simply needs to sleep it off," said Percy, with the air of a man all too familiar with such things. "We will find him a bed and make sure he is looked after. He will need to be carried upstairs." The footman was sent off to arrange carriage.

Rowlands's body unclenched. He gasped for breath, then he soiled himself. He began to cry, apologizing piteously for having lost control, and saying his stomach burned. He begged for water. I knelt down with the jug.

"Lord, his hands are frozen," I said. Wordless, Percy knelt and rubbed them. Rowlands's heart was racing fit to burst from his chest.

Moments later, several footmen appeared with a makeshift litter, but when they tried to lift Rowlands onto it, he cried out in pain.

"We shall take him to one of the club's bedchambers," Percy said. "They are very comfortable."

"Will you call a doctor?"

"In these cases, it is rarely necessary," said Percy.

I picked up Rowlands's gaudy coat and the jug of water and came after them.

"We have it in hand, Captain Avery," said Percy.

"Mr. Percy." I drew close and muttered in his ear. "I am almost certain that this is the cholera: the vomiting, the diarrhea, the thirst, the spasms. I have seen it fell a man in hours. You must get a doctor."

Mr. Percy rubbed his forehead; for a moment, his composure deserted him. Rowlands shrieked and vomited again, his hands, arched like claws, grasped mine.

"Please, do not leave me!" he gasped. The footmen began to look alarmed and mutinous.

Percy stepped back as if he had been stung. "I will arrange it. But we must get him upstairs." Rowlands was still clutching my hand. "I know it is a great deal to ask, but would you be good enough to stay with him until I return?"

"Of course."

He gave the footmen directions and unhooked a key from his chain. They lifted the litter through a door to a chilly corridor and a set of plain stone steps, evidently the servants' staircase. It was an agonizing journey: the stairs were narrow and steep and seemed to go round and round forever. At every pitch and turn the poor man cried out and twisted in pain, but at the third flight, we came into a corner anteroom and through a doorway onto a carpeted landing. I was directed to the first door to hand. A bedchamber with thick Turkey carpet, red velvet curtains, a marble washstand, a fireplace, a chair and a brass-framed bed, onto which the footmen rolled the patient, none too gently.

The door opened and Percy came in, followed by Morel and a formidable-looking woman in a nightcap and quilted bedcoat who was introduced as the housekeeper, Mrs. Quill. At that moment, Rowlands was seized by another convulsion and voided his guts.

One of the footmen was instructed to light the fire; the others were dismissed. I asked Rowlands if he could describe his symptoms. In a shrunken voice he told me that he was desperately thirsty, his throat and stomach burned, his head ached, and he could not feel his hands or his feet. When the spasms came he could not breathe.

Percy, Morel and Mrs. Quill, the housekeeper, muttered to each other. Mrs. Quill shook her head a great deal.

"All my housemaids are long abed," she said firmly, "and they are none of them sufficiently discreet. We do not want this widely known."

"Matilda is awake," said Morel. "She has been copying out Chef's recipes for the banquet. She is capable and prudent."

I did not like the idea at all but felt it was hardly my place to protest.

"We will need towels, clean linen, hot water and bowls. Will you see to it?" said Percy.

The housekeeper reluctantly assented, though, clearly, she felt it beneath her.

"And laudanum to dull the pain," I said.

Pursed-lipped, she left. Matty arrived not long after. She looked past Morel and Percy at the sick man.

"What is it?" she said.

"It may be the cholera," said Percy, "but we are not certain. He must be nursed and made as comfortable as possible. Will you help, Matilda? You are not obliged to, and it may be unpleasant, but it shall not be forgotten, I assure you. There is hot water from the basin. Mrs. Quill is bringing clean linen and bowls."

"Are you staying, Captain?" she said.

I nodded. "But I would not ask this of you," I said in a low voice.

"Then I will stay," she said.

"We must take care," I said. "In India, we were told not to come too close to cholera sufferers, for fear of inhaling a patient's miasma, and to wash well after contact."

The housekeeper returned, none too graciously, with linen, soap, buckets and a small bottle of laudanum. Then she, Morel and Percy, who said he must report to Monsieur Soyer, left. I mixed a little laudanum in brandy and forced Rowlands to take it, while Matty turned on the copper faucets above the basin. The steaming water flowing into the bowl distracted me for a moment. I had never seen such a thing and was both impressed and secretly alarmed that it might not stop and would overflow into the room. Matty brought over her bowl and cloth and set about cleaning, with great gentleness, this man she had never met, though every touch seemed to pain him. We asked him if he could think what might have caused it; he said he could think of nothing and confessed that he was very frightened. Then for a while he seemed to drift into slumber, and Matty and I sat quiet for a time. I offered her the chair, but she preferred to warm herself next to the hearth.

"I've never been into the club before," she said.

"What? Never?"

"I've never had reason to leave the kitchen, and the servants' stairs take us to our rooms. Women aren't to be seen. If a housemaid hears a member coming when they are cleaning, she must hide in an anteroom or a cupboard."

Rowlands cried out again. The convulsions returned more violently and, each time, he vomited or voided his guts and breathing became more difficult. By the time the club's doctor arrived, Rowlands's skin was wrinkled, as if all the fluid had been wrung from his body. The smell was appalling.

"Cholera," said the doctor briskly. "I am afraid it is too late to bleed him. Indeed, there is very little to be done at all. I doubt he will last the night. I will give him a little brandy now. You may give him more at the correct intervals."

Even as the doctor administered brandy, poor Rowlands cried out for water, and the moment the doctor left we gave it to him.

Through the small hours, Percy and Morel returned intermittently. Then, finally, Soyer came. He was hatless and without his frock coat and rings. He approached the bed as Rowlands was gripped by another spasm. He watched him for a while, then beckoned me to the door.

"Mr. Percy says there is no hope," he whispered. I shook my head.

He came and sat with us, wordless at last, while the poor patient stared at us, his eyes full of terror until, with a last convulsion, he expired.

PART TWO

Chapter Four

After Rowlands died, they insisted I stay what remained of the night at the club. I bade Matty good night, told her to wash thoroughly and said she had shown great kindness and presence of mind. Haunted by Rowlands's desperate face, I did not expect to sleep, but I slipped into unconsciousness almost at once.

When I woke, in the deep folds of a four-poster bed, I was unable to recall where I was. The first thing that came to me was Blake's incarceration, the second that it must be late and that I must have missed the early train to Swindon—once again, I would disappoint my wife. Then the horrors of the night returned to me. I stumbled up. I was astonished to find one of my own clean suits over a chair. A footman knocked and informed me it was ten o'clock and a bath had been drawn for me.

I had never seen such a thing as the bathroom. It was so lavish. The bath was polished marble, and above it was one of the shining copper faucets from which hot water directly issued. The pleasure and novelty of the water distracted me for a while from the memory of the night before. I dressed, folded my evening suit into a bundle and found my way to a grand staircase framed by vast mirrors.

At the bottom was a great square hall such as one might imagine in a grand Roman villa, encircled by a portico of handsome Corinthian columns in ochre marble, and with a mosaic pavement. Under the portico were leather Chesterfields on which members sat, murmuring together. Instead of the open air, a square skylight netted in gilded diamond panes provided a roof through which light poured in, and above the portico was a gallery that ran around the sides of the hall. The walls on the ground floor were picked out in polished-marble panels of oxblood, green and black, and divided by gilded pilasters. The place felt rich and warm. A footman whom I vaguely recalled from the day before accosted me.

"Captain Avery? Jeffers, sir—from last night." I remembered him then. He had gone for Percy when we had found Rowlands on the floor. "May we get you some breakfast?"

I could not think of food. "Thank you. I have a train to catch and am already late."

"Then would you follow me, sir? Just for a moment. You are awaited."

I wanted to be gone.

"Please, sir. They beg just a minute of your time."

"Lead the way."

He took me to a long library that must have run almost the length of the building. The walls were bookcases, every one filled with volumes, divided from each other by gilded pilasters. There were reading desks, deep leather armchairs and a Turkey carpet. By one of the fireplaces, four well-dressed, well-fed men were seated. Five men were standing: Soyer in black velvet, for once capless, and staring resolutely at the carpet; Mr. Percy; another man I did not know; and two liveried footmen.

At a gesture from one of the seated men, all those standing except Soyer departed. My first instinct was mild alarm.

"Gentlemen, what is it that you want of me?" I said.

"We wish only to express our gratitude, Captain Avery. We are the governing committee of the Reform Club—the most significant part of it." This from a man in late middle age, expensively if conservatively dressed in black, with thick, dark umbrella brows, and eyes that looked as if they had been outlined in pencil for some theatrical melodrama. "I am the club's chairman, Lord Marcus Hill. We are so distressed that you were forced to witness the terrible events of last night, and at the same time know that we were fortunate to benefit from your attention and kindness. Won't you sit down?"

It seemed churlish to refuse. "I am sorry I could not do more."

"We give you our thanks. Can we not offer Captain Avery a fortifying brandy or something to eat?"

"Thank you, no. Just now, my appetite is somewhat diminished."

"Of course. May I also say that your reputation, Captain Avery, and that of your talented colleague, Mr. Blake, precedes you. Just the other day I was speaking to an old friend of mine lately retired from the East India Company about your brave defense of the great Mountstuart."

I nodded politely and shifted uneasily in my chair. Soyer continued to stare at the carpet.

"I mean your reputation for courage and for"—Lord Marcus hesitated—"discretion. We would very much like your discretion, Captain. Were it to be widely bruited abroad that the poor gentleman died here in such circumstances, well, the gossip could be very unfairly damaging to the club."

"I had no intention of discussing the matter abroad," I said, a little irked.

"That is a great relief," said Lord Marcus. "And in fact we have something more to ask of you—to beg of you, really. Might we presume further on your goodwill by asking whether you would be willing to look further into the matter for us?"

"I do not understand. He died of cholera, did he not?"

"The fact is, Captain Avery, in four days the club is holding a banquet for a very important eastern potentate, Ibrahim Pasha. You may have heard of him? The Prince of Egypt? Many regard him as the key to peace in the Middle East. Lord Palmerston is hosting the occasion. It will be the pinnacle of the club's existence so far. Crowned heads will be present. Monsieur Soyer has devised an extraordinary menu. All the newspapers, including *The Times,* will devote pages to it. Nothing can be allowed to go wrong. Do you see, Captain Avery?"

"I cannot say I do, nor how it relates to Mr. Rowlands."

A small, red-faced man with a red beard jumped up impatiently. "Damn it, man, let us be clear about this. We need to know what the man died of! If something other than cholera did for him!"

"Captain Beare, please!" said Lord Marcus.

"Do you have any reason to believe it wasn't cholera?" I said. "If so, you will need a doctor or a chemist, not me."

"For heaven's sake, no more of this fimble-famble!" said Captain Beare. "We want you to find out if there's been foul play, or if the kitchen is contaminated and Soyer is fit to run it. And we want you to do it quietly, with no fuss!"

"How dare you! Of course I am fit to run it," said Soyer, suddenly furiously animated.

"That remains to be seen," said Captain Beare, waving his finger.

"There is nothing wrong with my kitchen!" shouted Alexis Soyer. "If you are looking for so-called foul play, look to yourselves."

"Soyer!" said Lord Marcus.

"I offer my unreserved apologies, milord," said Soyer immediately. "But my kitchen is the cleanest you will ever see."

"We have no doubt of that, Monsieur Soyer," said Lord Marcus mollifyingly.

"There he is, getting above himself again," said Captain Beare, shaking his head.

"Captain Beare, you are not helping," said Lord Marcus.

"I am sorry to be obtuse, gentlemen, but you will have to make things a good deal clearer to me if you want me to help," I said.

Lord Marcus rubbed his chin. I realized he was uneasy.

"Captain Avery, before I say any more, I must have your word that you will speak nothing of what you hear in this room. It is absolutely vital."

I did my best to hide my surprise. "I give you my word."

"The fact is, the banquet for Ibrahim Pasha is extremely important, and absolutely nothing can be allowed to obstruct or impede it. The matter is also exceedingly sensitive, the fruit of the combined efforts of certain members of both parties, Tory and Whig—I mean, liberal." He looked around, smiling.

"I beg your pardon?" I said.

"Of course, this must be kept strictly secret. As I said, the banquet must be a success. Ibrahim Pasha has come to England ostensibly on a private holiday but in fact on behalf of his ailing eighty-year-old father, Mehmet Ali Pasha, the ruler of Egypt. The banquet is a vital symbol of goodwill between Egypt and Britain, and the beginning of very delicate and secret negotiations among Egypt, Turkey and ourselves—an attempt to prevent war, no less. The truth is, the Russians are doing their best to start a war in the Middle East. They aim to draw Egypt into an alliance against Turkey. They have promised Egypt arms and territory if they will come in with them. As you know, barely two years ago Ibrahim Pasha took Palestine and Syria from the Turks and was almost at the gates of Constantinople."

"And it was our own dear Lord Palmerston who sent British warships to bombard his armies and force them out," said another man sardonically. He was younger than the others and fashionably dressed in a bright tartan waistcoat and a plum-colored coat. "Which is why relations are so delicate."

"Thank you, Molesworth," Lord Marcus said, with a rather forced smile. "We did so with the help of the Russians, you will recall, and signed an agreement on it. Now they are reneging upon it. We all want to avoid another war, at all costs. We have only just extricated ourselves from China, and Afghanistan is going none too well."

"Both wars Palmerston encouraged," said the man called Molesworth.

Lord Marcus went on, "If Ibrahim Pasha is seduced by the Russians, we will be obliged to help Turkey, the Middle East will be a disaster and Russia will almost certainly use this as an excuse to attack our northern borders in India. I have no need to explain to you, Captain Avery, the dangers attached to that."

"May I ask why the government is not arranging the dinner?"

"Yes, why is it not?" asked Molesworth.

Lord Marcus ignored him. "We do not want to alert the Russians, or the Tory party—who, in their usual ostrichlike way, want nothing to do with the outside world, and would do their best to stall any agreement with Egypt. The prime minister, Sir Robert Peel, however, fully understands the risks. He and Lord Palmerston both agree that something must be done. Thus, Palmerston—who is Britain's most respected figure when it comes to foreign policy, even if he is out of government—will be conducting the secret negotiations with the whole world watching, and none the wiser. He is also a sufficiently elevated figure to legitimately entertain Ibrahim Pasha, when the government are apparently ignoring him. So you see."

"See what?" I said, mildly irritated.

Lord Marcus opened his mouth. And closed it again. Soyer sighed.

The skeptical gentleman, Mr. Molesworth, spoke up. "The fact is, Captain Avery, something not dissimilar to Rowlands's death took place at the club some weeks ago. It is possible that this is not a coincidence, that neither man may have died of natural causes. That both may have been murdered. And that this is some attempt to disrupt or even prevent the banquet, which, of course, as Lord Marcus has repeated several times, must proceed smoothly."

At the word "murdered" the other members of the committee visibly shuddered. Molesworth seemed to me to enjoy this. He went on, "We need to establish what Mr. Rowlands died of, if there has been, as Captain Beare calls it, 'foul play' and, most importantly, where it comes from and who has perpetrated it. And it must be done discreetly, so as not to spread alarm. I think that is everything?"

Soyer spoke, and there was a hint of desperation in his voice, "Captain Avery, if you and Mr. Blake might be prevailed upon to help, I should be forever in your debt."

"Of course, the greatest likelihood is that nothing is amiss," said Lord Marcus soothingly. "But we have to be sure."

"What was the earlier case? The one similar to Rowlands's?" I said.

"It was not *very* similar," said Lord Marcus. "Some three weeks ago, one of our members was taken ill in the street after an evening at the club."

"After dining rather lavishly at the club," Molesworth corrected.

"Everett Cunningham was his name. He was not a young man and had a weak heart, but even so."

"He was perfectly healthy," said Molesworth, "if given to gluttony. He vomited in the street and was dead by the following morning."

"Did a doctor diagnose a cause of death?"

"The club doctor was sent to attend him. What was the diagnosis?" Once again, Molesworth seemed amused.

"I am sure we can find a record of it, if Captain Avery thinks it necessary," said Lord Marcus.

Another man stood up. He was exceedingly plump, with a soft, pink face reminiscent of blancmange. "Captain Avery, I am Edward Ellice, the club's founder," he said. He had an air of considerable satisfaction, proceeding, I suspected, from a considerable bank balance. "I should like to add that we would remunerate you well—very well—for any time and effort you expend on the matter."

"Thank you, Ellice," said Lord Marcus. "I believe also that Mr. Percy has arranged for your belongings to be brought here. Should you decide to depart for your home, you may do so immediately. Should you stay, as we hope you will, it would be a great convenience to us if you took rooms at the club—naturally, at our expense."

"But my account at the Oriental—" I said.

"—has been paid," said Mr. Ellice.

I blinked. I felt the familiar stirrings of excitement and was flattered by their persistence. Another week in London would not be too great a hardship, nor would the fee. Perhaps I might persuade Blake out of the Marshalsea and watch over Matty for a while longer. Then I brought myself back to reality.

"Gentlemen, I am sensible of the honor you do me—and my associate, Mr. Blake. But I cannot accept. Firstly, I promised my wife I would return home today. Secondly, I am a Tory born and bred. I should not really have set foot in the Reform at all, I meant only to visit the kitchen—"

"We will not tell if you do not," said Lord Marcus Hill. "More than a few men of your party have been tempted to cross the threshold by virtue of Monsieur Soyer's skills."

"Thirdly, Mr. Blake is indisposed, that is to say, he is not available, being engaged—"

"Surely he will come if you ask him," said Soyer.

"And if he cannot extricate himself, which is highly likely, you would be left with just me, and I neither know London well, nor have his skills—"

"Captain Avery, you are too modest."

"Truly, I am not." Truly, I was not.

"Please, Captain Avery."

I had always been bad at saying no. "My Lord, gentlemen, I assure you I would be little use to you on my own, but I will see what I can do about Mr. Blake, and I promise to put myself at your disposal, for one day at least."

"Excellent news," said Lord Marcus Hill.

"So," said the red-faced Captain Beare, "what is your first move, Avery?"

"Ah," I said.

I had not the faintest idea.

"As a matter of fact," said Molesworth, the skeptic, "I have taken the liberty of summoning a surgeon to conduct a postmortem examination of the body. I expect him here very shortly."

"A surgeon?" said Captain Beare suspiciously.

"A medic, and a brother."

"A brother?"

"A brother MP. A radical."

"Not Wakley, the member for Finsbury?" said plump Mr. Ellice.

"The very same," said Molesworth, amused.

"Oh, no!" Ellice dashed his hand against his forehead. "Wakley is the least discreet man. You have been very hasty, Molesworth. And a postmortem will involve a coroner and a police report, will it not? I thought the one thing we wished to do was *not* draw attention to Mr. Rowlands's demise."

"We cannot hide it, and Wakley is a coroner as well as a surgeon, and indisputably honest."

"Far too honest, if you ask me," said Ellice. "He is a troublemaker and a busybody."

"What do you think, Captain Avery?" said Lord Marcus.

"If there is any more to Rowlands's death than there appears," I said, with more confidence than I felt, "then a postmortem is the only way to discover it."

"I wonder if it would be possible," Ellice mused, "to have the postmortem but perhaps to delay making public its findings?" He gazed at me questioningly.

"You will have to ask Mr. Wakley. I think it unlikely and, even if Mr. Blake could carry off such a thing, as I said before, I would not know how."

"No, no, of course, Mr. Ellice should not have asked," said Lord Marcus.

I suggested that the club should be aired and fumigated to remove any lurking cholera. And that we send to Soyer's other guests of the night before to discover if any of them had been taken ill. The committee readily agreed to the former, and footmen were set to opening every window in the building—to the exasperation, I later discovered, of the members. As for sending to discover the state of the other guests, they were extremely reluctant. I let the matter go, promising myself I would revisit it later.

Then, with a good deal of relief, I retired to my room "to think." My belongings, such as they were, had already been laid on the daybed and a fire had been lit in the grate. Clearly, they had been confident of convincing me.

I made my letter to Blake as persuasive as I could: brief and straightforward as to the circumstances of Rowlands's death, the club's request, the possibility of conspiracy and Soyer's worry. I also made no bones about how at sea I was and how in need of his advice. I arranged for it to be delivered to Collinson, since I could not let the club know where Blake was, with a covering note mentioning that it might just change Blake's mind.

I turned—uneasily—to the letter I owed my wife, Helen. I explained that I had been asked to undertake a task in London which I felt I could not refuse. I rushed over the matter of my lodging at the Reform, of which she would disapprove, and instead mentioned Collinson, by whom I knew she would be impressed. I told her I would return home as soon as I possibly could, asked her to kiss the baby for me and signed myself her devoted and affectionate husband. To my sister Louisa I wrote more honestly, a fact that, as usual, provoked guilty feelings and yet seemed unavoidable, confessing that I had succumbed to the Reform Club's flattery, that I must spend a little more time in London for Blake's sake, and that I had little idea of what I should do.

I SHOULD HAVE LIKED to have slept, but I feared I would lose the rest of the day. So I took myself down to the kitchen to see if I could find Soyer, or even Matty. There was no trace of them, or indeed any sign of what had passed the night before. Instead, a group of fifteen or so ladies and gentlemen hovered in the middle of the kitchen next to the oddest-shaped table I had ever seen. It was about twelve feet long, though, given the size of the kitchen, it did not seem that large, and was shaped like a lozenge or a Christmas cracker without the ends, with some twelve sides. In its middle stood a great iron cupboard.

Percy appeared. "Welcome, ladies and gentlemen," he said. He had to shout a little to compete with the clatter and whistle of the kitchen. "Welcome to the kitchens of the Reform Club. I am Mr. Percy, steward of the Reform Club. I order and oversee supplies, see to their storage, marshal the accounts. And I am the cellarman, ordering wines and spirits—under instructions, of course, from Monsieur Soyer and the Wine Committee." He smiled, and brought out an enormous ring of keys. "Today, I shall be your guide on our tour." Even I had heard of the Reform's famous kitchen tours.

There was a hum of disappointment. Mr. Percy smiled sympathetically. "I regret to say that Monsieur Soyer, or 'Chef,' as we call him, is unavoidably detained. He would have moved heaven and earth to be with you, if he could.

"As you know," Percy continued, "the kitchens opened almost a year ago to instant acclaim, and so remarkable, so novel, and so impressive have visitors found them, that we have taken to giving regular tours for the discerning. In the last year, the kitchen has served almost twenty thousand meals"—he paused for the gasp of amazement—"and that does not include the thousands of hot beverages, *amuses-bouches* and breakfasts we also prepare. There are well over sixty staff, from potboys to kitchen maids to skilled cooks. The cooks, you will note, wear tall white hats called 'toques.' The staff are divided into sections. One, for example, prepares sauces, another roasts, another sees to the grilling and frying of meats, another prepares fish, another the soups and vegetables; another, known as the *garde manger,* prepares cold savories, such as aspics, terrines, hams and salads; and, finally, we have the *pâtissier* for sweets, desserts, ices and special cakes, as well as our own baker. Heat, light and ice are produced with the help of our six-horse-power steam engine, which sits in a purpose-built room well below the kitchens. We have gas pipes throughout the kitchen and the club. I can tell you that the club spent the sum of six hundred and seventy-four pounds on pots, pans, knives and utensils." There was another gasp of amazement at the vast sum. "By the end of your visit, I hope you will agree that the Reform's kitchens are a temple to science and innovation, to England's genius in progress and, if I may say so, the genius of Monsieur Alexis Soyer, who is responsible for so many of the brilliant and new ideas exhibited here." There was nothing showy about his speech; indeed, one might almost have described him as a little dry, but somehow this served to make his words all the more persuasive. Since I could spy neither Soyer nor Matty, I decided I would join the tour.

"Let us start with this strange but ingenious table," said Percy. "It is made of elm and it has twelve sides. Monsieur Soyer came up with it, so as to allow twelve cooks to work upon it at one time without getting in each other's way. But look underneath. There are special drawers for knives, chopping boards that slide out on casters, and copper buckets with mops so that the table is always clean. And see, around the two pillars in the middle of the table, the little shelves at arm's height contain boxes of herbs and seasonings which spin about. The iron box in the center of the table is a steam closet for keeping finished dishes warm. Everything is thought of, no space is wasted. This is typical of Monsieur Soyer."

Percy led us around the kitchen, pointing out each clever innovation: a tall and shallow fireplace for roasting game and poultry on spits under which the coals were piled vertically upon themselves, like a wall, to present more heat. The heat kept small ovens and trays of shallow water set in the sides of the fireplace warm so that sauces and soups could be kept at a constant temperature. In the corridor between the cold meat and sauce larders and the principal kitchen was a sloping iron table upon which salmon, turbot, Dover sole and half a dozen lobsters were kept chilled by the action of iced water coursing over them. Orders from the dining room upstairs were communicated by speaking tubes to a kitchen clerk who sat at a high desk tucked away in the main kitchen. Dishes were delivered to the dining room without delay by cupboards called "lifts," which were moved up and down a shaft by a series of pulleys operated both by hand and with the application of steam. Never had I seen anything so clever.

And the smells! In one corner, the scent of sweet, yeasty baking; nearby, the tang of juiced lemons; in another corner, gentle, soupy aromas emanating from cauldrons of simmering veal and beef that made the stomach groan; and in a third, the spitting, fatty savor of roasting meat.

Perhaps the most remarkable things of all were the two vast gas stoves: great, square, cast-iron boxes, the fronts of which were divided into five separate compartments, each with its own little door, not unlike a chest of drawers. The wonder of them was that heat could be produced instantly the moment it was needed, and extinguished the moment it was not; and that the temperatures could be regulated so that one compartment was blastingly hot while the one next to it was merely warm. The same was true of the top of the range, on which sat a series of trivets under which circles of flame were fed by gas flues. One stew pan bubbled wildly while that next to it barely simmered. The greatest miracle was that it was clean: there was no coal, with its noxious fumes, and no ash casting blackened dust over every surface.

"On these two stoves, ladies and gentlemen, we can cook a dinner for six hundred people in the time it would take a housewife to roast an ordinary joint. These stoves save the club not only time but two hundredweight of coal a day. Moreover, they produce no carbonic acid, the unfortunate result of burning charcoal, a trial and poison for every chef. It was carbonic acid," Percy said, lowering his voice, "that took the life of Monsieur's own brother Philippe, chef to the Duke of Cambridge, only last year. Monsieur Soyer believes that, one day, there will be a gas stove in every kitchen in England." We half-laughed, impressed but disbelieving.

"We are nearing the end of our tour," said Percy. "Come this way."

We followed him to one of the side kitchens, and there, standing before a paneled wall, stood Soyer, velvet suit, tilted cap, diamond rings and all. In his hand he brandished a wooden spoon—his one concession to his trade.

"Welcome, welcome, my friends," he said, "to the kitchens of the Reform, the most advanced, the most remarkable and well-arranged kitchen in the world! You may have heard of me"—he smiled coyly, for of course everyone knew who he was—"I am Alexis Soyer, the architect of this extraordinary enterprise. Here, you witness history. Here, we employ dozens of technical innovations which I have perfected in order to create hundreds of dishes every day, and we ensure that each one is produced perfectly and served in precisely the correct state, and at precisely the correct temperature, as I intended when first I invented it. What you see here is not merely novelty but the triumph of science, the kitchen of the future."

The audience applauded enthusiastically.

"Three things are of immeasurable importance in this place. One is cleanliness. Cleanliness is the soul of the kitchen," he said, wagging his spoon. "This kitchen is the cleanest you will ever see. The second is timing. You will see clocks on every wall. In cooking, precise timing is the difference between perfection and failure. Finally, there is the precise control of temperature. Here, we command the elements: fire, water, air in the form of gas and steam; and earth in the form of coal and charcoal. Ladies and gentlemen, in this kitchen, we are alchemists, magicians even."

Soyer half pirouetted on his shiny pumps and began to move the wall before which he had been speaking. It was, we now saw, balanced on well-oiled casters, and slid smoothly sideways, folding slightly.

We were suddenly buffeted by a heat so intense we had to step back.

"You are safe here. No harm can come to you," said Soyer. Before us was a great fireplace in which a vast mound of charcoal glittered and over which hung two enormous turn-spits, each large enough to roast a whole sheep.

"A little conjuring trick of mine," said Soyer, grinning. "You had no idea that the fire was here, *non?* Things in this kitchen are not always what they seem. The screen prevents the rest of the kitchen from becoming too hot. It is lined with tin on the fire side, so the heat is reflected back upon the spits and cooks the meat more evenly and quickly. But the fire is not merely for these. Behind it is a boiler which provides us with gallons of hot water for the kitchen. And around it, also benefiting from its heat, are boiling stoves, charcoal grates, small ovens for soufflés and pastry, and a steam closet. The spits are caused to turn by hot air from the fire. We waste nothing here. Waste, as I always say, is abominable ingratitude to God.

"And within our movable wall, there are little warming shelves." He swung the screen around to the side to reveal a small space in the thickness of the screen, and pulled from it a small tray of tiny tartlets, each one filled with a shiny yellow custard and topped with a dark cherry. "Please," he said, encouraging us each to take one. Eager gloved hands seized the dainty pastries. Even I did not resist. The first sensation was warmth and crispness but, just as one appreciated this, the tart melted on the tongue. The filling was an almond cream, not thick like a paste but whipped and airy. The cherry, which had slumbered in brandy since its harvesting, trembled then burst gloriously.

"And another?" said Soyer. We did not hold back. "When the Duchess of Sutherland came to view the kitchens, she was so impressed with my screen that she ordered one for her own kitchens!"

No one else seemed much surprised by this egregious piece of boasting.

"And now, *mesdames et messieurs,* you have seen the pots and pans and stoves, but you must, before you go, see what is cooking!"

He coaxed a woman to try a mouthful of a soup he was "concocting for a certain milord who will be dining at the club tonight." Indecorously plunging his forefinger, complete with its diamond ring, into the cauldron, he scooped it up and into his mouth. "Mmmm, a *leetle* more salt, I think, and a *leetle* of this magic dust," he said, smiling at us and reaching into a small box. "Perfect!"

He called to another lady, who had looked crotchety throughout. "How wonderful to see you, milady. It must have been, let me see, with the Dowager Marchioness of Downshire? It is a pleasure and an honor to see you once more. You must come and taste just a *soupçon* of this sole *à la maître d'hôtel.* As I recall, it was your late husband's favorite dish? Let us see if it finds favor."

The lady allowed herself to be drawn forward and even submitted to eating a mouthful of the fish from a spoon proffered by Soyer himself. Then she smiled beatifically and pronounced it "Delicious!"

"And now, dear friends," and Soyer bowed so low it seemed impossible that his cap would not fall off—and yet it did not—"I must leave you. A chef is always wanted in three places at once, and I must attend to my sauces." He raised an eyebrow in such a way as to suggest . . . I am not quite sure what, but several of the ladies could not suppress a nervous giggle.

"Our tour is at an end. I wish you sweet *adieux.* I hope we have informed and entertained you. If you are intrigued, if you are impressed, our work is done. We seek only to please." He bowed again, brought his fingers to his lips and blew us a somewhat operatic kiss, and began to back out of the kitchen. "*Adieu, adieu, adieu.* As your great playwright says, 'Parting is such sweet sorrow.'" He turned, and was gone.

The party on the tour dispersed, and I was left, a little bewildered, surrounded by kitchen maids and chefs.

Soyer suddenly appeared from one of the side kitchens and seized my shoulders, kissing me on both cheeks. I was shocked.

He laughed. "You are not familiar with the French way, eh? You will have to become accustomed to many grateful kisses now. I cannot thank you enough for agreeing to stay and help us! I am sure all will be well now. May we offer you a *soupçon* of anything? A dish of kidneys? A coddled egg? A little side of bacon, perhaps?"

My stomach turned a little, and I declined.

"*Non*, I can see, after last night . . ." he said, and for a moment the relentless smile was wiped from his face.

"Oh, no, Monsieur Soyer, it was wonderful, extraordinary, astonishing," I said, my epithets surprising even me. "Thank you! I have never tasted anything like it." It was all true and, at the same time, irretrievably clouded by what had come after.

"It was my pleasure," said Soyer, and his face fell again.

"Captain Avery?" A voice called from the other side of the kitchen. The footman whose face I knew. He fought his way across the kitchen. He was out of breath.

"Jeffers, sir? From last night?" he said.

"Of course."

"Been searching for you. Couldn't find you, sir," he said almost reproachfully. "There's a gentleman to see you, upstairs. A surgeon: Mr. Wakley."

Chapter Five

Mr. Wakley was a big man with a prominent, hawkish nose. Every part of him gave the impression of impatience and distracted concentration. His brow was knotted, his mouth was pursed and his chin taut. He drummed his fingers on the worn leather case on his lap, and at the same time tapped his foot on a rare edge of uncarpeted floor. This caused the other gentlemen in the room to shoot him irritated looks, which he ignored. The only hint of levity was his hair, which, despite his middle age, fell in great, lavish, dark gold curls about his face.

I had kept him waiting.

"I should like to get on," he said, rather more loudly than necessary, as two dozen eyes lifted to regard him crossly. "I have a great many things to attend to today. This is not the kind of case I should generally take on, believe me, nor do I care much for this place—as far as I am concerned, it has been the muzzling of the radicals. But since Molesworth asked me . . ."

"I do apologize, Dr. Wakley. Shall we proceed?"

"*Mr.* Wakley." He stood up, gathering his case, and followed me out into the saloon. "I am a surgeon, not a medic; there is a difference. I must say, I was most surprised to receive the call, for I am hardly clubbable and make no bones of regarding this place as the graveyard of the radicals." He said this with a grim little smile. "They have been seduced by fine dinners and thick carpets and marble halls and, once again, the Whigs, those antediluvian relics, are in charge. I am, sir, you see, a member of Parliament myself, and a radical. I suppose I am Molesworth's revenge. And who, sir, are you?"

I explained.

"Well," he said skeptically, "you are very young. So, the body. Where is it?"

"The body? In a bedchamber upstairs."

"And the name?"

"Mr. Rowlands, an MP."

"Not little Charlie Rowlands? Fancy dresser? Whiggish tendencies?" I nodded. "Dear me, not overly serious, but too young to die. He was a friend of Tommy Duncombe, my neighboring MP."

"May I speak plainly?" I said. I explained the circumstances of Rowlands's death, and the club's request.

"Does Duncombe know?"

I shook my head.

He sighed. "He must be told."

Our dialogue was interrupted by a man in black suiting who came bustling up to us.

"Mr. Wakley? I am the club secretary, Mr. Scott. And Captain Avery, I have not had a moment to introduce myself. You may not recall, but we encountered each other earlier. Do not hesitate to call on me if you require anything." He had a hurried manner, full of self-importance, as if he had much more pressing and significant things to be doing elsewhere, and flat, undistinguished features. He rubbed his hands a lot. "I am delighted you have made each other's acquaintance," he said.

"So, what have you done thus far?" said Wakley to Scott.

Scott said that, since the committee had wished the matter to be dealt with discreetly, he had thus far done nothing.

"You've done *nothing?*" said Wakley. "What kind of man are you? What of his family? Are they coming to collect the body? Have plans been made for the burial?"

Mr. Scott said he had not yet informed Rowlands's family of his death.

"Not told the family, sir! Outrageous! And an egregious waste of my time!" Wakley almost shouted. "A postmortem examination cannot be performed unless the family of the deceased request it or a coroner has ordered it. I assume you have informed the coroner?" he said, turning to me.

"I am sorry, sir," I said. "I rather thought you were one, and that, thus far, we had no reason to call one. The doctor who attended Mr. Rowlands diagnosed cholera, but we wished to be sure by having a postmortem examination."

"I do not like it much, but I see the sense in establishing quickly whether the boy did die of cholera or not. And I am the correct man for the job, being both a coroner and a surgeon—you would be surprised how few there are. I can fill out the relevant papers, but I ought to convene a court on the matter, and it would be unusual for me to perform the postmortem examination as well—though it is not illegal. Ideally, it should be done in a mortuary, or at the least in my own surgery. I cannot imagine there is anywhere suitable in this ridiculous palace." He gazed up at the saloon's grand glass dome.

"You"—he waved at Scott, for whom I now felt almost sorry—"find me a messenger boy. I will need my assistant to bring my instruments, and I will send a note to the Westminster coroner, whom I know, to arrange matters. Presumably, the party has not been told of Rowlands's death either? It should be the duty of the club to inform the party."

Scott shook his head. He looked rather crushed.

Wakley glanced back at him. "What? Still here? I need this *now!*" And he turned his back on the unfortunate secretary, who immediately scuttled away.

THERE WERE SEVERAL ROOMS outside the kitchen's main area which might serve as a place in which Wakley could do his work. Mr. Percy arranged for the body to be moved to one. It lay covered by a sheet on one of the butler's tables, its proximity to the kitchen mildly disturbing.

Wakley and I descended to the kitchen. The scene had changed entirely; it was nothing like the orderly oasis it had seemed only half an hour before. It was luncheon, and a state of furious chaos prevailed. The heat was now tropical and, everywhere, there was shouting. I gradually made this out to be demands for dishes in a curious combination of French and English: "*Deux côtelettes!* Two stewed rump! *Trois canetons! Une sole!* One ox tongue! *Trois turbots!* Two chops!"

Cooks bent, red-faced, over steaming and smoking pans, enveloped in clouds of heat, perspiring freely. Kitchen maids and boys dashed from table to stove to fire, carrying vast stew pans or sauce boats wrapped in white cloths, or trays of plates and bowls. Soyer, a white apron over his velvet suiting, his ridiculous cap askew upon his head, stood in the main kitchen by the kitchen clerk's desk, inspecting each dish.

"Is that the famous Monsieur Soyer?" said Wakley. "I should like to meet him."

I hesitated; Soyer was entirely engrossed, and dozens of dishes were awaiting his inspection. But I led Wakley over anyway.

"Monsieur Soyer," I said. "May I—?"

Soyer glanced at Wakley. "Do I know you, sir?"

"No," said Wakley genially, "but I am about to carve up your deceased dinner guest."

Soyer's smile wavered.

"Thomas Wakley at your service: surgeon, coroner, member of Parliament, editor and founder of *The Lancet* medical journal: 'We amputate nonsense and let in the light of truth and common sense.' I am to divine the cause of Mr. Rowlands's death."

"Mr. Molesworth's acquaintance! Enchanted to meet you," said Soyer.

"I have been following your work at the consumption hospital in Knightsbridge and the Clerkenwell poorhouse, Soyer," said Wakley. "Impressive results! In my opinion, your scientific systems should be adopted by every hospital and poorhouse in the country, and I shall be saying so in my next editorial."

"Why, Mr. Wakley, I am ravished and enchanted by your words," said Soyer. "They come at a moment of shadow, and they bring the sun with them!" And he suddenly embraced the surgeon and kissed him upon both cheeks.

"Well," said Wakley, extremely startled, "I think we should commence with the postmortem."

WAKLEY EXAMINED the room and decided it would do, though he complained that the light was dim. Rather peremptorily, he demanded gas lamps, a basin, water, a deal of clean linen, the permanent loan of four glass jars with stoppers as tight as possible, and several large dishes which "the kitchen would not be sad to lose." All this was quickly furnished with admirable efficiency, along with an iron post higher than a man and curved at the end on which a lamp could be hooked to provide overhead light. One of the kitchen clerks asked if we should like something to eat.

Wakley gave a brief, slightly scornful smile and shook his head. Uncertain of what would be required of me, I declined, too.

By now, Wakley's assistant had arrived. The two men removed their neckties and frock coats, rolled up their sleeves and put on white aprons. Over the table and bench in the room, the assistant laid thick tablecloths. Wakley placed his leather case of surgical instruments on one of these and opened it. Laid upon the red cloth interior was an array of formidable-looking instruments: two or three scissorlike tools, a saw with a red wooden handle; two tweezerlike implements; a thing very like a sharp shepherd's crook; and five knives with blades of varying lengths. From his bag, Wakley's assistant brought forth a ledger and pencil. Wakley washed his hands and instructed his assistant to draw back the sheet. Together they divested the cadaver of his clothes, often with a judicious snip of scissors. There was poor Rowlands, no longer a man, just a gray-faced, unfamiliar mannequin.

"Will you stay, Captain Avery? My assistant is a little squeamish." (At this, the assistant reddened and looked intently at his ledger.) "It is not for the fainthearted, but you will certainly learn something."

I did not relish the thought, but I had seen some unpleasant things during my campaign in India and had grown up on a farm, and I thought I should stay.

The young footman who had brought the last of the jars idled by the door, too, curious.

Wakley leaned over the body, looking first at the face, and especially the lips and mouth. I had seen Blake do much the same thing.

"Face is somewhat dehydrated and shrunken, but no bluishness," he said, and the assistant made a note. "It is congested, however. See, Captain Avery, it is darker than the rest of the body."

"Is that indicative of something?

"If you have seen cholera before, you will recall that the face falls in and the skin often takes on a bluish tinge. This gentleman is not blue—though that is not conclusive of anything—but the darkness of the face is unusual and may indicate something else."

He moved his attention to the rest of the body, which was wrinkled and wrung out, but not as badly as some I had seen taken by cholera. Slowly, he scrutinized every inch, muttering to himself and every so often passing unintelligible comments to his assistant.

"Ah," he said, as he reached the feet.

He returned to the face. In a swift and almost violent movement he forced open the jaw, bent over the mouth and sniffed. He sniffed again. "No especially pungent smells."

With the gaslight over his head, he thrust his fingers into the mouth, felt about and then peered in.

"Hmm," he said.

He turned to his instruments and picked up a knife and a pair of scissors.

"Scalpel and forceps, Captain Avery," he said, holding them up. "The light is not perfect. Might you be able to hold the lamp directly over the body, should I ask you, while my assistant makes the notes? If you cannot, I shall not think the less of you. I have seen the strongest man laid low by the contents of a man's stomach, and I should rather know it before you have passed out on the floor."

I assured him that I would be able, though I was not at all sure I would. With that, he made a deep cut into poor Rowlands's middle. Blood bloomed slowly on either side of the cut. Wakley asked if I would wipe it away gently, which I did. At this, the footman swiftly withdrew.

The next minutes were not ones I wish to recall in precise detail. That first cut went from the chest bone to the bottom of the pelvis. There was blood, but not quantities of it. Then Wakley made a cut at ninety degrees across the first long one so that he was able to fold back the skin of the chest and abdomen, and clipped the two flaps back. The chill in the room helped ensure the smell was not as bad as I had feared, though the legacy of the night before rendered me more nauseous than I had expected, and it took a good deal to maintain my equilibrium. As he inspected the body's cavity, sniffing gently and prodding various organs, Wakley asked me to bring the lamp closer. I did not look away. Having examined it to his satisfaction, he dictated a few lines to his assistant, and then, from his case, brought out a piece of catgut and, pushing the ribs gently apart, found a red, tube-like extrusion and tied a tight knot about it. He tied two further tight knots around a similar protuberance at the bottom of the pelvis.

"Captain Avery, would you bring that dish across to me? I shall now remove the stomach." From the corner of my eye, I saw him make two cuts on either side of the two sets of knots and lift out a large, sagging, red sack, which he set on the plate I held. I nearly gagged but placed the dish on the table behind me. I was suddenly and horribly reminded of Soyer's feast; Wakley's arranging of the body parts seemed a hideous parody of it. The thought made my gorge rise.

Wakley removed the guts in similar fashion. I provided the dishes and bowl and held the lamp. Then he went through the various organs—liver, kidney, spleen and, finally, the heart—prodding, examining, making observations that his assistant noted down, then removing each organ and placing it into a jar which I held for him and immediately closed as tightly as I could. He returned again to the cavity, scrutinizing the upper chest and neck and the bottom of the gut, and making several small cuts.

"I shall now examine the stomach. I think, perhaps, Captain Avery, you should turn away. You have done better than I expected."

I did not argue.

At length, he announced that he had finished.

"Interesting. I am glad you called upon me."

"And your conclusion?" I said.

"You were there when he was taken ill?"

"I was."

"I should like to know the order in which his symptoms appeared. Did he say he was thirsty?

"Yes."

"When? At what point? Was it before or after he had vomited?

I tried to think back. "Before. He was thirsty from the start."

"Did he vomit and then evacuate his bowels, or was it the bowels first?"

"He vomited."

"It is not cholera. Of that I can assure you. The body is, among other things, simply too wet. Cholera dries a body out. And you would expect to find the surface of the stomach and gut almost dry and velvety smooth. No, this is not cholera. Let me show you. Here, the liver. There are the beginnings of fatty deposits all across it. And here in the heart. You cannot see it so clearly in the jar, but the left chamber is full of liquid—blood has leaked into it. And the stomach, if you will give it a glance, is very inflamed. Here, see the patches of deep crimson and these clusters of small brown ulcers; they continue all the way down into the gut. I have taken some samples of the liquid from the stomach and the gut and will analyze them in my rooms, if I have time—otherwise, I shall send some to a chemist—and that will show it beyond doubt. But the organs do not lie, and I am certain I know what they say."

"What, Mr. Wakley?"

"I am at this moment fairly satisfied that this man died from arsenic poisoning."

By the time a quailing Mr. Scott arrived to inform us that messages had been sent to Rowlands's lodgings and family, Wakley had sewed up the body, wrapped it in a new sheet, made arrangements for it to be sent to the mortuary, boxed his samples and sent his assistant away with them to his surgery.

"Well, Captain Avery," said the surgeon. He was almost cordial. "What will you do now?"

My heart had started to beat loud in my ears when he mentioned arsenic, and I had been racking my brains for everything I could remember of the dinner. Who had sat next to Rowlands? (The MP Duncombe—who on his other side had had me—and the rude chef, Francobaldi.) What particularly he had eaten? (As far as I could recall, everything, and a good deal of it.)

"I must discover who poisoned him and what dish killed him."

"Hold on to your horses, young man! It is possible the meal killed him—the violence of his reaction could suggest as much—but though I cannot say I have much regard for the Reform, it seems to me unlikely that such a thing would happen here. In my experience, most deliberate poisonings take place in domestic settings—women murdering husbands and lodgers, and so forth."

"So you are saying he was not poisoned by Soyer's dinner?"

"It is possible he was. The inflammation and corrosion begin further down the digestive tract, and are noticeable in the stomach and gut, which might be commensurate with his ingesting the arsenic somewhere toward the middle or end of the meal, so the effect of the poison would have been a little delayed by the other foods he had already consumed. It is also possible that he was not. There are many ways in which arsenic could have entered his body without any deliberate act of malice. Quite apart from killing bedbugs and mice, and in taxidermy, you will know as well as I that arsenic is found in every area of daily life: in cures for malaria, for asthma, for leprosy, even, God help us, in self-styled restorative tonics, lotions to restore gray hair to its previous color and skin creams sold by quacks, noodles and knaves! Did you also know that it provides a color pigment called Scheele's green, which is found in paint, upon wallpaper and even on cloth?"

I said I did not.

"Some years ago a young woman died after wearing a green tarlatan dress to a party. She was overcome by the fumes from the arsenic dye on her skirts. Frankly, it is a scandal, one I myself have taken pains to expose, thus far to very little effect. The authorities, with their corrupt vested interests and their criminal apathy, do nothing."

"I do recall seeing Mr. Rowlands drinking from a small bottle of tonic."

"Aha! Perhaps he overdid his medication; or sleeps in a room with green wallpaper. Perhaps," he said, raising an eyebrow, "he has a taste for stuffing and mounting animal skins. Or perhaps he has a vengeful butler or mistress. There are, you see, signs that he might have ingested small amounts of arsenic over a longer period, which built up in his stomach and finally killed him. He had the beginnings of fatty deposits on his liver. His heart had leaked. These imply, though do not prove, a longer gestation. What do you know of Rowlands?"

"Almost nothing. I met him but once. Last night. He was a very keen trencherman."

"I assume you suffered no ill effects from the dinner? Have you discovered whether anyone else did?"

"As far as I know, we are all well."

"As far as you know? Oh, my dear sir, you have been deputized by the club. You must be methodical! You must be systematic! What will you do next?"

"There are seven members of the dinner I have not seen personally. I will discover if they had any ill effects."

"Good. And?"

"I will find out what I can about Rowlands."

"I would recommend a visit to Thomas Duncombe, my fellow MP in Finsbury. They were good friends. I can furnish you with his address." He pulled out a scrap of paper and scribbled on it. "What else?"

"I-I—"

"I advise you to discover all the sources of arsenic that may be found in the Reform, and if there might have been some accident."

"Yes, Mr. Wakley, but first we must tell Monsieur Soyer of your conclusions," I said. "We cannot waste time if the kitchen is polluted."

SOYER'S ROOM BORE almost no traces of the previous night's dining. It had been transformed into an office. The table had gone, and in its place was a large, handsome desk covered in papers. Two deep armchairs sat before the fire. The chef was standing by his desk. Next to him stood Mr. Percy, the steward.

"Ah, Monsieur . . ." He hesitated over Wakley's name. "Excuse me, we are planning a banquet. It is in four days' time—there is a mountain of arrangements. But your results. It was cholera?"

"I am afraid not."

Percy brought his hands together and gripped them tightly.

"I see," said Soyer. "What, then, caused the poor man's demise?"

"I cannot speak with absolute certainty. A number of tests must be performed, but currently I propose a diagnosis of poison, sir. Arsenic," said Wakley.

Soyer laughed furiously and sat down. "But it is impossible!"

"Will this news be widely reported, sir?" asked Percy in a low voice.

"I must lodge a coroner's report and inform the police—unless, of course, the source of the poison can be quickly located and proven to be accidental. Of course, the family must be told."

"It would be better if it was not widely known just yet, sir. I am sure you understand," said Percy. "We hold our banquet next week." He gestured at the papers on the table. "Crowned heads, sir, foreign visitors. It cannot be canceled."

"I have heard of it," said Wakley. "The Egyptian despot?"

"His son," said Soyer, a little sharply.

"Hmm, I cannot say I have much sympathy with Lord Palmerston and his grand ideas, but I see your problem. Please do not misunderstand me. It is quite possible that the man was not deliberately poisoned. It is also the case that your dinner may not have caused it. This young man"—he gestured to me—"and you appear to have suffered no ill effects. You should, however, know that one may find arsenic in the most unlikely places: in the green dye of paper flowers on a table decoration, in the green of sugar leaves decorating a cake. I heard of one chef using arsenic dye to make a green blancmange—with dire effects. Why, I could walk you around your kitchen and find a dozen places where arsenic hides."

"Sir, my kitchen is the cleanest in London!" Soyer protested. "In the world! For me, cleanliness is the soul of the—"

"I have no doubt that your kitchen is admirable, Monsieur Soyer," said Wakley, smiling; it was clear that he thought he knew better. "I am sure, for example, that it is entirely free of rats, cockroaches and such?"

"We employ a young man whose sole task is to catch vermin," said Percy.

"And to do so he employs arsenic and strychnine?"

"Well, yes," said Soyer. "But we are not fools. Great care is taken to keep such things locked away in special cabinets."

"Monsieur Morel, the housekeeper and myself are the only ones with keys," said Percy.

"The truth is that, even in the most excellent kitchens, such as this plainly is," said Wakley enthusiastically, "contamination may sneak in.

The matter is one of my very greatest hobbyhorses. The extent of it is a vast and unplumbed scandal, especially in London, where the ties with those who grow the food are becoming so tenuous."

"I am sure there is nothing—" Percy began, but Wakley plowed over him.

"For decades, chalk and alum have been added to bread, and burned corn and peas ground up to make coffee. Vinegar is rendered sharper by the addition of sulfuric acid, arrowroot is added to milk to thicken it, mustard is eked out with flour, strychnine is added to beer to add bitterness, and green vitriol to encourage a foaming head. And these are but the harmless manipulations."

"Good heavens!" I said. "Strychnine and vitriol in beer?"

"And in gin, too. Enough to impart hallucinations and a nasty disruption of the bowels. And I have seen far worse: Indian berry—very toxic—added to beer to make it more intoxicating. Custard flavored with laurel—a mortal poison; pepper made from floor sweepings, comfits from china clay. Double Gloucester cheese colored with red lead. Lead, copper, mercury, arsenic—deadly, all—they are everywhere. I myself can attest that lead salts taste quite delicious."

"Why is nothing done?" I said.

"Because we are ruled by noodles and knaves, and we mindlessly follow the religion of free trade to its most dangerous conclusions!" shouted Wakley, making us all start. "We let the market run its course, whatever its consequences. No regulation! God forbid that the public be protected from such things. It is not so in the rest of Europe."

"Not in this kitchen, Monsieur," Soyer insisted stiffly. "We use only the best grocers. Our flour is purchased directly from one mill in Shropshire, with which I am well acquainted. Our spices—"

"Oh, but yes! Gentlemen, yes! Even here!" Wakley's voice throbbed with passion. "Respectable grocers add poisonous chemicals to their food in order to make it look more appetizing or to extend its life: copper salts are added to bottled fruits and vegetables to make them a brighter green; sulfate of iron to potted meat and anchovies to make them red. All, of course, highly toxic." He walked over to the sideboard, picked up the jar of peas that Mr. Blackwell had left the night before and examined it. It was, it had to be said, an exceedingly lurid green.

"As I said," Soyer put in coolly, "I use only the best suppliers in London and the freshest food. As for preserves, we make our own."

Wakley smiled kindly. "Personally, I would not buy anything that has passed through a grocer's mill. But you are correct, the vast majority of adulteration is of cheap food. The poor must eat, and those who sell to them adulterate their products to keep their prices low. Do not even ask what happens to workhouse food: oatmeal is padded out with barleymeal, and children clutch their stomachs in pain as they cry with hunger."

"I quite agree, sir!" said Soyer. "And, to that end, in one week I will open a scientific soup kitchen to feed the poor in Spitalfields. With a hundred gallons of good soup made from fresh ingredients, I calculate I can feed between five hundred and six hundred people. And I have plans for a model kitchen that could supply enough for tens of thousands."

"Remarkable!" said Wakley. "Though we must take care not to let our niggardly government use such initiatives as yours as a fig leaf for its own failures.

"Now, I truly do not wish to insult you, but I would advise you to discover all the uses of arsenic in the kitchen. You may be surprised to find more than you expected. And, if you had any leftovers from your dinner, I should like to take samples so we might have them tested to see if we might locate the source of the arsenic."

"Alas, sir, we have been cleaning the kitchen since early this morning. We disposed of it—for fear that it might be tainted," Soyer said.

"That is a shame," said Wakley shortly. He picked up Mr. Blackwell's peas again, and shook his head.

"But you did say, did you not, that it was possible that poor Mr. Rowlands's demise had nothing to do with my dinner? And it is possible, is it not, that he may have ingested what killed him earlier in the day, or even over a longer period of time?" Soyer continued.

"It is possible, but I must suggest you do not dismiss the idea that there may be contamination in the kitchen entirely."

MR. WAKLEY TOOK his leave soon afterward.

I lingered, hoping for a few moments alone with Soyer. Mr. Percy, most tactfully, left the room.

"May I ask what will you do next, Captain Avery?" Soyer said, before I managed my own question.

"I must discover if anyone else suffered ill effects from the dinner: send to Mr. Francobaldi, Mr. Duncombe, Mr. Prestage, Mr. Blackwell and Mr. Jerrold. Oh, and Mr. Ude and Lord Alvanley."

Soyer's grin faltered. "Asking if they were ill? That is not a proposition I love."

"It must, however, be done," I insisted, spurred by Wakley's certainty. "I will be as discreet as I can."

"Let me talk to Ude. He can be—how shall I say?—a little quick-tempered. And I shall probably see Francobaldi tonight. Let me ask him," said Soyer.

"May I ask why?"

"For convenience," he said, and then, "and because, as you saw, Captain, he can be a little—what do the English say? Hasty?—and he is not always discreet."

"He was sitting next to Mr. Rowlands, and . . ." I coughed, rather than say more.

"Oh, no, Captain Avery!" said Soyer. "He can be unmannerly, he is often rude, but I should never have believed—"

"Mr. Duncombe was on Rowlands's other side."

"But they were the best of friends!"

A voice in my head said that this did not necessarily count for anything. The voice sounded very much like Blake's.

"Monsieur Soyer, I must know more about Mr. Rowlands. Can you tell me if anyone else at the table was familiar with Mr. Rowlands, or perhaps disliked him?"

"As far as I am aware, no one there but Duncombe knew him, though perhaps Jerrold had met him through the club."

"Did you know him well? Has he family?"

"He was not an intimate, *non*, but he was a keen member of the club, and came often. He was a bachelor, a genial young man of good taste. He enjoyed life. He appreciated my kitchen. I saw him at the theater often, and he was a habitué of the gaming tables and the races. He was a dandy and took particular care with his dress and toilet. In these things, of course, he resembled Mr. Duncombe, too, though they differed in politics, for he was a Whig and Mr. Duncombe is a radical. I do not know his family—quite wealthy, I think. I cannot think that anyone would want him dead. I suppose you should speak to Duncombe," he said uncertainly. "We can give you the address."

"Thank you. Wakley gave it to me."

He fidgeted and cast a look at his desk.

"Is there anything you wish to tell me, Monsieur Soyer," I said, "that might help me to help you?"

"You know, I can think of nothing."

I looked into his brown, guileless eyes. Blake could stare his interlocutors into revelation. I could not. Soyer shook his head emphatically back and forth.

"This morning," I said, "Captain Beare suggested something may have gone awry in the kitchen. He mentioned the possibility of foul play. I know his words offended you, but please, Monsieur Soyer, tell me, do you have any suspicions of your own? Is there something you fear?"

"No, no, that is ridiculous. Overdramatic. Beare is an angry little person, a skinflint with no taste, he wishes to dine only on bacon and beans (mine are, in fact, very good) and wants the kitchen to subsist on pennies. The truth is, my staff adore me. My fellow chefs are my dearest friends. I count some of the highest in the land as my patrons. I have no enemies, I tell you. And, as for contamination, my kitchens are the cleanest you will ever see, Captain Avery. I assure you. You may ask anyone."

"In the library, with the committee, I surmised that you were concerned that perhaps the kitchen might be in some way responsible for Mr. Rowlands's—"

"*Non, non,*" said Soyer emphatically, "it was just the shock of his passing. And of course, I cannot ignore even the slightest suggestion of uncleanliness in our kitchens. Our reputation must be above question."

"I quite see," I said patiently. "And what about the other gentleman who died? Mr. Cunningham?"

"I do not think I knew him. You would do better to ask the committee. He dined in the club, but never came to one of my dinners. I was told that, three weeks ago, he ate here one night then left, intending to walk home, as he did not live far away: Mayfair, I think. Somewhere along the way, he was taken ill. He fell in the street and was sick. It was some hours before he was found and brought home. He expired soon after. His sickness, when it was described, was not unlike Mr. Rowlands's. That is all I know."

"Can you think of anything he and Mr. Rowlands might have had in common?"

He shrugged. "Cunningham was much older. I do not believe they were friends. He was certainly no dandy. Between you and me, a rather dull man, I think. I suppose they were both to the Whig side."

I nodded.

"May I in turn ask you a question, Captain Avery? Have you yet heard from Blake? It would be so marvelous if he were able to free himself."

"I beg your pardon?" I said, alarmed.

"From his other obligations."

"Of course." I almost laughed. "I am afraid I have not heard from him. I am sorry, I did say that he would be unlikely to come. So, you are organizing a soup kitchen, next week? And the banquet in four days. How will you find the time?"

"There is always time if you make it, Captain Avery. I have a fine brigade here, and one rises a little earlier, gets to bed a little later, drinks a good deal of coffee. My mind teems with notions. I wish to be a chef for all people, and I am not blind. I create ice cream pagodas for great men but, all the while, the poor starve. I have seen the houses of the destitute silk weavers in Spitalfields, six or seven in one small room, families deprived of all basic necessities: no food, no fire, barely a garment to cover themselves, children without a morsel passing their lips for days at a time, forced to beg for a crust. I know I can show how vast quantities of nutritious food may be produced cheaply and quickly so those in want need not go hungry.

"I planned that, once the great banquet was done, my soup kitchen would follow. Mr. Prestage is making me a giant boiler to produce the quantities of heat and soup I shall need."

"You are indefatigable, Monsieur Soyer."

"As I say, there is always time. Though I am very busy, it is true." He suppressed a yawn.

"I will not detain you any longer."

"But I have an idea! Come out with me tonight. I planned to go to the Provence Hotel. Francobaldi will be there. We will see him together. And I had thought to call on Ude. You will see if they are well for yourself. And, in the middle, the theater."

"Well, I—" In truth, I already felt quite done up, and I did not relish the thought of breaking in on the solemn Monsieur Ude. "I should be delighted!"

"Excellent!" Soyer turned back to his desk and its papers. He picked up a little enamel box, from which he extracted what appeared to be a tiny pill and put it on his tongue.

"Even I occasionally require a pick-me-up," he said.

ANOTHER OF THE REFORM'S public rooms, this one off the gallery on the first floor. Thickly carpeted, richly decorated, all gilded cornices, marble columns and deep tub chairs, deserted but for four committee members—Lord Marcus Hill, Captain Beare, the sardonic Mr. Molesworth and the plump Mr. Ellice—and myself.

There was, of course, dismay at Wakley's verdict of arsenic poisoning and the possibility of contamination in the kitchen. Molesworth remained insistently detached and half amused by everything.

"Given the sensitive nature of the negotiations attached to the banquet, I think we cannot rule out deliberate mischief on the part of our enemies. We must consider whether the Russians might be at the bottom of this," said Ellice, somewhat dramatically. "They are well known to be devious, and famous for poisoning their opponents."

"That Muscovite exile who was murdered in Piccadilly some years ago was poisoned by the Russians," said Captain Beare darkly.

It all sounded outlandishly farfetched and implausible to me but, to my surprise, Lord Marcus seemed to take it seriously.

"Palmerston does say that there are at least three Russian secret police currently watching a group of Russian émigrés in Soho," said he. "They report regularly to the Russian military attaché. The government has them watched, but there is always the possibility that they might have recruited an English assassin. I must say that Ambassador Brunnov seems to me a very good sort. Very keen on good Anglo-Russian relations. I would be surprised if he were mixed up in anything like this."

I was skeptical, but I had been wrong before, very wrong. I moved the meeting on. I asked them if they could think of anything that connected Cunningham, the man who had fallen sick in the street, with Rowlands.

"As founder of the club, I should like to say a few words about Everett Cunningham," Ellice said, and then gave a long disquisition. I think I should have wept if it had been my obituary, for Cunningham seemed to have spent his whole life eating club dinners, reading *The Times* and occasionally sitting in Parliament as a Whig MP.

"The two deceased were both Whigs," I observed.

"We are all the same party now," said Lord Marcus smoothly. "Whig and radical, we are all liberals, all for progress."

"Are we?" said Molesworth. "I increasingly wonder if we have anything in common."

"William!" said Lord Marcus. "Please try to be a little more"—I guessed he would say "discreet," but instead he said, "courteous in front of our guest."

"So what will you do now, Captain Avery?" asked Mr. Ellice.

The question was starting to annoy me.

"I shall be searching out all possible uses of arsenic in the club and at Mr. Rowlands's lodgings in case he ingested it accidentally. I shall be visiting last night's dinner guests, with particular attention to those who sat on either side of him: Mr. Duncombe and the chef, Mr. Francobaldi."

Molesworth sighed. "The thought of Duncombe poisoning anyone is quite preposterous."

"Have you considered taking a good look at the kitchen?" said Captain Beare. "As I said earlier, I am not convinced all is quite as it should be down there. If I were you, I should be inclined to make a close study of the staff."

To protests from Lord Marcus and Ellice, he said gruffly, "Stands to reason it is the most likely place the arsenic came from, and the most likely place it would have been administered."

"We must consider the foreign angle," said Lord Marcus.

"Ellice's precious Russians!" said Molesworth.

"William, if you cannot take the matter seriously, I am not sure you have any reason to be here," said Lord Marcus.

"I take it extremely seriously," said Molesworth coldly. "It was I who brought Wakley in, which is why we now have the diagnosis. I thought time was of the essence. Why are we wasting Captain Avery's time? He should be pursuing his inquiries."

"When it comes to foreign matters, gentlemen, I am ignorant," I said. "Sir Theophilus Collinson is the only man I—"

"But Collinson is the very man to speak to," said Lord Marcus. "He will be at the banquet. A capital idea!"

"Are we done, gentlemen?" said Molesworth.

"There was one last incident of which we should apprise you," said Lord Marcus. "Mr. Duncombe came in today, asking if anyone had seen Rowlands."

"And he was informed of his death?" I said.

"N-o," Lord Marcus managed to turn the word into two syllables.

"No?"

Ellice said, "Mr. Scott was told that the matter required discretion. He said the gentleman was not on the premises."

"Gentlemen, there is discretion, and there is tying oneself into knots," I said. "I cannot see that any good can come of trying to hide Mr. Rowlands's death. It will come out, one way or another. The footmen seem to know of it, and the kitchen staff who spent the morning scrubbing and throwing away the leftovers will know something untoward has taken place."

"We must ask Scott to have a word with them," said Lord Marcus.

"The fact is," Mr. Ellice said, "it could be very bad for the club if the news were to be known too widely. The last thing we want is sinister half-truths and innuendo. If you are to visit Duncombe, perhaps you might ask for his discretion . . . ?"

I agreed, reluctantly.

"Captain Avery, it has been a most exhausting day for you. Might I offer you dinner?" said Lord Marcus.

"That is most generous of you, Lord Marcus," I said, much surprised. "I am so sorry, I have arranged to spend the evening with Monsieur Soyer. I thought it would be useful."

"With Soyer?" said Captain Beare. "Good God! You choose a servant over a lord! I urge you not to forget yourself, Avery. You have been engaged to look after the interests of the club, not those of Monsieur Soyer."

"Are not the two interconnected, sir?" I said coldly.

"And 'engaged' is not the right word at all, Beare," said Lord Marcus. "We are fortunate that the captain is good enough to help us. And it makes sense for him to acquaint himself better with Soyer, who is not merely key to our banquet but also exceedingly amusing and talented."

"Do not get too friendly with him," said Captain Beare. "I know him better than you, and I would not trust him."

Chapter Six

The revelation of Rowlands's poisoning had thrown me into confusion. Once the shock had subsided, once one started to think, there were so many possible threads to follow. When Blake was faced with an inquiry, he seemed to find his way through so smoothly. But how did he select the most persuasive directions, or decide what was significant and what was not? When I considered my own situation, I hardly knew where to begin. There was Wakley's proposition of accidental contamination and the possibility that a supplier might have delivered tainted food. There was Captain Beare's accusation that something was wrong in the kitchen itself—unlikely, it seemed to me, given the remarkable showing of the day before and Soyer's elevated reputation. There were Lord Marcus's damned Russians, but I had absolutely no idea how I might tackle them—a gun and my fists were my usual weapons; I had no talent for espionage. And there was my sense—or was I over-egging it?—that the club was full of political divisions to which it did not like to admit. But the world of English politics, however acrimonious the battles of words, was the most civilized in the world, and hardly a place of murderous intentions.

It was midafternoon. I felt I had to act. I resolved to call on the guests at the dinner to see if any of them had succumbed to sickness, if they might have anything to tell me about Rowlands, or if they might prompt my suspicions, and then to visit Rowlands's lodgings to see what more I could learn about him. I was glad to get away; the Reform's luxury was most alluring, but my new obligation weighed upon me and the place had begun to seem a mite oppressive.

The outing, however, was frustrating. Duncombe was out, nor was Mr. Blackwell at his address, and at Bramah and Prestage on Piccadilly I was told Mr. Prestage was at his iron foundry in Pimlico. I left messages asking whether I might call the next day, and wrote to Jerrold asking him to dine with me at the Reform the following evening.

At Rowlands's lodgings it became plain that among my duties would be breaking the news of his demise to his servants. I had some experience of this from India, but it was never an easy matter. I learned little save that Rowlands had been a man of expensive tastes and his servants had liked him enough to weep for him. The walls were neither green nor yellow; there were no green waistcoats in his wardrobe. The cook looked at me as if I were mad when I asked if the dead man's bed had been troubled by bedbugs. She asked if I knew if the servants would be let go on full pay. There had been no recent dismissals, no lady visitors (he had been most discreet about such things, his valet said, and visited just one very respectable establishment, whose address he furnished me with). He was, they intimated, a nice, easygoing young man who spent a good deal of time at his tailor's, hatter's and bootmaker's, riding in the park, attending the races and taking whitebait dinners in Greenwich, when he was not at the Reform or Brooks's Club, of which he was also a member—as any young gentleman of means about town would be. Of his friends, they named "that Mr. Duncombe" and several younger, fashionable gents about town. Of his engagement in politics, they were not sure, but they thought he was a Whig. As for his health, the valet said—between noisy blasts on a handkerchief—Mr. Rowlands had taken the occasional blue or white pill, he was quite partial to a tonic and used several pharmacists. There were lines of bottles of proprietary medicines in his dressing room, all of which I should have liked to have taken with me. As it was, I pocketed two small, unmarked vials when the valet's back was turned.

I could have called on Collinson to inquire about the Russians, but I could not stomach another sighting of him so soon, and I hoped to have my answer from Blake before I did so. I considered going to the Marshalsea but reckoned I would not have time to get there and leave before the prison closed. I resolved to go in the morning. Exasperated, I returned to the Reform and went to observe the kitchen, as Captain Beare had suggested.

Pacing the kitchens—the staff largely ignored me, though a few were curious and some disliked me watching them—I found myself in a part I did not recognize. There was a great dresser on which piles of clean crockery were stacked. To the side of it stood a boy, dripping with water and carrying a sack. He cowered in the shadow of three large receptacles tightly covered in hessian. A door next to the boy was flung open and a great, heavyset man appeared. He was not tall but forbiddingly stocky, with fists like hams and hair shaved to the skull, a great swollen nose and a complexion like raw veal. The dripping boy visibly shrank from him.

"You come back here!" the ogre shouted. He picked the boy up as if he were no more than a bit of rag, then dealt him a blow on the head that left him stunned. "Get in there," he said, and almost threw the boy through the doorway, following on behind and slamming the door behind him.

As I followed after them, another boy stepped out to detain me.

"Oh, sir, your honor, sir, you cannot go in there."

"Why not?"

"'Tis the scullery, sir. Gentleman don't want to see that."

"I am on Monsieur Soyer's business," I said.

The boy looked nervous. "No, sir, please. It's not for the likes of you." But I pushed past him—as gently as I could—and he was forced to stand to one side.

The stocky ogre was beating the boy with all the force at his disposal. The child was insensible, sagging like the sack he had dropped. At a line of basins, scullery maids were washing mountains of pans, their attention determinedly set upon their task.

"What is the meaning of this?" I shouted. The ogre tossed the boy onto the floor. A seam of blood trickled from the child's nose. Several of the scullery maids looked up.

"You taken the wrong door, mister," said the ogre. "This ain't no business of yours." The scullery maids shrank slightly as he spoke.

"Who are you?"

"Gimbell, head kitchen porter."

"The boy." I said, trying to get to the child. Gimbell barred my way.

"I tell you sir, t'ain't none of your business. He's the vermin boy. Disobedient, don't do his work, needed a lesson. He'll be right enough."

The scullery door opened. The boy who had tried to stop me was accompanied by a young man in a black suit with inky fingers, clearly a clerk.

"Ah, Captain Avery, Mr. Percy is looking for you! Time to go. This is Mr. G.'s realm. We should not trespass."

"Have you seen this boy?"

The clerk eyed the small heap on the floor. He smiled nervously.

"Mr. G.?"

"He'll be right as rain," said Gimbell unreassuringly. "You understand. We'll take care of him. Don't you worry. You there"—he pointed to one of the scullery maids—"bring him a cup of water."

The girl picked up a chipped cup and a cloth and came over to the boy. She crouched down next to him, trying not to soak her skirts, for the floor was very wet, and began to dab at his nose. He opened his eyes slowly and looked at her.

"No harm done," said Gimbell.

"Out we go, sir," said the kitchen clerk, hustling me forward politely. Reluctantly, I allowed myself to be pushed out. It was as ugly a scene as I had witnessed anywhere for some time, and not something I had expected to see in a place such as this. It was clear, too, that I was not supposed to have seen it. I wondered how much Soyer knew about his scullery. I could not like a man who countenanced such cruelty toward children.

I shot the porter as chilly a look as I could and left.

"Here," said the young man with inky fingers, and he stopped by the kitchen clerk's desk, where an almost identical young man was busily making notes. "Mr. Percy will be with you directly." He trotted away before I could press him on what I had witnessed.

I suspected Mr. Percy was not coming at all and it had merely been a ruse to get me from the scullery. Still, the principal kitchen was not without interest. It was almost six o'clock and dishes were being prepared for the evening. A line of chefs was laboring in comparative tranquility, whisking, stirring, sprinkling, and constantly tasting a row of viscous liquids: sauces, broths and soups. In the middle was a young man with unruly, straw-colored hair and an air of great calm, working on a large bowl of yellow, creamy liquid. There was something both winning and proficient about him. He lifted the bowl up and gazed closely at its content, sniffed it, tasted it, then beckoned one of his fellows to taste it, too, then smilingly passed it on to him to finish. Then he proceeded to inspect the others' creations: bending low over them, tasting, seasoning, making suggestions in what I realized was French. Meanwhile, simpering kitchen maids (did I mention this paragon was also, though visibly dripping with the heat, quite handsome?) came to collect the concoctions from him to take them to some warming closet, or brought some piece of meat or fish to be dressed.

I shifted myself around until I was now in the corner of the roasting kitchen. There were fires and ranges on all sides, and it was fiendishly hot and ruled, I quickly gathered, by a small and furious gray-haired man with a neat mustache who was passionately dissatisfied with every morsel that emerged from oven, pan or spit. The younger cooks, meanwhile, repeatedly tried to get each other into trouble. One young man in particular, with black, greasy hair and a smirk, seemed to be at the center of these games and took special pleasure in them. For the rest, tempers seemed on the edge of breaking. That any completed dishes could emerge from such place seemed a miracle, and yet every few moments joints and filets issued forth and went off for dressing.

All at once the small, gray-haired man screamed at the top of his voice. He was brandishing a big knife at a miserable young cook and seemed to have taken leave of his senses. For a moment I thought he might stab the cook or bring the blade down upon his fingers. Instead, he smacked the boy with the side of the knife, then threw it down, picked up a plate and smashed it upon the floor, before stalking away. The greasy young man smirked.

I turned to find myself the object of Monsieur Morel's melancholy gaze. "May I help you, *Capitaine?*"

"I hope I am not intruding?" Helpfully, he did not dispute it. "I wished to learn a little more about the workings of the kitchen," I said.

"Have you learned anything"—he paused, and folded his arms—"useful?"

"Well, I wished to ask about the scullery—"

"You saw the great buckets covered in sacking? It is a great shame. So much food put to waste. If there is even the smallest possibility that *le pauvre* Monsieur Rowlands was harmed by something he ate, nothing can be left."

"Of course," I said, wondering how I might escape him. Then my savior appeared. "Monsieur Soyer!"

Soyer was watching a man marching through the kitchen. He turned and revealed himself to be the secretary, Mr. Scott. Unaware that we could see him, he came and stood very close to a kitchen maid who was busily beating some concoction. He looked over her shoulder as if to examine her work but at the same time he pressed his palm hard into the back of her skirts. It was impossible that the girl did not notice, though her face gave nothing away. I hoped the volume of her skirts meant she did not feel it.

"Mr. Scott! What brings you to our subterranean kingdom?" Soyer called out brightly.

Mr. Scott took a startled step from his prey. She slipped quickly out of the kitchen.

"I hear you have disposed of all the food, Mr. Soyer," Mr. Scott said. He carried a large ledger, which he now opened. "A terrible waste. It will look appalling on the books."

Soyer shrugged. "What would you have me do, Mr. Scott? Our kitchens must be beyond reproach."

"But still, Captain Beare and the rest will not like it."

"If the committee wishes us to take all precautions . . . Moreover, Mr. Scott, as you know, I have made considerable savings in the last few months. If only the rest of the club was managed as carefully."

Mr. Scott's eyes narrowed, but he said nothing.

"Have you met Captain Avery?" said Soyer. "Mr. Scott, Walter Scott—just like the great author." Soyer paused in a way that seemed subtly denigrating. "The club secretary."

"We have met," I said. I could not resist. "Are you any relation?"

"To the writer? No, Captain Avery," the secretary said with a stiff little smile. "But, as I said before, do not hesitate to come to me, should you have any questions. I oversee the entire club."

"Was there anything else, Mr. Scott?" said Soyer. "I am exceedingly busy." He gave a small, dismissive wave that was meant to insult.

"No, Mr. Soyer, I simply wished to see how the kitchen was conducting itself. I, too, am very busy." Scott turned on his heel.

"*Incompétent*," Soyer muttered, smiling all the while. "I hope you are still going to allow me to entertain you tonight, Captain Avery? I plan to depart at nine."

I nodded. I had wondered why he was so keen to take me out. Now I believed it was to win me over to his side.

The kitchen no longer seemed to me the charmed, delightful place it had the day before. There was much I needed to understand.

"I wondered if you might spare me Matty—Matilda—for one hour?" I said.

He did not ask why, but gave me a watchful look and said, "I believe she is working in the pastry kitchen. I shall need her in one hour or two for some clerking. My foolish secretary left yesterday."

I strolled over to the pastry kitchen. Matty was cleaning out a cupboard. Mr. Schmidt, the *pâtissier*, was, as I had seen him last, entirely preoccupied with a most elaborate cake decoration.

"Mr. Schmidt, Captain Avery at your service. I must speak with your kitchen maid Matilda. A matter of Monsieur Soyer's. Most urgent."

Schmidt barely looked up but, about him, the cooks' and *commis*'s attention stirred. Matty's face was deep in the cupboards. "If Mrs. Relph can spare her," he said, his voice deep and foreign. "Ask of Mrs. Relph."

Mrs. Relph was the older pastry cook I had seen with Matty before. "Mrs. Relph," I called across the whistling steam, "it is important."

Mrs. Relph gave me a most suspicious look and nodded, her lips tight with disapproval. Matty emerged from her cupboard. Without raising their heads, the young men about her seemed almost to twitch with awareness of her.

"Follow me, Miss Horner," I said.

We walked out into the corridor, and as far from the kitchens as we could go. Her face lit up.

"How are you?" I said. "Did you wash carefully after . . ."

"Of course. I thought you had left," she said.

"I have been asked to stay."

"Something's amiss?"

"This is confidential. The committee are concerned about Rowlands's death. A doctor came to examine the body."

"It wasn't cholera?"

I shook my head. "I have no idea where to begin," I said. "Unless you can help me. I am a soldier, not a private inquiry agent. I do not understand this place. I need a guide. I have you for an hour. We should speak outside."

She looked up from under her brows. "I can't, don't ask me. I'm finished with all that. I'm happy here." When I had first met her, Matty had been a police informer.

"Lord, Matty! I know nothing about this place. I am all at sea, and even you, my only friend here, will not help me." I pressed my thumb into the place between my eyebrows where it ached. "Something is not as it should be. Please, help me. Explain this place to me. I'm sure you would not refuse if Blake asked you." I knew this was unjust. "Or perhaps this place has secrets and you are frightened to speak of them."

"It has not," she snapped. I had riled her. "Where is Blake?"

"I cannot tell you."

"Come on, Captain. I can keep a secret."

"I cannot. It is not my secret to tell. But I will tell you what the surgeon said."

TRAFALGAR SQUARE is a peculiar spot: one of those rare places in the city where there was space to stop and contemplate the moving city without being deafened or jostled or crushed by successive waves of humanity. At the same time, it was quite bare of all vegetation. Not one tree marred its vistas. Perhaps its architects had thought the natural world would distract from its grand constructions. It was late November when I had last seen it, and the column that would eventually support Lord Nelson's statue had grown another thirty feet above its vast square plinth.

Matty stood on the steps of the church on the eastern side. She looked like a little starling in a brown cloak and a black-and-brown bonnet. It was pleasant to walk, and I felt it churlish to press her.

"Matty—"

"Look at me, in my warm cape and my proper bonnet. The club has given me so much, and I love my position. It is better than I could ever have hoped." I knew she did not want to speak of it. I felt a brute for making her. I pulled her round to face me.

"I am truly sorry, Matty, but I need you to tell me about the club. All of it."

"What did the surgeon say?"

"Rowlands was poisoned—with arsenic."

"Bloody hell!" The news winded her. "What will happen? Will we be closed? Will there be jobs lost?"

"I cannot tell. We do not know where it came from. It could have been the kitchen, or Rowlands might have dosed himself. It could even have been someone from outside trying to cause damage."

"Like that Francobaldi, or something to do with the Egyptian banquet?"

"You are very quick. Tell me about Francobaldi."

"He's always sniffing round Chef. I don't like him. He pretends to be friendly, but I reckon he'd do anything to get one over on Chef."

"That is interesting." I marked Francobaldi as someone to observe.

She gathered herself. "Not that he'd kill a man, though, I'm not saying that, but . . . Why isn't Blake here? He's Soyer's friend."

"I would tell you if I could, I swear it. I hope he will come. Heaven knows I need him to come. In the meantime, I must know about the kitchen. Yesterday, it seemed to me to be a beautiful mechanism that worked perfectly. Today, I saw a boy beaten senseless and one cook almost stab another. And at least one member of the committee is convinced that something is not well in the kitchen. And the committee told me they think another member of the club may have died of something similar some weeks ago."

My words silenced her; quite the opposite effect to that I had hoped for.

"Do you not see that the only way to return matters to where they were is to discover the source of the poison as quickly as possible?" I said pleadingly. "And even if nobody in the kitchen is directly responsible, then it is at least possible that it came from there."

We walked for a minute or so, I biting back my impatience. "For example," I said at last, "is it usual for boys to be knocked insensible in the scullery?"

"Sometimes. Gimbell does it there so no one but the kitchen boys and the scullery maids see. And he enjoys it."

"So Monsieur Soyer doesn't know?"

"Oh, he knows. They all know. Maybe not how bad he is, or how much he drinks. They just reckon it's not their business to interfere. It's how it works. They say a kitchen needs a porter who will frighten off the beggars and the thieves and train up the potboys and keep them in line. They need to learn obedience. Gimbell does it, so no one else has to. He's reliable, to their way of seeing."

"I cannot like a man who allows such things on his watch."

"I don't like it; I don't say I do. But it's part of it, the kitchen, good and bad. Mr. Percy says the kitchen's like a ladder—or an army. You'd understand that. Chef at the top, then Monsieur Morel, the *sous-chef,* then the senior chefs who run the different stations: sauces, fish, roast, grill, vegetable, desserts—all that. Then the *chefs de partie,* their seconds-in-command, then under them the cooks and the junior chefs—the *commis*—and the apprentices, and then us, the kitchen maids. Mr. Percy says Chef must be concerned with the whole ladder. He cannot always look at what is happening on the rungs."

I understood it. I did not like it.

"Do you know anything about the boy who kills vermin? And where they keep the arsenic?"

"Not much. He's a bit simple, does his job well enough. Very careful—had the fear of God put into him. All the poisons are locked in a special cupboard. We can't get at it. Mr. Percy has the key."

"I have not asked you about Pen. Blake said he did not stay."

Her brother. Her face fell. A less happy subject. "You'd never recognize him—he's grown like a weed. Found regular work hard to stick to." She rubbed her mouth. "They still give him a little portering here, but . . ." She trailed off. "Couldn't force him to stay. And I see him on my afternoon off."

"How does he live?"

"On this and that. Costers give him a bit of work. Staying in some lodging house with his mates. Says he prefers it. I give him a bit of tin and food from the kitchen." She gave an unhappy smile.

"Did Gimbell beat Pen?"

"Yes. Said he smelled disobedience on him. Pen's a rum one, I know that, but Gimbell went for him. One day, after he'd had a few, he took Pen into the scullery and beat the living daylights out of him. Mr. Percy himself caught hold of me, or I would have killed him. He said this is how it is in a big kitchen. To be perfect every day, we must do exactly what we're told or we fall short and then we fail. You have to take it from those above you, even from Gimbell. You have to learn how to get around him. Them as"—she corrected herself—"those who keep their heads down and stick it, they'll do and they'll rise. Those who can't, they lose their chance."

"So Pen left."

"He says he prefers the streets. Can't stay indoors. Maybe he'll learn." She rubbed her eyes.

"And you and Gimbell?"

"I've had clouts off him, but I kept my head down and I'm out of there now."

"And the small man with a gray mustache in the roasting kitchen? He nearly stabbed a man today."

She knew him. "Monsieur Benoît. An artist with meat and fish, Chef says. Maybe he is, but he's a bastard—sorry for my language," she said, "but he is. And there's that cook, Albert. Dark hair. Troublemaker, likes to make the other cooks look bad."

"I saw him."

"He's a bastard, too—sorry, but he is. I wouldn't work on meat if you paid me. One time, Monsieur Benoît pressed an apprentice's hand on a hotplate till he screamed. Two weeks the boy couldn't work."

"Did Soyer know?

"He kept his job for him."

"And the boy came back?" I said, horrified.

"Of course. You don't get a chance in a kitchen like Soyer's twice. Besides, he was French, where else would he go?"

"Could you imagine someone in the kitchen who felt mistreated taking a bribe, perhaps in return for adding something they shouldn't to a dish?"

"No! No one would do that! Everyone wants to work for Chef. Everyone loves Chef. This is the best kitchen in England."

"Where apprentices have their hands burned and it takes two weeks for their wound to heal and boys are beaten insensible?" I said angrily.

"You don't understand!" she said, just as angry.

I collected myself. "Could someone steal into the kitchens without being seen and add something to a dish?" I asked, more calmly.

"I cannot see how. We all know each other. Well, perhaps it is possible," she said thoughtfully. "People come in new sometimes, a potboy, an apprentice. But they stay. Or they usually do. And there are the carters and carriers and errand boys that hang around the doors. Some of them I recognize, but not all of them."

"Any more kitchen tyrants and monsters to apprise me of?"

She scowled. "The kitchen is full of stresses and strains. When service is on, and there are three hundred for dinner and everything must happen at the right moment, and everything must be perfect, and the kitchen is all steam and pistons and heat, it's like bedlam, and it's true, chefs become angry, cooks and *commis* play jokes, or plot against each other, or torment the apprentices. It's just how it is. The chefs are hard taskmasters, the cooks want approval and promotion. If they don't get it, there'll be someone snapping at their heels. And there's always dinner to be made."

"It sounds to me as if the bullies and bruisers thrive."

"That's not true. The best cook in the kitchen is Monsieur Perrin, the sauce chef. Did you see him? He's in charge of all the sauces and soups, over men twice his age. He never loses his temper, even when there's a rush. Everything he does comes out right. Everyone likes him." She smiled fondly. I recalled the golden-haired prodigy.

"And handsome, too."

"The kitchen maids say he has lovely soft eyes"—she blushed a little—"and they love his accent. They're all in love with him, but he hardly notices. Everyone likes him. 'Cept maybe Mr. Morel."

"Why?"

"I don't know. I've heard it said he's jealous."

"Jealous of what?"

"Perrin—he does everything well. And everyone likes him."

"And they don't like Morel?"

"No. He's different, Morel."

"How?"

"He's quiet, keeps to himself. But he's able, always busy. And sad."

"Sad?"

She shrugged. "What's the word? Melancholy." She pronounced it carefully, but with a certain satisfaction. "And sometimes he'll lose his temper suddenly when the kitchen is very stretched and it seems as if everything is going to come crashing about our ears. But it never does."

"Are there no English cooks?"

"Everyone knows the English can't cook! There are a few apprentices and junior chefs, and most of the potboys and kitchen maids are English. It's not what I expected—all the foreigners—but I like it."

"So Mr. Percy is the most senior Englishman."

"Been here since the club opened. He's cool-headed, that's the thing. He's been kind to me, likes hard workers. Doing two jobs now, since the butler left."

"The butler left?"

"A few months back. Mr. Percy does the ordering and oversees the dining room. He likes it that way. He's got lots of staff—footmen and underbutlers and clerks and all."

She took my arm and led me down toward the scaffoldings of the Houses of the Parliament.

"So," I ventured at last, "Monsieur Soyer."

"I have never met anyone like him."

"I, too, have never met anyone like him," I said. "I think one of him is probably enough."

She gave me a sharp look. "I know he seems a bit . . . with his clothes and his airs and all, but he's a good man, a genius I reckon, and he gave me a chance I could never have hoped for. He insists on the best, and we make brilliant things. He works harder than anyone. He'll sit sketching an idea for hours. Just thinking. Or standing over a sauce, tasting, adding, starting again. On and on. He never sleeps."

"I understand that he gave you a chance, Matty, but he let Gimbell beat Pen."

"He's not perfect, but every kitchen maid and apprentice knows how lucky they are to be at the Reform."

"A man on the committee told me there might be foul play in the kitchen and that he did not trust Soyer."

"I can't speak for upstairs, but I'd say that's nonsense."

"But you have heard things?" I coaxed.

"I've heard they're fools. Percy says they are jealous of Chef's success and think he outshines the club. Who is it who says this?"

"Red-faced creature, Captain Beare."

She nodded. "Fancies himself as chairman after milord steps down. Has it in for Chef. He says Chef's got above himself, that he's a servant and should remember it. Says the food bill is too high. Wants everything cheaper."

"Do the others think this?"

"No. No. Some of them want things cheaper, but Chef has champions, like the chairman, Milord Whatshisname—"

"Lord Marcus Hill."

"That's him." She smiled wickedly. "Likes his dinner and his comforts. Just married. Forty-three he is, and his blushing bride is twenty-one and very rich."

"Matty!"

"She is! And I'll give you a dishonest man. Mr. Scott." Her lip curled.

"The secretary?"

"The same! If he's not dishonest, then he's good for nothing. The housemaids call him Haymarket Hector. He'll touch any bit of you he can get at. He pays girls to come to his rooms."

"Matty!"

"What?"

"It is just that a lady does not talk that way."

"'A lady'! You *high-po-cright*!" She snatched her arm away.

"I beg your pardon?"

"You heard me, *high-po-cright*. I know what it means."

"I think perhaps you mean 'hypocrite.'"

She marched off ahead of me, furious. "You know what I mean. It's a word I've read and never said. You want my, my *observations*, but then you, you *censure* me for the way I deliver them!"

"I am sorry. I admire your honesty, I do. It is just that you are rising, learning, if not to be a lady, then a respectable woman, and such women do not speak so, in public."

"Don't think I speak to everyone the way I speak to you. I don't. I thought you would understand."

"I apologize, with all my heart."

"Blake gave me a dictionary. I wanted to learn new words. I suppose it must seem foolish to you."

"Not in the least. I find it admirable." I was mortified. The last thing I wished to be was discouraging. But it was true, I did want her observations, the more acute and personal and worldly the better, something I could not imagine asking of any other woman.

"There must be someone to whom you can complain about Scott?"

"Sometimes, Captain, I wonder how you get about in the world."

"I wonder," I said, "if the Reform is a suitable place for you."

"Now that's enough! I was on the street before. I am safe, I am well fed and I am more than satisfied. I have friends. I bless you and Blake every day."

"I see that it must seem contradictory to ask for this, and then to wish to see you protected."

"Yes, it is."

"All right. Is there anything more you should tell me?"

I fancied that she hesitated. "Can't think of anything."

I glanced up at the skies. The wind blew in our faces. Across the Thames, rain clouds approached.

"What are you thinking, Captain?"

"I am thinking I promised to have you back in an hour. I am thinking that I do not know what to think. I fear I am not made for this work. I must hope Blake comes."

"And if he doesn't?"

"Then I'll tell them they should find a real inquiry agent."

She steered me back toward Trafalgar Square and Pall Mall. For some minutes, we were silent.

"I don't need protecting, you know," she said.

How wrong she was.

Chapter Seven

I was fatigued and had little appetite for a night with anyone, let alone Alexis Soyer. I lay down to sleep, but I could not. It was the first time I had had to think all day, but my thoughts, rather than dwelling on the matter at hand, or even on Blake, turned to Helen and my guilt at failing to return as I had promised. I must confess that I had in part accepted the Reform's offer out of a reluctance to go home. I had had such hopes of the birth of our son, but the baby, rather than drawing my wife and me closer, had somehow widened the rift between us. I had gradually become aware that she found the baby difficult and my hopeless devotion to him grating. Sometimes, I thought she seemed frightened of being left with him—though there was the wet nurse and my sister, and the servants on hand. I wondered if the child we had lost in Afghanistan haunted Helen, but we never talked of it. It seemed to break some unspoken agreement to raise the matter. In the meantime, I knew she found the country dull and was dissatisfied by the society and entertainments I provided for her.

There was no resolution to this, of course, only another bout of self-recrimination. So at half past nine o'clock I presented myself at Soyer's office. He had called us a cab, and immediately bundled me in. He was in remarkably good spirits and very talkative.

"There is no doubt," he said, "that it has not been the best of days. But now you are here! And I have such an evening arranged! We shall make a brief visit to my dear friend and mentor, Ude, to see he is well. How glad he will be to see you, my friend! And tomorrow, perhaps Blake will join us."

I could not see why Monsieur Ude should have any interest in remaking my acquaintance. We dismounted before a very substantial brick-and-white stuccoed four-story town house on Albemarle Street in Mayfair.

"Monsieur Ude lives here?" I said doubtfully.

"Ude has made so much money he could rent Buckingham Palace if he so wished."

We mounted the steps, and he beat an enthusiastic tattoo upon the door knocker.

Monsieur Ude occupied the first three floors. It did not seem to be enough. Every inch was hung with paintings and sketches, every surface crowded with valuable objects—one could tell they were valuable by the way Madame Ude gasped every time anyone touched or brushed past them.

They had just finished dinner. In the drawing room, the old lord from the night before, Alvanley, clearly none the worse for Soyer's cooking, sat deep in an armchair, oblivious save to the glass of something tawny in his hand, which he sipped appreciatively. This was surprising, as there was a considerable clamor: dogs were barking and dashing about the room, a parrot was squawking, and Monsieur and Madame Ude had evidently been engaged in an extremely acrimonious and noisy discussion in French.

Madame Ude embraced Soyer; Ude—like Alvanley, looking perfectly well—kissed him on both cheeks, then fixed me with his large saucer eyes, both doleful and beady at the same time.

"*Maître*, you are well! I needed to know."

"Should I not be?"

"I know I can count upon your discretion," Soyer said more quietly. "There are problems at the club."

Ude led us into the dining room and closed the door.

"*Problèmes? Lesquels?*" he eyed me, unfriendly. "What does he do here?"

"Captain Avery is helping me. I trust him. *Maître*, one of the guests died after the dinner last night."

"*Eh, bien*, at Crockford's, gentlemen were forever expiring at the gaming tables—the heart, the liver, excess, overstimulation." He permitted himself a small smile. "These Englishmen, they do not recognize their age and they have no care for their livers." He patted Soyer on the shoulder.

"But Mr. Rowlands, he was a young man and it was at my table."

"But it cannot have been the dinner—which, Alexis, I must tell you, was extremely good—for we are all well."

For a moment, Soyer basked in his praise. "Yes, but there are questions that remain unanswered, and the committee—"

Ude made a rather uncouth spitting noise. "Committees! It is always the way with these clubs. They cannot leave us to do our work. They are ingrates who wish to be in charge over all things, and always they complain about money. They drive us away, we who lend these places their luster. It was thus at Crockford's. And I"—his voice rose imperiously—"I who cooked for Bonaparte and two French kings; whose recipes were admired by Lord Byron! So you should not lose heart."

"Thank you, *Maître*."

We left soon afterward. Soyer took heart from Ude's words and was much cheered and, though I found the man prickly and ill-humored, I put him, and Alvanley—who had continued to sip his brandy throughout—at the bottom of my list.

"And now, to eat!" said Soyer. We took a cab to the bottom of Great Windmill Street, where he insisted there was an excellent vendor of fried fish.

"You know, it is a secret of chefs in this city that when we have finished cooking our elaborate dishes, we love nothing more than three penn'orth of hot fried fish."

Soyer greeted the fish seller by name, and they struck up a conversation about the fish (whiting), where it was landed (Gravesend) and the constituents of the batter (flour and water). "I will be taking the recipe one of these days," he warned, as he handed me my portion, wrapped in old news sheets, doused with vinegar and finger-burningly hot.

"Did Ude truly cook for Napoleon?"

Soyer grinned. He was devouring his fish with his fingers. "He cooked for Napoleon's mother, I believe, and for King Charles X once or twice, when he was in exile in London."

"Now," he said, when we had finished, "we shall visit the ballet at the Haymarket."

"But Monsieur Soyer, you are not in evening dress."

"No more I am! Do not concern yourself, it will take but a second to arrange." He delicately wiped his fingers on his handkerchief and retrieved two short tags on the bottom of his short jacket, and tugged upon them. At once the jacket ripped away to reveal an unfurling velvet frock coat with soft, wide lapels. Then he pulled upon what looked like a thread hanging from his trousers. The trousers were likewise swept off, and underneath were a pair of silk trousers that billowed like some Arab pasha's. With a flourish he pulled away the front of his waistcoat to reveal another covered in gold braid. It was so ridiculous and yet so wholehearted I could not help but laugh.

"Aha! I amuse you at last, Captain Avery." From his bag he brought a silk cravat and a pair of cream-colored kid gloves. "And my boots, another invention. They have hollow heels, in which I keep my coins. Ingenious, yes?" He removed his red beret from its precarious perch and from his bag drew out what appeared to be a flat, black disk. He tapped it and it flipped and transformed into a silk top hat. Bizarrely, the crown was set at a slight angle so, just like the beret, it teetered to one side.

"Monsieur Soyer, may I ask you why you wear your hat thus?"

"But of course, Captain Avery. It is my signature. I call it *à la zoug-zoug*. Of all things, I abhor a vertical line. Even my cards are not square." He drew out a small silver case shaped like a diamond. "I must stand out from the crowd, Captain Avery, I cannot help it. The English find me entertaining, I know, and sometimes even ridiculous." He sighed melodramatically, and then grinned. "But this has its advantages. I always knew I could cook, but that has never been enough. Always, my mind has teemed with notions, ideas, inventions. I knew there was—and is—so much more I could do. My fame and the noise about me gives me a stage for my inventions, my future plans, the books I intend to write, the good I intend to do."

He took my hand. "I must have this matter of poor Mr. Rowlands resolved."

"I understand," I said. I felt the seed of liking for him begin to germinate. He was grandiose and vainglorious and very un-English but there were moments when he was irresistible.

After the ballet we repaired to the Provence Hotel, which was on Leicester Square, where there was a raucous gathering of cooks and their entourages, mostly French. The night was advancing, and I could not help but be surprised that the chefs were so rowdy and merry at this hour: from what I had gathered, both Morel and Soyer would be in the kitchen early.

As Soyer had promised, I soon spied Francobaldi, the rude guest from the night before who had sat on Rowlands's right side, and Morel, who was playing cards. Soyer quietly took Francobaldi aside and murmured to him. They spoke for some minutes, then Soyer returned to me and Francobaldi to his table of merrymakers.

"He says he is quite well, no ill effects, but I was forced to tell him rather more than I should have liked."

"Does he know that Rowlands died?"

"I do not think so, but he guessed someone had been taken ill. Now your work is over, take a glass of claret with me."

My work was far from over, I had come to learn more about Francobaldi, and to watch Soyer among his peers. But I accepted. It was good, the claret, and I was tired, and I had several glasses, and then cognac, and sat quiet, letting the talk, most of which was in French, flow over me.

Francobaldi was easy to observe. He wanted attention, but he was disconcerting, too. He seemed to pulse with an energetic nerviness which manifested itself at first as coarse humor. His companions took this in good part; they were evidently familiar with it. I glanced at Morel, who, the opposite of Francobaldi, seemed happy to merge into the evening. He sat at his card game, betting moderately, but occasionally he would look up from his hand to gaze on the rest of the company with a silent intensity. I could not help but wonder what he was thinking.

Then Francobaldi got into a dispute with another chef, Monsieur Comte, who was chef to some marquess. It was, I gradually worked out, a disagreement—or perhaps a misunderstanding—over some wine the two had agreed to buy together at auction and then share. At first they traded explanations, then suddenly Francobaldi stood up and, staring down at his opponent as if he were the merest piece of dirt, asked him with a kind of pent-up passion "what he meant by it."

Monsieur Comte, the older man, rolled his eyes and explained, clearly not for the first time, why it had cost more than they had initially agreed. This only inflamed Francobaldi all the more. He asked him through clenched teeth if he meant to ruin him. Comte shook his head emphatically, and Francobaldi began to curse him with profanities of the sort one expected to hear only in the lowest places:

"Is that what you fucking think, you idiot? Either you are a fucking fool or a fucking swindler! Is that what this is? You are trying to bloody ruin me, to make a fucking fool out of me?"

He loomed over Comte—and he was a big man, broad-chested, almost like a wrestler. Comte, now genuinely anxious, began to plead that he had had to go up a little more to acquire the wine. Francobaldi continued to heap abuse upon him. His voice rose and rose, becoming ever thicker with anger, until he lost all control and screamed at Comte, and the rest of the gathering looked away in embarrassment.

"You are talking fucking nonsense! We agreed on certain terms! Do not think you can cheat me!"

He hit Comte on the side of the face, knocking him off his chair and onto the ground. The man staggered up, accepted a discreetly offered napkin, and quickly withdrew, with an aghast look at Francobaldi.

No one protested at Francobaldi's act, though the room was quiet for several seconds. Soyer watched Francobaldi—who had marched off to fill his glass before slumping into a chair and subsiding into a sullen silence—and laid a hand on my arm as if to restrain me. I could not have said entirely what Soyer was thinking, but I should have said the uppermost feeling was pity. Everyone began to chatter and drink again and the conversation returned to its previous volume.

I looked back at Morel. He was watching Francobaldi with a look of pure enmity.

Soyer suddenly became the center of attention, telling an anecdote I suspected his audience had heard before, about how, when he first came to England, he had gone hunting and had set off after a dog, rather than a fox. The story ended with his horse pitching him headfirst into a hedge. Francobaldi laughed and rejoined the party as if nothing had happened. Soyer, meanwhile, insisted upon reciting some of the—truly awful—poetry he had composed to woo his wife, then announced he would sing us a song, whereupon he stood on the table and embarked on a rousing chorus of something called, *"Pan, pan, pan, voilà, mes amis!"*

Following this, the whole company erupted into song, so much so that the fearsome French lady proprietor came in her dressing gown and nightcap and told the party to quiet down. It was near two when we staggered out of the Provence. Soyer led a party down to the Strand and said he was going on to some supper rooms in Covent Garden. I was utterly fatigued, having hardly slept the night before, and insisted I must to bed. Soyer told the silent Morel to find me a cab, though I protested I would walk back.

The Strand was quiet, save for the odd coffee seller and a few lone unfortunates wedging themselves into doorways.

"Are your evenings usually so eventful?" I asked Morel.

"The work is hard in the kitchen, sir. It is perhaps inevitable that, at the end of the day, some of us must open the engine door and let out some heat."

"Like Mr. Francobaldi, you mean?"

"Francobaldi's fire is unbanked at all times," said Morel, his tongue suddenly loosened. "He is without any self-control, and it takes very little to rouse him. And five minutes after such an outburst he will remember nothing of what he has done."

"He does seem very quick-tempered."

"He wants to be compared to Monsieur Soyer. In truth Comte is no better. They all do. Francobaldi has none of his genius. He is a copyist, at best. I would never have invited him to the dinner. Chef, however, is kind.

But you mark my words, in a week or two something from that dinner, something we have spent months laboring to bring into the world, will appear on Francobaldi's *carte*."

"He steals recipes?"

"He wishes to be the best, he will do anything to accomplish it."

I mused on this, and what I had witnessed at the Provence, and concluded that Mr. Francobaldi had moved rather closer to the top of my list.

"CAPTAIN AVERY!" The knocking and calling eventually dragged me from sleep. My head hurt. It felt early. "Captain Avery, I have a message for you."

Head thick with last night's drink, I stumbled to the door.

"A message for you. It arrived late last night. It was marked 'urgent,' but you were not at the club."

"Ah, thank you—"

"Jeffers, sir, from yesterday and the evening before?"

"Yes, of course." He passed me a pale white envelope, good quality but dirtied at the edges, and creased, as if it had been through several hands.

I tore it open. A single leaf of paper. A sentence. Not his handwriting.

I regret to inform you that Jeremiah Blake has disappeared.

I HAD DETESTED the Marshalsea from the first; it was a squalid place. But now the sight of its dull, gray buildings, its dull, gray cobbles and its hopeless men, combined with my throbbing head and a certain bad conscience at finding the message so late, made me furious.

The yard was full of debris: several upturned benches, an odd shoe, shreds of soggy paper. The warden was exceedingly flustered and continually buttoned and unbuttoned his coat.

"This really is a most unusual occurrence. I should go so far as to say—indeed, I would stress—that nothing like it has happened in years."

"I do not care whether it is common or uncommon, sir."

"But, really, Captain Avery, you must understand we could never have imagined . . . I hope you will make this clear to Sir Theophilus Collinson when you make your report. Obviously, we will help you with any means at our disposal. Perhaps I might offer you some refreshment?"

"You think I am here on Collinson's behalf?"

"Well, naturally . . ."

"I want none of your miserable hospitality. I only wish to know what happened, and I can assure you that Collinson will not be assuaged by pathetic excuses."

The warden nodded, ashen, and began to rub his hands in serpentine knots. I knew my ability to make him squirm derived entirely from my association with Collinson. I did not care.

"Yes, sir, of course. This way, sir. It has taken us a little while to piece together the course of events. It was yesterday afternoon, when most of the inmates were out in the yards. Along here, if you please, sir."

He led me to the third set of buildings, where Blake's room had been. We went down a few steps, into a foul-smelling, dark room with two small high windows. The floor oozed wetly. There were stalls in the far wall and a long trough.

"Washing stalls," the warden said, smiling feebly. "Mr. Blake was washing himself. It seems that another inmate, a man called Nathaniel Gore, called him out and wanted to fight him. Mr. Blake at first refused, but then Gore apparently came at him with a long knife. Mr. Blake was stabbed in the thigh. The witnesses said the blood spurted most dramatically. The terrified onlookers ran into the yard, shouting that Mr. Blake had been killed. The Marshalsea is, as a rule, a place of peaceful debtors, not violent men, so again I cannot stress how unusual this was. We have seen nothing like it in years. The inmates became most excited; they lost all sense of propriety. They began to run about, screaming that they would be killed and that there was a madman loose in the prison. We had to shut the gates, and it took us some time to quieten them and restore order."

"So he is dead? You knew Nathaniel Gore had a grudge against Mr. Blake. Even I knew he was a danger. You have a great deal to answer for. I imagine Collinson will have you dismissed."

"Sir, if I may," said the warden, his fingers tangling in such tight circles I thought he might break them, "that is not the end of the story. As I say, it took some considerable time to calm the uproar, and so there was a delay before a group of trustees managed to reach the washroom. Aside from the bloodstains on the ground"—he gestured at a dark, black patch of floor—"they could find no trace of either man. It appears that Mr. Gore left the jail just after the start of the commotion. Like the other inmates, he was permitted to leave the prison, as long as he remained within the 'liberty' of the prison and returned by sunset. The turnkey did not realize he was the cause of the uproar. As for Mr. Blake"—he coughed slightly—"he, too, has disappeared. No one recalls seeing him. A number of frightened inmates did leave the prison before we shut the gates. They all returned later, but neither Gore nor Mr. Blake have been found. We did not realize until the prison closed, then we made a thorough search, but . . ." He ground to a painful halt. "We did write to you last night . . . Of course, we have informed the New Police. Absconders rarely get far."

My exasperation at Blake's rashness leached into vexation at the warden. "How bad was Blake's wound?"

The warden shook his head. I demanded that I take possession of Blake's things. The warden himself walked me to Blake's room, his assistant trailing behind, during which time he admitted, without any prodding, that the Marshalsea's guards and trustees were neither as numerous nor as alert as they should have been.

The warden left, the assistant waited in the doorway. The old shipping clerk with whom he had shared was lying on the mattress with his arm across his eyes. He did not acknowledge my presence. Blake's few pieces of clothing lay neatly folded on the floor; his books were stacked in a corner under the table. I picked through them, hoping there might be something, some hint. But I could find nothing, just the books themselves and some notes I could not read, on account of their being in Blake's shorthand.

I rested my elbows on the table and took my head in my hands and shut my eyes. I was tired and bilious from the night before, and my head throbbed.

"Are you quite well, sir?" The warden's minion stood anxiously at the door.

"I should like a minute, if you please," I said, without opening my eyes. The door closed, and the room was quiet.

"In the spine." The shipping clerk's voice was hoarse, as if it were not often used.

I looked up. He had not moved at all.

"Iss in the big book. In the spine." The words emerged from behind his arm. "Left it just before he went down."

I picked up the thickest volume. It was called *Extraordinary Popular Delusions and the Madness of Crowds*. I poked my finger into the space between the book's binding and the spine and carefully fished out a small piece of paper of almost transparent thinness. I unfolded it. It read:

Don't fret.

I took up the rest of Blake's belongings and left as quickly as I could.

Chapter Eight

I must do without Blake. The truth of it, now that the evidence was incontrovertible, was harder to accept than I had expected. My intention was to inform the Reform Club that I could not continue with the inquiry, and return to Devon. Even now, I cannot say exactly why I agreed to stay on. I had not revised my opinion of my abilities. It was a confusion of reasons. After the first shock of Blake's disappearance, the temptation to eke out my London freedom a little longer and my no doubt ill-considered appetite for incident and inquiry began to reassert themselves. It occurred to me that I had already picked up too many threads to drop them now. I was concerned about Matty. I found myself feeling I owed something to Soyer. I had a number of suspicions that warranted further inquiry. And finally, at the back of my mind there was the quite baseless conviction that, if I remained at the Reform, Blake might eventually appear.

What I would say to the Reform about his absence was another matter. I did not want to tell them about the Marshalsea. There was still a small, probably foolish part of me that hoped he might emerge unscathed from the matter. And for what were, I know, personal, petty reasons, I felt news of his incarceration would not reflect well on me, erasing what small standing I had.

I told Soyer first. It was almost luncheon, and today the kitchen was bright, orderly, calm: once more a beautiful mechanism. At every station, heads were bowed over bowls, saucepans, cauldrons and plates. Deliveries had arrived and were piled up on top of each other. Among the *sauciers*, young Perrin was bent low over a chopping board, shredding herbs with extraordinary precision and at great speed. He looked up and nodded politely. I could not help but observe that there was something, as Matty had described, surprisingly soft and attractive about his eyes.

Soyer was standing with Percy, inspecting three pallets full of cuts of meat. Soyer suddenly reached into the lowest box, pulled out a great piece of burgundy-colored meat edged with a thick slab of yellow fat and examined it.

With an expression of utter disgust, he tossed it back onto the top pallet.

"*What is this?*" His voice rang out across the kitchen, throbbing with anger. The cooks and kitchen maids watched covertly.

"I have told your master before, I must have whole sides of beef!" he shouted at the carter who had delivered it. "I will not take delivery of these great lumps. I must have the best quality. These could be anything!" He picked up a joint and brought it to his nose, then flung it angrily away. "I would not serve this to my dog! Take them away, and do not bother to bring your wares here again!"

I have to say, to me, the anger seemed quite out of scale with the offense. I could see nothing wrong with the meat, but then I was not the most famous chef in London. The carter's response took me aback even more.

"Master says you can take 'em or leave 'em. Says you're damaged goods yourself, Mr. Soyer. Says the club owes him money. Says we'll see how long you'll be in a position to buy anything much from anyone."

"How dare you speak to me like this!" Soyer said—coming up close to the man, who was a big, heavyset creature in hobnail boots, and much larger than he—and placing himself mere inches from his nose. "You are a nobody! Leave this place and do not come back! Take your shoddy goods with you!"

I thought the carter might strike him, but he retreated, muttering crossly, then Percy took his arm and drew him to the pallets, murmuring while Soyer stalked across the kitchen to his office.

"May I ask whom you serve?" I said to the carter as he lifted his pallets.

"Hastings Bland of Smithfield, best beef in London," said the man. "Don't matter, I reckon. He'll get his money one way or t'other."

Frenchmen are of course famous for their passionate moods. Or perhaps he was somewhat the worse for wear from the night before. Or perhaps there was more to it. The carter's words had pricked my curiosity. I resolved to add the name of Hastings Bland to my list of inquirees. In the meantime, I went after Soyer.

"CAPTAIN AVERY! What a fine evening it was!" he said, getting up from his desk, all smiles. None the worse for wear at all, it seemed.

"It was indeed, and I have a slightly sore head to prove it," I said. "Might we speak? I imagine you might be preoccupied after that meat business . . ."

"That? Oh, no." He laughed gaily. "One must keep the suppliers on their toes. It was nothing. What was it you wished to ask me about?"

"I am afraid there is no possibility that Blake will be able to come. He is deeply engaged in another matter—a case. I am deeply sorry."

He faltered for a moment but recovered himself at once and said brightly, "But I have quite reconciled myself to this! You, Captain Avery, will help us, and when all is done, we shall tease and reprove him together."

Morel put his head around the door. "Chef?" he said. "*Des nouvelles.*"

He stood tautly, as if he was struggling to control himself, and his voice was breathless. "I told you last night, *Capitaine*, that Jo Francobaldi would have something of ours on his bill of fare?"

Soyer sat back in his chair. Now he seemed resigned rather than angry.

"He gives a dinner tonight at the Union Club. He gave the menu to the *Morning Chronicle*. He serves what he calls a *château au pâte*, a pastry castle. Within are small chickens stuffed with mushrooms, ox tongue and sweetbreads. On the so-called 'battlements' are gold-plated *attelettes* on which are skewered truffles and crayfish."

"But it is Monsieur Soyer's pastry crown to the letter!" I said.

"It is," said Morel, "and three days before we were to make it a centerpiece of our banquet. This time, he goes too far. Alexis, this time we must act."

"It has happened often before?" I said.

"Five, six times that we know of," said Morel. "More, perhaps. Clever, understated dishes of complex flavors. But never before so soon after eating one, and never quite so boldly as to copy a centerpiece."

"You must call him out," I said, appalled. "There are the people who ate the pastry crown, who can swear he has stolen your receipt. I should be happy to."

"*Bien sûr!*" said Morel. "He is baiting us! We must publish our menu from the dinner first."

"We will not," said Soyer, "because we cannot afford to bring attention to ourselves at this moment. He must have realized this from my words last night. In any case, Captain Avery, the stealing of recipes is a strange thing. We chefs all borrow notions from each other, embroider upon them here or there. It is a brave man who claims to have invented something completely new. Indeed, to the public, I think there is little more foolish and ridiculous than the sight of one chef accusing another of having stolen from him. I do not mind being laughed at from time to time, but I will not be seen to descend to such a level."

"But he goes too far!" said Morel.

"I say," Soyer said, with just the merest emphasis on the "say," "we let it pass."

"Of course, there is his temper," said Morel, examining the surface of Soyer's desk.

"I do not fear his moods. Come, André, let us consider how sad it is to be so desperate, how *tragique* to have to resort to such subterfuges to draw praise and attention, and remind ourselves that we have ten such ideas that are as good or even better. We triumph every time."

Morel examined Soyer's desk more closely. He was still deeply incensed.

LORD MARCUS HILL, Ellice and Beare took Blake's absence even more complacently, a fact that fed my own uncertainty.

"Well," said Lord Marcus, "much as we regret that Mr. Blake will not be able to help us, I cannot think of anyone more fitted to understand the club's situation and sympathize with its members—and with Monsieur Soyer, of course."

He meant, of course, that I was a gentleman, and professional inquiry agents were not.

"I fear you overestimate my experience and abilities, Lord Marcus," I said, "but I will do what I can."

"That is capital. The club is delighted!" said Mr. Ellice.

"How was your evening with Soyer?" asked Captain Beare. "Did you improve your acquaintance? Has he confided in you? Did he tell you about how he was censured by the committee for dishonesty; how his kitchen mutinied against him? Eh?"

"Beare!" said Lord Marcus, looking pained. "Really, this is not helpful."

"Is it not? What is your move *now*, Captain Avery?" said Captain Beare.

I MARCHED DOWN to the kitchen and plucked Matty away from the dessert station again.

"What is all this about foul play and the committee censuring Soyer for dishonesty? And a mutiny among the staff? Is it to be like last time, then? I give you my trust, and you feed me truth, or not, as it pleases you, drip by drip?"

Perhaps it was not fair to take my anger out upon her. The true locus of my exasperation was Soyer, whom I believed had done his best to charm me in order to distract me from pressing him on difficult matters. At every turn, it seemed I discovered that questions I had asked had not been answered truthfully.

"Look, Captain, I could not be more grateful to you," said Matty stoutly, "but I am done with being a nose. Can I not just be a kitchen maid? This place has been good to me. I have chances. Don't make me spoil it all with rumors and whispers."

"I had thought better of you. That you would not shirk from your duty. A man is dead. The sooner we can resolve the matter, the sooner your kitchen may return to its former state of perfection." My sore head and my frustration made me bullying and churlish.

"But what if that man's death has nothing to do with the kitchen? You ask me to rake up old stories that do no one any good, for nothing."

Her words gave me pause; she might not be wrong. "How can I know if they are not connected if you will not tell me about them? It seems to me that you are doing your best to bury your head in the sand like some ostrich bird."

"You are right. I don't want there to be any trouble in the kitchen. If there is trouble in the kitchen, death and such, then we lose our livelihoods, all of us, and I am tossed back onto the street."

"Matty."

"You tell me where Blake is," she said, folding her arms, "and I'll answer your questions."

"I cannot. He made me swear."

She held her folded arms more tightly and glared at me. I do not know what another man might have done. I capitulated. In truth, I trusted her.

"He was in the Marshalsea," I said, or rather blurted. It was a relief to speak it. "Unjustly. A long story, a dispute with his patron. He could have freed himself, but he would not. Now he has disappeared. There was a riot. It seems he walked out and did not return."

"Reckoned I couldn't keep a secret? Just a cheap servant girl?"

"Do not be so foolish. I have told no one else, and I have broken my promise by telling you."

"Where is he now?"

"I have no idea. On a boat somewhere, perhaps."

"What do you mean?"

"The last time I saw him, just before I visited you two days ago, he told me he would not be there long. This was what he meant. I went to the prison this morning. I found a piece of paper hidden in the spine of a book telling me not to worry."

"So he planned it. Where would he go?"

I shook my head. "Beyond the grasp of the law."

"I don't believe it. He would not have left a message if he did not mean to help you. To help us."

"Jeremiah draws admiration and loyalty. I've never been sure how much he reciprocates it. And if he were to appear, he would be at once arrested and find himself back in jail, or worse. Now it is your turn. Tell me about the committee and Soyer."

"A few months back, the committee accused him of being on the take."

"'On the take'?"

"Stealing from the club. Padding the bills. Skimming off the top. It put him in a great rage."

"Was he guilty?"

"The committee could find nothing against him, but he was—what's the words?—'censured for insolence,' not dishonesty. He was furious at their accusations, and he said some things. They reprimanded him; he gave his notice. Lord Whatsit had to persuade him to stay."

"Is Soyer honest?"

"What a question!"

"If I am to do any good, I must know the truth. I do not wish to insult him or you—Blake would do the same."

Her mouth pulled downward. "Look, I think he's honest. Committee found nothing, and he's the best-paid chef in London, they say, and he makes more money from his inventions and his special dinners. He had a print made of the kitchens and charges a half a guinea—a guinea colored—and it's sold over a thousand copies. I think it was more that he was protecting others."

"Other members of the kitchen? Who?"

Again her mouth pulled downward.

"Matty, I am not seeking to put people out of their posts, but I should know. Blake would ask."

She did not answer.

"Matty?"

"The cooks say it is not really stealing. Wages are not high, work is hard and long. For me, I don't need much. But others, they've got families and rent. Whatever it is, it is not bad, I'm sure of it."

"What kinds of things are taken?"

"Leftovers, mostly. Sometimes they sell a little something on, sometimes they feed their families. Sometimes a pat of butter might go, or a bottle of something. The one who was mainly at it was the butler, and Chef sacked him. Percy's in charge of ordering now, and he's very proper."

"Is there anyone in the kitchen who is mad or bad enough to put poison in the food?"

"No one! The kitchen feeds people, it doesn't kill them."

"Perhaps it does not. And what about this mutiny?"

"It's a stupid word for it. My first week, there was a grand dinner in the club. Chef was all dressed up to meet the guests. Just before service, the underchefs and the kitchen maids refused to work. I never learned exactly why—I was too new—but I heard they had all been working almost without a break for three days. He had changed the menu twice; Morel was tearing out his hair; Benoît was throwing pans on the floor. Chef went back to the kitchen, put his apron on, wheedled them round, took them through the dinner himself. It was a grand success, but afterward he fell into towering temper. Frightening, it was. He sacked five or six there and then."

"Do the lower staff dislike him?"

"No! They love him and respect him. They want to be noticed by him. One word of praise from him . . . And he is generous. Gives out leftovers. Things people can sell, even, or at least until recently. In return he demands perfection. He is hard to please."

"So he is letting them sell the club's food?"

"Don't twist things," she said angrily.

"Why did they mutiny?"

"Perhaps sometimes he demands too much."

FOR MY SINS, I did not relish the thought of returning to beard Soyer at once. So I instead went to fulfill the appointments that I had made the day before.

In my head I ran through those who had been present at Soyer's dinner: Alvanley and Ude, whom I had seen and were well. Francobaldi, who seemed to be actively offering himself up as a possible suspect. Mr. Blackwell the bottler, Mr. Prestage the engineer and Mr. Duncombe, who had sat on Rowlands's left side but was his good friend, I would now visit. Jerrold, I would meet for dinner. Then there were myself, Soyer and Morel.

The premises of Crosse & Blackwell was a handsome yellow brick and stucco mansion on Soho Square, not far from Blake's lodgings. Mr. Blackwell told me that he and his partner, Mr. Crosse, had just refurbished the whole building, at no small expense. The new sign over the eight-paneled front door read "Italian Warehousemen and Oilmen by Appointment to Her Majesty." In the shining plate-glass windows there were elegant bottles of maraschinos and marsalas arranged on velvet cushions. Small jars of essence of anchovies stood next to large jars of bright green vegetables: cucumbers, green tomatoes and peas. A few days before, I would have regarded these with relish. Now, the combination of my sore head and Mr. Wakley's discourse on copper poisoning had extinguished my appetite.

This was unfortunate, as Mr. Blackwell, who declared a) he was delighted I had come, for he had been hoping to meet me again, and b) he was in remarkably good health and had never before met or heard of Mr. Rowlands, was very keen for me to try a selection of his relishes and pickles.

"May I ask how you get the vegetables to look so very green and fresh?" I said innocently.

"It is because they *are* green and fresh," said Mr. Blackwell. "We merely pickle them as soon as they are harvested in our special mixes of vinegar or brine to maintain their quality."

"Do you, may I ask, use copper salts in your mixes?" I ventured.

"Well, I cannot really tell you as our recipes are a company secret."

"You can tell me. I won't tell a soul," I said, entirely dishonestly.

"Let us say, just the tiniest smidgen. A little copper is, in fact, rather good for the body," he said confidently.

"I do not think it is, you know."

"My dear sir, you are a civilian in these matters—what can you know about such things? I assure you, every ingredient feeds a body with goodness. Now let me tell you about my plan."

His plan, he told me plainly, was to persuade me to endorse "Imperial Sauce," a new concoction of anchovies, onions, vinegar and "several secret ingredients from the East." The idea had come to him late in the night after the dinner. He intended to sell it alongside Sir Robert Peel's sauce. "It really is the prime minister's favorite," he said. The label would read "the choice of true heroes—enjoyed by Jeremiah Blake and William Avery"—or the other way round, if I preferred. I protested that we were really not sufficiently famous to sell bottled relishes. Mr. Blackwell said that he had it in mind to finance a book about our adventures in India, which would make us marvelously famous. He had "the very author in mind." My first thought was how much Blake would hate the idea; with a jolt, the fact of his absence was borne upon me again. Then I felt queasy.

"Will you not have a bottled cucumber? See how deliciously fresh they look!" said Mr. Blackwell.

I fled.

My purported reason for visiting Bramah and Prestage on Piccadilly was an interest in Soyer's inventions, which the company had manufactured. In truth, I wanted another look at Mr. John Joseph Prestage.

"None the worse for our banquet, I see!" I said, more heartily than I felt.

"No, indeed. Mr. Soyer truly surpassed himself this time," said Mr. Prestage, whom one look revealed to be in robust and rubicund health. "It was a feast made in heaven," he said. He asked that I excuse his red face; he had been at the firm's iron foundry in Pimlico.

"I was just overseeing the finishing of the great boilers we have made for Mr. Soyer's soup kitchen," he said, and proceeded to bore me with descriptions of camshafts and cogs, paddles and gearwheels.

"It certainly was a fine evening," I said, trying to restrain a yawn. "Are you well acquainted with Monsieur Soyer and his circle?"

"I shouldn't say his circle, precisely, but I certainly esteem him highly. A true inventor. We're proud to manufacture his inventions."

I made clumsy attempts to bring the conversation round to how well he had known Rowlands, which I eventually ascertained was not at all, and I also learned that the club and its members had remained notably resistant to Soyer's attempts to raise money for his soup kitchen in subscriptions.

"I would have thought Mr. Duncombe and Mr. Rowlands, as MPs, might make an example," I said finally.

"I think Mr. Duncombe has pledged an amount, though the gentleman does have something of a reputation for overextending himself financially," said Prestage carefully. "As I said, I had never met the other gentleman before that night."

I nodded assiduously over Soyer's inventions—a small gas range, a large gas range, steam-heated fish pans, special teapots, an array of the "tendon separators" that I had seen that first night—for what seemed like hours, until I was at last able to make my escape.

It was too early for Mr. Duncombe, who, I had been informed, rarely rose before noon. Also, I did not relish the thought of having to deliver the news of Rowlands's death to him.

So instead I revisited Monsieur Ude in nearby Albemarle Street. I considered it possible he would not receive me, but I needed a view of Soyer from outside his kitchen, and clearly Mr. Francobaldi would not do.

Madame Ude greeted me kindly—"Dear Alexis's friend!"—while small dogs dashed about her ankles and, behind her, a parrot hung from a wire swing entwined with paper flowers and curling fronds.

"I was hoping to have a word with your esteemed husband. It is a matter of some importance."

"Oh, Monsieur Ude!" she said, giving a sudden grimace. "No doubt he is about. Louis!" she shouted snappishly. "Louis Eustache!"

"Merde, merde, merde!" said the parrot. Madame Ude's smile faltered.

"I do not wish to speak to anyone." Ude's voice emerged from another room. "I am dining, I am thinking. Send them away." Madame Ude went in and upbraided him in loud, angry whispers. She reappeared, all smiles again, and led me into the dining room. Ude sat at the table in shirtsleeves: a fine white shirt and a silk damask waistcoat. An empty brandy glass and a fine crystal decanter half full of amber fluid sat on the table before him. The parrot, which had hopped its way in behind me, fluttered onto the alarmingly crowded sideboard. Reaching into his waistcoat pocket, Ude fished out a pair of small wire spectacles and put them on. He undid a button on his waistcoat and eyed me with his skeptical, saucerlike eyes.

"So, what is it that you want?"

"To talk to you about Monsieur Soyer."

He raised his eyebrows. "So, one day he brings you to my house, the next you come behind his back, sniffing, for what, *scandale?*"

"Not behind his back, Monsieur Ude." *Not exactly,* I thought. "He told you he has problems and he has asked me to help him." He gave me a most dubious look. "I must confess I know almost nothing about your world. If I am to help Monsieur Soyer, I must know as much as I can. He trusts you. You are"—I grasped for the right phrase—"a chef among chefs. The younger men look up to you and aspire to your reputation. You are their father."

Ude looked not entirely displeased. He pondered for a moment, picked up the decanter and poured himself a small glass of brandy. As he did so, his sleeve rode up and along his plump arms were revealed a myriad of pale scars.

"The badges of my profession," he said, with a certain satisfaction.

"You have known Monsieur Soyer a long time—what would you say about him?"

He gave me an owl-like look over the tops of his spectacles.

"He is a most talented chef. His food is excellent. He is a grand logistician and innovator. He looks forward. He is a showman. The English, they like a spectacle, and he knows so well how to provide that. But most of all, *org-an-iz-a-tion.*" He rapped out the word like a tattoo. "He is capable of arranging things brilliantly on a mighty scale. This, perhaps, is his greatest genius. He works very hard. He is very, very determined. He has known hardship and pain. His family was—how would you say?—very, very modest. His natural demeanor is to be cheerful, which is not very French. What else? He loves his wife."

I wanted to ask about the accusations of dishonesty, but I thought it would get me nothing but a request to leave. Or maybe, I thought guiltily, I was simply being chicken-hearted. Blake would not have hesitated.

"Is that how the other chefs regard him?" I said.

The great owl-eyes fixed upon me again. "How should I know? I can speak only for myself. But I will say to you something about the kitchen. The English have a joke about French chefs. 'I ate at this chef's establishment. I asked for the salt. The chef came out, he was tearing his hair, he was shouting, and all because I asked for the salt. How droll! How ridiculous!'

"I do not know where this story started. But they said it of me, and now they say it of Alexis, of young Francobaldi, and others. Perhaps they will be saying it in a hundred years' time. The young chefs, my fellow countrymen, feel they must smile at this joke, but they hate it. They give great thought to the realization of something that is a perfect balance of taste, of seasoning, of beauty. Then, without having tasted it, the customer at the table demands, 'Where is the salt?' and sprays it liberally over everything.

"I may exaggerate a little. But these boys, they regard themselves as artists, whereas you English regard them as servants—and foreigners." He cocked an eyebrow. "If they are very talented, very amusing and very nice, Society may play with them for a while, but when they are tired of them, Society sends them back to the servants' hall.

"Of course, many of these talented young men come from very modest backgrounds, like Soyer. Some can hardly read and write, especially in English, so perhaps it is not so surprising."

"Were you the same, Monsieur Ude?"

"Me?" Ude said, "*Non*. I knew I was an artisan. I regarded money as the most honest acknowledgment of my skills. I made sure I was well paid and now I live as I like, independent of them. When I left Crockford's, it was not because of some spurned dessert or a disagreement over an ortolan, it was an argument about my salary."

"Does Monsieur Soyer have enemies?"

"How should I know?" he said briskly. He did not like the question.

"Please understand why I ask this," I said. "It is possible that someone wishes him great harm. In which case, I must find them."

He added yet more brandy to his glass and took a long sip.

"It is often said that the kitchen is like an army. You are a soldier, *non*, Captain Avery? You will understand. To feed a multitude, to create excellent food consistently, there must be order and organization, and strict discipline.

"The kitchen is like an army, but it is also a battleground. The work is hard and the payment is low, unless you rise to the top. And you must rise quickly, you must be noticed young, or you will be left behind. No garlands and prizes for you. To rise, you must compete with others just as ambitious as you, and trounce them. In Paris and here, Alexis has trodden upon the dreams of many men, some twice his age. He likes to say that we chefs are a happy band of companions making our way in London, but . . ."

He turned his unblinking gaze upon me again, stood up, picked up a small glass from the sideboard, poured a tot of brandy in it and handed it to me. "*Tuez le ver,* kill the worm, Monsieur. In English I think you say, the hair of the dog that bit you."

I drank it down in one go. He undid the last button of his waistcoat.

"Are you a religious man, Captain Avery?"

"Only conventionally so, sir," I said honestly. "That is to say, I was brought up in the Church of England."

He smiled. "*Moi non plus.* Me neither. But I was raised Catholic, and it has left its mark, as such things do. Sins, Captain Avery, sins express real truths about men. And every profession, it seems to me, has its typical sin. A version of what we in France call its *déformation professionelle*. For you soldiers, Captain, the sin is anger. For a soldier, anger is so tempting, is it not? Because it is not always a sin. Sometimes, a man must be angry in order to fight, *non*? And we know in our hearts that it is easier to feel anger than to feel fear. Somebody watching a kitchen in full service might think that there is much anger in a kitchen. The heat and the urgency produce this. But anger is not the chef's besetting sin. You might then conclude that it must be gluttony, since all our days we are surrounded by incitements to eat and drink. But this too is not so. The chief sin of the chef and of the kitchen, Captain Avery, is envy."

It was time for Duncombe; I could delay no longer. A left turn off Albemarle Street and a right took me into Dover Street. On the other side, there was a grand mansion set far back from the street with a high stone wall with two grand gateways and an even grander porter's lodge, all forbiddingly closed. A brass plate announced it to be the Russian Embassy.

The thought came to me that I should go in, even as I told myself it was a foolish idea. I think, in hindsight, my milk-liveredness regarding Duncombe and the news I must deliver, as well as my general uncertainty about how to deal with the whole poisoning matter, shamed me. I had never faltered in battle. So, though I had no idea what I should say or to whom I should speak, I rapped as loudly as I could on the porter's lodge. This instantly drew the attention of every passerby. But no sound issued from inside the Russian compound, and no one came.

I tried again, more vigorously, and called out, "Hi there! I wish to visit the embassy. I am on important business!"

After some time, a door in the gate opened with a reluctant squeak.

"Yes?"

"I must speak with someone in the embassy."

"Who, sir?" A supercilious English porter.

I struggled for an answer. I did not even know the ambassador's name.

"The military attaché."

The porter's eyebrows shot up. He looked me up and down, his gaze lingering at my feet. "No carriage, sir?"

"No."

"And you are, sir?"

"Captain William Avery. I am on official business."

"I do not believe we are expecting a Captain Avery," he said.

"Are you going to deny me entry?" I said combatively, though with every passing second my blundering seemed more and more idiotic. No preparation, no plan, no idea what I should say.

"This way, sir," he drawled, drawing out the "sir" until it felt like a snub.

Through the courtyard, up a flight of steps to a porched entrance. The hall was laid in black and white marble, furnished with elaborate gilt furniture and dominated by a huge, full-length portrait of the czar (Nicholas? Alexander? I could not remember) in a blue jacket with gold epaulets and a chestful of medals. The place was empty save for two footmen (English) in curled gray wigs and knee breeches, to whom I was passed. One took charge of me, while the other went in search of an official.

Eventually, a gentleman appeared.

"May I help you, sir?" It was my first encounter with the strange, vowel-extending nasal quality—"*hee-yelp*"—of the Russian accent. Despite this, I at once understood that he was both bored and unimpressed.

"I, ah"—*wish to know if you are poisoning members of the Reform Club*—"I am trying to find a Russian gentleman I encountered at the

Carlton Club. Excellent chap. I thought perhaps the embassy would, you know, have a record of Russian gentlemen in London, and their addresses?"

The official sighed audibly. "We could take a calling card and forward it to the gentleman. We cannot simply give you the address. Do you have"—*hee-yav*—"the name?"

"Mr., ah, Ivan, ah, -ovitch." It was the only Russian-ish name I could think of.

"That is a very common name. Do you have his first name?"

"Ah, Alexander." Was that the name of the czar?

"I will consult my list." He disappeared, trotting back a few minutes later.

"We have no record of anyone by that name."

"Oh."

I thought the pantomime at an end, but he took pity on me. "We have a Peter Ivanovitch and a Sergey Ivanovitch?"

"No, he was definitely Alexander. How strange. He was, I believe, a friend of the Russian military attaché, whose name I cannot now remember."

"Kiril Michaelovitch Annekoff," the official said, without thinking. "He is currently on maneuvers with your army. I could take your card and inquire of him."

"Oh no, I will write to him. At the embassy? Could you write down his name?"

The official looked suspicious and resentful, but obliged. I was sure he knew something was not quite right, but was not sure what. I left quickly, cursing my foolishness, and made for Duncombe's address on Queen Street.

Within a few minutes, I was certain I was being followed. A man came up behind me on my left and must have remained at the same point some yards behind me for some time, neither passing me nor falling back. When I turned my head slightly, I could see only an outstretched foot.

Bloody Russians, I thought. I increased my pace and there he was again, the same distance behind me as before; I slowed down, and he did likewise. I continued for a minute more and then turned upon him.

He was very rough-looking, in a workman's corduroy trousers, a ragged moleskin jacket and a soft cap which came down low over his ears. He wore a pair of old gloves such as a costermonger would wear so his hands appeared whole. He smelled distinctly unsavory. He began to cough.

"Not here," he said. "Not until we are further in and there are more people on the street."

Chapter Nine

Too late now," I said, remarkably nonchalantly, I thought. "How in damnation did you know where I was, Blake? No, do not answer. I have an appointment in Queen Street. You look like a beggar, and you stink. And you are supposed to be wounded."

"We'll meet after, then," he said.

"Will we, indeed?"

"We will," he said. "Bit rash of you to storm the Russian Embassy all on your own. Nice to you, were they?"

I did not laugh.

"Take a cab to Dean Street when you're done and tell the old dragon to let you in," he said. "I'll come in round the back. She'll not hear me."

"And why should I come?" I said.

"You'll come," he said, and shuffled away.

Filled with equal quantities of outrage and relief, I determined not to give him another thought until I met him. Naturally, I arrived at Duncombe's residence in Queen Street thoroughly discomposed. I was taken to a fine sitting room on the first floor, decorated in green and cream and full of large vases and bronze statuettes posed on French furniture. Everything was very expensive. On the walls there were portrait sketches—one was of Duncombe himself—and over the fireplace a painting of Old Testament prophets which I should have said was Italian, though I knew little of such things.

Mr. Tommy Duncombe swept in, smiling beatifically. He was somewhat red and creased about the eyes, but the rest of him appeared to have sprung starched and dewy from the dawn. He wore a fresh, white, billowing shirt under a light blue velvet waistcoat, under a navy blue velvet frock coat with satin lapels, and blue-and-white striped trousers and elegant patent boots. He grasped a bottle of seltzer water.

"Captain Avery, what an honor! I am afraid you find me just risen, and a little the worse."

"You have been ill?" I said. It was by now four o'clock.

He smiled sheepishly. "No, I was out till the early hours at Crockford's. Nothing more than a sore head, entirely self-induced. Please, be seated. I am so pleased to make your further acquaintance. Mr. Blake isn't with you?" he said hopefully.

"I am afraid not."

"As I mentioned the other night, I believe that you and Mr. Blake did a good deal to secure the cause last year."

"The cause?"

"Of Chartism, of course. It is about to reach its zenith. In a month I shall be presenting a new petition demanding the vote and the other five points of the Charter to the House of Commons in May. We have raised the country: we expect to have over three million signatures. The petition will be so long I do not know how we will actually get it into the Chamber!"

In other circumstances, I would have dwelled on the sheer unlikeliness of this butterfly dandy's devotion to his proletarian cause, but Blake's reappearance and the news I was about to deliver rather eclipsed it. As if he had read my mind, he began to speak of his friend.

"I must say, I am rather concerned about Rowlands. I have not seen him since our dinner. It was a remarkable evening, was it not? I called at the club yesterday, and they said he was not there, but he was not at home either."

"I have some bad news, Mr. Duncombe." I cleared my throat. "Mr. Rowlands passed away some hours after the dinner."

"What did you say?"

I repeated the words.

"Rowlands died?" he said dazedly, and took a gulp of his seltzer water. "But I asked at the club yesterday. He was scarcely twenty-five . . ."

My own age. "Thomas Wakley performed a postmortem investigation upon the body yesterday morning."

"Oh, good lord! How did he die?"

I told a half lie. "We are waiting for the results. I am so sorry to bring you such bad news. But if you could bear the thought, I would be very grateful if you could help me with some questions I have. Of course, if you would rather I left . . ."

"Oh, not at all. I must just . . ." He looked away. When he looked up at last, his eyes were quite wet.

"Ask away, sir," he said.

"You knew Rowlands well?"

"He was a good deal younger than me but a keen patron of the turf and the tables. He was a sweet-natured boy but a dyed-in-the-wool Whig, though I tried to persuade him otherwise." He took another swig of his water and called, rather hollowly, for a coffee and a brandy. "Why do you ask me this? Did something terrible happen to him? Was he attacked?"

"Do you have any reason to think he might have been?"

"No. Just your questions . . . I did think he looked rather ill at dinner . . ."

"Mr. Duncombe, the Reform Club have asked me to look into Mr. Rowlands's death, but to do so discreetly. May I have your word as a gentleman that my words will not go beyond this room?"

"Well, I suppose so . . . yes, of course."

"Mr. Wakley has some reason to believe he was killed by arsenic poisoning."

"Good lord!"

"Can you think of anything which might explain this, or cast any light on his circumstances? Had anything disturbed him in the previous weeks? Was there anyone who disliked him? A feud? A gambling debt, perhaps?"

He looked aghast again. "He could be contrary, even inflammatory, but only about politics. He made a speech against extending the suffrage, and another in praise of Palmerston and the war in Afghanistan which raised the hackles of many radicals. Though we are supposed now to be one party, there is, I must admit, not precisely a feud but what you might call a *froideur* between the radicals and the Whigs. He exasperated some of my younger radical friends, but not unto murder. And I am proof that such things can be bridged, we were great friends—and friends with Mr. Disraeli, who is a Tory. There was no particular girl. A couple of ballet dancers at the Haymarket. Nothing serious."

I coughed. "Debts?"

"Well, yes, but we all have debts. And his were nothing"—he smiled—"on the scale of mine."

"Any habits? I mean, can you think of anything that might have exposed him to arsenic?"

"What, you mean such as licking green wallpaper? Tom Wakley's hobbyhorse? No, nothing of that sort." He sat up. "Are you suggesting it was

Soyer's dinner?" He took another pull from his water. "Do forgive me for this; I find it helps my dyspepsia."

"Mr. Wakley says it might have been something at the dinner. But as far as I can ascertain, no one else was taken ill. Did you experience any, ah, queasiness?"

"No, save a certain biliousness the next day. But I am not in the first flush of youth and my digestion is not all that it should be. If not the dinner, then what?"

"Was Rowlands in good health? His dressing room was full of pills and tonics."

"Good enough. I mean, he ate and drank a good deal. No doubt more than he should. But I am no slouch in that quarter. As for pills and tonics, well, you should see my dressing room! It is something of a craze at the moment for us city idlers. We stay up too late and then attempt to restore ourselves with hocus-pocus potions and remedies."

"Well, we should have the results soon. And may I say again, I should be most grateful if, for the moment, you were able to remain silent about the circumstances of Mr. Rowlands's demise. I shall give you news as soon as I have it."

"You have my word on it, Captain Avery. His people are from Yorkshire. I know them . . . I suppose I should write to them."

As I WALKED to Blake's lodgings, I began to rehearse the recriminations I would throw at him, growing more incensed with each passing minute. I was so deep in my furious but eloquent telling-off that I did not even hear his neighbor Miss Jenkins rush out of her shop and call to me. When she caught me gently by the arm and asked me if I had heard from Blake, I shook my head discourteously.

Blake's landlady began to grumble as soon as she set eyes on me. She had not seen him in a month. She was out of pocket. Did I think I could simply turn up at any time of the day or night (it was approximately five o'clock in the afternoon)? I informed her that I had a list of items that Blake had requested, and that I knew perfectly well the rent had been paid (which I did not). At this she wheezed and reluctantly let me past.

His rooms had become even chillier and more unloved since last I had visited. Books piled on the table, a dried-out piece of bread on a shelf and two oranges dusted with mold. I threw these out of the back window and left it open for him to climb in. There was no wood in the grate—a matter I suspected the landlady knew more about than she let on. I rattled downstairs and gave her a penny for a bucket of kindling and some logs, and lit a fire.

I did not hear him come in through the window at all and, when I saw him in the bedroom doorway smeared with dirt, I was muttering crossly to myself. I had planned to be taking my ease in a lordly fashion on the settle when he arrived.

He was amused. "You got my books? And something to eat?"

"We shall attend to my questions first."

"I could not have told you. You must see it."

"No. No, I do not," I spluttered. "Evidently, I am never to be trusted with your confidence. And what are you planning to do? Live as a fugitive? Leave the country?"

He held his hands up in supplication. "It's good to see you, William. You found my note?"

I choked back a gust of rage. "Of all the stupid, hare-brained ideas! Collinson will never forgive you, and you will be a fugitive forever!"

I jumped up—I could not keep still another moment—and began to pace. "Could you not just have nodded your head and got out of prison with Collinson's say-so? Would it not have been so much easier?"

"Keep your voice down."

"Could you not?"

"No. I couldn't."

"I assume the knife I provided was the one that Nathaniel Gore—if that is his real name—used to attack you?" He looked a fraction abashed. "So it was. And who is Nathaniel Gore?"

"Someone who owed me a favor. Where are my books?"

"At the Reform. How the devil did you get out?" I threw myself on the settle.

"There's a small door in the washrooms. Leads to the cesspool, and that to an open gutter into the Thames. The trustees have to be able to get at it when it gets blocked, otherwise the whole prison becomes an open sewer. I had a key. I walked through it down to the river, and swam to the bank. The currents are strong but it was low tide."

"And that is why you stink. Could you not have just walked out the front gate?"

"Acquiring sufficient hot water was not straightforward."

"I would have expected you to have several changes of clothes and a full purse secreted somewhere about the city."

"Well, I did not."

"And Mr. Gore?"

"On a ship bound for New York."

"And your plan?"

"Look, William, I was thinking to put myself beyond Collinson's reach. I thought I would leave the country. But I am here."

"Why?"

He said nothing.

"Are you here to say good-bye, or to help your ludicrous friend Soyer?"

He rubbed his ear. "There's a ship to New York in four days. A boat to France tomorrow, if I'd rather." He began to pick clothes off the floor.

"You cannot go," I said. "Soyer needs you. Matty needs you. I cannot do without you. Besides, you look sick. Blake, I know you have thought about this. Else there would have been no note. Else you would not have met me here."

He picked up a book. Then he sat down on the edge of a chair, pulled off his foul gloves and held his palms out toward the fire, rubbing the stumps of his missing fingers. Something crawled out from his jacket.

"Fire and fury! You have fleas."

"Have you really nothing to eat?" he said, and looked so ill that I felt my fury begin to slip from me, which I found most provoking.

"Here." I had bought two crushed pastries from a French bakery. He tore into them like some starved beast.

"If I were caught," he said, "you would be charged with aiding and abetting me. As would anyone else who recognized me and had not turned me in."

"We will find a way to square it with Collinson. I am sure we will. I am lodging at the Reform. Come back with me. You could stay in my room tonight. Have one of their hot baths. Water comes steaming from the faucet. It is marvelous. At least be well and clean when you leave."

He stared at the fire.

"I could hide you. You could take on a disguise." In a flush of inspiration, I said, "You could be my manservant!"

"I bloody could not."

"Once you were fumigated, of course. Why not? It is a good notion. You can be in attendance to me, see everything. I am sure you can come up with a disguise. Do they know you at the Reform?"

"I visited Matty once or twice."

"Would they know you?"

"Even if they didn't, how would you get a tramp into the Reform, Captain Avery?"

"We will find a way. By the by, Blake," I said excitedly, "what if we solved Soyer's matter together? We might get you off the hook. Collinson loves his subterfuges. We could say you absconding was all a plan to get you into the Reform in disguise to survey the scene anonymously. The Reform committee are desperate to have your help. If we were to meet with success, Collinson would have to withdraw his charges."

"Have you not noticed that life does not generally play out like a fairy tale?"

"I truly think if we can resolve this and you are willing to accept the credit—"

"Enough fantasy. Tell me about this murder at the Reform." You will remember I had written to him in the Marshalsea.

What did I do? I obliged him, of course. I told him everything, from my arrival at the Reform to the moment when I departed from Duncombe's.

"Whom I rather took to," I said.

"A champion of the poor who is thousands in debt and puts small tradesmen into penury while he plays the tables at Crockford's with money he does not have and hands out thirty-pound tips."

"Soyer likes him," I said accusingly.

"Soyer's a fool and a snob," said Blake.

"Isn't he? Vainglorious, affected, full of airs, distinctly evasive about the truth, and he fawns on a title so dreadfully it is unseemly. Perhaps we should simply take the boat to New York."

"But I like him. And his wife. And his cooking."

"His cooking? You? *Côtelettes de mouton à la Reforme? Potage* Lord

Marcus Hill? Pound cake filled with marzipan cream made to resemble a plucked chicken?"

"You have not tasted his boiled beans and bacon."

I snorted.

"He is not ridiculous in his native tongue." He leaned back and shut his eyes. "He is, in his way, a brilliant man. He would have made a great general. Instead, he organizes a kitchen like a military campaign and invents something useful every week. If the government put him in charge of national nourishment, no one in the country would starve."

"And now someone has died in his kitchen and the club worries that there might already have been another victim."

"And they are fretting because of their banquet."

"Not just that—but yes."

"And, as Wakley says, arsenic is everywhere, and it may have nothing to do with Soyer."

"And I must resolve it in three days."

"What do you think, then?" he said.

I gave him a pleading look. "I do not know. I cannot seem to cut the matter down to any size; the possibilities just seem to loom and grow. Do I look at the guests at the dinner? At the servants who cooked it or brought it to the table? At Rowlands's friends and enemies—and what of the other man, Cunningham? Or the Russians, who may be plotting to have the banquet canceled, about whom I know nothing? Then there is the possibility of accidental contamination, but it also occurred to me after I saw Soyer quarrel with the meat man this morning that a supplier might deliver something unfit to eat if they were sufficiently dishonest or sufficiently angry. And there is the club itself: hundreds of members, dozens of staff—full, as I discover, of rivalry and resentment. Where do I begin? Where do I stop?"

Blake's landlady chose this moment to shriek up (she never climbed the stairs if she could help it) and demand why I wasn't done by now. I called down that I was all but finished, and swiftly took up a bag, into which Blake threw a number of items.

"I'll climb out of the back window. It's nearly dark now, so I will not be seen. You lock up behind you."

"And?"

"You will have to find a way of getting me into the Reform. I'll give you a head start. Then I'll have one of those hot baths and sleep in your room."

I said, "You have to come through the gate in the side street—"

"Carlton Gardens—I know it," he said. "I'll meet you in Crown Passage; it's a narrow lane on the opposite side from the Reform in St. James's. Come and find me." He sauntered, too cocksure for my liking, toward the back room.

Then he said, "Do you have those bottles you took from Rowlands's rooms?"

I examined my pockets. They were still there: one a tiny pot of Delftware, the other a tiny glass vial. He scooped them up onto his palm.

"Can I keep them?"

"If you can make your way down the wall without breaking them."

I did not bother to stay to watch him reach the ground safely. He seemed so sure of himself that part of me half wished him a broken ankle on the way.

MATTY WAS SLICING FRUIT: perfect grapes, pineapples and oranges. Next to her, Mrs. Relph was stirring a cream of the palest lemon hue.

"I require your presence, Matty."

Matty looked up irritably. She came up to me and bobbed.

"Mrs. Relph is losing patience with me. I can't be disappearing all the time like this. People are starting to talk."

"It is important," I said, equally cool. "I need you now. And I shall have words with Mrs. Relph."

"No—" she said, but I was already there.

"Mrs. Relph, I shall have need of Matty today, and maybe for the next few days. It is on Monsieur Soyer's business. I would be most grateful if you would release her when necessary."

"Yes, sir," she said frostily, wiping red, calloused hands.

"Is there something more you would say, Mrs. Relph?"

"No, sir." Her face had the closed look of the servant who knows better but will not say.

"Please, speak."

"All right, sir." She looked me square in the face and lowered her voice. "Since you ask. Besides that it becomes exceedingly difficult to complete tasks if she is constantly to be called away, the fact is, sir, Matilda is a good, steady girl, a clever girl with good prospects, and your presence and attentions are causing talk. I daresay you turn her head a little. But if she is to do well in this business, as I hope she will, she must hold on to her reputation and keep herself straight. It is hard enough with the men here. It's hard enough with the attention Chef shows her. Your presence encourages more of that."

"I see," I said stiffly. "I am sorry, madam, if I am regarded as a disruptive influence. I do not wish to be. And believe me, I am well aware of Matty's fine qualities, which is why we need her."

I TOLD MATTY THE NEWS.

Crown Passage was a grim little alley. Blake was crouching in a doorway. I pulled him up and helped him into my plain country coat, watched the fleas leap upon it and wondered if it would ever be fit to wear again. It hid most of the poorness of his clothing and much of the stench, and a woolen cap with earmuffs covered much of his face. I pressed a small pie that Matty had taken from the kitchen into his hand. Dusk was falling as I led him down Carlton Gardens. In the balustraded wall around the club there was a gate. Most of the time, it was manned by one of Gimbell's brawnier favorites, but Matty had, against my better judgment, lured him away with the promise of a meringue and a teasing smile, and sent out a little potboy, who, knowing no better, opened the door wide for us.

We rounded the dark sides of the basement, dodging as best we could the scullery boys who scuttled in and out with slops and the delivery men wrestling pallets of greens, to the furthest and littlest-used entrance from the street. Though I had fought in numerous skirmishes in India, I found I was nervous. If we were discovered, what explanation could I give? Blake would be done for.

We waited in the shadows until Matty opened the door.

"Blimey, you stink!" she said in a hoarse whisper. Then, "How could you do this to yourself? Why could you not just do what the milord says? I thought you were steady, Blake, and then you do the stupid thing. How will you get out of this? And then to have Avery lie to me about it! You thought I could not keep a secret? Who else has more reason to, and better practice?"

"I concur with everything Matty says," I said.

"Just your knowing where I am makes you an accomplice, Matty."

"Precious little care you are taking to keep yourself safe," she replied. "We need to bide our time until the kitchen clerk goes for dinner, then we can get up the stairs."

She ushered us into the corridor, then pushed us into a cupboard too small for the three of us—Blake's odor was almost overwhelming—until she was sure that no one was about, and we emerged, gasping.

"We've a moment or two to get up the servants' stairs."

Whistling and footsteps sounded from round the corner. There was nowhere to hide Blake save the lift that carried food from the kitchen to the dining rooms upstairs. Matty pointed to it desperately.

"He will never fit."

Without a word, Blake threw off my coat and climbed in, miraculously folding himself up. Matty shut the doors quickly and began to draw on the pulleys. Round the corner came the prodigy, Perrin.

He was right upon us when he said, "Ah, *la belle* Mathilde," and gave her a look that was at once suggestive and soulful, and in heavily accented English said, "Do you take the clerk's job?"

"Just for a moment, Chef." She smiled back, rather more warmly than necessary, while wrestling with the pulleys.

He turned to me and evidently thought the worst, raising his eyebrows. Then he pressed his apron to his nose.

"*Bon sang!* What is that, *cette puanteur*!"

Matty answered at once. "There was a tramp, a beggar, got in here. The captain took him out, but he left something behind." She laughed and pointed at my coat. "I'll burn it and fetch a mop as soon as I'm done here."

He nodded at me, still half amused. "*Bon, ma belle,* make it soon." She grinned and blushed, and as soon as he had gone began to work the pulley the other way.

"Captain! I can't pull it back down." The ropes would not move. I leaned down with all my own strength, but to no avail. Then the kitchen clerk appeared at the end of the passage.

"You'll have to go upstairs and find him. I can't go into the club," she hissed, and fled.

I snatched up my coat and dashed up the stairs to the porter's lobby and thence into the saloon, almost sending footmen flying, then walked as swiftly—with the illusion of unhurriedness—as I could to the far corner of the building where I assumed the lift must emerge. I found a small anteroom where two footmen were wrestling with the lift door. They looked at me with great bemusement.

"Good evening," I said. "The lift is broken. The fault is downstairs. The ropes, I think. It must be fixed. Before dinner. You must go!"

"But we cannot both leave our post."

"But you must. You were both asked for."

Reluctantly, they left.

"Blake! Open the door!"

There was a muffled choke. I pulled the lift open. Blake blearily opened his eyes, and tumbled out hands first into a heap on the floor.

"Too old for that," he muttered.

The servants' staircase was just outside the anteroom, so I bundled Blake up in my coat and half carried him up the two flights of stairs to my room. Thankfully, we had no further encounters.

I requested a bath (one I should not have minded myself), and a footman delivered a note which proved to be from Wakley. It confirmed the diagnosis of arsenic poisoning, and added that he would send a longer report on the morrow. Blake took the bath, emerging a good deal sweeter-smelling and reassuringly pink-fleshed, though still alarmingly whiskered, and wearing my bedrobe.

He had taken out Rowlands's two small bottles and placed them on the desk. Now he unscrewed each and sniffed them.

"What do you think?"

He was silent for a while, his brows bunched in concentration. He upended the contents of the glass bottle onto his finger and licked it.

"Fowler's Solution," he said.

"The tonic?"

He nodded. He poured out the contents of the small blue pot onto the desk. A smaller pile of white grains. He stared at them. I reached over to touch them, and he pushed my arm away.

"I reckon it's white arsenic."

"Good lord! How can you tell?

"I'll need milk and an egg."

I summoned a footman to go down to the kitchen and request milk, an uncooked egg, bread and butter and a hearty soup. Food was not permitted in the rooms, but I said Monsieur Soyer had offered me the kitchen's resources, and it was an emergency. Blake lay down and rested.

I was to meet Jerrold downstairs, and dressed for dinner. The footman delivered a tray. Blake sat up suddenly, as if surprised from a deep sleep.

On my table was a bottle of sherry. He poured a generous shot into a glass and took a swig. Then he took from the bag I had brought from his rooms a small pack of tools and instruments. He unwrapped it and extracted a pair of small tongs; with these he picked up a single grain of the powder. Before I could stop him, he placed it upon his tongue.

"Blake!"

Immediately, he gagged, spat it out, took a great mouthful of sherry and then spewed it out into the sink. He took a mouthful of the milk, swilled and spat that, too. He broke the egg and tipped it into a glass with more milk, which he swallowed. Then he sat down on the bed, rubbing his mouth gingerly.

"Well?"

"That's arsenic: sharp, like a sting in the mouth."

"And you thought it a fine idea to try it yourself, in your state, to discover this. And I am supposed to be rash."

"I knew what I was at. Arsenic is the active ingredient of Fowler's."

"I had no idea. My aunt takes it for her lumbago."

"It's flavored with lavender water, and is mostly quackery."

"So Rowlands was dosing himself with two kinds of arsenic."

He shrugged. "Arsenic's a treatment for the clap. He may not have known it was also in the Fowler's. But there's enough here for him to have killed himself and a few more besides."

"So it was self-induced." I felt my chest sink with relief. And then, "But what about Cunningham?"

"Perhaps it was cholera and a bit of dyspepsia. We'll talk tomorrow. Now, I shall eat my bread and soup and sleep, and you will have your dinner."

It was with an almost jaunty step that I made my way to the dining room.

Chapter Ten

The Reform's dining room was known as the Coffee Room. It was another great long chamber, divided into three parts by gilded columns and pilasters, adorned with carved, gilded swags, wreaths and cornices, furnished with red silk curtains and Persian carpets, and set with tables laid for four and six. At each table sat gentlemen—mostly in dark frock coats, though here and there one saw flashes of green or blue—drinking and dining. Douglas Jerrold and Henry Mayhew were sitting together, Mayhew more smartly dressed than usual, in a correctly buttoned waistcoat and a properly knotted necktie.

"How are you, Douglas?" I managed to get in first. "No ill effects after Soyer's dinner?"

The older man stood up, pushing his unruly hair back from his face.

"None at all, my dear Avery. Now, an invitation to the kitchen is one thing," he said, smirking, "but ensconcing oneself at the club is quite another. You are a damned Tory, Avery! I am surprised they have not run you out of the place."

"Don't be ridiculous, Douglas," said Mayhew, refilling his glass with a plum-colored nectar. "This place was lost to politics the minute Soyer's first dish reached the table. It is a palace to fine living, and the zeal of the radicals is quite blunted. See the butterfly brigade over there—Duncombe with Molesworth and their friends—out in their brightest plumage, tucking into their veal chops." He pointed to a table of dandies showing off in gold braid and yellow velvet. In among them I saw Thomas Duncombe and William Molesworth. Molesworth ignored me; Duncombe acknowledged me with a discreet wave.

"You have arranged the table with the Coffee Room clerk?" Jerrold added, looking suddenly anxious. "He is a tartar, I'm afraid, a stickler." At the Coffee Room's entrance, a severe-looking man at a lectern was gesturing furiously at me. "Very hard on members' guests. He insists they must sign in the book before dinner. No exceptions."

I went over and explained that the club committee had arranged for me to stay at the club. The Coffee Room clerk said my name was not in the book. I said Mr. Percy and the secretary would vouch for me. Rules were rules, he said. The committee had no special rights when it came to guests; he had heard nothing of it from the secretary. I spied the footman whose name I could not remember divesting himself of plates. He came over, reintroduced himself—"Jeffers, sir"—and confirmed that I was a guest of the committee. This cut no ice. I was a stranger, the Coffee Room clerk said. He could not allow me to eat if my name was not in the book. Jerrold came and asked if I might be his guest, but he, too, was forcefully rebuked. He was allowed one guest: Mr. Mayhew.

By now we were beginning to attract attention.

"We shall find you a sponsor," said Jerrold decisively, and he cast about the room. Duncombe looked over, and I bowed my head, I cannot really say why; I simply had a strong feeling that I did not want to be beholden to him. Mayhew, meanwhile, was raising and lowering his eyebrows at a tremendous rate, gesturing at someone sitting behind him. Jerrold at first pointedly ignored him but, after a few minutes of vainly looking, he gave in.

"He would not be my first choice," he said with a sigh, "but we shall ask him anyway. He came on his own, and he should agree if we ask him sufficiently humbly. Let us hope he is not in one of his crochets."

The man in question was perhaps thirty, an eye-catching figure with a powerful face, a squashed pugilist's nose and a bulldog chin. He had a startling mop of wavy hair, almost pure white, and wore round spectacles. He leaned back precariously in his chair, and there seemed to be a dozen empty glasses before him on the table.

"Thack!" Jerrold said, with as much warmth as he could muster.

"Young Douglas." The man, at least ten years his junior, brought his chair down and stood up. He was extremely tall.

Jerrold twitched at the greeting and smiled long-sufferingly. "I wonder if you might do us a great favor tonight. This young gentleman is being put up at the club by the committee, but Scott, the secretary, has failed to inform the Coffee Room tyrant. I have used up my visitor for the day, and the clerk insists he cannot be fed. Would you be so good as to make him your guest for the night?"

The man looked down at me. He hesitated.

Jerrold added, "Of course, I expect to pay for his dinner."

"In fact, the committee will pay," I said quickly, "or I will. Either way, everyone will be reimbursed."

"Thack, may I introduce Captain William Avery. He has been in India."

"Ah, I was born in India. One of the Chinjalee Averys?"

"No, sir, I am afraid not."

"I wonder you have not heard of Avery, Thack," Jerrold prompted, almost tauntingly. Between the two men, matters were not entirely easy.

"He was the toast of India, saved a maharajah from a tiger, fought the Thugs with Xavier Mountstuart and won a sheaf of medals in Afghanistan before being invalided out."

"Well, naturally, I have," said the man, a mite huffily. "I follow happenings in India."

"Avery," Jerrold ran on, "this is William Thackeray, a member of our very humble profession, that is to say, a journalist"—at this, Thackeray winced—"of considerable talent and acuity. He writes for *Fraser's Magazine* and had a novel published last year, *Catherine*."

I tried to think if I had read anything from *Fraser's* at all. It seemed my dinner might very well depend upon it.

"I did enjoy *Yellowplush*—yes, the *Yellowplush* stories in *Fraser's*," I said. "Highly amusing."

Thackeray's face broke into an extraordinarily attractive smile.

"You have hit the very nail, Avery," said Jerrold drily. "There, you will have to stand him dinner now."

THE FARE WAS SIMPLER than Soyer's dinner, but no less satisfying for that. A velvety vegetable soup, followed by three small plates of French olives, anchovy filets and crisp, bitter radishes with butter. Jerrold and Mayhew ordered roast beef served with early spring vegetables, some small potatoes basted in butter and chopped herbs, and I chose Soyer's famous dish, lamb cutlets *à la* Reform, as well as a late winter salad of herbs and cress. Percy, who periodically patrolled the Coffee Room, came to carve their beef, a great roast of which rolled up on a silver platter, his knife sliding through the meat like a diver penetrating water.

"Is everything to your liking, Captain Avery?" he said.

Mayhew looked impressed. "Good God! Two days, and the staff are greeting you by name. And you're a Tory. What's the secret?"

"Pity he was not about to face down the Coffee Room clerk," observed Jerrold.

We drank sherry, then an excellent claret. From time to time, Mr. Thackeray, sitting with his friends at the next table, glanced over at us.

"Douglas says there are rumors flying round the club," said Mayhew at last. "Come on, Avery, what's your secret?" He chased the last morsels round his dinner plate.

"What sort of rumors?" I said.

"Douglas says that someone died at the club, later that night, after your dinner."

"For a moment I wondered if it was you!" said Jerrold waggishly. "After all, you disappeared from the dinner table and never came back. You and young Rowlands. Now, tell us how it is that you have become such a favorite at the Reform."

I choked and looked up from my plate guiltily. There was an awkward pause. "I cannot really—"

"My dear fellow—" said Jerrold. Another pause. "Not Rowlands?"

Blake always said my face was distressingly easy to read.

"I found him collapsed on the floor."

"Dear me. Do you know what it was?"

The wine had loosened my tongue. "The committee has pressed me to look into it, because everything must be perfect for their banquet, though I protested I was not really their man, and Blake is away."

"Was it something he ate?" Jerrold said, laughing. "It seems the club has gone from pampering Whigs to killing them off. Rather a severe sentence, would you not say?"

"Well, it is most interesting," said Mayhew brightly, his wineglass empty and his cheeks flushed. "Douglas says that beneath the calm surface of the Reform, a thousand feuds and rivalries lurk. Each faction vies for domination. The committee versus the members. The committee versus the kitchen. The radicals versus the Whigs. A perfect place for a murder."

"Why, it is a marvelous place!" said Jerrold, only half mocking. "The finest food in clubland, the most glorious building. A place that salutes talent, not birth, and takes everyone: nonconformists, Roman Catholics, Jews—and hacks! And when they put their minds to it, the members are supposed to be thinking up a program to improve the world. What could be better?" He paused. "Fewer dull Whigs, I suppose. *Et voilà*."

"So, Avery," said Mayhew casually, "is there a story in Rowlands's demise for us?"

"No, not at all, and I am not supposed to have told you any of this. The committee has asked me to be discreet. But I do not believe Soyer's table was the culprit, for here we are, and Duncombe over there, none the worse for wear. My suspicion is, Rowlands was dosing himself with arsenic and took too much. I believe the matter is more or less resolved, and tomorrow I should be on my way home."

"Duncombe? Does he know?" said Jerrold.

"I had to tell him this afternoon. He was most upset."

"He seems quite jolly to me now," said Jerrold tartly. Duncombe was now cheerily sharing some wine with two rather dull-looking men at another table.

"My dear Avery, you really should be more circumspect—you are altogether too trusting. We are newspapermen—it is our job to publish what others wish kept quiet." He hooted at my worried look. "Do not fear, we'll keep your counsel. But, in return, you must tell us where Blake is." His sharp little eyes gleamed.

"Some mysterious investigation about which he will say nothing," I mumbled. "Tell me about Mr. Thackeray. I gather it is not an easy acquaintance."

"We have a history," said Jerrold. "We met in Paris in the thirties. He was busy losing a fortune, I attempting to scrape a living. He has a sharp tongue—though not quite as sharp as mine—and a satirical eye." He grinned. "He considers himself a gentleman and feels journalism debases him and consequently looks down on the rest of us. He is rather inclined to look down in general. He thinks me lower than him because he once saw me eating my peas with a knife."

"Douglas makes him nervous because he is as clever as he."

"He has had his tragedies," Jerrold went on. "He has a mad wife—a sad story—and two small daughters. Ran through his inheritance in a matter of years. Now he has to scramble for commissions like the rest of us to pay for his wife's asylum bills. He is prone to moods. He can be greatly entertaining or as crotchety and rude as you like, and is a member of a great many clubs and out every night."

"He cannot decide if he approves of *Punch* or thinks it beneath him," said Mayhew.

"He is coming over," said Jerrold.

"May we join you?" said Mr. Thackeray. He had brought his chair with him, and two smiling followers. We exchanged pleasantries and they sat themselves down. Mr. Thackeray folded his considerable length into his chair and said his friends had heard of me, and he wished to learn more about the gentleman with such good taste in literature for whose dinner he had just paid. He beckoned the Coffee Room clerk and demanded a bottle of claret and some port, lit a cigar and asked me about India.

I mumbled a vague reply. I did not want to talk about India.

"Now, Thack," said Mayhew, bending confidentially into the table, "you are a clubman *par excellence*, and you must have some excellent gossip."

Thackeray chuckled, looked over his spectacles and puffed on his cigar.

It was one of his friends who answered. "Did you hear that blackguard Dr. Blackman is being forced to resign for cheating at cards?"

"Indeed, the bugger had ten pounds off me two weeks ago," said Thackeray.

"I am told Worplesdon was seen voting for the Tories," said Jerrold.

"Ha, ha! No more Reform dinners for him!"

"John Wilkie was found asleep in the library with his shoes off, but he is in with the committee and so may live to tell the tale."

"He has a new doxy and so gets no sleep these days."

"Who's the lady?"

"Mrs. Keeley, and she is no lady."

"Oh, the actress!" said Thackeray, delighted. "I heard said she didn't care for 'docking.'"

"That is because she cannot do it in public, and she performs only for applause," said Jerrold.

They both grinned widely. The air began to warm up.

"What do you know about the committee?" said Jerrold.

"Oh, the committee! I'm told that Charles Barry is taking them to court for his fee."

"I have heard it, too. I did not set too much store by it."

"I have it on good authority . . ."

"But why?" said Mayhew innocently.

"The club is in debt. All this"—Thackeray waved his cigar toward the gilded columns and the painted cornices—"costs far more than was originally estimated. Three times more, if what I've heard is to be believed. Barry says he is owed more for all the redesigns and extra time he spent; the committee disagrees."

"What if the committee will not pay?" said Mayhew.

"Perhaps the entire club will end up in debtor's prison," said Thackeray. "What a thought! It might make a good squib for *Punch*. The members of the Reform troop into the Marshalsea one by one."

"From what I hear, the committee could do with a few days in the chokey," Jerrold murmured, smiling. "What is all this about arguments with Soyer? The members would be in uproar if they were to wake up one day and discover he had left and the committee the reason for it."

"That's the one thing we agree on, Douglas," said Thackeray. "There are some fine idiots on the committee."

"I came across Captain Beare yesterday," I said.

"Beare is exactly the man," said Thackeray.

"He is an unimaginative little person who considers food a weakness," said Jerrold. "He has decided his one chance to lord it over his fellow men will be as chairman of the club's governing committee."

"I am sure Soyer can be a handful," Thackeray mused. "Though I yield to no man in my admiration of his stewed rump steak with oyster sauce, and I am very fond of him. He has his moments and, for all his genius, he is, in the end, just a cook."

"My dear Thack, what a snob you are," said Jerrold, not altogether warmly.

The air began to cool again.

"What do you make of Mr. Ellice?" I ventured.

"Oh, Ellice!" said Thackeray. "Ellice claims he invented the club and believes it belongs to him. In truth, he fought the idea for months and now pets the child—adopted—as if begat by himself!"

A gentleman at another table looked round at this. Jerrold smiled mischievously, leaned forward once more and lowered his voice.

"William Molesworth, over there, founded the club." He gestured at where Duncombe and his friends sat in their rainbow colors. "Have you not seen him flinch every time Ellice takes the credit? He persuaded Ellice to put a very considerable sum of money into setting it up; now Ellice thinks he owns it. Molesworth's idea was to start a club that would gather together all the so-called progressives—the radicals, the religious nonconformists and dissenters, northern factory owners who favored notions of reform and progress, and the Irish members—all those who broadly call themselves liberals—along with the Whigs, to build one party to oppose the Tories. At first the Whigs' leaders refused; they could think of nothing more demeaning than to descend to the radicals' level. However, they were eventually brought around, not least by the Tories' triumph at the last elections. The radicals expected that, having pulled all sides of the argument together, they would be at the helm. They would draw off the best and most progressive of the Whigs, the old party would decay and they would lead a coalition of progress and change."

"How wrong they have been," said Mayhew.

"In what way?" I said.

"The Whigs did not fade, they have won. They have kept hold of the party," said Thackeray nonchalantly, "while the radicals have never been a party and all wish to be leaders; moreover, their numbers were sorely reduced at the last election, not least because Whig landlords still have control over a large number of corrupt parliamentary seats, and like to put in men they regard as the 'right sort.' The radicals have been outnumbered by the Whigs, and their claws pulled. The forces of conservatism are in charge here—and luxury, excellent food and good company have worn down political zeal. Not that I mind excessively." He grinned. "And, finally, the Whig leaders like Palmerston stay away—they keep to their rich aeries at Brooks's Club and Crockford's, where they gamble their fortunes and hatch policy, while at the Carlton the Tory leaders may be seen a dozen times a day. If I were Molesworth, it would stick in my gullet."

"I am amazed," said Jerrold, thoughtfully, "that the radicals are not angrier."

"Some are," said Mayhew excitedly, taking a deep swig from his glass and casting his eyes in the direction of Molesworth and Duncombe's table. "I have heard that some are furious at the direction the club has taken. They thought they would rule the party; instead, they find their numbers depleted and the Whigs once again in the ascendant. They blame the club for promising their dominance but delivering their downfall, and for blunting political ambition by encouraging lotus-eating. I have even heard it said that some would like to see it fall, for it would leave them free again."

"Ah, yes." Thackeray waved his cigar as if sketching a picture in the air. "I see it all: the radicals in their sky-blue frock coats rising up and pulling down the curtains, knocking over the portrait busts and—whisper it—pouring salt into the soup! Before repairing home to change for dinner."

"Not all the radicals are silly young dandies," Jerrold said. "Not that they are likely to do anything. That is not the British way. They will mutter and complain, and that will be that."

"Too true," said Thackeray. "And, for all its faults, the Reform is the queen of clubland: the fairest, the most convivial, and with the finest bill of fare. Soyer was on form tonight. I forswore the beans and bacon for once and had an excellent veal chop and *œufs en gelée*."

"There's that banquet here in a few days," said Mayhew unsteadily, and I saw that in the space of minutes he had slipped from sober to sozzled. "If I were an angry radical, I'd go along and upset a tureen of soup in Ibrahim Pasha's . . . lap. I'd throw forks and bread rolls at Lord Palmerston. I should do my best to bring down the house. I'd have done for Rowlands before he did for himself!"

It occurred to me that Mayhew's speculations might be closer to the mark than he realized.

"So that story is true?" said Thackeray.

"You had heard already?" I said, alarmed.

"He told me." He pointed at one of his friends.

"I was told this afternoon that he had died," said the friend.

"What carried him off?" Thackeray said. A smile stole across his features. "Did he expire under the weight of his gold watch chains? Was he mesmerized by one of his patterned waistcoats and walked into the road, only to be run over by a draper's cart?"

Jerrold shrugged, one of his crooked shoulders leaping much higher than the other, and gave me a philosophical look.

"What does Captain Avery know about the matter?" said Thackeray, sitting up.

"I happened to be with Mr. Rowlands, whom I hardly knew, when he was taken ill," I said.

"We heard it was after one of Soyer's dinners. Fancy! The great chef's cooking finished him off!" Thackeray clapped his hands and laughed delightedly.

"No, sir!" said I, rather more vehemently than I had intended.

"Oh, do not misunderstand me. I love Monsieur Soyer extremely. His culinary creations delight me, his manner and convivial habits amuse and enchant me. One day, I shall put him in a novel!"

"Anyway," said Mayhew indignantly, "Rowlands did not die of his dinner, he was poisoned. With arsenic. He was dosing himself."

"Henry," said Jerrold, "I think we had better get you home."

"Arsenic, eh?" said Thackeray. He nodded knowingly. "One hears it is rather the thing in certain excitable parts of society."

"Really?" I said.

"I know it only on hearsay, of course. But the story is that some fashionable young bucks take a grain a day. They claim that, in the right dose, it improves the complexion and the digestion, and bestows great energy and staying power on the ingester, both outside, and—so it is said—inside, the bedroom."

"Good God! Is there anything in it?"

"Damned if I know. But in Ireland once I saw a man wipe a little arsenic on a racehorse's arse to make him run. The effect was"—Thackeray spread his arms as wide as he could— "voltaic!" He threw his head back and laughed.

"Did he win the race?"

"He did indeed."

I RETURNED TO MY ROOM in excellent spirits. The matter of Rowlands's death seemed resolved. Blake was snoring quietly. He would be free in the morning to go where he would. Wrapped in the sheets, he looked almost frail—and unusually at peace—his gaunt face wiped clean of frowns and questions. I wedged the occasional table against the door to prevent anyone entering, took the cast-off coverlet, wrapped myself in it and lay down next to him. As I drifted off, I recalled that I had failed to write to Helen again, as I had promised myself I would, but the thought could not keep me from sleep.

PART THREE

Chapter Eleven

A dozen heavy blows, painful and insistent, penetrated my dreams. Then came the calls.

"Captain Avery! Captain Avery! Are you there? Are you awake?"

Blake sat up, eyes wide.

"Into the wardrobe," I ordered him. He looked at me askance but climbed in nevertheless.

I went to the door and pulled the table away from it.

"What time is it? I did request that I not be roused early this morning. Is it very late?"

In the doorway, Mr. Scott in a bedrobe, his countenance gray with anxiety, and Mr. Percy, grave, trim, dressed, composed.

"It is not yet five, sir. I am sorry," said Mr. Scott, wringing his hands.

"There has been an incident," said Mr. Percy. "We would be grateful for your presence."

"An incident?"

"One of our members is sick," Scott said. He made an awful gasping noise.

"Two are sick," said Mr. Percy. "Very sick. Symptoms similar to Rowlands's the other night. They dined at the same table in the Coffee Room last night."

"I dined there, too."

"Will you come?"

"I will dress at once."

Mr. Scott looked cheered. Percy gave me a small, relieved nod.

When the door was shut, Blake climbed out of the cupboard and back into bed. I dressed.

"I was so sure we had resolved Rowlands's death last night. Mr. Thackeray mentioned how certain fashionable young men were taking arsenic, and I remembered Rowlands was taking Fowler's, too. I was certain that he had poisoned himself by accident, and Cunningham's death was something else. Now there are two more. Blake?"

"I'm asleep," said Blake.

"What do you intend to do? Will you leave?" I said.

"Mnnfwah!" said Blake. He turned violently onto his side so that his back was facing me.

"Blake!"

"If they are dead, don't let anyone touch them, or anything around them."

My spirits lifted. "Of course. How shall we arrange it?"

He pulled the covers up over his head. "Later."

A SLEEPY FOOTMAN ushered me down to Mr. Scott's room. The secretary sat at an expensive polished mahogany desk. His chair was upholstered in burgundy velvet. The desk itself was remarkably disorderly:

papers piled up, papers slipping onto the floor, more papers sprinkled across it. Scott himself was still in his bedrobe, unhappily rubbing his hands. Mr. Percy stood to one side, looking as if his patience had been mightily tried.

"Please, Mr. Scott, calm yourself," said Percy. "You must tell the captain what has transpired."

Haltingly, Scott explained that the first man had been taken ill on the way to his carriage. His footman had returned to the club for help. He had been carried to a chamber, where he vomited and was convulsing and terrified. The club's doctor had been called and administered an emetic. Almost immediately thereafter, the second gentleman, who had dined with him and was still drinking, had also fallen sick and had decided to take a chamber for the night.

"Why did you not call me before?"

"We hoped it might pass, and we did not wish to trouble you," Scott babbled. "There is a good deal of spring influenza and the like around. Guests have been taken ill before here, and recovered."

"But these are the same symptoms as Rowlands had!"

Scott blinked and shook his head.

"May I see the gentlemen?" I said stiffly.

Scott nodded, then began to rub his hands again. "Oh, sir, how shall we manage? The story is bound to leak out. Mr. Percy thinks we should close the kitchen, but the members will complain. And it will create the most terrible hole in our finances. We simply cannot afford it. And the banquet draws ever nearer. Three hundred guests to feed, every leader of the party, and all the great and good present, too. How shall we do it?"

"Please, Mr. Scott, calm yourself," said Percy. "We shall simply take a step at a time, and Captain Avery will help us. The banquet is in two days. If there are difficulties with the finances, I would be more than happy to go through the accounts with you."

At this, Scott stood up, turned haughtily to the steward and said in a strangled voice, "May I remind you of your station, Mr. Percy. You may occupy a significant position at the club, but you are a servant, nevertheless. I am the secretary, an official of the club. Do not presume to talk to me thus."

Percy inclined his head in a most dignified manner and turned on his heel.

"Mr. Percy!" Scott called out. "I was hasty. I apologize."

Percy returned. His face was like granite, and Scott, flustered, could not look at him.

"Would you please take Captain Avery to see the, ah, afflicted gentlemen?"

I REMEMBERED the club's doctor from the night of Rowlands's death. He was just the same as he had been on that occasion: at once avuncular and smilingly fatalistic. We stood under a gaslight in the hallway outside the door of one of the sick men as he whispered to us that there was very little hope.

I asked if we might see the patient. He raised his hands in horror—it would be impossible. I asked him what was wrong with the patient. In a most complacent tone he said he could not be sure. Blake would have bristled at such an answer; now I did.

"Are you certain of that, sir?" I said. And then, more quietly, "I am speaking to you at the request of the club itself."

There was a call from within the room, and he rushed inside, closing the door behind him.

"What now, Captain Avery?" said Percy.

"We must see the gentleman."

We stepped in as quietly as we could. The room was lit by two candles. On the bed, the patient was in the throes of the most hideous and dramatic convulsion I had ever witnessed. His spine had bent backward upon itself so extremely that his head and feet almost met, and he did not seem to be breathing. Then suddenly he was released, his back snapped forward and he was straight once more. The doctor glanced at us balefully but said nothing. For a moment, the man recovered and breathed again. Then, as we watched, his body was once more seized by a terrible spasm, which left him gasping and choking. For a dreadful minute his whole body seemed to be electrically charged. Then he fell back upon the bed, insensible. The doctor bent over him.

"It is over," he said at last.

"I need to speak to you, sir," I said.

"Not now." This ill-temperedly.

I drew closer to the bed. The dead man's face had been pulled into a grotesque rictus, as if all the muscles had been dragged upward. As if death mocked us, with a livid, hideous smile. Around his lips was a foamy white stain. His fists were still clenched in death.

The door opened. A footman.

"Sir, the other gentleman will not open his door."

"You have another patient, doctor," I said. "You"—I pointed at the footman—"stay here."

"WE MUST GET into the room," I said.

Percy nodded.

I backed away and hurled my full weight at the door. It did not budge at all.

"Captain Avery," said Mr. Percy quietly, "I have a key."

The man lay very still on the bed, the sheets wildly twisted about him, as if he had taken part in some crazed struggle. Something—his foot—

gave a little jerk. I approached. I saw the same white stain around his mouth as I had seen on the dead man. I bent over him.

"He is alive!" To my intense relief, he was breathing, shallowly. His foot gave another jerk.

I left the doctor with his new patient and dispatched Percy to find Scott and make arrangements to summon Mr. Wakley. Then I returned to my room. Blake was still lying in the bed.

"I need you," I said. "You must advise me, at the very least."

"I need a day's more sleep."

"Blake!"

He sat up, groaning. "What's the damage?"

"One man dead. Another, I hope, recovering. Vomiting, convulsions."

He rubbed his face and scratched his head.

"All right. I'll stay. I've thought what to do and, though it galls me, I suppose I will have to be your fartcatcher."

"My what?"

"Your valet, your footman, your manservant, just as you suggested. Make sure you do not enjoy it too much."

"My servant?"

"Mmm." He looked at me from under his eyebrows, unsmiling.

"Just now, you are the most sinister servant anyone could imagine. And how will I pass you off? I had not mentioned you before."

"I came up from Devon," he said. "I arrived last night, stayed in a tavern, planned to accompany you home, but now will stay. You'll say that you summoned me the day before yesterday, when you assumed the matter would take a few days. Then you thought it would be swiftly resolved, so did not think to tell the secretary, as you expected to depart today. I'll lodge in the servants' quarters here. I can observe the staff. We'll make inquiries together."

"But surely they know you here?"

"Soyer will know me, and he must be warned. He has no guile, or none without notice. No one else will."

"It must be poison, don't you think?"

"Looks like it."

First, he took a razor to his hair, cutting it shorter round the sides, then brushed it into a side parting, causing the thicker side to fluff up in a most un-Blakean manner and teasing the other down over the scar across his eyebrow. From the bag I had carried from his rooms he brought out a plain black loose frock coat and waistcoat, a clean white shirt, a pair of dark gray trousers, well-polished boots and an old but well-made leather bag. Out of this came a beaver hat, a pair of wire spectacles and white gloves, the middle two fingers of which had been stuffed so as to hide the damage to his hand. Having dressed, he drew out a little case in which there was a small pot of gum Arabic and what appeared to be several dead black flies. One of these he affixed to his upper lip, transforming it instantly into a surprisingly credible mustache. His shoulders rolled forward and he bowed his head, rather than meeting the world with his usual bold glare. Blake was gone, and in his place was the picture of a steady, unobtrusive manservant.

We discussed how we should manage the thing. It was obvious that I would have to lead our inquiries. Blake suggested a number of questions for the doctor, which I attempted to receive in good part, though, in truth, the exchange set both our teeth on edge.

We tiptoed out into the corridor, avoiding the footmen who were starting to pad about the place, took the servants' stairs to the saloon, then scuttled in an ungainly fashion across its mosaic floor and thence to the basement. There was a sleepy kitchen boy on duty. I saw Blake out into the yard and returned upstairs; a few moments later, he knocked upon the door carrying his leather bag and asked for me. Together, we went to see our victims.

. . .

THE DEAD MAN'S name was Addiscomb. Blake prowled around the body, his observation patient, slow, unnerving. He pored over it, bringing himself very close, and sniffing and occasionally even prodding with his finger. Then he took out a small notebook and began to scribble. Once he had examined the body, he looked over the room inch by inch until I was almost twitching with restlessness.

"Show me what to look for, or at least teach me, so we may be done quicker."

He did not look up.

"Tell me, then, what you have found?"

"Not much to be found. This is murder from a distance."

"Murder?"

"What else?"

"I suppose you are wonderfully well acquainted with poisons," I said, only half-jokingly.

"I know a little about arsenic and nux vomica, which they grow in India. It's called strychnine here. I'd say that's what did for our corpse."

"Not arsenic?"

"No. The way the face is contorted, the bluish tinge of the skin, I'd say it was strychnine."

"Two different poisons?"

"So it would seem."

"What does it mean? Arsenic one day, strychnine the next?"

Blake shrugged. "Most poisoners find one means of killing and stay with it. There could be two poisoners, but that seems farfetched. Most poisoners don't want their crimes discovered, but this one wants us to know these were not accidents. He has used a second poison so the Reform will know that this was deliberately intended. And if the story leaks out, no one will care if it was arsenic or cyanide or antimony or lead or whatever, they will just remember that Soyer and the Reform Club poison their customers."

"So Rowlands's death was no accident?"

Blake shrugged.

The other victim, the Honorable Henry Rickards, Addiscomb's friend, seemed to be recovering.

"He woke briefly and asked for darkness and quiet," said the doctor. "His convulsions, such as they were, seem to have passed. I hope he is over the worst. I gave him bromide of potassium. He is now sleeping deeply."

I asked the doctor if he had known either of the gentlemen. He said he had not.

"They were both poisoned," I said.

He looked about him as if someone might be eavesdropping. "Let us not jump to conclusions."

I looked at him, incredulous. Blake brushed off, somewhat overenthusiastically, an invisible speck from my shoulder. That is to say, he prodded me.

"I was led to understand," the doctor murmured, "that the club is keen to avoid any unnecessary awkwardness at this time."

"I beg your pardon? Who has told you this?"

"Why, the committee—"

"So this has happened before?" said Blake. The interjection was all the more surprising, as it was uttered in an accent in which London vowels were mixed with an unmistakable (and impressive) Irish brogue.

"No—"

"What were the dead man's symptoms?" said Blake impatiently.

"Your manservant is very impertinent!"

"Isn't he?" I said. I turned back and frowned at Blake. "However, I do find him a great help in my inquiries. His methods are thorough, though a good deal less courteous and pleasant than my own. So I request politely that you answer the question. If it helps, consider the question from me; the committee has appointed me, and I require the truth."

The doctor's eyebrows flew upward.

"The dead man's symptoms?" said Blake.

"Severe nausea," he said grumpishly. "Sensitivity of all the senses. Light, sound and touch all pained him and seemed to start the convulsions. Involuntary spasms, beginning in his legs. Stiffening and jerking of muscles. By the time I arrived, his body was already convulsing and he was frothing at the mouth. One of the servants had given him a salt-and-water emetic."

"Died of asphyxiation?" said Blake.

"Probably."

"Seeing the contortion of the face, I would say it was a certainty," said Blake.

"Your servant fancies himself some manner of physician, does he?" said the doctor.

"Strychnine. I've seen it before," said Blake.

"And the sick gentleman shows the same symptoms?" I said.

Reluctantly, the doctor agreed.

"Have you attended any similar cases at the Reform?" I said.

"Is that any of your business?"

Blake whispered in my ear.

"It is. Are you a member of the Reform, sir?"

"I am, and proud to be."

"The committee will take a dim view of any attempts to inhibit my investigations."

"Moreover, sir"—this was Blake—"you allowed the administration of a salt-and-water emetic for what was undoubtedly a case of strychnine poisoning, thereby killing your patient more quickly."

"But I was not to know! And I was told the club wished to be discreet."

"By whom?"

"The secretary, Mr. Scott."

"My question again, sir." I said. "Have you seen anything like this?"

He shook his head.

"What about Rowlands? What about the gentleman who fell ill in the street and was not found until the next day?"

The doctor glowered. "If you mean Mr. Cunningham, he had a weak heart."

"It will be a very easy matter to visit Mr. Cunningham's family."

"It is possible that he ate something that did not agree with him."

"Is it conceivable that it was poison?"

"The symptoms were not the same as these men's at all," he said, giving me a wary look.

"Good God, sir! Do you really think that such a thing could seriously be kept a secret and, more than that, should be? Does this not suggest to you that there is a matter that must be addressed and resolved?"

The doctor shrugged angrily.

"You may have heard of me, doctor. My name is Captain William Avery. I won two medals in Afghanistan, saved the life of a maharajah in India, and was with the poet Xavier Mountstuart in his final battle before he died. My threats are not empty ones."

"It is not impossible that they were poisoned," he said stiffly. "The gentleman, Cunningham, he had vomited. But it was certainly not strychnine."

"I have some work for you. I should like an accurate résumé of what you recall of the previous cases, and another of your observations of the dead man today. I should like you to collect what you can of the dead man's bodily fluids for the coroner. I am ordering a postmortem. I expect you to agree to it."

"Do you indeed?" he said, bridling.

"No matter if you do not. Mr. Wakley will be coming anyway. But it will not look well if you do not. The club will be grateful for your services." I smiled politely.

"AH, BLAKE, I WAS GOOD! 'You may have heard of me, I am Captain William Avery, my threats are not empty ones.' I was marvelous!"

"Can't call me Blake."

"Maguire, then." He had chosen it himself.

"Remember it: Maguire. You did well, but you had a lever on him—his negligence and his appetite for approval from the club."

"And I recovered your rash intervention."

"Hmm."

"What next?"

"I'd like to meet Mr. Scott."

I ASKED Mr. Scott if he knew the two men Addiscomb and Rickards.

"I knew them both a little; very respectable gentlemen. Often dined here. I believe they were both members of Parliament."

"Whig or radical?" I asked.

"I'm sure I do not know—hardly my business."

"Well, they were both poisoned by strychnine," I said, reflecting on the fact that half an hour before, I had barely heard of it. "In my opinion, the club must be closed."

"But we cannot, it is impossible! The club's reputation. The banquet!" He began to wring his hands again.

"Three men dead, Mr. Scott. Another at death's door. I'd say the club's reputation will be ruined if you do not."

"It is a matter for the committee," he blustered.

"Have you sent to Lord Marcus?"

"I was about to. I am sure he will come as soon as he hears."

"I urge you not to delay. You must inform the families of the dead man and that of his sick friend, too. And Mr. Wakley must be summoned to examine the body and, this time, he must be paid. And I will require a list of all the diners in the Coffee Room last night, and where they sat. In due course, we shall probably have to contact them."

At this, his expression—previously aghast—became distinctly mulish.

"Have you summoned the police?"

"I rather hoped that you might manage it so that it was not immediately necessary."

"What magic do you expect me to conjure? Another man is dead," I said. "You will have to do it, Mr. Scott."

Scott began gloomily to shift papers back and forth upon his desk, to no discernible effect.

"Have you got all that?" I said, trying to rein in my impatience.

"I am sure I will remember," he said.

"If it is too much, I am sure Mr. Percy could spare one of his clerks?" I could not resist.

"No, indeed, I will manage," he said curtly, with a forced smile.

Then I introduced my newly arrived servant, Maguire, and requested lodging for him. Scott barely noticed Blake.

THE KITCHENS had an uneasy, distracted yet foreboding air. The scents of lye, chloride of lime and vinegar had replaced the aromas of stocks and roasts. Everywhere, kitchen maids and apprentices were gloomily scrubbing and wiping. The poultry kitchen's game shelves had been cleared of birds, stew pans that had formerly bubbled with stocks were empty. New deliveries were stacked up in great towers, but no one paid them any mind. By the scullery there were three vast sacks full of slabs of cooked meats, crushed vegetables, half-finished desserts. Mr. Gimbell stood by, holding a vast, steaming cup of coffee in his fist and perspiring freely as his band of scullery maids and boys darted in and out with buckets of water and mops.

I spied Matty scrubbing the marble slabs in the pastry kitchen. She looked up, saw us—her eyes almost popping when she recognized Blake—then quickly returned to her work.

Those not scrubbing or disposing were gathered in small knots, whispering darkly among themselves. Above the hum of steam and voices, Monsieur Benoît, the roasting chef, raged at some unfortunate minion. He boxed the young man on the ears, then stalked off to the butchery. The rest of his cooks clustered around black-haired Albert, who was regaling his audience with some no doubt unsavory anecdote.

"Troops aren't happy," Blake murmured. He held his hat under his arm and looked about the kitchen, as if in reverent awe.

Matty went for clean water and, as she turned to do so, another girl collided with her. I recognized her as the kitchen maid who had brought the tea tray and looked at Matty with such dislike on my first visit to the kitchen. Water splashed over both of them, and the other girl shrieked and turned furiously upon Matty:

"Watch yourself! Think you're so grand you doan have to look out for anyone else!" She pushed Matty in the chest, the hardest blow she could, sending her tumbling to the floor. The girl's eruption broke through the odd, muted air of the kitchen, and about the two an expectant audience fell silent. Blake took hold of my sleeve, thinking I might intercede. But Matty got herself up quickly and gazed fiercely at the girl with her fists clenched.

She said in a low voice, "I don't want no trouble, Margaret. Never have. But if you want to make something of it, I won't back off, believe me. I'd rather keep my place here, and I fancy so would you."

A whoop went up from a gang of young men who had been hanging about the game larder.

The other girl took a step back. "If there will be any place to keep," she muttered. And then, "You take care, Matty Horner, I'm watching you."

Perrin, the prince of the kitchen, came over and clapped his hands.

"Enough, girls! Enough! You, Alfred, Robert"—he pointed at the noisy young men—"*taisez-vous*. This is not a day for dispute."

I fancied both girls blushed slightly as they bobbed their apologies and went their own ways. There was an unnatural quiet for a moment, then the drone of chatter began again.

In the doorway of the main kitchen, his arms folded tightly across his chest and absentmindedly biting his thumb, Morel watched Perrin.

No one gave Blake or me a second look.

SOYER HAD DISAPPEARED. We found him by one of the entrances where food deliveries were made. Morel had followed him. A tower of fruit and vegetables had arrived, piled in pallets. Several porters stood by, their smuttiness standing out in the white cleanliness of the kitchen. Soyer was entirely absorbed in the crates. He looked over them then pointed out the third pallet down.

"I wish to see this one," he said peremptorily, and the porters lifted the top pallets off so he could examine the produce. A cornucopia of potatoes, lettuce and carrots were exposed. He dug his hands through them. Then he raised his arms in the air as if he were about to declaim a speech in a theater.

"*Non. Non, non, non!*" he cried. "Not good enough! The potatoes are spoiled, the winter lettuce is wilted. This is not up to our standard. It will not do."

The carrier scowled. "My master said—"

"I do not care what your master said, *I cannot serve this at the Reform!*" Soyer's tone became progressively higher and angrier. "I will not pay for it, and if your master cannot give me what I need, I will go elsewhere!" He drew his arms down to his sides, as if he were fighting to contain a great fury.

"But—"

"No blandishments, no bribes, no threats cut ice with me, you may be sure. Take it away!" And he folded his arms and pushed his chest out.

"My master says you owe him money!"

Everyone about the pallets seemed to breathe at the same time. Soyer ignored them. The phrase echoed in my ears. It was almost precisely what the butcher's man had said.

The porters piled the pallets back on top of each other, angry but powerless, and carried their spoiled goods outside. Soyer strode off to his office.

I looked at Blake. He seemed to me to be hiding behind his spectacles and his mustache, unobtrusive and as unreadable as ever.

I KNOCKED on Soyer's office door and went in, Blake sliding in silently behind me. There was Francobaldi, insufferable and commiserating. Soyer fiddled with a pencil as Francobaldi spoke, upending it and righting it again and again. His fancy lavender frock coat was folded over the back of his chair. Even his hat looked limp. His spark of liveliness, that which drew attention to him in any company, seemed all but extinguished. There was no fire in the grate, the gaslights were out; the room was downright funereal.

"Why, Captain Avery," Francobaldi said, in his ripe Continental tones, "here you are again, like the proverbial 'bad penny.' Can it be that you have moved into the club for good? I must say, your timing is terrible, ha ha ha." He laughed heartily.

I smiled coldly. "I might say the same for you, Mr. Francobaldi."

"Well, perhaps I should take my leave. Soyer," he said, "chin up! As they say."

The door closed. Soyer stared at his pencil.

"What was he doing here?" I said.

"He brought a present to thank me for the dinner." He spoke listlessly and pointed to a bottle on the desk. "It is a passable burgundy. Naturally, I could hardly keep the news from him. I have no doubt he will tell everyone, especially as I particularly asked for his discretion."

There was silence.

"It seems that death surrounds me," said Soyer. "My brother last year, and my mother-in-law. Then Cunningham and Rowlands. Now this." His voice began to rise alarmingly. "I do not understand how it happened. I have worked so hard. We went so thoroughly through everything. But there is a poison in my kitchen, and I cannot root it out, and I do not know how to stem it. And I do not know what to tell them, even if I may trust them. Oh, Emma, *si tu étais ici*! If you were only here. Her good sense would guide me. But she is not! And then there is the banquet, which now I dread. I am sorry, *Capitaine*, you find me at a low ebb."

"Courage, Monsieur Soyer! We will find a way through it," I said, finding myself unexpectedly moved. "I have some news—good news. But you must prepare yourself. And please, you must be quiet."

Chapter Twelve

I drew Blake forward and removed his spectacles. He stood straighter and ruffled his hair. Soyer stared for a moment, then his eyes grew round and his hat almost fell off his head. He threw himself at Blake and kissed him on both cheeks, which Blake submitted to with surprisingly good grace. When he at last let him go, Soyer said, "But I should hardly have known you—"

Blake picked up Soyer's invention, the tendon separator, and began to turn it over in his hands.

"So you have made it. Very clever."

"But this is nothing! Blake, you are here! My faith is restored. We will root out this blight. I feel sure of it now!" He looked extremely cheered.

"Avery and I will do what we can to help you, Alexis," said Blake, "but the police are bound to come, and I cannot make promises. And no one can know who I am."

"You are in disguise!"

"I am in trouble."

"My dear fellow! But all will be well now, I am certain!"

"We are saying I am Avery's manservant. My name is Maguire," Blake said. "It's important. If I am discovered, I will have to leave at once."

"Maguire. I will remember."

"Where is Emma, Alexis?"

"She is in Belgium. A major commission. I have not written. I do not wish to upset her. She is—" He arched his hands about his belly to show she was with child.

"May I offer my congratulations," I said. I could not have imagined a more inopportune moment for such news.

"What next?" said Blake.

"I must close the kitchen, at least for today. The Lord knows what will happen with Lord Palmerston's banquet. Two days away, and planned for so long! We had already started on some of the dishes, and have had to dispose of them all. Sauces that take days to prepare. There are untouched deliveries that arrived this morning. Do I discard them, too? And what of all our dried goods? Flour, grains, preserves, wines, spirits? They might all be tainted." He sat back, thoroughly discouraged. He hesitated. "Do you think this might have been some terrible accident? And Rowlands, too?"

"If you can think of a way that strychnine could accidentally find its way into someone's dinner."

"Strychnine? But it was arsenic!"

"Strychnine. And there is the second man, who appears to be recovering. With this and Cunningham, I can't see Rowlands's death as an accident. But we'll have to wait for Wakley's conclusions."

"Monsieur Wakley said that it might have been an accident," Soyer persisted.

"Did he?"

"He said that arsenic and other things may creep into food, when we do not realize . . ." He stopped. "I know it is an absurdity."

"Arsenic and strychnine are not hard to come by if you're killing rats, or if you're a doctor or druggist. In India, they use strychnine in very small amounts to stimulate the appetite. Have you ever toyed with that?"

"But of course not!" said Soyer. "We use strychnine for one thing—killing vermin. As we do arsenic. They are both kept locked in a special cupboard."

"Then it seems to me that it is most likely to be deliberate: someone wants to cause harm to the club, or you, or wants to prevent this banquet. Does anything occur to you—any small thing—that might help us?"

"*Non.*"

"Did you know these men at all—Addiscomb and Rickards?"

"Perhaps by name. I think they ate here a good deal. But I cannot recall ever having met them."

"I need to ask you, Alexis"—Blake watched Soyer closely as he spoke—"can you think of any way that poison could have got into food served from this kitchen?"

"You are accusing me? *Alors, pourquoi ferrais-je ça?* Why would I do that? My reputation stands upon what I serve. This is my calling! A chef has a sacred duty to provide goodness and nourishment to those who come to him for sustenance. I mean, the idea is absurd!"

"Calm yourself, Alexis. That was not what I was asking," Blake said, but I was not sure I believed him. "I want you to try to imagine all the possible ways in which poison might be added to food or drink here."

"Are you asking me if I trust my staff? You think I should distrust them? I do not go about looking for traitors. I could not work in such a way. My staff follow me because they know that even the lowliest is engaged in a great enterprise and they know that I shall see that they are cared for."

"Even the ones on a few shillings a week, hardly enough to feed themselves?" said Blake.

"Even they. I ensure that no one leaves the kitchen hungry."

"It is a practical question. How does poison get into the food?"

Soyer persisted in eluding it. "A mistake, perhaps? Someone confusing one powder for another."

"Which you said could not take place in your kitchen."

Soyer threw up his hands. "An assassin steals in unseen and sprinkles it upon the plate!"

Blake sighed and answered the question himself. "The fact is, it is most likely that the poison is being administered in the kitchen or when the food is en route to the dining room. It is also possible that it has come from a supplier, already contaminated, deliberately but erratically, so that only one or two are affected."

"Or it could take place at the table."

Blake ignored this. "Tell me, how do your staff regard you?"

"I like to think that they are satisfied in their work, and they see me as their captain, perhaps even as a father."

"But, on occasion, they have mutinied," said Blake.

"Yes," he said impatiently, "it is true. I demand the highest standards. Perhaps I ask too much. But I try to reward as well as demand."

"I have noticed," I said hesitantly, "a good deal of rivalry in the kitchen, and feelings run high."

"Bah! Any kitchen is thus. Every apprentice wishes to be a *commis,* every *commis* to be a *cuisinier,* every *cuisinier* to be a *chef de partie.* That is what galvanizes the kitchen, making each strive to do better. Those with real talent rise over the heads of the others. It is conflict, it is life."

"And sometimes it is violent," I said.

"Sometimes."

"I have seen the younger chefs bait and fight each other in a manner that the army would not accept, not on duty."

"It is never excessive."

"I saw the roast chef, Monsieur Benoît, beat one of his apprentices with a knife, and nearly stab him. And Gimbell beat a boy senseless."

"*Ça arrive,*" said Soyer. "One is training young men for perfection. One must be harsh until they learn. There is nothing remarkable in this."

"What if some young man here nursed an anger toward you for condoning this? Or one of your cooks' admiration turns to frustration and from frustration into madness?" said Blake.

Soyer raised his hands. "I do not know. I should not believe it."

"What about suppliers?"

"What of them?"

"Forgive me, sir," I said, "but I saw you lose your temper twice and return deliveries that were not up to your standard. Might one of them wish to be revenged upon you?"

"The idea is ridiculous!"

"What of one of your rivals? Francobaldi? He is jealous enough of you, and he wishes you no good."

"He would never go that far."

"Do you owe anyone money?" said Blake.

"Please!"

"I am serious. Have you got yourself into trouble? Gambling hells? Women?"

"Blake! I work all hours, and hardly have time for such things. And, besides, I adore my wife!"

There was a short silence.

"Well," Soyer said, "nothing that would cause any problems, I assure you."

"Enough speculation," said Blake, "We must get to work. Someone must write to all the diners to see if others are ill."

"*Mon Dieu,* Blake! The club would never agree to that, and I—"

"You what?" Blake said sharply.

"No, you are right." Soyer cast his eyes down. "But I tell you, such an inquiry, it will kill the club, and the kitchen. You know what reputation is in this city."

"You think news of this won't have crept into the broadsides by tomorrow morning?"

"No one who counts reads them or believes them. Please, might we wait before we inquire after the health of everyone who ate here? I do not wish to be heartless, but surely, if the dinner had harmed them, it would be too late by now?"

"We would discover whether the victims were deliberately chosen or if the poison was more widely spread, and how it might have been administered."

"I understand." Soyer looked as if all the air had leaked out of him. Then he rallied. "But it has been my experience that, if someone does become sick after eating in a professional dining room, one does hear of it eventually. Could we not wait, just a little?"

"This is not what I returned for," said Blake. That hard, blank expression had come back. "For obfuscations and misrepresentations."

"But it was to save your friend's reputation," I said. "Can we not wait a day? There is plenty to do."

"When the police come, it may look bad for you if no effort has been made to find out if anyone else is ill," said Blake. "But we could wait. We must discover what our men ate and thus narrow down where the poison might have come from. And we must take samples of the leftovers. Take spoonfuls, put them in clean jars and stopper them. Wakley has tests for arsenic and strychnine. It may yield nothing, but it's worth a try."

"Percy will find out what they ate," said Soyer. "He can lay his hands on their bills of fare and accounts." He went over to the door and had Percy summoned.

"And we will speak in turn to everyone in the kitchen who might have touched or prepared the food and drink," said Blake.

"But that could be everyone!" said Soyer. "And the footmen and the clerks!"

"Then we will speak to everyone."

Soyer's mouth jutted into a pout.

"Will not the police do that?" I said.

"The kitchen is closing. We will speak to them while they are all here."

There was a light tap at the door. Blake quickly replaced his spectacles and smoothed down his hair.

Mr. Percy entered, as correct as ever, though there were gray shadows under his eyes. "The cleaning is going apace, Chef. But the staff are talking. What would you have us do when the cleaning's done?"

Soyer sighed and turned away.

Percy peered, as courteously as was possible, at Blake. My heart began to thud. Percy was an observant man.

"May I present my manservant, Maguire, Mr. Percy? He has come up from Devon and will be helping me with my inquiries. Mr. Scott, I hope, is arranging a room for him."

"Pleased to meet you, sir," said Blake, in his full London Irish. "It is a marvelous place this, so. Even today it quite takes my breath away." And he offered his gloved hand and grinned in a manner utterly unBlake-ean.

"Pleased to meet you, Mr. Maguire—you're not from Devon?" said Percy politely, but now he was gazing at Soyer rather as an anxious aunt watches over an errant nephew.

"No, sir. Met the captain in India. Followed him to Devon. Captain, if you don't mind my saying, wasn't Mr. Soyer going to ask Mr. Percy to discover what your men ate last night?"

"Yes, yes," said Soyer. "Can you discover what Mr. Addiscomb and his friend ate and drank?"

"Certainly."

"Did you know either of them, Mr. Percy?" I asked.

"I knew their faces, but I must confess this is not really my area. Although I manage the waiting staff and am up in the Coffee Room now we have no butler, my chief role is to make sure everything runs smoothly downstairs and that the food and wine is ordered and paid for."

"Captain, you were going to ask if Mr. Percy could furnish us with a list of the members of the kitchen so we may speak to them before they leave," said Blake.

Percy glanced up. I wondered if Blake had gone too far, but the steward's gaze returned at once to Soyer.

"Could you perhaps draw up a list?" I said.

"Certainly, sir, but if I may say so, you will have your work cut out: that is over sixty people," said Percy.

"I realize this, but we must act. Maguire will help. I trust him, and he is very well organized, and speaks good French and some Italian."

"And the captain has furnished me with the right questions."

If Percy was surprised, he gave no sign of it.

"May I ask Mr. Percy where he is from and how he came to work for Mr. Soyer?"

If Percy was affronted, he did not show it. "I am from Shropshire, sir. Worked my way up in service, then came to London and worked for a number of titled gentlemen as butler, then steward. I came to the Reform three years ago, when Chef started cooking but before the building was completed. He was kind enough to try me out for my ability to run a household and my knowledge of wines and spirits. I hope I have not let him down."

"Is your family in service?"

Percy shook his head. "My father had a drapery business in Oswestry. He prospered, then he was injured in an accident some years ago. Lost all his fingers, got into debt, lost the business. So I went into service. It was not what I had planned, but I was a hard worker and rose quickly."

"Mr. Percy has been a rock since we started at the Reform," said Soyer. "I could not have done without him."

"I will see to that list," Percy said diffidently—I wondered if he was a little embarrassed—and withdrew.

"Tell me about him," said Blake.

"He and Morel, my *sous-chef,* are my chief and invaluable aides—especially since we lost the butler and since I seem unable to retain a secretary and Mr. Scott is quite *inutile.* Percy came to me when I was setting up the kitchen and asked if I would consider him. He had excellent references from his former employers and I saw his worth at once. He is very *effectif, très bien organisé,* admirably calm, utterly correct and reliable. Other establishments have tried to lure him away, but he has refused them all. He is loyal to me, and he values his position. He is not married, but has, I think, family in Shropshire."

As he spoke, Soyer began to recover some of his former vitality.

"And Morel?"

"André Morel I first met when he had just arrived from France and could barely speak English, some six or seven years ago. I saw and understood his great skills, encouraged them, and brought them on, and when I at last came to the Reform, made him my deputy. He puts everything into the kitchen—he is an orphan, no family to speak of—and owes everything to me."

"He must be the same age as you?" said Blake.

"A little older, if you must know. But he is an excellent lieutenant. I am a prodigy, you see, I was born to lead, to innovate. I must have a Morel, someone utterly reliable who ensures that all runs perfectly every day. This he relieves me of. I, on the other hand, shoulder the reversals and the demands; he cannot always leap over the obstacles, as I do. He worries over them. I relieve him of that. Everyone who knows him respects him, knows his worth."

He went to the sideboard and began to rearrange the things upon it. "I cannot think what I should do next."

"You should talk to your troops," said Blake. "Put fire back into them and fear into your enemies."

"You are right," said Soyer. He forced onto his features his usual ready smile and started to rebutton his waistcoat and retie his limp cravat.

"And tell them we're going to talk to them. Now, while memories are fresh, and before anyone should take it into their minds to disappear. Go out and stand in that panopticon of yours, and address your kitchen. Show that you are not to be easily dislodged. After all, you are Alexis Soyer, the Napoleon of chefs!"

"I am!" He placed a few rings on his fingers, picked up the lavender velvet frock coat from the back of his chair and adjusted his hat.

"*Aux armes!* To the barricades!" He hesitated. "What shall I tell them?"

"Whatever you like. Customers are dead. Kitchen's closed. Avery and I need to speak to all of them."

Soyer looked horrified. "I cannot say that!"

"I'd say they know it already. Tell them the boiler's broken, if you must. Or that the club must be cleared for the banquet. Whatever you like. Personally, I think some honesty is best."

Soyer nodded doubtfully, and walked out into the kitchen.

"What is a panopticon?" I said to Blake.

"It's a circular prison—or, rather, a plan for one—in which an observer can see all the inmates from one central position but they cannot know when precisely they are being watched and so must act as if they are watched all the time. None was ever built, but I always reckoned there's a point in Soyer's kitchen from which he can see almost everything, though I've never quite found it."

"So a panopticon would be a good thing?" I said cautiously.

"It is a monstrous engine of eternal scrutiny. It would be a nightmare. But it might catch a poisoner."

Soyer stood on a chair.

"My friends, my colleagues. Each and every one of you," he said. His voice, deeper than usual, penetrated to the far corners of the kitchen, even above the noise of the steam. "Come and heed me. I must speak to you."

Everyone shuffled slowly toward their chief.

"My friends and colleagues, a kitchen is a marvelous place. A place where, aspiring to the example of the great creator, we invent and prepare things of surpassing ingenuity, beauty and delectability. And the kitchen is a marvelous place in another way: a place of raging heat and light, certainly, of hard work and sharp words, sometimes, I grant you. But also a place where such work, and devotion and talent, is rewarded. You may be from the lowliest background, but if you work and show talent here, you will rise, and no one will stop you. I was born into a family of modest means in France thirty-two years ago, and see how I have risen. There, Morel, my great lieutenant, a man of talent whose abilities have raised him to the top of his profession; and, in among you, I espy young Monsieur Perrin, and Monsieur Benoît, too, and so many others with greatness in them.

"In this place, we have been engaged in a great venture, perhaps the greatest: to make the best kitchen in England, and one not merely for one fortunate lord or prince but which any of those who visit this great club may enjoy, serving dishes both simple and satisfying but also those that are refined, ingenious and delicious. And how triumphantly we have succeeded! The day after tomorrow our genius will be demonstrated beyond question at the banquet we shall prepare for the Prince of Egypt, Ibrahim Pasha; all the newspapers shall trumpet our genius. Let me be clear. None of what has been achieved could have been done without the efforts of every single one of you. You are all, from lowly potboy to brilliant chef, a vital, moving part of our glorious engine.

"None of what we do is easily won, we know that. And so, I have to tell you that, as we face our greatest triumph, we also face our greatest challenge, but it is one which, I swear to you, will not defeat us."

At this, the gathered began to fidget, for they knew that he was coming to the matter.

"*Mes amis*, my friends, we are under attack from something pernicious and evil-intentioned. Something tainted, something that wishes us no good, has entered our kitchen. Something that wants to take from us all we have won with such hard work and such devotion. Something that could see our livelihoods put at risk, our reputations brought into question. I know that we, none of us, want that, nor will we allow it. I will do everything to defeat this, and I know you will, too. We shall cook nothing today. We shall continue to clean and, one by one, we shall all speak to our friend Captain Avery and his—and his aide, Mr.—Maguire, who are helping us to counter this evil. The kitchen clerks will take your name, and you will be called. Tell anything you can think of that may help us. Any small detail may be of use.

"Some may say we cannot return from this. Some may say this is impossible. But"—he paused dramatically—"remember what I have told you before: 'Impossible is a word only to be found in a dictionary of fools!'"

Blake murmured in my ear, "Napoleon."

"Impossible," said Soyer, "is the refuge of poltroons."

There were some isolated cheers and clapping.

"Most of you shall be finished by noon, and I shall pay you all for a full day! And those who remain later will be paid time and a half! But I expect to see you all back here early tomorrow!"

The room clapped more enthusiastically. There were more cheers.

"One final request. I ask for your discretion. There are those who envy us and would be only too pleased to spread evil rumors and to see our reputation and our kitchen destroyed. We fight for our survival, for our positions and our livelihoods. We fight for the Reform Club, the greatest dining room in London—*non*, in the world!"

He blew his audience two kisses and dismounted from his chair amid more clapping. In twos and threes, the staff returned to their huddles, and some began to wander toward the kitchen maids' dining room.

"Perhaps," said Percy, "I may furnish Mr. Maguire with refreshment? I am sure we can endeavor to find you something entirely safe to eat."

"Oh, I am perfectly well just now. We should get on with our inquiries. But if I may say so, I am quite amazed by the kitchens here." Blake beamed uncharacteristically. I confess I found it rather annoying.

"May I say that you seem admirably unperturbed," Percy said. "Not a pleasant surprise to arrive this morning and find yourself in such circumstances."

My shoulders began to tighten.

Blake said, "Ah, Mr. Percy, I am used to it, for I was a military man and the captain has a nose for trouble. I should like to compliment you, too, on your sangfroid."

"That's most kind. I recognized you as a soldier the moment I saw you—it's in the carriage."

"Fifteen-odd years in John Company," said Blake, with another easy smile.

"Must have been quite a change, India to the English countryside?"

"A bit quieter, a lot cooler. But we get along all right."

WE SET OURSELVES UP in the butler's room while Mr. Percy rooted out the list of the dishes that Addiscomb and Rickards had eaten, since Scott had failed to do so.

They had begun with *potage à la* Victoria, a cream of artichoke soup. Then Addiscomb had had roast rib of beef, turnips and greens, and Rickards lamb cutlets *à la* Reform. These had followed with a salad of winter herbs with ham, and *celeri à la moelle de bœuf,* celery with beef marrow. Dessert was jelly with mixed fruits and pineapple cream. They had drunk two bottles of claret, some sherry, coffee and some port to end with.

I had had the lamb cutlets, too.

"We sold a great many of all these dishes last night: at least twenty roast beefs, maybe thirty cutlets, perhaps eighteen *potages à la* Victoria. The jellies are always popular."

"And no one else the worse for wear, so far as we know, Mr. Percy?" I said.

Percy looked a little pained. "So far as we know."

"It's unlikely, then, that someone sprinkled arsenic into a great saucepan of soup, or rubbed it all over a fine beef joint?" Blake said with a small smile. He was never usually so cheery, nor used so many extraneous words.

Percy could not find it in himself to be amused. Then Morel walked past.

"Monsieur Morel!" I called. "Might I have a moment of your time?"

Answer came there none. I bounded out, only to collide with the man himself, sending him sprawling and causing the portfolio he was carrying to fly open and sheets to spill out across the floor. He knelt down and began to scoop them up, stuffing them back in as swiftly as he could.

"Let me help you," I said.

"*Non*, leave me," he said brusquely, then, "it is better I do it myself. They have a particular order."

"What are they?" I said, proffering the sheet that had slid the furthest from him.

He seized it from me. "Nothing."

I stepped back. "I did not wish to upset you."

He recollected himself. "They are a few notes, incomplete, for new dishes. They must be kept safe."

"I see."

"My apologies." He rubbed his forehead. "I am not myself. I find with this new"—he could not bring himself to say "death"—"and Francobaldi always here, I am suspicious of everyone."

"I understand. Could you spare us a few minutes to give us the benefit of your knowledge of the kitchen and its habits?"

Reluctantly, Morel followed me into the butler's room.

"Mr. Maguire, my manservant and aide, will ask a few questions. I shall observe." I leaned against the unlit hearth and tried to look commanding.

"Monsewer Morel," said Blake—and Morel winced at his pronunciation—"is it possible to discover precisely which parts of the kitchen prepared the food the gentlemen ate last night?"

Morel looked at the list of what the poisoned men had eaten and shrugged. "Almost every part of the kitchen will have worked on one aspect of these dishes or another, from chopping vegetables to making the stocks. Monsieur Perrin's *sauciers* make the sauces and finish the main dishes, and the *potager* who reports to him makes soups. The roasting section under Monsieur Benoît would have cooked the beef and lamb; the *entremetiers* prepare the vegetables dishes, the dessert kitchen made the desserts, but, within that, one *commis* will set the jelly, another will have cut the fruit, a third will whisk the cream, a fourth will flavor and set it."

"It seems most likely to me that the poison would have been added between the particular dishes being arranged on their plates and being served to the diners," said Blake.

"It could also have been added at some point at the table, into the wine, perhaps," I said.

Now he was my servant, he could not be seen to ignore me. "Yes, of course, sir," he said. "But, begging your pardon, Monsewer Morel,"—Morel winced again—"is there a method for putting the dishes together and bringing them out?"

"As I said, every dish is made up of many parts: the meat or fish, the sauce, the stock and vegetables that made the sauce, and so on. These will be tasted repeatedly before they are placed on the plate, then the *chefs de partie* of each section, or their deputy, will either finish or check every dish. In the principal kitchen, Chef or Monsieur Perrin or I, or, on occasion, Percy or the kitchen clerk on duty, will pass each dish before it is taken to the lift to the Coffee Room. It is then collected by the footmen and taken to the table."

"Who was passing dishes last night?"

"We all took a turn, I believe—myself, Perrin, Chef, Percy."

"Who carries the plates to the lift, sir?"

"Cooks and junior chefs bring them to the delivery windows or to us, then either kitchen maids or apprentices will carry them to the lift. Desserts and confectionary are taken on wheeled tables, as the distance to the lift is further. Once they are upstairs, the footmen take them to the tables."

"Do you think the poison could simply have been sprinkled on top of a dish, or would it have needed to be stirred in?" said Blake.

"Since I have never poisoned anyone, Monsieur," said Morel faintly, "I cannot tell you."

"Then can you advise me on what might be a suitable dish for such contamination?" Blake persisted.

Morel sank his head into his hands.

"I know far less than Monsieur Morel about these things," Percy broke in, "and nothing of poisons save for using a little arsenic on bedbugs, but as I consider it, coffee could work, or something that requires flour, for it could be mixed into that. The richness and sharpness of certain desserts might disguise bitterness, don't you think, Chef? For example, the pineapple cream—"

"And wines and spirits?" Blake interrupted.

"It is certainly possible. The sherry and the port would already have been opened; one might add a pinch of something. The claret, too, would likely have been decanted before it came to the table. My underbutlers do that, and the kitchen clerks keep a note of what is opened."

Blake nodded.

"No one in the kitchen has been ill, then? Not at all?" he said.

Percy and Morel glanced at each other.

"Is there something I have not been told?" I said.

"I'm sorry, sir, it simply did not occur to us that it might be connected," said Percy. "Three weeks ago, two kitchen maids fell ill, and a junior sauce cook—an infection of the stomach, we thought. Now I think of it, it may well have been the night Mr. Cunningham fell ill."

"And you did not think to say! Does Soyer know?"

"Sir, we were only told about Mr. Cunningham yesterday. And I am sure Chef had no notion of it. It is a large staff. I am truly sorry. I will point them out to you when you speak to them. But may I ask, how long will the club have to remain closed, do you think?"

"Until we discover the cause of this," I said.

"May I speak plainly, sir?"

"By all means."

"Mr. Scott will insist the club cannot pay wages if it is not drawing in money. We know the finances are in a tangle, not least because of—well, it's not my place to say—and it is the staff who will suffer. I have a little put by, but there are plenty with families to feed, or who have nothing to fall back on because they are foreigners. Perhaps you might have a word with the committee?"

"I will do what I can."

Mr. Scott appeared at the door to announce that Lord Marcus Hill was waiting for me.

I followed him out. He was watching the kitchen maids cleaning.

"Mr. Scott," I said sharply, "you failed to get me the list of what the gentlemen ate last night. I had to ask Mr. Percy instead. I hope you have managed to undertake the other tasks?"

A kitchen maid bent over to scrub the floor. Scott stared at her in a manner I can only describe as hungry. "I am doing my best," he said, not moving his eyes, "but I have to see to the accounts. We are losing money dreadfully since we are not open today. I must know what is coming in, and how much is being spent on food and spirits. Monsieur Soyer can be rather evasive on the matter, Captain Avery."

Percy cast his eyes up at the ceiling.

"Summoning Mr. Wakley and informing the families take precedence over your accounts, Mr. Scott," I said irritably. "And calling in the police.

"Mr. Scott!" I said again.

"Oh, yes, right away—" he started, and, seeing my expression, set off across the kitchen.

"I hope you will not take it amiss, Captain Avery," said Percy feelingly, "if I say that, in my opinion, Mr. Scott's suggestion that the kitchen is evasive is perfect nonsense. I must admit I am not cool on the subject: we in the kitchen find his claims to oversee us both irksome and lacking."

"And dishonest, Mr. Percy?" said Blake.

"Disorderly, I should say, Mr. Maguire," said Percy, sighing. "Not up to the mark."

Blake fussed about me, dusting down my frock coat and straightening my collar. "Don't offer Hill too much," he muttered into my necktie. "Get what you can from him."

Chapter Thirteen

It was the footman I knew who conducted me to the Strangers' Room.

"Been at the club long—?"

"Jeffers, sir," he cut in, "from the other day?"

"Yes, I do remember," I said, a touch irritated.

"Since it began, sir, and proud to be here."

"I do not suppose you knew Mr. Addiscomb and Mr. Rickards?"

"The gentlemen that passed away, sir?"

"One is recovering," I said. "I suppose everyone knows now?"

"Oh, yes, sir. And as a matter of fact, I did know them, sir. Served them regularly."

"Anything to report?"

"Well, sir, since it is you that is asking, they were not the liveliest gentlemen, and neither were they young. Liked their dinner, and dined here at least once or twice a week, often together. Mr. Addiscomb was very appreciative of Monsieur Soyer's menus. Liked to say it was the finest dinner in London."

There was a fire in the Strangers' Room, the only one in the whole club, I guessed. Lord Marcus Hill, his hair combed flat against his brows, his emphatic eyebrows arched with friendliness and concern, stood in front of it.

"The committee is about to meet, and I wished to see you. I am told Henry Rickards is recovering. Have you come to any conclusions?"

"I am all but certain Mr. Addiscomb and Mr. Rickards were poisoned, but, while Rowlands was killed with arsenic, I believe these two had unknowingly taken strychnine. I have called Mr. Wakley back so as to be sure."

"That troublesome radical—" said Lord Marcus.

"—a respected surgeon and coroner," said another voice. I started. Mr. Molesworth was standing behind me. In true butterfly dandy style, he wore a yellow-and-black tartan silk waistcoat, a black silk cutaway and yellow trousers. The opposite of mourning. "And he is both knowledgeable in and skilled at such matters."

Hill waved his hand. "If you say so."

"I assume you now believe Rowlands was murdered?" said Molesworth.

"It seems likely. And from the doctor's reports, it seems highly likely that the man who fell ill in the street, and later expired—Cunningham—had entirely the same symptoms."

"Do you have any thoughts as to the perpetrator?"

I could not quite bear to say no, so I listed everything we planned to do and all the lines of inquiry we planned to pursue.

"So you have no idea at all," said Molesworth.

"What about foreign intervention?" asked Lord Marcus.

"The Russians, you mean?" I said. "We have so far found no one in the kitchen whom we believe could plausibly be working on their behalf. But I will look into the matter further as soon as our interviews with the staff are done. I will be consulting with Sir Theo Collinson." The thought oppressed me. I cleared my throat. "Gentlemen, may I in turn ask you both a question?"

"Ask away," said Lord Marcus, his thick brows rounded in surprise.

"I should like you to tell me what you know about Mr. Addiscomb and the Honorable Henry Rickards. I can find no one who knew them well."

"Addiscomb is—was—a member of Parliament; Rickards used to be. He retired from his seat at the last election," said Lord Marcus. "They were old friends."

"Did you regard them as friends?" I said.

It was Molesworth who answered. He gave a sort of gasping laugh. "No, indeed. They were dyed-in-the-wool Whigs."

"Like Cunningham and Rowlands?" I said.

"Do you believe that to be significant?" said Molesworth.

"This is nonsense! Cunningham has barely been active in the Commons since 1832," said Lord Marcus.

"Did they have any obvious enemies?" I asked.

"What a question!" said Lord Marcus. "This is a place of conviviality. A broad but friendly church. There are no enmities or divisions played out here."

"Pardon me, Your Lordship, but I have heard that there is a good deal of hostility between those of the Whiggish persuasion and the radicals."

"I must ask where you heard such nonsense. Gossip in the kitchen? Not from Soyer surely?"

"I do not think Monsieur Soyer has the slightest interest in the politics of the club. It has come from other members."

"Well," said Lord Marcus peevishly, "that may have been the case some years ago, but I really do not think it is so now."

"My dear Lord Marcus," said Molesworth, "you must know that such gossip is common currency. As a radical myself, I cannot deny that I am disappointed that the club seems to have abandoned its original principle of furthering reform."

"Mr. Molesworth, what would you say about these men?" I said.

Lord Marcus looked quite petulant. Molesworth ignored him.

"I do not like to speak ill of the dead, but they were notable for their old-fashioned notions and their particular opposition to change. They poked fun at my radical colleagues, sneered at their political convictions and their dress. It was unedifying in men in late middle age."

"At radical dandies like Duncombe, for example?" I did my best not to stare at Molesworth's canary-yellow trousers.

"Some may refer to him thus," said Molesworth.

"Captain Avery, this is ridiculous. A distraction. These are not grounds for murder. This is the healthy cut and thrust among men of politics. It is the way of the world."

"Let us move on," said Molesworth, languidly inspecting his perfectly gloved left hand. "As far as we know, we have three dead men, one very ill, and no obvious suspect. We have called a meeting of the committee. We must act before circumstances catch up with us. There will be talk. We must decide how long the club should be closed, and whether Monsieur Soyer should resign."

"Resign!" said Lord Marcus Hill. "But he makes the Reform Club what it is."

"A sad fact for a political club," said Molesworth coldly. "The truth is, Monsieur Soyer's name is bound to be attached to this scandal."

"What about the banquet?" asked Lord Marcus.

"It must be canceled. It is not safe for it to take place—unless Captain Avery can produce a plausible culprit by the end of the day. And that"—Molesworth paused—"seems most unlikely."

"But it would bring the most dreadful humiliation on the party. Upon our leaders. Upon the club."

"It might bring humiliation on Lord Palmerston, but it would be worse if some of our guests actually died as a result of it, don't you think?"

"Your Lordship," I said, "I think that Monsieur Soyer—"

"We have heard quite enough of what you think, young man," said Lord Marcus. "You say you have other inquiries to make? I suggest you go and make them."

"But his presence will be required at the meeting of the committee later," said Molesworth. "He must come and explain himself."

Without looking at me, Lord Marcus walked heavily out of the room. Molesworth followed lightly behind, in his delicate leather pumps.

WE HAD BEGUN our interviews with the senior chefs of each station, since they knew their own staff intimately and might be helpful in that respect. Alas, we were too optimistic. By the time I returned to the kitchen, Blake had reached Herr Schmidt, the German pastry chef.

Blake had suggested we look out for the Germans. Many lived under Russian rule and, though he found the whole notion of a Russian conspiracy implausible, an agent would most likely sound German. It was quickly apparent that Schmidt could not possibly be a Russian spy. He had spent twenty years as a pastry chef in London, found Blake's questions mystifying and simply wished to get back to work—he had castles to build, creams to whisk: the great masterpiece he had planned for Lord Palmerston's banquet needed attention before he left. No, he had noticed nothing odd, seen nothing strange, he was bewildered by the question: it was a kitchen, and they were there to create pleasure through the medium of nourishment.

The fish, vegetable and *entremets* chefs had been much the same: mildly suspicious, bewildered, impatient to get back to their kitchens, somewhere between admiring and envious of their colleagues' talents, satisfied by most of their underlings, exasperated by a few, reverent of Soyer.

Monsieur Benoît, the roast chef, who came next, refused to speak English, then was highly displeased to discover that Blake spoke excellent French. His answers, when they came, were reluctantly given and imperious. Monsieur Soyer respected him as an artist and furnished him with the best ingredients. His cooks and apprentices were fools and scoundrels to a man. They were far too stupid to manage anything as complicated as poisoning someone, unless of course they had done it by accident, which would be perfectly possible, save that he, Benoît, would most certainly have caught it, as there was nothing he did not see. As for his fellow chefs, they were good enough, skilled even, though most were sheep who followed their master, not one original thought in their bodies. And as for that Perrin, the *saucier*—Benoît began to swell with indignation. A mere boy! A charlatan! A pretty scallywag who pretended to invention but who simply copied what Soyer gave him! He smiled too much! Those who claimed him as a great talent were utterly mistaken, he was merely ambitious and designing. He would be found out soon enough. He would come to a bad end.

Blake steered Benoît, his nostrils almost steaming with fury, from the room.

His successor was Perrin himself. He was the kind of man one almost wants to dislike, but he was utterly disarming. Quite as preoccupied as his fellow chefs and thus quite as useless, he was cheerful and courteous with it. He pronounced the notion of the poisoning bewildering and unthinkable: "But why would anyone in this kitchen do that? It makes no sense. It must be a mistake. No one here would do such a thing." He was complimentary about his cooks and apprentices, and told Blake, "But your French is excellent!" He asked me how I had liked the sauce on my lamb cutlets the night before. "Do we put in too much ham and make it perhaps a *leetle* too salty?"

Once he had left, I said, "He is so perfect, I wonder if he is too good to be true."

"A pretty boy," said Blake, "with soft eyes."

AT OUR REQUEST, Morel and Percy had made a list of those who had been taken on within the previous three or four months: a good ten names, two of which were German. One of these was Albert, the dark, greasy young man who had taken so much pleasure in his colleagues' distress at the roasting station, and whom Matty had named as a bully. They gave us the names of the kitchen maids who had fallen sick three weeks before. They also, reluctantly, picked out two cooks and an underbutler whom they believed to have gambling debts, and five or six more who were struggling to feed extended families and might be susceptible to bribery.

"Some of the potboys all but live on the street," Percy added, "though they have little to do with the preparation of dishes. Many are foreign and have no family here to fall back on. I believe most of us are devoted to Chef and would not dream of ill-doing, but life in London is precarious, and it is possible that someone in a weak moment might be tempted or pressed to do something they would regret."

It soon became repetitive, wearing work, coaxing recollections from shy kitchen maids and proper answers from excitable apprentices to see if there was one telling detail that might enlighten us. Nothing sprang out; no one could recall anything that sounded genuinely suspicious, or that might correspond to an act of contamination, though there were a few accusations that we felt obliged to note. Most of the meat cooks confided to Blake that they considered Monsieur Benoît mad and capable of anything. All the sauce cooks admired Perrin. One underbutler said he did not trust another underbutler; the kitchen clerks did not like each other one bit. A vegetable chef swore he had seen one of the fish cooks sprinkle a strange powder over the lobster; since none of our victims had eaten lobster, we nodded and passed on. Two put-upon young junior cooks admitted in low, shamed tones that they hated Albert, the young German roast cook, more than anyone else in the world and would not have been surprised to hear he had committed any crime. As for the new recruits, six—including one of the Germans, a pastry apprentice with a face full of pimples—were obviously too young and innocent to be anything other than potboys and apprentices. Of the rest, three were French and had learned their skills in other kitchens. The other German, who worked in the *entremets* section, was clearly intelligent and able. Blake, while agreeing he should be watched, said it was unlikely he was our man, as he was Jewish. The Russians, he explained, "were great persecutors of the Jews."

We were interviewing the vermin boy, under the supervision of the ghastly Gimbell, about the management of the poisons cupboard, when Mr. Wakley arrived. It was almost a relief to see him surge into the room—there was no other word for it—with his long, golden tresses tossing.

"Well, young man," Wakley said, pumping my arm, "good day to you! I was wondering how you were progressing, but this is a facer! Another death, and one sick abed! And, I hear, another death some weeks ago that may have been connected. One death may be regarded as just about acceptable, but three is downright carelessness!" And he laughed heartily at his own joke.

"You find us in the midst of interviewing the kitchen staff," I said. "My manservant and general factotum, Maguire, has come from the country to help me." I fancied that Blake bent over somewhat more than he had and buried his face into his spectacles and his collar. Wakley glanced cursorily over his side-combed hair, his glasses and his mustache, and for a second he hesitated, as if something caught at his memory. I had the most dreadful thought that they had met before.

"I should mention, young man, that I felt obliged to deliver my conclusions on the death of Mr. Rowlands to the police. I am now certain that Rowlands was an habitual user of arsenic in greater quantities than one would usually expect; but I am certain also that he ingested a fatally large dose of arsenic hours before he fell sick."

"Were you able to tell what the source was?"

"No. Arsenic has a habit of creeping, even after its host is dead. It was everywhere in his stomach. A few mouthfuls of Fowler's Tonic would not account for it, and so I must conclude that something else—probably on Monsieur Soyer's table—delivered it."

"I have made sure that the dead man's room has not been tidied, and neither has he been moved, so there will be ample opportunity for you to take samples of, of"—I swallowed—"the various bodily fluids. And I believe the club doctor acquired similar samples from our recovering patient."

"There, you are learning, Captain Avery."

"We also have reason to believe that the new corpse and his friend were poisoned after eating at the club, but by a different poison—strychnine."

"Good heavens! Two poisons! That *is* unusual. Though both are easily obtained for domestic use." Thankfully, he did not ask how I, so obviously green in such matters, could have known this. "Well, no reason to delay a visit to our corpse. There is a footman ready to take me upstairs, apparently. I shall meet with you later."

"What do you do with the mice and rats you do catch?" Blake was asking the vermin boy.

"Burns 'em, sir. But I sells the mice tails to a lady in Lambeth." He looked sheepishly at Gimbell, who gave him a shove.

In the midst of our interviews, Soyer suddenly appeared in the doorway, wreathed in smiles.

"I would be grateful for a moment with you both," he said.

Once he was in his office, his shoulders bowed and his smile vanished. He took from a pocket in his waistcoat a key, went to the sideboard and turned it in the lock of a small drawer. Out of this he drew two pieces of paper, on which there was a deal of black ink. He placed them on the table, his hands trembling, and gazed at Blake.

The paper was of good quality, thick and white. The words had been cut out and stuck down, half were handwritten, the rest from publications: newspapers, bills, broadsides.

The first letter read:

This was not the first and it will not be the last. The Lord giveth and the Lord taketh away, and all shall be taken from you.

"When did this come?"

"The morning after the dinner, after poor Rowlands died. It was addressed most formally to 'The Chef of the Reform.' I opened it, as Grove, the secretary, had walked out the day before, and I alone saw it."

"And you did not think to mention it to me!" I said sharply.

"*Je suis désolé, Capitaine.* Truly. I know it was a mistake. But I did not know what it meant. I have always received a few letters that are—let us say—a little eccentric. I thought perhaps it was some angry radical or madman. And I confess, I was both worried and fearful that any unnecessary whisper of *scandale* at this time would be so bad for the banquet. I went to Lord Marcus to speak of Rowlands. I had the letter in my pocket. I discovered that he was already concerned about Rowlands's death; he had called the committee. It was then that he told me about the gentleman who died after falling ill in the street three weeks ago, that it may not have been his heart. At the same time, he counseled caution. The two events were not likely to be connected but might harm us if they were to be widely known. Lord Marcus is my great champion on the committee; I did not wish to alarm him further. Then we thought of Captain Avery,"—he turned to Blake—"and you. And I assumed, with your great talents, it should all be swiftly resolved."

"Yet you kept the letter," said Blake.

"*Oui.*"

Blake picked up the second.

"It arrived half an hour ago," said Soyer dolefully. "It was delivered to the porter upstairs, but he did not recognize the messenger. A boy. Here is the envelope."

The envelope was fine and creamy white. Again, it was addressed to "The Chef of the Reform." There was no stamp. The strange pattern of handwritten and printed words read:

This was no accident. You knew there would be more. And there will be. You cannot stop this. You and your foolish ambitions will be washed away in a raging torrent. A flood to cleanse the ordure.

Soyer gazed at the letter. His uppermost emotion seemed to be sadness. "To have such an enemy. I had no idea. I thought they loved me."

Blake shrugged. "No one has only friends. And it may not be meant entirely for you."

"I do not understand."

"Addressing you as the Chef of the Reform rather than Soyer suggests some distance. Perhaps it is intended to alarm and upset you in order to disrupt the banquet. Its actual target may be the Reform itself, rather than you personally."

At this, Soyer's distress seemed to abate a little.

I HAD TWO QUESTIONS for Blake as we made our way back to the butler's room. Had he encountered Wakley before, and did he truly believe that the letters were not personally meant for Soyer?

To the first question he said: "Yes."

To the second: "They may be. But no purpose is served by upsetting Soyer further."

Matty was lingering in the doorway. She was most agitated.

"Percy says I'm not on the list to question," she said. "You've to put me on the list."

"But, Matty, we know it wasn't you."

"You've got to put me on the list. You don't understand. Don't make me different from the others. They're starting to talk. Please."

"Who—" I started to say, but she closed the door.

The staff still to be spoken to had by now mostly collected in the kitchen maids' dining room, where they waited to be summoned. Platters of fried fish—sent out for by Soyer—had been laid out on the table. The mood was now a combustible mix of impatience to leave, uneasiness and growing suspicion.

This was apparent in the Irish underbutler we next interrogated. "Did you know, sir, that a couple of kitchen maids were taken sick after staff supper about three weeks ago? Very ill they were."

"I had heard," I said. "What do you have to say about it?"

He shrugged. "Ask them. Hannah and Margaret. They'll tell you. Anyway, sir," he went on, "poison's a woman's weapon. Everyone knows that. Stands to reason it's a woman. A man would stand up for hisself, not creep around in the shadows, cowardly like. That's what everyone's saying—or thinking—out there."

The kitchen maid Hannah, whom Percy and Morel had named as one of the two girls who had been taken ill, came in after him. She was a small, sallow woman, with wisps of straggling hair escaping from her cap.

"Pea soup, chicken stew and dumplings. And a bit of pound cake, I ate, sir. The pains started half an hour after. They was unbearable. My throat burned. I was thirsty, but I couldn't hardly swallow. My stomach hurt worse. A gripping pain that took me and caused me to twist about. I hurt all over. Then, well, there was stuff I'd rather not say to a man, sir. But it was bad, sir. Terrible for a day—them squeezing, seizing pains in my stomach and all over. Then it began to pass, but I wasn't right for a fortnight. And I'm still not right. Nice plump cheeks, nice plump arms, I had before, sir. Now I'm like a skinny old goat. Feel like I'll never be myself again. Now they're saying it was poison. And when I think back, there was a bitter taste in the stew. Or maybe it was the pound cake."

The next girl to come was Margaret, the kitchen maid who had almost knocked Matty off her feet. She, too, insisted she had been poisoned. The sickness had not affected her as it had Hannah, and she was a handsome girl, though in repose her face was hard and her manner insolent. She said that after eating the maids' dinner that night she had felt a burning sensation, an unquenchable thirst, stomach spasms. They were saying it was poison, she said, and she thought they were right.

"And do you have any idea what might have caused it?" I asked politely.

"I do."

"And?"

"Pound cake. Only me and Hannah ate it."

I nodded.

"And is there anything else you recall from that day?"

"Plenty. 'S a woman's tool, ain't it, poison?"

"So it is said. Though in this—"

"Then you should look at the kitchen maids. Can't be me or Hannah, we was victims." She glanced at me provokingly.

"Who, then?" I said.

"Well." There was a pause. "Matty Horner. She was helping with the maids' dinner that night; she served it up. The staff cook had to go. And I reckon she made the pound cake." She seemed almost to dare me to contradict her.

"Do you have anything more than suspicion, Margaret?"

"Told yer, sir. She made the pound cake; it made me sick. And I know she weren't in her bed the night that Mr. Rowlands died. One of the footmen said. What was she doing? She won't say."

"I can assure you, Miss Horner committed no wrongdoing that night; indeed, quite the opposite."

The girl gave me a bald look.

"You'd know then, sir," she murmured. Then, after a moment, "She's a dark one. Not what she seems. Only been here months, and look where she is. Wound certain people round her little finger. She'd do anything to get on. And she got that place in the pastry kitchen 'cos the apprentice she replaced died."

"It is no secret that you dislike Miss Horner, is it, Margaret?" I said.

"Look, I'm not the only one that thinks it," she replied.

She was not. The next kitchen maid also made dark allusions to Matty, and the cooks after her. They repeated the rumors. She had helped with the cooking on the night the kitchen maids had gone sick; she had been in the kitchen on the night Rowlands had died. She had not been to bed that night and wouldn't say what she'd been up to. Considerably disquieted, I called in Percy.

"I do not know where it started," he said, the gray pouches under his eyes more marked even than earlier. "But Margaret has been talking and talking. She has a certain sway with some of the kitchen maids. There's only a few of them left now in the dining room, sitting there, fretful and idle. 'The devil makes work,' as they say. Matilda is new, some begrudge her her success, everyone wants a culprit as soon as possible."

"But this is nonsense."

Mrs. Relph walked in without announcing herself. She clutched a shawl tight around her shoulders.

"It may not be my place, sir," she said in a tone that made it clear she very much thought it was, "but you will have heard what they're saying out there about Matilda. Rumor takes hold quick, sir. I hope you will call a stop to it because, if I may say so, sir, it will get worse, and you've helped it."

Percy nodded. "These interviews, Captain Avery, maybe they were not wise."

"Perhaps, but we could not have predicted this, and since we have started we cannot give up now. Where is Matty?"

Mrs. Relph said, "I took her into the dessert kitchen. I won't have her sitting there listening to those wicked girls!"

"How is she?"

"She bears it as well as can be expected. She is a brave girl."

"She is, and I thank you, Mrs. Relph," I said. "Truly I do. I had no idea that this would bring such a thing upon her. But I am certain we can scotch these insinuations. They are purely circumstantial."

"See you do," she said shortly.

THE NEXT to be summoned was the roast cook called Albert who so provoked his peers. He sauntered in, something essentially insolent in his very gait. It occurred to me that Monsieur Benoît was so caught up in his little world of cooking and fury that he probably had never even noticed the young man's natural insubordination. He reminded me of a sort I had encountered in the army: the soldier who believes himself sharper and bolder than the rest and thinks he can get away with anything.

"I can help you, Captain," he said. "I know who the guilty one is."

"You're German," said Blake.

"I am."

"Who is it, then?"

"It is the girl," he said nonchalantly, examining his hands. "Matty."

"And how do you know?" I said, keeping my voice as cool as I could.

"She is—what do the French say?—*putain*, bad girl." He smiled.

I did not know the word, but I did not like his overfamiliarity.

"That's a foul word for a hard-working kitchen maid," said Blake, quietly. I wondered if the young man could feel the iron in his voice. "Do you have any reason to say this?"

Albert waved his hands as if to illustrate his words. "The others say she was here in the kitchen the other times when men got ill, but I have the proof." He smiled again, now triumphantly.

"Proof?" said Blake, his face a genial mask.

"I hear what they have eaten, the men, the one who died, the one who is sick. *La crème d'ananas*. The pineapple cream. Matty, she made it! And ask how many they sell last night? Only two!" He sat back, pleased with himself.

"How do you know this?"

"Look for yourself. In the ledger. It is easy enough."

"And why would she do this?" asked Blake.

He fixed the young man with a look. Albert smiled at first but after a few moments dropped his gaze, and his answer was ill-tempered.

"Why? I do not know. People are bad. And she comes from the gutter."

"You know there are those here who say that you could have committed this crime?"

"I? Who says this?" Albert essayed a careless grin but managed to look only sulky.

"Where are you from, Albert?"

"Württemberg. All the best cooks are from here."

"And how did you find this out, about Matilda?"

"I keep my eye on things. I know things." He grinned again.

"We may need to speak to you again, but for now you are dismissed," I said coldly.

He stood up with a swagger and made for the door.

"He is German," I said, almost hopefully.

"He is from the west, near the French border, nowhere near Russia—if he is indeed from Württemberg. We'll ask the other German cooks if he has a regional accent."

"Good God! Something you do not know?"

The door opened, and Matty crept in. She sat upon a chair, then pulled her feet up under her skirt and fastened her arms tight round her skirts as if to make herself as small as possible. She would not look at us.

"Those girls were sick the night I helped to make the maids' dinner." Her voice was dull.

"Why did you not say, Matty?"

"It didn't seem like anything at the time. It just seemed like they had a tummy upset. I didn't cook the food. Well, I helped with the pound cake. And I was there in the kitchen the night Rowlands died. But I was nowhere near the food—Chef had me writing letters, 'cos his secretary had left, and I hoped to speak to you, before you went. After that, I was with you and Rowlands."

"We know that you had nothing to do with it, Matty," I said.

"Last night, the pineapple cream separated," she went on. "I was sent to recover it. Egg white and yolks beaten in by hand. It took an age, and there wasn't much of it. It was to be served for lunch today."

"But the two gentlemen had it."

"I only heard that when Mr. Percy got the list of dishes. The kitchen clerk said they were the only two who had eaten it. Footman offered it to them late, as a special." She shifted in her seat. "Margaret says they'll arrest me."

"They cannot; this is mere coincidence."

"I told you before: no one wanted it to be the kitchen but, if it is the kitchen, everyone wants a culprit quick, so we are saved and things return to how they were. Everyone knows I was on the streets, and no better than I should be. Even people with nothing against me, even those who like me, are looking at me funny."

"We know it is not true, Matty. We will explain it."

"You can't stop it. I'm tainted, whatever happens. Even if they let me go and I came back, I'd be marked. I should have known it was too good to last."

I had never seen her so defeated.

"Matty, this is nonsense. A mistake. Do not lose faith. And see, we have letters from the real culprit to Monsieur Soyer," I said.

"Letters?" she said.

"Show them to her."

Blake brought them out of his pocket and laid them on the table.

She stared at the printed letters and written words as if mesmerized by them.

"What is it, Matty?"

"The written words that have been cut out."

"What of them?"

"Can't you see? They're my writing."

Chapter Fourteen

The committee is ready for you, sir," said the footman.

"I shall be a moment," I told him. "They will be voting on whether to dismiss Soyer," I said to Blake. "What shall I say?"

He turned me round and began to brush down my shoulders and my lapels. "Do you think he should be dismissed?"

"No." Then, "I do not know. My instincts say that it would be an injustice. But there is a chance that it might all stop if he were gone. Then again, it might not."

"Do you think finding the culprit will be easier if he is gone?"

"Of course not."

"Then he needs defending."

"And who am I to do that?"

"You're a hero with real decorations. Most of these men have spent the last twenty years on their arses. Lay it on with a trowel. Remind them that if they cut the head off they haven't cured the body, they've killed it."

He was still fussing over my lapels. I pushed him away. "Blake, you are not my actual valet!"

He clicked his teeth. "Have you seen yourself?"

I said, "Your mustache is askew."

THERE WERE APPROXIMATELY twenty men in the room, most in middle age, heads short of hair but faces with graying whiskers, each man vehemently arguing with another. It was like a convention of bad-tempered, frock-coated uncles. Lord Marcus was holding hard to the shreds of a smile but was unable to quieten his fellow committee members. Mr. Molesworth, as usual, looked amused. Captain Beare was smug, and the flabby-faced Mr. Ellice looked fretful and angry. To one side, listless and useless, stood Mr. Scott.

Lord Marcus raised his hands to plead for quiet.

"Gentlemen, as I said, we have already taken steps to resolve the predicament in which we find ourselves. Two days ago, we secured the services of Captain William Avery, of whom many of you will have heard. I have every confidence that he will swiftly discover the root of our troubles."

"He has not done very well so far!" someone called out.

"Who is Captain Avery to address us thus?" said another.

Mr. Ellice levered himself from his chair and, almost proprietorially, propelled me forward with his haunch-like arm. "Perhaps you would introduce yourself?"

Wincing a little, I listed my accomplishments.

"Did you not have a colleague?" someone shouted. "A man with one eye?"

"No, with one finger?"

"Yes. Mr. Blake, I am afraid—"

"—Mr. Blake is unavailable," Lord Marcus interceded.

"The other characteristic of Captain Avery, of course," said Mr. Molesworth, "is that he is a Tory."

There was a surge of grousing and griping. Lord Marcus Hill eyed Molesworth crossly.

"Captain Avery has an excellent reputation, for discretion as much as for the success of his inquiries," he said. "Would you not have us secure the services of the best?"

"If he is a Tory, he should not be within the perimeters of this club at all!"

There were a number of "ayes." Someone shouted, "When was the last time you discussed politics within the perimeters of this club? I should say never! You are always far too intent on your dinner!"

A guffaw of laughter.

I felt quite ready to leave the meeting and the club forever. Then I thought of Matty, and Soyer, and Blake's chance to redeem himself.

"Gentlemen, it is true that I am a Tory born and bred. But my colleague, Jeremiah Blake, is a radical—more a radical, I daresay, than any of you. That has not prevented us from working most fruitfully together, or from my admiring him—despite his many, many, many faults—almost above any man."

There was a certain amount of grumbling, but my words seemed to placate my audience.

"Tell us what you have found," said Lord Marcus.

"Gentlemen," I said, "as Lord Marcus said, I was asked to look into the death of Mr. Rowlands. I have established beyond doubt that Mr. Rowlands died of arsenic poisoning and was a serial imbiber of arsenic-based tonics—"

"Are you claiming that Mr. Addiscomb and his friends were also indulging in arsenic eating?" someone called out.

"No, no, not at all," I said. "I merely wish to show that I can work quickly and effectively. I heard of this new death only hours ago." I paused. "I am in the process of interviewing all the kitchen staff. A highly respected coroner and surgeon is examining the body as we speak. The police are on their way. I am confident we will discover the perpetrator of these crimes and his reasons."

"Before the banquet?"

I swallowed painfully. "I will do my best," I said.

Once again, order dissolved into shouts and arguments.

Now Captain Beare raised his voice.

"I thank Captain Avery for his most edifying report," he shouted gruffly, "but to sum up—we must mourn the passing of Everett Cunningham, Charles Rowlands and Ralph Addiscomb, while Henry Rickards lies abed, fighting for his life. Two kitchen maids nearly died over three weeks ago. And the fact remains that our kitchen, under the command of our so-called culinary genius, Alexis Soyer, is responsible."

Roars and boos. I wondered how Beare knew about the kitchen maids.

Once the committee quietened, Molesworth stood up, remarkably placid, raised his hand and waited for the room to attend him.

"As you know, I am rarely to be found on the same side as Captain Beare. But on this occasion it seems to me that our priority must be the protection of the club itself. This state of affairs will soon be public knowledge. As Captain Avery says, the police are on their way. Unfortunate though it is, it seems to me that there is one thing the club must do, and that is to cancel the banquet and to divest itself of Monsieur Soyer."

There was another great explosion of debate.

Mr. Ellice stood up as energetically as his considerable girth would allow.

"This is absurd! As the founder of the club, I say we cannot cancel the banquet."

Almost without thinking, my eyes slid over to Molesworth. He did his best to hide it, but he flinched when Ellice reiterated his claim to the club.

"It was to be the pinnacle of the club's achievements," Ellice was saying, "our apotheosis. Every newspaper in the land is already primed to write of it, and is scrambling to discover the menu. Are we willing to let it come to nothing? Can you not see how humiliating it would be to have to cancel the banquet at this late stage? How it would besmirch Lord Palmerston's standing? No foreign consul would ever take us seriously again. If we cancel it and dismiss Soyer, it will certainly put a great hole in the reputation of the club, and the party. We would be regarded as ridiculous—unfit to organize a dinner, let alone a foreign policy." I must admit I was surprised: I had not imagined him capable of such energy.

"Could we not find another chef?" asked one of the members.

"Find another chef? We cannot simply 'find' some other chef to orchestrate a dinner for three hundred. There is no one with Soyer's reputation or abilities. He has spent months and months planning this dinner. It will be an unrepeatable event."

"A monument to Soyer, more like," said Captain Beare. Several members snorted.

"In any event, the cancelation of the dinner is not within our power," Ellice said, breathing heavily. "It was, after all, ordered and organized by Lord Palmerston and the party."

"Are we not paying for it? Is it not on our premises?"

"We have already recouped our costs in the contributions of the diners."

There were a few minutes of bickering.

"The fact remains," said Molesworth, "that three of our members have died of poisoning after consuming food from the club's kitchens. The only persons who truly lose by the cancelation of this dinner are the Whig leaders. Some of us believe that Lord Palmerston would benefit from a little dent in his reputation. Perhaps then he would be a little less keen to start his little wars."

"If I may put in my ha'penny worth, gentlemen," said Lord Marcus,

"I think we are being precipitous. We have already agreed to close. May I ask that we set aside our personal prejudices and divisions and think only of the club?"

"Are we not doing that already?" said Molesworth.

Lord Marcus straightened his shoulders and set his chin. "Mr. Molesworth, I beg you to put aside party advantage. You know well where your arguments tend."

"And where is that?"

"To a renewed division between Whigs and radicals which can do neither side any good and which may lead to the possible dissolution of the club."

"If there are any more deaths, that will come to pass anyway," Molesworth snapped.

The meeting erupted again.

"I move we go to a vote to ask Monsieur Soyer for his resignation and to cancel the banquet," called Molesworth.

"Gentlemen! Quiet, please!" said Lord Marcus. "Mr. Molesworth, I am the chairman of the committee, and I decide on the motions and when they take place."

"You cannot deny us a vote."

"But I may decide when it will come."

Heated exchanges regarding Soyer's future continued for several minutes. At last, I raised my hand.

Lord Marcus stood. "Let us give Captain Avery the floor."

"Gentlemen, since you have not actually disputed my continuing engagement in these matters, I assume that you agree to my staying on to investigate. May I make a small point? Decide what you must about your banquet, but consider, if you were to rid yourselves of Monsieur Soyer, you would be left with a kitchen in which poison still lurks and with no one to lead it. Who knows the kitchen, the staff and those who supply it as Monsieur Soyer does? Personally, I feel his advice and experience are vital to my inquiries."

"Are you quite certain"—one man stood up and coughed—"that Soyer himself is not the author of these crimes?"

"I would stake my reputation upon it."

"Do you suspect anyone, Captain Avery?"

"Well, I—" Every time I answered such a question, I felt I was giving a hostage to fortune. "We are inquiring into a number of possible reasons for the poisoning. But it seems to me that the stout-hearted British way would be to stand by Monsieur Soyer."

"To stand by our French upstart!" one man quipped.

"Might I request that you consider one more thing?" I felt awkward raising the matter, but I had promised Mr. Percy. "The club's senior staff have asked me to request that you consider paying wages while the club is closed. As you can imagine, the kitchen is very anxious; morale is low. I believe that such a promise will raise their spirits and ensure cooperation, while, of course, ensuring they do not go hungry."

The audience grumbled again. Mr. Ellice shook his head. Captain Beare said irritably, "To ensure cooperation? It is from them that our troubles come in the first place. They should need no encouragement to cooperate!"

Lord Marcus beckoned Mr. Scott and asked him to report on the club's finances.

Bowing and scraping in an almost unbearably ingratiating manner (though the committee apparently did not find it so), Scott told his audience that the club's finances were under a good deal of pressure. It simply would not be practical to pay the kitchen staff if the club were closed.

The entire committee nodded their heads.

That being decided, Molesworth asked whether they were ready to vote upon Soyer.

"Is this entirely necessary?" said Lord Marcus. "Do we truly wish to lose our greatest asset?"

"And there is the matter of the banquet," said Molesworth.

"May I also add, as a little fillip to our proceedings," Mr. Scott suddenly interrupted, almost fluttering his eyelashes at the committee, "that I believe the club's predicament may be resolved sooner than expected. Captain Avery has—no doubt out of scruple and caution—forborne to inform you that there is a suspect. I am told that witnesses have come forward with evidence which may implicate a certain kitchen maid. The police are coming, and they will certainly be interviewing the girl and making inquiries. It is just possible that an arrest may soon be made."

Shouts, cheers, ejaculations of shock. I wondered how Scott knew about Matty.

"May I venture that, while the committee may feel it necessary to cancel the banquet, we may not need to keep the club closed for long."

Lord Marcus proposed the two votes.

Thus I saw exactly how Mr. Scott kept his job.

WHEN I RETURNED to the kitchen this time, it was eerily quiet and dark. Most of the staff had left; in all but the main kitchen, the flaring gaslights had been extinguished. Here, Soyer stood in his apron before one of the large gas ranges. Next to him were three long golden French loaves, the ones known as baguettes. Monsieur Perrin bustled around him.

At the twelve-sided table sat Mr. Percy and Morel, and slightly apart from them, Mrs. Relph, talking quietly to Matty. To one side, Blake was examining a row of broiling stoves and warming pans, no doubt trying to determine their mechanisms.

Everyone but Soyer looked up expectantly.

"Captain Avery?" To my surprise, it was the usually reticent Morel.

"Monsieur Soyer won a vote of confidence," I said, "but the banquet has been canceled."

Morel cast about almost wildly, put his hand to his forehead, then let it fall.

"It is the correct decision," said Soyer, and came over and patted Morel on the shoulder.

"There is more—"

"*Eh bien,* Captain Avery, it must wait. We will eat, then we will decide what to do next."

"But—"

"Let us have a little calm before the storm," Soyer said. And I thought: *he knows.* "*Capitaine,* will you sit with the kitchen staff and risk my cooking, like these brave souls here? And you, too, Mr. Maguire—if the captain will allow it?" I nodded awkwardly. "We shall have a good late lunch. There is bread from Durand, the best baker in St. Martin's Lane. Morel and I bought it ourselves. Coffee, also purchased by me and made by my dear Morel. Fine, clean, simple food! And an *omelette aux fines herbes* with a little salad to whet the appetite. The eggs and cream are from Durand, too."

It occurred to me that I had never seen Soyer cook. He took a long phosphorous match and placed it against a pipe in one of the compartments on the top of the vast stove. In a moment, a flame danced up. He did the same with a second compartment, and set a frying pan on each. With nonchalant elegance, he cracked a dozen eggs one by one into a white china bowl, then filled his fingers with salt from one of the little crocks nearby and cast it across the mixture. He did the same with a pinch of ground pepper, then poured from a jug a stream of thick cream into the eggs. He beat them briskly with a fork in wide circles, his hands moving with the same easy grace and precision as I had noted in Perrin. The eggs seemed almost to leap into the air as the whisk lifted them up and brought them back into the bowl. Soyer placed a perfect square of lemon-white butter into each frying pan and brandished each pan in turn over its flame. The butter began to emit a very gentle hiss. Then he seized the white bowl and poured out the mixture, dividing it between the two pans and stirring each gently with a wooden spoon. The butter in the pans hissed louder. For a few seconds he simply watched the mixture settle, then he added a pinch of herbs to both and began carefully to agitate the pans, one and then the other, and, taking up a metal tool rather like a flat spade, worked quickly around the edges of each, prodding, scooping and tucking. After some minutes he picked up each pan and tapped it on the stove, then he turned a knob on the front of the range and, miracle of miracles, the flame was at once extinguished.

He set down the pans where the flame had been. The egg mixture continued to sizzle and steam. When the hissing ceased, he took his metal tool and folded each omelet upon itself. Then he tipped each pan, letting the concoction slip elegantly onto a large blue plate. This he brought to the table: two perfect, soft, unblemished yellow semicircles, smooth and shiny as porcelain. Mr. Percy divided them neatly among eight plates. Perrin put a little salad onto each plate and broke the bread with his hands, and we all came to the table.

"*Un repas paysan,*" Soyer said, "the food of peasants. Honest, and none the worse for that." He picked up his bread, pulled opened the crust so the soft, velutinous white inside was exposed, pushed it into a piece of omelet, then lifted the dripping morsel to his lips and bit upon it.

I cannot say that I did not hesitate, just a little, before I ate. I looked up to find Morel watching me, and took a large mouthful. It was perfect. *If I am to die,* I thought, *this would not by any means be the worst way.*

"Mr. Maguire," I heard Percy murmur to Blake, "we do not stand on ceremony down here. Please, remove your gloves while you eat—as long as your master is agreeable."

"Kind of you, Mr. Percy," said Blake. "Truth to tell, my hands have suffered over the winter. They are somewhat unsightly and best kept covered. I rub a liniment of fuller's earth onto them. The gloves help."

I watched Blake's hands. As usual, the two middle fingers of his left glove were stuffed with cotton to make them appear whole and, of course, they did not bend. He had acquired a habit while he ate in company of keeping his left hand either in his lap or moving it quickly.

"My friends," Soyer said, "I should like to tell you a story, about the time I escaped the Paris mob during the July Revolution in 1830. Morel and Percy know it well, I fear. They must endure it once more. It was a bloody time. I was working for the First Minister, the Prince de Polignac, not a popular man. Much hated, in fact, at the time. I was barely twenty, with a dozen chefs beneath me. One night, the prince gave a grand banquet at the Foreign Office. Rioters and revolutionaries encircled the building and broke in as we were serving the *entremets*. They began to shoot at us and accused us of being traitors, and at the same time they grabbed at the food, tearing birds from the spits and overturning tables of pastries. Two of my fellow chefs were shot; one fell before my eyes. The doors were blocked, and there was no way out. *Alors*, what did I do? It is a sweltering night, but I had a cool head and a good singing voice. I rip off my apron, climb upon a table and I begin to sing our national song, '*La Marseillaise*,' '*Allons, enfants de la Patrie, Le jour de gloire est arrivé!*' My voice rises clear and strong and, gradually, others join it. The room begins to calm, the rioters cheer, lift me on their shoulders and carry me up the stairs to the great hall, still singing. Finally, I see a way out and manage to escape into the crowds." With this, he took a mouthful of baguette and gave us all a triumphant smile.

"My friends, be of good cheer. I believe we will win through. We are hard-working, quick and clever. We will find the truth."

I looked about the table. Percy, calm, the picture of reliability. Morel, casting the odd pained look at Perrin. Perrin himself placid, his eyes on Soyer. Matty, barely eating, her head bowed over her plate, shrinking from attention; Mrs. Relph, watching her anxiously. Blake, uttering occasional ejaculations of appreciation, no doubt for some particular, unguessable reason, and watching constantly from behind his spectacles.

"I am sorry. There is more, and I must tell it to you," I said, pushing my plate away. "The committee has decided that the club cannot afford to pay the servants for the days when the club is shut. Again, I am sorry."

Soyer stepped back and raised his hand like some revolutionary on the barricades.

"I shall pay their wages if the club will not."

"There is more."

"Speak it, my dear *Capitaine,* we are braced for anything!" said Soyer.

"The committee learned that Miss Matty—Matilda—had been accused by some of the staff. It has insisted that the police take her for questioning as soon as they arrive."

I looked at Soyer, and I saw that he already knew. Matty turned away from the table and covered her face with her hands. Mrs. Relph gave me a furious look, as if it were my fault, and placed her hand on Matty's shoulder. Young Perrin sprang up.

"*Mais c'est fou!*" he said. "We all know this is impossible. Mathilde, do not despair. We will defend you!" He brought out a fresh handkerchief from his top pocket and offered it to her. She refused it, but nevertheless granted him a small, desolate smile.

These were the words I should have said.

I added hurriedly, "It should go without saying that I regard these accusations as largely malicious and entirely without truth. We will scotch them as soon as the police arrive. And Bl—Mr. Maguire and I will devote all our efforts to finding the real culprit."

I could not say that Soyer owed his very position to Mr. Scott's offering up of Matty as a suspect. In their relief at having an apparently plausible culprit, the committee had voted overwhelmingly to retain him, while ordering that Matty be immediately handed over to the police.

Mr. Scott arrived not long afterward to say that the police had arrived and that the committee had decided that Matty be—his word—detained until the police were ready to speak to her; a footman would watch her. Soyer, Perrin, Morel and Percy all protested, but Matty, looking at no one, rose and said she would like to be on her own and would go and sit in the butler's room. Mrs. Relph insisted upon accompanying her. The footman was persuaded to stand outside the door. Scott's good humor was thoroughly repugnant.

In the empty saloon, two constables and a pale, slight man in a gray worsted suit and low-crowned hat looked slightly cowed by their marbled surroundings. Scott began to make introductions. The man in the gray worsted turned. We recognized each other at once.

"We know each other, Captain Avery and I," he said. "The surroundings are more salubrious this time," he added, and gazed up at the Reform's great glass dome.

I had no desire to be reacquainted with Sergeant Loin of the Westminster division of the Metropolitan New Police. He was a beady-eyed fellow who had made a good deal of trouble for Blake, though he had at the last behaved decently enough over the Holywell Street murders—and gained a good deal of unearned credit at Blake's expense. I feared he would see through Blake's disguise.

"I hope you do not have any foolish notions about 'solving' this matter, Captain Avery. Mr. Blake has a license for such work; you do not."

"I have been helping the club in an unofficial capacity," I said. "But you are out of uniform, and out of your district, too, I think."

"Indeed not, sir. The Metropolitan Police are setting up a new Detecting branch for the whole city, and I am one of eight policemen seconded to it. We go about in plain clothes. Such matters are very much my department now. It is you, Captain, who would seem to be in the wrong place. May I ask how it is that you come to be here?"

"By chance, Monsieur Soyer asked me to dinner on the night that Mr. Rowlands, who later died, was taken ill. We assumed it was cholera, of which I had seen a deal in India, and so, in the absence of a doctor, I stayed to help."

"And you are still here."

"The club had some doubts about Rowlands's demise and asked me to look into them. I do not believe there is a law against that."

"Then there was another death last night."

"And here you are, Sergeant Loin."

"And Blake?"

"Is not here. I called Mr. Wakley, a respected surgeon and coroner, to make an examination of Mr. Addiscomb, the latest victim. He is looking at the body now. He performed a postmortem examination upon Mr. Rowlands two days ago and has the results."

Loin was taken aback. "I know about Mr. Wakley. It's a good thing you called him in, Captain Avery."

"Glad to be of service." I could not restrain a little sarcasm.

"The body must be removed to the police deadhouse. The secretary—Mr. Scott, was it?—was vague about the whereabouts of Mr. Rowlands's corpse."

"It was taken to his lodgings yesterday. I can furnish you with the address."

"Thank you," said Loin awkwardly. "I believe there is a suspect? A girl?"

"The girl is not the culprit, just the object of malicious gossip."

"I'll be the judge of that, Captain. She's still here, though, and Mr. Soyer?"

"She is," said Scott, "and secured. The captain has a soft spot for her, but we must take precautions."

"Secured? She is quite harmless, and certainly not guilty of what you suggest."

Loin looked from Scott to me and back. "We will, naturally, be inspecting the club," he said, "and, in due course, I shall interview the staff and the relevant members."

"I believe most of the staff have departed," said Scott smoothly, "as the club is now closed. But Captain Avery has spoken to everyone in the kitchen. I am sure he will be only too pleased to share his findings with you."

"I am sure he will," said Loin.

"Now, Sergeant." Scott's manner managed to be both grand and obsequious, as if he could not decide whether to placate the policeman or condescend to him. "I do hope we may rely on your discretion? We are very keen that these unpleasant matters do not become common currency beyond the club. As you see, we are doing all we can to remedy the situation, and the club will be closed until we are certain we have scotched the problem."

"I'll do my duty, sir," Loin said. "I've no reason to gossip. But I think you'll find it hard to keep a lid on this." Then he said, "Have we met before, Mr. Scott?"

Scott licked his lips and smiled. "No, indeed. I am sure I should remember."

"I shall take a moment with the captain, Mr. Scott," said Loin. "Then I should appreciate it if you would take me to our victim."

He walked over to one of the colonnades and beckoned me to follow.

"You'll oblige me by staying put, Captain," he said in a low voice. "I'll want to speak to you later."

"I have certain errands," I said coolly, "but I can make myself available."

Loin ran his fingers around the brim of his hat. "I heard about Blake," he said, even more quietly. "Absconding from the Marshalsea is not a common event."

"Is that why you asked me if he was here?"

"I'm sorry for it. My first thought was why would a man as clever as he do such a thing?"

"Mine, too."

"You've heard nothing, then?"

"No. I imagine he has taken a boat somewhere. He does not feel bound to England."

"No doubt," he said, nodding vigorously. "Did I mention that the club has asked us to place constables outside the front and back of the club, night and day? It occurred to me you might wish to know." He coughed.

"LOIN IS HERE." I told Blake.

"Of course he is."

"I do not joke," I said. "He is investigating the deaths. If anyone sees through this"—I gestured at his spectacles and mustache—"it will be him. We will have to keep you out of his way."

"If I hide, I learn nothing." He took off the spectacles, rubbed his eyes and yawned. He looked pale and tired.

"You are not well. You should rest."

"Too much smiling, that's all."

I should have liked to have let him sleep, but there was too much to get on with. "What are we to do about Matty?"

"Not much we can do. Loin'll question her; the evidence is circumstantial. He's not a fool."

"Surely there is something—Scott is so energetically touting her."

"If she's arrested, the matter is resolved and the club reopens. It suits them all."

"Therefore, we must find the true culprit as soon as possible. And then we can recover your name and Collinson will have to relent. Have you drawn any conclusions? I confess I saw no one among the staff of whom I thought, *It truly might be you*. But there were so many of them, I worry that I did not ask the right questions. Or that they might have lied and I could not have told. But you—you see into people, you know the questions to ask." I was gabbling.

"I'm no mind reader, William."

"You must have some thoughts? We have questioned over sixty people."

"There's no virtue in rushing if there's no clear conclusion."

"But—"

"I do not have an answer, William."

"*No* thoughts?"

Blake rubbed the bridge of his nose then touched the ragged edge of his ear. "Some. No conclusions." He sighed. "I need to see the kitchen at work. And there's little prospect of that unless Matty's arrested. And, William, I'm tired."

"We must spread our net wider," I said excitedly. "Let us look beyond the kitchen. Wakley talked of contamination and adulteration. I myself witnessed two suppliers with good reason to be very angry with Soyer. He sent back their goods and insulted them; both claim he owes them money. There may be others. Mr. Scott mentioned that the kitchen is pressed for money. And there is the matter of whether it is quite honest; I do not think Matty told me everything."

"All right." Blake yawned. "Wakley can take samples of the dried goods. And we'll visit the kitchen's chief suppliers."

"Then there is the chef Francobaldi. Ude said that envy is the chief sin of the kitchen. Francobaldi has a temper that is quite out of control, and he is consumed with jealousy of Soyer."

"So we'll see Francobaldi." He suppressed another yawn.

"He drinks late at the Provence Hotel."

"I know the place."

"And there are the Russians."

"Ah, the Russians."

"And the club members. There are those like Beare who seem determined to rid themselves of Soyer. I do not know if it means anything, but the other matter of note is that all the victims were Whigs. Collinson says the relations between the radicals and the Whigs are personal and bitter. I have seen it, too. What if the radicals are determined to bring the place down and split from the Whigs? These deaths certainly threaten a momentous collapse."

"Who would do it? From what you say, Molesworth might exploit such a situation, but would he cause it?" He let his eyes shut.

I hesitated. "I cannot help but feel that Molesworth knows more than he says. I would not put it past him to be part of a plot. And what of Duncombe, who is so pleased that the Chartists are to present a new petition in a month? Such a friend of Rowlands, and sat next to him that night at dinner. He was in the Coffee Room last night, too.

"And I have," I said, "a list of those who purchased supper at the club on the night when Cunningham died. Duncombe was there." And, as I spoke, a vision suddenly appeared in my head of Duncombe chatting with two dull-looking middle-aged men.

"Good lord! I believe that Duncombe drank a toast with Addiscomb and Rickards at their table last night."

"We will visit both Duncombe and Molesworth. When I've had a kip."

IN THE KITCHEN I found Wakley had returned from his examination of Addiscomb and Rickards.

"Well, this is all most unusual, Captain Avery!" he said, almost enthusiastically. "I have just been informing Mr. Percy that I am all but certain that, just as you suggested, Addiscomb and Rickards were poisoned with strychnine. I think Rickards will live. But two types of poison. Most unusual!"

Percy, correct as ever, was laboring not to look too put out by Wakley's keenness, but I could not help noticing he could not stop fussing with his cuffs.

"Mr. Wakley," I said, "is it possible that some of the kitchen's goods might have been contaminated before they arrived here?"

"Of course it is possible!" he said. "Though, if that were the case, one might have expected more diners to fall ill."

"Mr. Percy, may I ask you in confidence whether you have ever discovered adulterated goods here?"

"Never," Percy said, a touch overbrightly, "our suppliers' reputations would not stand it."

"I have seen Monsieur Soyer send deliveries back," I said.

"Oh, we argue with all the suppliers on occasion—it is understood. It is the way Chef reminds them that he will only take the best. And, in fact, I do recall Cadbury and Pratt of Bond Street once tried to foist bad milk upon us. We never used them again. They were adding far too much boric acid, to make it last longer."

"It is an old trick," said Wakley, sighing. "In my opinion, all boracized milk and cream is dangerous. But thousands disagree. In large quantities, it is, without question, poisonous."

"I should like Mr. Wakley to make tests on some of the kitchen's dried goods and wines. If that is agreeable, Mr. Percy," I said.

Wakley said, "I am prepared to do it, but I must make it plain I shall have to make my results available to the police."

"I would expect nothing else."

"As it happens, in my case I have a number of small receptacles for collecting such things. There will not be enough, but let me give them to you, Captain Avery. You grow into your task."

He produced four small, pristine medicine bottles and four new corks tied together to stopper them with. They were pretty little things. I slipped one into my pocket and gave Percy the rest.

"I cannot imagine it will yield much, gentlemen," said Percy, "but I'll happily see to it straightaway." He disappeared into the butler's pantry to make up the samples.

After perhaps half an hour, Mr. Scott and Loin appeared in the kitchens. Introductions were made. Blake had slipped into the butler's pantry to help Percy fill up jars. I should not have concerned myself about Loin recognizing him. Soyer, emerging from his office with Perrin and Morel, wearing his lavender velvet frock coat, with his cap askew and his dozen rings, provided such a spectacle that Loin barely looked at anyone else.

"Mr. Wakley has reported his findings to me," said Loin. "We appear to have two deaths from poison and one man recovering."

"I hope he will be reporting them to us, since the club commissioned him," I said.

"Is it to you, Sergeant Loin, that we owe poor Mathilde's current confinement?" Soyer said coldly.

"I've ordered nothing so far, Mr. Soyer," said Loin, "and I know nothing of the girl, but I should like to talk to her."

"Whatever Mr. Scott has told you," Soyer said, deliberately ignoring the secretary, "it is quite impossible that Mathilde is the culprit. We, the senior members of the kitchen"—he gestured to Morel, Perrin and Percy—"are all quite persuaded of the fact."

"I will have to be the judge of that, sir," Loin said, "as I told Captain Avery."

"The girl has been a great favorite of Monsieur Soyer's," Scott said to Loin in a "confidential" voice that we could all hear. "She's a clever little thing. Too clever, I'd say. Ambitious. Personally, I've always found her rather sly."

"If she is so clever, Mr. Scott, why would she endanger her position with such an act?" I said.

Scott pretended to consider. "The lower orders are always hard to fathom. She is a street girl. What do you expect?"

I believe every man in the room save Loin would happily have knocked him down.

"Is this some form of revenge, Mr. Scott? She spurned your advances, so now you go after her?" I said.

"Captain Avery, you go too far," said Scott, more calmly than I would have expected. "I should watch that mouth of yours. You cannot be unaware of the rumors surrounding yourself and the girl."

"How dare you!" I said, my fists twitching.

"I have some questions for Mr. Soyer," said Loin hurriedly. "Perhaps we might speak privately?"

Scott spoke over him. "A case of gagging on your own medicine, I think, Captain. Of course," he went on, addressing the whole room, "should she prove guilty, the club could reopen, your staff could return to work, Chef, and the banquet for Lord Palmerston would go ahead."

"Mr. Soyer?" said Loin.

"Anything you wish to say to me may be said before these gentlemen," Soyer said coolly.

Loin nodded. "I should like to confirm that you have closed the kitchen?"

Soyer spread his arms out and raised his eyebrows as if to demonstrate what a foolish question it was.

Loin bristled. He asked where the previous night's dinner had been prepared. Once again, Soyer spread out his arms.

"We prepared food for two hundred guests last night," he said. "There were nine different items on the *carte*. Each dish is prepared in a different part of the kitchen, and each has parts contributed by perhaps three or four people."

"What did the victims eat?" said Loin.

Percy brought out the list. "Would you care for some refreshment, sir?" he asked Loin.

"Thank you. I'll have coffee," said Loin.

Loin began to bombard Soyer with questions. Did he have an idea of what in particular might have poisoned the men? How clean was the kitchen? What about the gentleman who had fallen sick in the street, and Mr. Rowlands? Had he known them personally? Soyer, feeling himself under attack, began dramatically to protest the absolute cleanliness of his kitchen.

In the midst of this, a bespectacled manservant emerged from the butler's pantry carrying a tray. It was Blake. At the sight of him I stopped breathing.

Silently, Blake placed a pot of coffee with one cup and a small jug of fresh milk on the table. Loin was so taken up with Soyer he barely noticed him. Looking up from his task, Blake gave me a wicked smile.

"Would you care for me to pour it?" A bland servant's voice. The gloved hands hovered over the coffeepot.

"Please," said Loin. Soyer was in full flow.

Blake poured out the coffee.

"Milk, sir?"

"Please," said Loin irritably.

I almost choked. At any minute I expected his hand to reach out and seize Blake's gloved wrist.

"Will there be anything else, sir?"

"No."

With a small bow, Blake withdrew. I breathed again.

Loin's questions became increasingly exasperated, Soyer's answers increasingly outraged. I was relieved when Loin turned abruptly to me.

"Mr. Scott says you have the details of the evidence against the suspect. I'll have your account now, if I may. Briefly, though."

"It is not evidence," I said, "it is gossip and coincidence."

"Sergeant," said Soyer stiffly, "I shall excuse myself. I have pressing matters to take care of. I shall be in my office."

Loin waved him away in a manner deliberately disrespectful. Soyer stalked off. Perrin and Morel would have followed him, but Loin held up his hand. "The other gentlemen, though, I'll be wanting to speak to them, too."

From the kitchen maids' dinner to the discovery of Matty's handwritten words in Soyer's letters, I described the accusations against her, pointing out the obvious objections as I went along. I described what I knew of Mr. Cunningham's death, a matter which discomfited Mr. Scott, and I took a gloomy pleasure in his aggrievement.

"Mr. Cunningham was old and had a weak heart," he protested. "There is no proof that he died as a result of eating here."

"At that point, I believe Matty had not yet begun to work in the pastry kitchen," I said, ignoring him. "She was still a kitchen maid. Moreover, it is my belief that the notes sent to Monsieur Soyer are not genuine. The club's banquet for Ibrahim Pasha has been canceled, but I believe there are those who are determined that it take place, no matter what the consequences. What better way to reinstate it than by producing a suspect? And how easy to acquire a paper in Matty's hand. They are all over the kitchen."

"And do you have a notion of who might do such a thing?" said Loin, who clearly thought I was addled.

"I do not make rash accusations before I have evidence," I said, staring at Scott.

"Matty? That's the girl's name?" said Loin.

"Yes, Matty Horner."

Loin was astonished. I had forgotten he had known her; of course, she had been a police informant.

"Blake asked Soyer if he would take her on as a scullery maid after Holywell Street. She has been doing very well."

"MATTY HORNER? Is that you?"

"It is, Sergeant Loin," she said. She sat upright in one of the armchairs in the butler's room where first we had had tea together. Mrs. Relph sat on the other chair; she had the ability to maintain a perpetually outraged expression. At this moment, I was actually glad of it. Matty had tidied herself and arranged her hair. She looked up with a calm that seemed to me to most closely resemble hopelessness.

"Well, this is a turn-up," said Loin. "You've filled out and grown, Matty. Regular family reunion, isn't it, Captain Avery? Only one we're missing is Blake."

There was a silence.

"I'd hoped to see you out of trouble for good, Matty . . ."

"Yes, sir."

He gave me a brief glance and gestured to Mrs. Relph. "I shall be speaking to Miss Horner alone."

. . .

I FOUND BLAKE in the kitchen maids' room, dozing. I shook him awake.

"For God's sake, what were you thinking, coming in to serve Loin like that?" I said. "I thought I should choke. I'd give you a blinker right here and now if I could! I swear you wanted to be caught!"

Blake smiled placidly. "It went off all right."

"All right? You could have been taken there and then. I cannot believe you would be so foolish."

"Young Will Avery all sober and so grown up."

"It was a stupid, irresponsible thing to do."

"You must have had a moment's pleasure watching him take the coffee from my hand, and no notion it was me."

"My heart was in my mouth. We cannot take such risks. We should not be wasting time. We should be chasing Francobaldi and visiting Duncombe and Molesworth."

He said, "I cannot leave until Loin and his constables go and he has finished with Matty." Then, "You know, I think your concern feeds my levity."

I left in a fit of pique and went to see Soyer.

"Are you busy?"

"I am never idle!" he said with a brittle cheer. "The banquet is canceled. I cannot run my kitchen, nor find the one who wishes me harm, nor keep a poor, innocent girl from the police. So I will find something else to occupy me. I am planning the soup kitchen. If I cannot cook here, then I will bring forward its opening. The giant boiler I ordered from Bramah and Prestage is ready. Where better to put my energies?

"With this kitchen, I believe I could feed thousands more effectively than has ever been done before. I have a number of recipes for cheap and wholesome soups thickened with rice and pearl barley. I call them 'panadas.'" He gestured at the papers on his desk. "Such quantities are not for the fainthearted, however. I must work out every last detail. I plan to provide food for at least three hundred and fifty hungry mouths on our first attempt. But tell me, is there anything I can do to help you? Have the police asked for anything?" His lip curled. It was the only intimation of how angry he was.

"I should like to visit some of your suppliers, with your permission."

"*Eh bien*, if you like. If you think it may help. Do whatever you must."

IN THE KITCHEN Perrin and Morel stood in uneasy silence on opposite sides of the twelve-sided table. Matty and Loin had not emerged.

"There is a message for you, *Capitaine*," said Morel. "A boy came just a moment ago. I did not like to disturb you. There is a person who wishes to speak to you waiting outside. They would not give their name."

Mystified, I thanked him, took my coat and emerged into the gray afternoon light. I traversed the yard, took the steps up to the street and came out onto the corner of Pall Mall. I could see no one waiting in any direction save a couple of constables standing outside the club.

"Captain Avery?" one said.

"Yes."

He took hold of my left arm, the other constable my right. "I am arresting you for debt."

Chapter Fifteen

I spluttered and protested that this was outrageous. I demanded the name of my accuser and insisted I owed money to no one, which was more or less true. None of it made the slightest difference.

An hour later, I was in the Marshalsea Prison, in a grubby little room which stank of decades of other men's sweat, my only consolation that I had it to myself. I had had to pay all I had to secure it.

My arrival had been utterly demeaning. The gatekeeper had recognized me at once, and laughed, then spat before my feet. The prison governor was waiting for me. The last time I had seen him, after Blake's disappearance, he had groveled in embarrassment. Now, he enjoyed my humiliation.

"Who has done this to me? This is trumped-up nonsense!"

"Welcome, Captain Avery. Who would have thought we should meet again so soon! And in such circumstances! But I have the summons here." He waved a piece of paper at me. "It is quite legal."

"I cannot believe this! Surely the law says I must be told who claims a debt from me?"

"I am sure you will find out soon enough." He smiled loftily. "In the meantime, you may as well make yourself comfortable. The trustee will take you to your room. It is one of the better ones, but it will cost you."

"I was dragged off the street. I have urgent matters to attend to. My friends have no idea where I am!"

"Would you rather they did?"

That was a good question, to which I had no good answer.

And so here I was, in this noxious little room with its mildewed walls and its dirty little window. There was a deal chair and a gray wooden pallet covered in nothing but other men's stains, and that was all. I had just enough left in my pockets to purchase a candle, but not enough for dinner or a blanket. This was debtors' prison.

I had come to hate the Marshalsea when I visited Blake. Incarceration within its walls was a thousand times worse. It was a cold night. I wrapped myself as best I could in my coat, and passed the hours alternating between rage, frustration and boredom. Not knowing the name of my accuser or why I had been imprisoned added a ghastly edge of desperation. I racked my brains for outstanding debts of any size. I could think of nothing. Money was not plentiful, but I had thought we were scraping along. The truth was, however, it wasn't just the poor who lived on the edge of debt. In Devon, almost everyone I knew lived on the line between almost-prosperity and debt—a bad harvest, a purchasing arrangement fallen through, and misery beckoned. In the dark, I began to imagine that there might be some great financial arrangement that had slipped from memory. Had I mortgaged the house in Devon, or borrowed on the harvest and simply forgotten? Had Helen bought dresses or furniture I did not know about? When would I find out? Would I be left to rot? Blake had said there were men who had been in the Marshalsea for thirty years for debts which no one now remembered.

Toward morning, I finally fell into a shallow sleep filled with fevered images of faces and torsos twisting in terrifying convulsions. I awoke sweating and gasping as the door of my room opened and the trustee stepped aside to reveal . . . Sir Theo Collinson.

"What?" I wheezed, shaking those fearful pictures from my head.

He swept in like winter, his brows bunched over his eyes like furious hillocks. The effect was mitigated somewhat by the fact that his stomach preceded the rest of him by several inches.

"How did you know I was here?"

He cast his eyes over the room and, with a moue of distaste, settled himself gingerly on the chair.

"It really is most unpleasant, is it not? I have told you before, Avery, I know everything," he said. "I have eyes everywhere."

I heartily hoped this was not the truth.

He sighed. "I put you here."

"You! But—"

"Avery, do you think I am stupid?" he said slowly, and there was cold, calm malice in his tone. "Have I ever given you any reason to suppose that I am stupid?"

"No, sir." My blood began to chill.

"Then how did you and he imagine that you could provoke me in such a way and get away with it?"

"I do not know what you mean."

With the same ghastly, cold calm he said, "Where is he?"

"Where is who?"

His eyebrows twitched. "Do not play with me, young man. No one plays with me and gets away with it. Remember who put you here."

With some difficulty, I fought my rising agitation and answered, "I do not know. On a boat to Timbuctoo by now, for all I know. Or dead."

"We both know he is alive! *Where is he?*"

Anger was my savior. "How the devil did you get me incarcerated here?"

"I think you do not understand just how powerful I am," he said, his voice chilly and calm again. "I could have you moldering here for months."

"But I owe you nothing."

"Indeed? Here is the bond to show you do." He handed me a sheet of paper with a passable imitation of my handwriting on it which said that I owed Sir Theophilus Collinson the sum of £150.

"This is a forgery! I never signed this!" For the second time in a day, I was consumed with outrage.

"And how long do you think it would take to prove it? And how much do you think it would cost? For every witness you might find to confirm your version, I could provide three to swear to mine."

"Good God, Collinson, I did everything you asked of me, and more. I have heard nothing from you these two days, and now I get this?"

"Come, Avery," Collinson said, suddenly all softness. "You understand. Blake has defied me, he is out and free, you are in London. Where would he go if not to seek you out?"

"You overestimate my influence with him. Do you think he would stay, Sir Theo? He would be a fugitive forever. He would not mind leaving London at all."

"Oh, well, you will have your little game." His small eyes seemed to shine with malevolence. "In the meantime, reflect on this. I can keep you here as long as I like. But it will be easier if you do as I say. You will go to him, wherever he is, and you will tell him that he will perform the task I give him. That task has now changed. He is to find the perpetrator of the Reform poisonings. I do not care how he does it, but it must be done. If he refuses, you will be in here for as long as I wish it. And I will find him, and his punishment will be worse than yours. Is that understood? You should think twice about trifling with me."

He gave me a few minutes for his words to sink in. I was bound, there was no question. It felt insupportable. I wanted to rage, but I would not give him the pleasure of it. Blake's perversity in refusing to give in to him no longer seemed perverse at all.

"Now I am going to have you released. For a while, at least," he said. "Do not think of heroics. Remember you have a wife and child. And you have already committed yourself to the Reform. What you are doing there, I cannot imagine. We both know you are no investigator. You are neither the class for it nor, let us be honest, do you have the mind."

"And what do you know about it?" He was not wrong, but I saw no reason why I should take his insults.

He gave me a pitying look. "I told you, I know everything." He shifted awkwardly in the chair. "Incidentally, how many are dead just now?"

"I thought you knew everything."

"Lord Marcus Hill wrote to me," he admitted. "And certain members of the government have asked me to look into it. I expected a visit from you regarding the Russians. You have been avoiding me, Avery."

"There are three dead if you include Cunningham, and one recovering. That is, as far as I know."

"And are you nowhere near apprehending a culprit? Have you made any advances at all?"

"I have established that Rowlands may have been dosing himself with arsenic," I said, anger making me proud, "and that the gentlemen last night appear to have been poisoned with strychnine. I arranged a postmortem examination for Rowlands—tests are taking place. There was another postmortem today. I have interviewed all the kitchen staff and, when I was dragged off the street, I was about to visit Soyer's suppliers."

"Not bad, but no real results, I see. There are the Russians, of course. And you should be acquainted with the club's other troubles." His eyebrows twitched with anticipation. "Should I apprise you? I do not know," he mused.

"I should," I said reluctantly, "be grateful for anything you can tell me."

He shifted on the chair, trying and failing to make himself comfortable.

"Well, of course, the club is in debt; the architect, Barry, says it owes him a good deal. It seems the members will have to step in; good thing there are some very wealthy ones. Then there are the factions. You would have thought they would all simply be happy to eat their fine dinners and slumber in their chairs, but they are not.

"Have you come across William Molesworth? He and his radical friends are not at all pleased that the club they started has become far too deferential to the Whig grandees. It is not beyond imagining that they contemplate a break with the Whigs and a departure from the club.

"On the other side, there are Whigs such as Ellice and Beare who answer to Palmerston and are very comfortable where they are, believe the party has done quite enough to bring about change for one century and would not mind one whit if Molesworth and the rest took themselves off. They would happily wish them to the devil. Frankly, I cannot really see why the die-hard Whigs do not simply join the Tories. But there are old bonds that hold them to the party, and they accept they must win over the middle if they are to counter the Tories in the long term. Palmerston regards the radicals—when he can be brought to think about them at all—as a thorn in his side. Then we have the so-called liberals, the moderate middle; among them, Lord Marcus Hill, who acts the peacemaker rather well. Didn't think he had it in him.

"The radicals intended to lure the middle to their side, edging out the Whig leaders. They underestimated that the middle had plans of its own, namely the repeal of the Corn Laws, and were happy to defer to the Whigs. Some of the radicals are considering, with the new Chartist petition coming in May, to combine with some ghastly working-class rump. Not, of course, that there is any chance of the petition succeeding." He smiled his lupine grin.

"As far as I can tell, all the poisoned men were Whigs," I said.

"Were they, indeed? Something to consider. Moving on, what do you know of the 'international angle'?"

"I know that the committee are desperate for the banquet to proceed, partly for the club's reputation, but also because Lord Palmerston hopes to prevent an alliance between Egypt and Russia and a possible war in the Middle East."

"Avery, you do surprise me. You know, I used to think you were quite stupid," he said affably.

"Do I have to listen to your insults?" I said.

"I cannot help making my own entertainment." He smirked. "A little indulgence of mine. I assume, then, that you know about the negotiations, that the Russians are highly suspicious of the prince's visit and that, if they have come to know about Palmerston's intentions, they will certainly do their best to subvert them.

"Perhaps I should also point out that Ibrahim Pasha has plenty of other enemies who would not be sad to see him dead: factions at the Turkish court, groups within Egypt. Especially as his father, Mehmet, who is eighty and sick, cannot last much longer. Should Ibrahim Pasha expire, it would suit his enemies very well if responsibility were laid at the door of a famous French chef or a British political party. It could be in the Russians' interests, too: it would certainly destroy any possibility of an accord among Britain, Egypt and Turkey. And what a fine case they would have if it were known that, in the weeks before the dinner, there were several poisonings at the club. Shock and horror, thunder and blood, the Reform Club dissolved, the party in ruins. Ibrahim Pasha conveniently dead."

"Is this your own view, or one more widely held?"

"It is, let us say, *a* view. I merely put what I hear and surmise before you."

"It certainly makes it all a good deal more confusing. But none of this matters, as the banquet has been canceled."

"My spies tell me you have already made a rather clumsy attempt on the embassy. I think the best policy would be to leave it to us. Baron Brunnov, the ambassador, is, like all Russian nobility, very grand. He certainly would not receive *you*. I suspect, in any case, that he is ignorant of any felonious goings-on. He is, however, most displeased by Ibrahim Pasha's visit. There *is* a Russian spy at the embassy, the military attaché—the Russians have little imagination in these matters—and a number of secret police whose purpose is to watch certain Russian émigrés report to him. But we already have eyes on them.

"You and Blake will keep to the Reform. In my opinion, the Russians' most likely stratagem would be to have an agent on the staff. Look at any Germans, in particular."

I did not say that Blake had already thought of this.

"I cannot do anything while I am stuck in here."

"As I said, I am about to have you released. We shall both return to the Reform. I have a meeting arranged with the committee. Then you will pass my message on to Blake. Now be a good boy, and help me out of this chair."

"I am not a boy, nor yours to command in everything." The words felt particularly bitter in my mouth.

He let it pass. "Then I ask you as a gentleman, and the younger man, since I find myself unable to get up."

. . .

I FOUND BLAKE in my room at the Reform.

"Christ! Where have you been?" I had rarely seen him so animated. "Morel said you were there one minute and gone the next. I went all around St. James's. Searched every tavern and gambling hell."

I explained.

"That bastard shaver," was all he said.

I could not look at him. "Blake, you should leave, take the boat to America." I turned the faucet and watched the hot water course into the basin. "I must wash and change; there is a meeting with the committee. Then, I'm damned if anything is going to keep me from Duncombe and Molesworth."

"I've news, too," he said soberly. "Loin took Matty for questioning. He hasn't arrested her, but she spent the night at Vine Street station."

"But there is no evidence!"

"Loin thought there was enough to keep her in."

"The committee would be delighted if she was arrested," I said gloomily. "Have you seen her?"

He shook his head. "Mrs. Relph went with her. If she's not been released, we'll visit her later."

Then he said, "Collinson must have something up his sleeve that he thinks I truly won't stomach. He wouldn't have come down on you so hard otherwise."

What it was, we were very soon to find out.

DOWNSTAIRS, Collinson's hefty presence dominated the golden-lit saloon.

"Gather them in, gather them in, Mr. Secretary, as fast as you can. You had better make a good showing, or I cannot vouch for anything. And I require coffee and some spirits. I assume you can provide them without poisoning me?"

Mr. Scott nodded vigorously, his expression slightly appalled.

"Captain Avery, you finally honor us with your presence," said Collinson.

Lord Marcus Hill and Molesworth were waiting, looking very disgruntled. I wondered if they even knew I had been gone. I gave Molesworth my particular attention, as covertly as I could. He was clearly displeased. Collinson, having ignored them up to that moment, suddenly arranged his features into a silkily reassuring smile.

"Marcus! William! Though I know matters are at a low ebb, may I tell you what a pleasure it is to see you. I am, in this case, not the general but only the messenger. You should know that Lord Palmerston will be here at eleven thirty sharp. He will not require lunch, but I should tell you he is not in the best of moods."

"Palmerston?" said Molesworth. "But he never comes here."

"The banquet," said Lord Marcus, frowning.

"The banquet," echoed Collinson. "He is displeased with the club's decision to cancel it. He will not accept it."

"He will have to," said Molesworth.

"He says it would be too great a blow to the prestige of the party, a diplomatic insult to Ibrahim Pasha, and that it will harm his own position and reputation."

"Not all of us would find that so unfortunate an outcome," murmured Molesworth.

"He says," Collinson went on, "that it will make the party and the club a laughingstock."

"And what if it kills one or two of his guests? What then becomes of his precious reputation—and ours?" Molesworth drawled.

"As I say, these are not my words, they are his. And he will be here, I should say, within the hour. Is Soyer about? I think he should be present."

"Sir Theo, we cannot host the banquet. Can you not weave your magic?" said Lord Marcus.

"I am afraid we are too far gone for that. When he arrives, I suggest you have a quorum of the committee and, of course, Soyer. Where is he?"

Lord Marcus Hill looked at Scott, who looked blank.

"At home?" I ventured.

"I suggest you collect him, Avery."

"Yes, sir," I said, grateful for an excuse to leave, though I had no idea where he lived.

BLAKE WAS DOZING again on my bed. I shook him awake.

"Lord Palmerston is coming to the Reform at eleven thirty. He is going to insist the banquet take place. The committee are horrified. I have been deputized to bring Soyer. I have no idea where he lives."

"Palmerston, eh. That's a facer."

"What—no, you cannot know him?"

"Executed a small commission for him once. Doubt he'd remember me."

"A small commission?"

He let his mouth twitch upward but said nothing.

"What shall we do?"

"Go and fetch Soyer."

Chapter Sixteen

Soyer's lodgings took up the first floor of a rambling brick town house on Charing Cross Road, with a battered front door and rackety stairs. Inside, Blake stopped before a solid, if equally battered, black door, at which he knocked briskly. There was no answer. He rapped again, and at last we began to hear sluggish noises. The door was opened eventually by a maid in an apron and a headscarf holding a duster.

"Begging your pardon, sirs, but he don't want to see no one."

Blake smiled briefly at her as he pushed past and walked to the end of the short, paneled corridor. I felt obliged to apologize for his brusqueness, and followed.

We came into a cluttered parlor that could not have been less like Soyer's domain at the Reform. A chaos of clothes, plates, squashed cushions and papers—papers, especially—and general debris littered the floor. On a chair was an elderly plate with a dried-out cheese rind. Soyer's *zoug-zoug* hat lay forlornly in a corner. Beneath the disarray the lineaments of an attractive room could be glimpsed: the dining table was a fine piece of walnut, there was a handsome Chesterfield and new curtains hung at the long, small-paned windows.

In the middle of this, clothed but very crumpled, his hatless head on the Chesterfield, his mouth dribbling slightly, lay Soyer.

Blake gave him a shake, and he took a great snorting breath and sat up suddenly, blinking several times.

"Didn't think you slept, Soyer."

"Blake—I mean—" He looked about anxiously, in case someone had heard him.

"It is just Avery and I, come to fetch you. Lord Palmerston is arriving at the club at eleven thirty."

"Lord Palmerston! *Merde!*" He sprang up, yawning, and rubbed his face. "What have we to serve him?" Then remembrance caught up with him, and he said, "But it is not what you call a sociable visit, is it?"

Blake shook his head. "Avery says he wants the banquet to go ahead."

For a moment, Soyer's face lit up with hope; almost at once, this was extinguished. "But it is impossible! And I cannot come—I have too much to do."

"Too much to do?" I said.

"I told you yesterday. My soup kitchen. I will not put it off a moment longer. I decided to bring forward the commencement. My suppliers and volunteers are all ready. It will produce its first meals tomorrow night."

"The same day as the banquet."

"The banquet is canceled."

"Palmerston is going to insist that it take place," I said. "You must be there to make your case."

Soyer yawned. "I will clothe myself." He stumbled across the room and out into the hallway. Blake followed him.

"Have you written to Emma?"

Soyer disappeared through another door. "She will return in two weeks, maybe three."

"You have not told her about the club?"

Soyer did not answer.

"She will not thank you for it, and you need her here."

Soyer called out, "I will not fail before her. I promised her success."

Blake shrugged. "You are a fool, Alexis."

"*Sans aucun doute*. In many things."

Soyer appeared at the door. He was dressed in dark gray—a loose coat with velvet lapels and trousers of the same somber hue. The colors of mourning did not suit him as his peacock duds did. He rubbed his eyes.

He went into the parlor, picked up a small enamel box, extracted from it a grain and placed it on his tongue. The box disappeared into his pocket.

"What's that?" asked Blake.

"Dr. Alighieri's proprietary powder tonic." He took a deep breath, thrust out his chest, squared his shoulders and seemed in an instant to slough off his former fatigue and sobriety.

We left Blake in Trafalgar Square, then Soyer and I went on to the Reform. Lord Marcus and Molesworth were in the Strangers' Room. Ellice and Beare had now joined them. Collinson had remained in the saloon. Molesworth had positioned himself before the window.

"Lord 'Pumice-stone' arrives," he observed. Ellice shook his wobbling chops disapprovingly.

Lord Palmerston, former Whig Home Secretary and architect of the recent war with China (which his supporters said was a triumph for free trade, his enemies that it had forced a nation into dependence on the demon opium but which everyone agreed was about to end in British victory), drew up in a fashionable phaeton, his coat of arms painted on the side. He emerged from the carriage at a leisurely pace, sauntered up the steps of the Reform, as a footman raced to open doors for him, into the porter's lobby and on to the saloon.

He was old—he was, after all, fifty-seven—if well kept, and exceedingly sure of himself. He was generally held, even now, to be handsome. I did not see it myself, though his features were very defined. A high forehead and luxuriant curly hair, gray at the temples, side whiskers running down almost to his collar. Straight brows, the eyes brown and knowing, the skin beneath bunched and lined. A thin, pointed nose—no doubt his supporters called it aquiline. The mouth composed into a supercilious almost-smile. It was clear he considered himself the superior of everyone around him. A tight-fitting black frock coat with velvet lapels, a just-glimpsed gray silk waistcoat. A silver-topped cane and a top hat in his hands. He was, of course, famous for his *amours* and dalliances, and his wife, the former Lady Cowper, was said to be no better. They had no children, but it was widely rumored that he had fathered three of hers while she was still married to Lord Cowper.

I wondered what my father would have made of him. Something upon the lines of "Get him in yer sights, shoot him 'twixt the eyes."

"Lord Palmerston, it is a great pleasure to welcome you to the Reform Club," said Lord Marcus, coming forward to greet him.

"A pleasure to be here, Marcus," said Lord Palmerston noncommittally, at the same time looking around as if he owned the place. "How is your delightful young bride?"

"She does very well, and asked that I remember her to you."

"Lovely creature. Sir Theo," he said, catching sight of Collinson, "I see you preceded me. As in so many things." He gave a small, dry smile. Collinson bowed and gave one of his own.

Palmerston turned again. "Monsieur Soyer, always a pleasure."

Soyer smiled his brightest, liveliest smile and bowed deeply, his hat once again miraculously failing to topple off. "*Ah non*, milord, the pleasure is all mine."

"May we show you into the library?" said Lord Marcus. "And provide you with some tea, or spirits? As you may know, our offerings at the moment are, unfortunately, rather limited . . ."

"Thank you, Lord Marcus, I should like a glass of port but I am rather short of time. We must speak. Monsieur Soyer, Mr. Ellice, Captain Beare, and you, too, Collinson. At once." Molesworth, I realized, he had not summoned. Molesworth looked confused.

"Of course, sir," said Lord Marcus.

"If I may, Your Lordship," said Collinson smoothly, "you might also wish to interview the young man who has been looking into the, ah, circumstances at the Reform, Captain Avery."

Palmerston nodded absently. "Him, too, then," he said.

The doors of the library began to close. Molesworth was left standing outside. Before they had shut entirely, I watched his face move from incomprehension to absolute fury.

A number of chairs had been set out informally, but it was clear that Lord Palmerston planned to stand, while we were expected to sit like schoolboys, and so we did. The half smile had disappeared; now, he was all cold-eyed business.

"I shall be brief. The Ibrahim Pasha banquet must go ahead. No ifs, no buts."

"Your Lordship," said Lord Marcus patiently, "the matter was debated at length by the committee, and it was decided that, under the circumstances, it would be too dangerous—"

"The banquet will take place," Palmerston interrupted. "The party's dignity requires it, the country's security demands it. If it is canceled, Ibrahim Pasha will take it as a personal slight, and all our careful diplomacy will be undone. Egypt will go with Russia. We will be obliged to back Turkey. There will be war, an ugly one. We will have to participate to maintain the balance of power, to protect our land routes to India. And we cannot afford it; matters are difficult enough in England. We must win Ibrahim Pasha over. Then there is the shame the party will face—I need hardly say what the papers will make of it—if the banquet is canceled. Whatever divisions there are among us just now, they must be reconciled. We must show a united front at a time when the Tories would see us fall apart. Any and all obstacles must be overcome, and these absurd rumors must be laid to rest. We are, after all, British."

"What rumors?" Lord Marcus asked carefully.

"This nonsense about someone dying at the club."

"But, milord," Soyer said, "men *have* died and—"

"One man—and, as I understand it, it may well have been his own fault."

There was a silence. Incensed, I looked over at Lord Marcus, who did not meet my gaze.

"If you please, Your Lordship," said Soyer, "even if the man had not died, I think it is now simply not possible. Practically, we have lost days of preparation. Many of my dishes take days, I cannot produce what we planned by tomorrow evening."

"Come now, Soyer, are you not the man who says, 'Impossible is a word to be found only in a dictionary of fools'?"

Soyer smiled nervously. "I believe that was Napoleon, milord."

"Your Lordship," I said urgently, "it was not just one—"

"Why is this man here?" Palmerston said, as his eyes briefly alighted upon me.

"He is the gentleman who has been investigating the matter for the club," said Collinson matter-of-factly.

"I must speak, Your Lordship—"

"Who is he?" Palmerston said.

"He is Captain Avery," said Lord Marcus. "He won several medals in India and Afghanistan, rescued the Rao of Doora from a tiger and was with Xavier Mountstuart when he died. And last year, he, along with his colleague Mr. Blake, resolved the Holywell Street murders, and the business with Lord Allington's sister."

"Well, what is it you wish to say?" asked Palmerston.

Lord Marcus gave me what I should have described as an imploring look.

"It was not just one dead man, Your Lordship. Two were taken sick not three nights ago; one died. Another died almost four weeks ago. We are in the course of resolving the matter and have several leads, but what we know for certain is that it was poison, and not cholera nor any other disease, that killed the men. In my opinion, it would be extraordinarily rash, if not actually dangerous, to hold the banquet."

"Marcus?"

It was Ellice who spoke; he bowed deeply. "Your Lordship, Captain Avery tends to exaggerate the matter."

I gaped.

"It is possible that there have been one or two casualties. However, the club's distinguished physician disputes that it was poison. He believes the cause to have been cholera, or some other gastric disease. The kitchens have been scrupulously cleaned twice over. There is no real cause for concern, but we wished to take the greatest care and so we thought it wiser to call off the banquet."

"I see," said Lord Palmerston.

"And should it prove to be the case that there was poison, we have a very plausible suspect. One of the kitchen maids who is just now being questioned by the police. There seems to be a good case against her."

"Mr. Ellice, this is monstrous," I said. "You cannot at one moment claim that nothing has happened, and at the next say that an innocent kitchen maid is to blame!"

"Captain Avery, is it not true that you have done your best to impede the inquiry into this girl? That you have some prior connection with her?" Ellice managed to make "connection" sound like a dirty word. "Things are at stake here that you do not understand. The fact is that, if poisoning has taken place, we can be quite confident that we have the culprit, and that we should have no further problems on that score. In my opinion, we should go ahead with the banquet, Your Lordship."

"I am not confident!" I said, furious at his lies and at his accusation. "This is nonsense!"

"So, which is it, three dead or one? Poison or no poison?" said Palmerston irritably.

"Three dead of poison!" I said. "I should add that I am convinced that the poisonings are deliberate and that their aim is to harm the Reform Club. The banquet provides a perfect opportunity to wreak havoc. How would it be if the prime minister or Ibrahim Pasha himself were poisoned?"

"Oh, that is not at issue. Ibrahim Pasha brings his own food taster." Lord Palmerston laughed to himself. "So, three possible deaths—"

"Which, as founder of the club, I refute," said Ellice.

"—compared with how many safely fed? Hundreds, Monsieur Soyer?"

"Yes, milord," said Soyer. I was aghast.

"What do you think, Collinson?" said Palmerston. "You pride yourself on giving good counsel."

"I, sir, I am not the custodian of a party or a club."

"Always on the fence, eh, Collinson?"

I could hardly believe what I was hearing. Collinson looked at me and half smiled. He had known this was coming, and his prison maneuver had put me into a position where I must comply.

"This is what shall be done," said Palmerston. "The club will issue a public assurance that all rumors regarding any poisoning here are entirely untrue."

Lord Marcus looked shocked. "But—"

Palmerston fixed him unblinkingly with his hooded eyes. "You have said as much. This must be done. For the sake of the party and the club. Monsieur Soyer, you will prepare the banquet."

Soyer nodded obediently.

"You will have to do your best to catch up. We know you are a man who can work miracles—for you have often told us so. Call in your cooks and, if you distrust them, dismiss them and find new ones."

His Lordship glanced back at me. "I recall you now. Blake and Avery, of course. I have encountered Mr. Blake—he ran a few errands for me some years ago. A most unmannerly fellow, if effective. Is he here? We might make a little headway with him."

"Alas, Your Lordship, he is missing," said Collinson. "So we are left with only half our brave duo. But he will work wonders, I am sure."

"Well, then, Captain Avery, you have until tomorrow night to discover whether your suspicions are based in truth and, if so, to apprehend your poisoner. I am sure you will manage it. In the meantime, it cannot be beyond the abilities of the club to take every precaution to ensure that nothing untoward takes place during the banquet. You were brought in to resolve this, Captain. What would you do?"

I said the first thing that came into my head. "I would form a military cordon. I would have soldiers observing the food from the moment it came in—or before—until it was served to the diners."

"A military cordon from the farmyard to the fricassee, as it were." The phrase seemed to please him, and he paused for a moment. "An excellent notion."

"But, sir, the club really does not have the resources . . ." said Lord Marcus faintly.

"Find them," said Palmerston curtly. "The Reform has some very wealthy members, yourself included, Marcus. I am sure the money can be found and arrangements made."

"But a military cordon?"

"Use your initiative. Captain Avery must have connections."

"I was in the East India Company Army, sir, not the British Army."

"Pish. Surely this is why you are here. You will arrange the security of the food. Marcus, you could provide a few troops. You had a commission in your younger days, and I seem to recall there are one or two generals among the members."

"Perhaps you yourself might use your—"

"We are in opposition, Marcus. I cannot be seen to overplay my hand. I am accused of ordering our forces about rather too much as it is." He brought a finger up to his lips and considered. "But I will do what I can. Now, are we all agreed?"

Like cowed schoolchildren, they nodded. And, for my sins, I nodded, too.

"THIS WAS WHAT it was about," Blake said, tight-mouthed. "Collinson knew they would let the banquet go ahead." He was as angry as I had ever seen him. "I will not collude with this bloody deluded exercise in idiocy. And not just idiocy but willful gambling with the lives of others. They fear embarrassment so they take the stupidest risk possible."

"I know, but Lord Palmerston says that peace depends upon it."

Blake snorted. "Lord Palmerston's reputation depends on it. I used to believe that reason was—what did Thomas Paine call it?—'the most formidable weapon against errors of every kind.' But men aren't guided by reason, but by ignorance, self-righteousness and stupidity."

"Reason is your weapon against them, Blake," I said. "And it is true that, if we leave now, we leave the poisoner the field. He can do what he likes."

Blake shook his head. "We are blackmailed into condoning their monstrous act."

"I do not condone it. It is rash, vain, stupid, dangerous. But I cannot go anywhere. As Collinson reminded me, I have a wife and a newborn child. And if I stay, at least I can do my best to prevent more deaths. If the dinner were not taking place, I would still be searching for the poisoner. I would have confronted Duncombe and Molesworth by now."

He gazed at me from under his brows, a pensive, sullen look.

"But Blake, you should go. There is no justification for this banquet, and you cannot live under Collinson's hand. I see that now."

He ran his hands through his hair.

"I escaped from prison and gave up passage to America so that a band of spoiled Whigs can give a lavish dinner at which they'll likely poison themselves and an oriental tyrant. And we are supposed to save them."

"There's Matty."

He gave an angry half laugh. "If there's another death and Matty's in jail, she is at least vindicated," he said. He slammed his palm against the wall. "So, we have until tomorrow night. I suppose Soyer gave in at once. Naturally, he did. He cannot resist an appeal from a fucking milord."

"Blake."

"This place," he said bitterly.

"The world, you mean."

He gave another angry laugh.

Chapter Seventeen

The kitchen had come alive again. The gaslights blazed, the sounds of steam were everywhere. Kitchen maids frantically scrubbed and swept, potboys carried buckets, chefs had begun to chop and set stew pans on the gas ranges. Soyer stood at the center of the kitchen, as if he had never been away, his hat was at its familiar angle, he had changed into his mauve velvet jacket, and his fingers were laddered with rings.

Catching sight of us, Soyer turned quickly away. Within a minute, he had disappeared into his office with Morel and Percy, and closed the door. We were not to be so easily put off.

Papers were spread over every inch of Soyer's desk, and the three were bent over them. Beside me, I could feel Blake glowering. Morel was in no better humor.

"I do not see how we can have every item watched as it issues from farmyard to serving plate," Percy was saying.

"Ah, here is Captain Avery," said Soyer, careful not to catch Blake's eye. "He has been given the task of arranging the safety of the food. We shall speak in a moment, *Capitaine*. Would you allow us a moment?"

I stayed where I was. Soyer gave an overly bright smile and continued, "You are right: there are things we require—the lamb and beef, bones and vegetables for stocks, and so forth. We will purchase them from the most respected and prestigious suppliers. If soldiers can be provided, then they will be in attendance. We will order as much as we can direct from makers and farms—poultry, vegetables, and so on, and as much flour as we can from the Saxford mill. Percy, have we the table arrangements? Do we know how many guests we shall have at the dinner itself?"

"The pasha will come with his *chargé d'affaires* and his taster; there will also be three Egyptian officials present, including the consul general, along with Lord Palmerston and Admiral Sir Charles Napier, who will conduct Ibrahim Pasha to the Reform. There will be, in addition, nearly three hundred guests at the dinner.

"A band of the Scots Fusilier Guards will play various Turkish airs, among them 'The Sultan's March,' as well as 'The Roast Beef of Old England.'"

Blake cleared his throat. "Excuse me, Mr. Percy, are Turkish airs quite the thing? After all, Ibrahim Pasha is from Egypt, tried to conquer Turkey and failed."

"The band knows no Egyptian airs," said Percy, uncharacteristically testy. "Are there any? Turkish, Egyptian—they should be grateful we have embraced their general area." He paused and cleared his throat. "My apologies, Mr. Maguire, matters are rather more pressed than usual. Where was I? Tureens, platters and vases will be silver plate; bowls and plates will be porcelain with a simple gold band. The principal illumination will be from fifteen slender silver candelabra standing some three feet high, and the best beeswax candles. These will alternate with equally tall silver gilt vases of exotic flowers and plates of the finest fruits of the Orient: grapes, figs and peaches from hothouses in Wiltshire. The first courses will arrive promptly at seven."

"Very good," said Soyer.

Percy nodded. "Do you have the recipes, Morel?"

"I do not keep recipes. I never use them. Everyone knows that," said Morel irritably.

Did I imagine it, or did Percy give me a meaningful look?

"The copies are here, Percy," said Soyer. "Mathilde ordered them some days ago."

There was an awkward silence. Morel tapped his fingers noisily on the sideboard. "Well, does anyone know where she is? Has anything been done to aid her?" he asked.

"She is at Vine Street police station, where she spent the night, sir," said Blake.

"We will do our best to have her released," said Soyer. "But, for the moment . . ."

Morel bit his lip. "*Je voudrais vous parler, Chef.*"

"Would you mind?" said Soyer. The door shut upon Blake and me. Morel's voice, raised in indignation, sounded through the door.

"*Mais c'est impossible!* We have lost too much time! *C'est pas possible, c'est pas possible de surveiller tous les ingrédients.* We cannot watch every cook and apprentice! We cannot guarantee the safety of anyone who eats the food. It is mad, and you know it! Moreover, by acknowledging this danger still exists, we admit that we know young Mathilde cannot be guilty, and yet she is in prison! I beg you, Alexis, refuse them!"

Soyer's voice came in more quietly and indistinct, then Percy's, deeper and reassuring. Then Morel again. "I cannot do this. This is wrong."

I felt myself warm to Morel.

Soyer spoke again, and this time he was not gentle.

Morel flung open the door and pushed past me, striding off across the kitchen. We turned back into Soyer's room.

Soyer startled like a frightened animal. "Percy, can you leave me? I have things to discuss with Captain Avery."

Percy's eyes flickered. "Of course, Chef."

The door closed. Blake stared at Soyer, who, for once, was silent, but gradually seemed to curl up in shame. At last he said, almost imploringly, "I could not refuse. This is my position, my kitchen, my calling. This is a political club, and when Lord Palmerston demands, we must say yes. We must."

Blake nodded very slightly, very slowly, and let his eyes bore into Soyer. I almost pitied Soyer; I knew precisely how he felt.

"This is my *métier.* I cannot simply leave when I wish. I mean, I must cook for this banquet."

Blake said nothing.

"I know there is no excuse for it. I should have refused, but he would not be refused. And when I saw how Ellice was, I thought, *They will have their dinner anyway, and they will take my recipes, and they will have Morel or Perrin execute them, and they will get the credit.* I know it is vanity, and fear. I must have the world's approbation. I know it, and I am not proud of it. But I have worked upon these dishes for months. I have poured everything into them. It was to be the crowning moment of the Reform's existence, and mine . . . And I thought, *At least if it is my banquet, if I execute it, then I can do my best to prevent disaster,* and Blake—and you, Avery—will help me, and there are no men more tenacious, more brilliant in pursuit. I know if there is a death I shall be ruined forever." He bowed his head. "Tell me what to do. *S'il te plaît,* Blake, I beg you."

At last, Blake said, "And Matty? You did not even mention her to us."

Soyer sank his head.

"If there's a suspect in jail, the banquet can go ahead, can't it?" said Blake.

"That is unfair."

"What will you do about it, then?"

"Anything, whatever you say."

Blake looked disgusted. "And your precious soup kitchen?"

"I have made excellent arrangements. I will send a few of our junior cooks. I know it will run perfectly without me."

"I want you to know that we stay because Collinson has forced our hand—I won't bother to explain why—and to make sure Matty is safe, and because there cannot be any more deaths. We do not stay for you."

"*Non*, Blake, *je comprends bien*," he said humbly.

I said, "You must supervise everything you serve. Lord Marcus says he and Palmerston can provide a hundred Scots Fusiliers within two hours—their band is, in any case, to play at the dinner. Once the food has arrived in the kitchen, you must arrange it so that there will be no point when it will not be supervised. Even in the dining room with the waiters."

"Soldiers in the dining room?" said Soyer. "Surely this will raise suspicions? If this was to get out, my reputation would be finished. And what is to stop these soldiers telling all kinds of stories after the dinner?"

Blake glared at him.

He bowed his head. "Yes, of course," he said.

"I'll bet Percy can arrange some clever choreography so the soldiers will appear as some extra honor paid to the pasha. You will have to think of some way to persuade them to keep quiet. And there is little we can do to check on food coming in from your suppliers. You must apportion a certain number of dishes to each cook. They will be in charge of them. They will taste them at every stage of their construction. It is not foolproof, but it is the best that we can manage."

"I understand, but who can arrange this?" Soyer said frantically. "I am no soldier, and already two days late in my preparations. Perhaps you . . . ?"

"It's not hard. Each soldier will mark one cook. Cold rooms and storerooms to be guarded at all times. In addition, there must be a system whereby the staff check each other's work. And everything must be tasted. Over and over."

"They will not like it, any of it."

"If they wish to keep their jobs and to prevent more deaths, they will do what they're told."

Soyer looked downcast.

"We have a poisoner to catch and a dozen calls to make," said Blake irritably. "You chefs all claim that a well-run kitchen is like an army. You should be able to manage it."

Soyer gave the most ridiculous, noisy sigh I had ever heard.

Blake ground his teeth. "Avery and I will talk to the soldiers. You must, however, call your senior chefs together and convince them that, despite the apprehension of a suspect, there is still a chance the poisoner is at large and they must be vigilant and accept the scrutiny of the soldiers. Then you will do the same to the whole kitchen. Percy and his clerks can arrange who takes charge of what dishes. I imagine there will be some, like Monsieur Benoît, who will not make things easy. And you must do something about Matty."

"I will have her sent a good lunch."

"Alexis!" It was almost a snarl.

"I do not know! What must I do?" said Soyer pleadingly. "I will write to Lord Marcus saying I'm certain she is innocent. I will write to the police officer, the station . . . What must I do?"

Blake gave in again. "Send her a good lunch and a note, and make sure it gets to her. We will find the real culprit."

Once Soyer had left us, I said carefully, "You changed your mind."

"What do you mean?" said Blake irritably.

"You were kinder than I expected."

He muttered something that I could not quite hear, set his cap on his head and stalked away.

In the butler's room, Percy gave me a list of the club's chief suppliers. It was dispiritingly long. "Our biggest suppliers are those from whom we purchase vegetables and fruits at Covent Garden: Solomon's or Bentley and Adams's. For meat, we were using Hastings Bland in Smithfield Market and, for poultry, Slater in Leadenhall Market. But our trade with Bland's has declined; we have not ordered from them tonight, and in future we shall be using Robinson's."

The first of the deliveries that Soyer had angrily sent back had been from Hastings Bland.

"Why are you no longer using Bland?"

"He's a difficult cove, a Smithfield slaughterman turned butcher. We dealt with him direct, as he had good meat, and prices are better if you buy direct. But he was not sending us good enough meat and was argumentative over the bills. Tiresome. As for our smaller suppliers, just now we use Grove's of Bond Street and Jay's of Hungerford Market for fish; for specialist poultry, Bailey's in Davis Street; and for fine game, Newland's in Air Street. We use Mold's for foie gras, truffles and mushrooms; items may also be ordered from Paris. Butter and cheese from Roberts of Swallow Street. We use a number of wine merchants, most recently Davey and Pane in South Audley Street."

"And for milk and flour?"

"Wilson's brings fresh milk to us from just past Clapham. Flour comes from an excellent flour mill in Shropshire."

"How do you choose your suppliers?"

"They are quite simply the best in London. Chef would accept no less."

Outside in the kitchen, a small knot of soldiers had already arrived.

Morel and two of the kitchen clerks were attempting to herd them into a corner near the butchery, but even there they seemed to be in the way. Blake took Percy aside, and they muttered for several minutes.

"We'll take the soldiers up to the hall for the moment and gather some footmen to corral them," Blake said when he came back.

Morel strode past. He managed to look both anxious and morose.

"Monsewer Morel!" Blake grinned and clapped him on the back. Morel winced.

"Mr. Maguire, I regret that I do not have the time to engage you in discussion just now. I have the aspics and creams for sixteen *entremets* to oversee and I do not know what we are to do with all these fighting men."

"Maybe you should put us to work, Monsewer Morel," said Blake, his smile broadening.

"You and your master have your work," said Morel curtly. "We would simply like you to complete it."

We had both been officers. It did not take us long to organize the men, give them their orders and furnish the two lieutenants who had accompanied them with a set of instructions.

It was now about one o'clock.

"What do we do now?

Blake set his jaw. "We'll do as we planned. We'll check the suppliers to see if we can trace any contamination. We'll hear what they think about the Reform's reputation. Then we will tackle Francobaldi and, if necessary, Collinson's Russians, if they are truly a threat. Collinson sees conspiracy everywhere, and he loves to overcomplicate. In any time that's left, I shall be in the kitchen, watching."

"What about Duncombe and Molesworth?" I said.

"All right, Duncombe and Molesworth, too."

"We should visit Matty first." I thought of it as a small mutiny before we gave in to Collinson's will. "Or, rather, I should visit Matty. After yesterday with Loin, I cannot risk you in the presence of policemen."

He shrugged. "I'll stay in the kitchens."

VINE STREET was a dismal alley behind the eastern end of Piccadilly, and its police station a dour, flat-fronted brick building with great iron bars across its windows. One could hear shrieks and shouting coming from within.

Inside, a noisy crowd of drunken men and unfortunate women were protesting as constables rounded them up and herded them into the cells. I pushed my way to the desk, where I asked to see Miss Horner.

It was a cold, rank little room with an iron door, one small, high window and a bench against a wall. Matty sat on this, her knees clasped to her chest and wrapped about with a blanket. She was pale and tired, and her usually neatly coiffed hair had half tumbled out of its pins.

I hardly knew what to say.

"I am so sorry I was not there when you were taken."

She shook her head. "Loin saw to it I had the cell to myself and gave me a blanket." She spoke on one low note and did not meet my eyes.

I unwrapped a pie I had brought and gave it to her. "Eat," I said. She took a mouthful, almost mechanically, as if she were hardly aware of what she did.

"Has he told you how long they plan to keep you?"

"No. He just said he'd come back today to talk to me."

"Be of good cheer, Matty. We will get you out of here, I promise you. We will find the one responsible for all this and have you set free."

She looked at me now, dully. "It's like I told you, Captain. No one wanted it to be the kitchen but, if it has to be, then the quicker the culprit—any culprit—is found, the sooner it all returns to how it was. They want it sorted so they can open the club and have their dinner. They don't want to look further than me."

"Then their poisoner will still be at large. And Blake and I will not rest until we have him."

"Or her," she said, with a thin smile.

The constable rapped on the door. "Time's up."

"Matty, I promise you," I said. I put my hands on her shoulders and looked into her eyes. "I promise you, we will not abandon you."

She closed her eyes and a tremor ran through her, but she did not cry.

When I returned to the front counter, Loin was waiting.

"How is she?" Loin said.

"How do you expect? She thinks the world has conspired to take from her the little she has won for herself and that nothing can stop it."

He had the grace to look discomfited. "The evidence against her is circumstantial. I'd doubt there's enough to charge her, but I've no other leads and I've had words from above. I must treat her as a suspect."

"What words from above?"

He shrugged.

"There are plenty of other leads," I said. "You are in the Detecting branch. Detect! The club is full of feuds. Did you not see that all the dead men are Whigs? What about the radicals? There are plenty who have no love for the Whigs. Or, worse, what of the divisions between the Turks and the Egyptians?"

"The fact remains that, if food has been poisoned, the most likely source for it is the kitchen," said Loin.

I PLODDED DOWN PICCADILLY, back to the Reform, my steps increasingly reluctant.

On the steps of the club, a woman in a brown cloak and red-trimmed bonnet was remonstrating with the porter. He looked exasperated. No doubt he had been turning angry gentlemen away all day. Below her on the pavement, her maid stood amid a sea of baggage. A few paces away, a constable stood awkwardly, pretending to ignore the scene. I should have known her figure anywhere but so utterly unexpected was the sight of her that it took me a moment to believe it. She turned, saw me.

"William?"

It was my wife.

Chapter Eighteen

"Helen! Good heavens!" I said.

"You took your time!"

"Helen, my dear—"

"The porter would not let me in, nor tell me whether you were here," she protested, her voice wobbling slightly. "He insists the place is shut. And here is a constable of the famous Metropolitan Police who would do nothing to help me. I suppose that is what one must expect from Whigs. If your father knew you were here!"

"I'd rather you did not tell him."

"I arrive in London and go to the Oriental, thinking to surprise you, only to be told your belongings were moved three days since. And not a word to me."

I tried to put my arm about her and steer her away from the porter. "I did write, my dear," I said, in a low voice. "I just rather skated over the matter of the Reform. If you had asked Louisa, she would have—"

"You told your sister before you informed me. Of course."

"I did not want to concern you, with Frederick unwell. And it is an awkward matter, requiring discretion, not a social one, I assure you."

"I suppose it's all to do with the sainted Blake?" she said, rolling her eyes. I changed the subject.

"You look lovely, my dear. But what are you doing here? Where is Frederick? How is he? Is he eating well?"

"I look perfectly dreadful, and the baby is perfectly well. He has the nursemaid and wet nurse and Louisa, who is, of course, marvelous with him." Too late I saw that I had been tactless to press her on the baby. "I thought, since you had escaped to London, why should not I? I had a fancy for a few days in town. You promised me a visit years ago, and I am still waiting."

"I'm sorry," I said guiltily. "But you did not travel on your own?"

"Of course not. Sir Henry Darrow was kind enough to escort us. He had business in London. He was very gentlemanly. We spent the night in the railway hotel in Swindon. It was remarkably uncomfortable."

Sir Henry Darrow was an older widower who had taken a shine to Helen.

"And now the man will not let us in. I am exhausted. What are you going to do?"

"Sir." It was the porter, descending the steps to us. "I'm very sorry, but the lady cannot stand here. This is a gentleman's club."

"This is so insulting. I am a lady. I should be treated with respect," said Helen, somewhere between fury and tears, a place I knew better than I wished.

"You know me," I said to the porter. "I am staying here at the behest of Lord Marcus Hill and the committee. Could you at least let my wife into the hall to rest while we resolve what to do?"

He shook his head. "More than my job's worth," he said, or some such unhelpful nonsense. "And I'm afraid, sir, that the lady must take herself off the steps and away from the door. We cannot have a commotion on the steps."

"Then you must send a message at once to Mr. Percy or, if you cannot find him, Mr. Scott. Tell them Captain Avery is in need of immediate assistance."

"I'll do what I can, sir," said the porter dubiously.

"Oh, for goodness' sake, William, be a man!" said my wife, but she marched down the steps to where Sarah, her maid, stood forlornly among the baggage.

Her words stung me. I began to gather up the cases and bags.

"Morning, Sarah," I said. "Long journey."

"Marning, master, it was."

"Follow me," I said. "I shall take you in. We shall enter through the kitchens."

"The kitchens!"

Mr. Scott appeared at the front door, looking most disgruntled. I had never been more glad to see him. He was followed by Lord Marcus Hill.

Lord Marcus raised his thick brown eyebrows almost to his hairline and said, "Why, Captain Avery! Are you quite all right?"

"Lord Marcus, may I present my wife, Helen, who has traveled from Devon most intrepidly to give me a delightful surprise. Our arrangements, however, turn out to be a little at odds, as I have of course given up my rooms in Mayfair. My dear, this is Lord Marcus Hill, chairman of the Reform Club."

Lord Marcus swept down the steps, followed by the porter. He was all smiles. "My dear Mrs. Avery, it is a great, great pleasure to meet you. May I?" Helen offered her hand; he brought it to his lips. "Your wife is enchanting, Captain Avery."

She was very pretty. She looked up at him through lowered eyelashes and smiled. My uppermost feeling was relief.

"And you have arrived to discover you are without shelter! And it is all our fault!" He spoke in that slightly exaggerated attentive way that certain still-presentable older men speak to younger women. "We prevailed upon your husband to help us in our hour of need and pressed him to decamp to our humble lodgings. How thoughtless of us. And you must be so tired after your journey."

"I am quite fatigued, Lord Marcus, it is true," said Helen, tilting her chin and opening her eyes very wide. "But I have been so very foolish. I wished my arrival to be a surprise to my husband. I did not think before I came. And now, you see . . ."

"I think we absolutely must make an exception for Mrs. Avery and let her rest in the lobby while we hatch a plan to resolve the matter. Don't you, Scott?"

Scott, who had been skulking behind him, said, "Well, the rules—"

"Fiddlesticks to the rules," Lord Marcus snapped. "The club is closed, and the lobby is the least we can do. You"—he summoned the porter with a deft switch of his hand—"take Mrs. Avery's bags. Scott, bring some tea."

He took her hand and escorted her up the steps. The porter took as many of the bags as he could, until he began to stagger. Sarah, the maid, remained upon the pavement, unsure whether she should follow.

"And something for Sarah, too, my dear," I called.

"Of course, my dear," she said, turning her head very slightly.

"Captain, I think I may have a notion to please everyone," Lord Marcus said, and, seeing me holding a bag, "But where is your manservant?"

Helen said, "Your manservant?"

I interrupted her. "Mr. Maguire is on an errand. He will be back shortly." I took her hand and squeezed it urgently. "Helen, my dear, we have much to discuss later. Would you excuse me for just a few brief moments? I will join you in the lobby."

She gave me a look both mutinous and complicit.

I rushed down to the kitchens. Blake was standing in the corridor by Soyer's office, whence he could see into three kitchens at the same time.

"My wife has arrived. I was not expecting her. I do not know where she will stay, but I must resolve it. Lord Marcus mentioned my manservant. She does not know that you have escaped from prison, but she knows I was in London to see you and I cannot think that she will not recognize you."

"I'll make my way out of here. I'll be in Crown Passage, the Red Lion Tavern."

"I'll tell her I cannot stay long. But I will have to dine with her tonight," I said. "Perhaps after, we might manage a late visit to the Provence to find Francobaldi? And we must see the butcher, Hastings Bland at Smithfield."

When I reached the lobby, my wife was sitting in an armchair, attended by Lord Marcus, Mr. Scott and Mr. Percy.

"William," said she, "you did not tell me that Alexis Soyer cooks here! And these gentlemen have been speaking so highly of you, I found myself blushing!"

Lord Marcus took my arm and drew me aside. "Captain Avery, I should like to apologize for my earlier ill temper. May I say how grateful I was for your sensible and timely support at the committee meeting. Most British! It was a dreadfully close-run thing." Then, more loudly, "I think I have a capital solution to our quandary. My brother and I own a building off St. James's Square, very close to here. There is within it a small apartment in which we occasionally lodge foreign dignitaries who come to visit the party. I should be *honored* if you and your delightful wife were to occupy it. As I was just telling Mrs. Avery, it is very well appointed—three fine rooms with gaslights and heated water. Somewhere for the servants to lay their heads."

"Well, I—"

"Oh, William, do say yes!"

"Do, Captain Avery," said Lord Marcus. "I think it will resolve matters perfectly. I feel this is the least I can do for you. I can arrange for it to be made ready for your arrival in a matter of hours. In the meantime, dear lady, I would offer you a tour of our famous kitchens—they are a veritable wonder of the world—but I must confess they are shut today."

"To tell the truth, I am very tired."

"The club does have strict rules about the admission of ladies," said Lord Marcus, "but since it is closed today I am sure that, just this once, we may permit Mrs. Avery to withdraw to her husband's room for a few hours to recover from her journey."

Scott nodded grudgingly. "Though it might be best not to bruit it too much abroad."

"I am overcome by your kindness, Your Lordship!" said Helen, and smiled charmingly.

HELEN LAID HER BONNET on the bed and arranged herself on the chaise longue, her cloak wrapped tightly around her shoulders.

"I am so sorry you have had such a time finding me. But now you may rest." I began to talk rather too fast. "The rooms are very comfortable, are they not? I have sent Sarah to draw a bath for you—they have faucets where the hot water comes steaming straight out; it is the height of luxury. The fire will be lit shortly."

She frowned. "You are going somewhere."

"I must, Helen. I have work to do. It is why I am here. But I will be back before long to change for dinner. And perhaps I need not leave at once. How are you? Are we dining out?"

"I am perfectly well, of course. We are invited to dinner by Lady Falkland. I wrote to say I was coming up and she insisted we must come."

I knew that if I pressed her further, I should either upset her or make her angry, but I could not stop myself. When we were alone, the distance between us seemed to yawn, and at the same time I felt her fragility so deeply. "Truly? No gloomy days? Bad thoughts? Is that why you came?"

"No," she said shortly. "I told you, I needed a change. Lord knows Bainton is dull enough."

I sat down beside her. "How are you? Please tell me. How is the house? How is Freddy?"

"All perfectly well. Do not press me, William, it makes it worse."

"My dear." I felt myself put too much into the words. "I am sorry."

"No more apologies." She gave a laugh. "I need some things. A new dress, gloves and a bonnet and a shawl, and some alterations to my old things. Surely we can afford it? We are not paying for our lodgings."

"Of course, my dear."

"Shall I meet Mr. Soyer?"

"Most certainly, but it would be better to wait until after our work is done. He is very preoccupied just now. In a few days," I said.

"Where are you going now?"

"To the kitchens."

"To see Mr. Soyer?"

"I can explain."

"Not now. I am tired."

"You do not wish to know what I am doing?"

She waved her hand vaguely. "Later, perhaps. I hope it is not dangerous."

"It is not. But I do have work to do here—neither social calls nor dangerous—but they will take me away from you, for the next two days, and then I should be free."

"No matter. Just tell me: where is Blake in all this?"

"Not here."

She pulled her shawl closer about her. "I am not a fool, William. When did you acquire a manservant?"

"We judged it would be more useful for our inquiry if Blake was in disguise. No one knows."

"His idea, I suppose. Getting you into trouble again. Very well. I shall see you later."

I felt a rush of contrition. "Good-bye, my dear." I kissed her forehead. She did not look at me.

"WHAT SHALL we say to these suppliers?" I said ill-temperedly to Blake as we strode up to Piccadilly. I still believed we should have seen Duncombe first. "'Tell us whether you are sending poisoned goods to the Reform'? They are hardly going to confess that they have been lacing the butter."

Blake rearranged his hair over his scar and set his cap back on his head. "You're an entrepreneurial gentleman of means moving up to London."

"You mean, in trade?" I said, my dismay palpable.

Blake ignored me. "Money talks loudest. You plan to set up a small club catering to your friends' epicurean tastes, and you are looking only for the best. Once you are talking, you will mention you acquired your list of suppliers from the great Monsieur Soyer himself. See what they answer. We simply want a feel of these places. It'll be enough."

"I am a soldier, not an actor!" I protested. "I cannot carry such a thing off. It is demeaning."

"There's not much acting involved. These types do not expect much from their grander customers; they prefer them ignorant."

We worked our way through the small emporiums around Bond Street and the farthest end of Piccadilly. I would ask for the senior clerk, set my questions, Blake standing respectfully at my elbow. I would be prevailed upon to try a little cheese or cured meat, or inspect a game bird or taste a slice of pie. Then I would mention the Reform. At the first establishment, there was a short and awkward pause, followed by a speech in fulsome praise of the club: how honored they were to supply it, what an exemplary customer it had been. The same momentary hesitation was evident at the second, and at the third the manager said, "Of course we hope Monsieur Soyer's unfortunate . . ." before he remembered himself and came to a halt.

At Davey and Pane in South Audley Street, the elderly wine merchant had a particularly antique but charming manner. I introduced myself in the usual way and asked about the wines and sherries while Blake quietly looked about. The place had the air of a church and the smell of a schoolroom, with its wood panels and highly polished tables. There was not a bottle in sight. The gentleman asked me if I was a Devon man. I answered in the affirmative, and he said he had grown up there and knew the Bainton Averys; he had been supplying a great-uncle of mine (my one rich relative, whom I hardly knew and liked little better) with wine for years. He brought out a number of small glasses and fine old bottles and insisted I taste them.

Blake scowled at me. "We do not have time for this," he hissed, and pressed a scrap into my hand.

Ask about sharp practice and get a move on, it said.

"My dear sir," said I, when he returned, "may I ask you a question?"

"Ask away."

"I am somewhat of an innocent when it comes to this business. I know there is sharp practice about—of what should I be wary?"

"Sad to say, sir, supply is not as honest a business as it should be. But it has ever been so. May I be blunt, sir?"

"Please."

"You should watch your accounts and keep an eagle eye on your chef or butler. There are certain practices . . ."

"Please enlighten me."

"It is not uncommon for a butler in charge of a large establishment to demand commissions—or 'presents,' as they are called—from his suppliers in return for his custom. Another trick: each month, a butler or steward will come to the supplier and demand that an extra few pounds or more be added to the monthly bill. This sum he will offer to divide with the supplier; if the supplier refuses, the customer will not merely take his custom elsewhere, he will denounce him and claim his goods are shoddy or that he is dishonest. So, if the supplier refuses, he loses custom; if he accepts, he is drawn into fraud. It is most tiresome. If you really wish to have the best and to pay the right price for it, you must watch out for such things, or make a kind of peace with your staff."

He gave me an almost fatherly look, as if he was quite sure that I should certainly fail to take his advice.

"This must give rise to a good deal of bad blood?"

"Most tradesman are inured to it, sir. Some are happy to profit by it. Some find it wearing."

"There must be establishments where this is not the case? I should be most amazed and disappointed if Monsieur Soyer at the Reform were engaged in such things."

His answer was carefully politic. "Of course, I cannot comment on individual cases, but the Reform is good enough to use our cellars, and I am certain they do not find them wanting."

I left with two very fine and expensive bottles of claret I had not intended to buy.

OUR LAST VISIT WAS to Bentley and Adams's greengrocers, in Covent Garden Market. They had made the second delivery that had so enraged Soyer he had sent it back.

I had first walked through Covent Garden the previous November, marveling even in that dark season at the streets dyed green by the trodden corpses of leaves and the fat, ripe perfume of flowers and fruits. In early spring, the effect was even more dazzling: lines of early flowers, many impossibly hothoused, and pyramids of exotic fruits—melons and pineapples—I had never thought to see outside India.

Bentley and Adams stood out from its row of stalls by virtue of its long frontage and the elaborate arrangement of its fruits and vegetables. Outside, there were boxes of potatoes and carrots, onions and cauliflowers, leeks and beetroots, piled upon each other. At the stall's entrance a display of handsome asparagus and rhubarb, young carrots, radishes, the first small lettuces and a few very early peas. Below, boxes of luminous oranges and lemons. Clearly, the stall regarded itself as well above the cut of the other vegetable merchants.

Inside, it had the air of a counting house. A clerk in a long white apron and shirtsleeves sat on a stool at a high desk. There was a counter of plain, polished wood, which Blake said was for the servant trade. "I shall speak for us this time," he said. "They expect to deal with servants." I waited in the doorway.

There was a genial man in a spotless apron and a smart jacket at the counter. Blake gave his story. Mr. Bentley, for it was he, liked to talk.

"Oh, Mr. Soyer, what a man! A genius, I should say. What he can do with one of my modest old leeks, or just a potato, well, it's a miracle, a piece of magic, I tell you."

"You've tasted his food? You are very fortunate."

"He has been so kind as to invite me to his snug at the Reform to sample some of his dishes. I won't hear a word said against him."

"Does anyone say a word against him?" said Blake.

"Why, no . . . I meant it simply as an expression."

"I have heard he can be very fussy, sends goods back for no good reason, doesn't pay his bills," said Blake insinuatingly.

"May well have been one of my deliveries!" said Mr. Bentley cheerily. "You must understand, Mr. Soyer is a perfectionist. One expects a little bad weather from such a man now and again, especially in a long-existing business arrangement. Sometimes we do not quite hit the mark, and he will take only the best. I am proud to supply him."

"Does the Reform pay its bills on time?" asked Blake in a confidential tone.

"I do not know what business it is of yours," said Mr. Bentley, startled.

"None at all. My gentleman is a great admirer of Soyer, but he has heard certain rumors."

Mr. Bentley picked up a bundle of asparagus. Blake leaned against the counter, looking entirely at his ease.

"Well, perhaps I should not say," Bentley said, "but the kitchen *is* a little slow to pay. I had heard the club was overstretched. I expect to get my money in the end. I trust the man and have good reason to."

"How d'you mean?" said Blake.

"His soup kitchen for the poor in Spitalfields. The silk weavers have suffered terribly, you know, from competition from the mills in the north. It's a great shame. Mr. Soyer has set up a subscription to pay for it, but most of the money will come from his own pocket. I know, because me and Solomon's next door have supplied most of the vegetables. Tons of onions and carrots."

"ENOUGH!" I SAID, as we departed the green-stained streets of the market. "No more grocers. Nearly a whole afternoon, and what have we accomplished?"

"You think we got nothing? We know the club is delaying payment and the suppliers are antsy. We know how the servants work scams. We know that at least one supplier whose produce Soyer has sent back is not raging against him."

"Can we not try Duncombe?" I said. "He must be out of bed by now."

"Captain Avery!" Duncombe made a great show of welcoming me. "Such a pleasure to see you again! I was just on my way to change for dinner, but I should far rather receive you." He seemed quite immaculate to me, in a narrow-waisted frock coat of silver gray, with a pale blue silk cravat and a waistcoat in blue-and-gray silk paisley.

"May I offer you a libation?" He looked past me with a gleam of anticipation. "This isn't, by any chance, the famed Mr. Blake?"

Blake and I fell over each other's words in answering in the negative.

"My manservant Maguire," I mumbled.

"My mistake," said Duncombe. "It is simply that I really am most intrigued by your erstwhile colleague. And I must apologize for my condition on your last visit—not worthy of a gentleman at all. Though may I say that despite the sad news that you bore, I was truly glad to make your better acquaintance."

"Not at all, Mr. Duncombe, think nothing of it." Neither of us mentioned having seen the other at the Reform the evening of Addiscomb and Rickards's poisoning.

"Madame Rumor whispers that the club is closed for a second day. I trust you will manage to resolve matters, Captain Avery. Indeed, I have guessed why you wish to see me, and, though I know the evidence may seem to add up, I must plead not guilty. It was not me, or not me alone."

"I see," I said, bemused. "I have not yet accused you of anything."

"But you were about to," he said, leaning forward confidentially.

"You have heard then about . . . ?"

"Well, naturally."

"I see," I said, entirely put off my stride. "And you thought that I—"

"Well, why would you not jump to conclusions? I would have. I know you saw me with Molesworth at the club the other night. The truth is, I did play a role. Though I am dreadfully sorry for it."

I thought of that table of Duncombe, Molesworth and the butterfly brigade, and I saw him drinking with Addiscomb and Rickards.

"So you were involved? You admit it?" I said, amazed, and feeling an almost triumphant light-headedness.

He sighed. "I must take some responsibility."

"And who else?"

"Molesworth, principally, then some of our younger radical friends went further than they should have. You saw them the other night. Though I also imagine some of the staff have acted."

"I am astonished!" I said. "Why did you do it? Was it to break apart the club? To be revenged on the Whigs? On Lord Palmerston?"

Duncombe looked penitent. "Nothing so extreme. Simply to do some mischief, though some of the young ones are, admittedly, very angry."

"Some mischief! Is that what you call it?"

At this point, Blake coughed.

"Captain Avery, I think you are taking on a little," said Duncombe. "And really, my own part was quite small."

"Quite small? It cannot have been so small, Mr. Duncombe. We know that you were at Soyer's dinner when Mr. Rowlands was taken ill. I saw you drinking the healths of Rickards and Addiscomb two nights ago, only hours before they were taken ill. And we have discovered that you dined at the club some weeks ago, on the night on which Mr. Cunningham died."

"Captain Avery, I am confused. I thought Cunningham had a bad heart. What is this about?"

"Do not deny it, sir."

"Is it true, then, that another member died two nights ago?"

Blake coughed again and said, "Excuse me, sir."

I said, "You know it is, sir."

"I had heard rumors."

"Mr. Duncombe, you cannot take it back now. You seem extraordinarily composed, given the terrible damage you admit you have caused."

"I think that is going a little far, Captain Avery."

Blake poked me in the ribs. I ignored him. "Too far! You killed your friend and protégé in order to—"

"I what, Captain Avery?"

"You heard me, Mr. Duncombe."

Duncombe's expression turned from pleasant confusion to dawning horror. "Captain Avery, what is it precisely that you think I have done?"

"Mr. Duncombe, what is it you were admitting to?"

"Not that I had any involvement in the death of my friend! Or anyone else, for that matter."

"I thought—" I said, "I thought you were confessing that . . ."

"I see," said Duncombe, in a strained voice. "We were at cross purposes. I must say, I am aghast that you could think such a thing of me."

"I am sorry, sir." I could barely meet the man's eye. "A misunderstanding. But it does seem that you were the only member present on the three occasions when someone has died at the club."

Duncombe looked mortified. "I assure you that is a coincidence. I do not even recall being at the club on the night when Mr. Cunningham died. I had heard he had passed, but I do not even remember when it was."

"I did see you take a drink with Mr. Addiscomb and the Honorable Mr. Rickards?"

"Yes," he said in a hushed voice. "But I have always had acquaintances on every side of politics. It is not a crime. I have known Rickards for years. We were both in the Dragoons many years ago."

"I think, perhaps, I should take my leave, Mr. Duncombe."

Leadenly, I made for the door. I think, if a bolt of lightning had struck me at that moment, I would have been grateful.

Before I could depart, however, the door opened of itself and Molesworth came in.

We stared at each other.

"Avery," said Molesworth curtly. "And who is this?"

"My man Maguire. How do you come to be here, Mr. Molesworth?"

"That's an impertinent question. I did not know the club had engaged you to quiz committee members."

"I will do whatever I must to find the man responsible for the poisonings." I was a little taller than he, and he only some five years older than me. I did not feel at a disadvantage.

"I thought it had already been decided that it was the girl."

"She has not been charged, and I am certain she is innocent."

"In that case, we both agree that the banquet should not proceed."

I looked back at Duncombe. "I consider it most significant that you are together. You knew about Addiscomb and Rickards because he told you. And you, Mr. Molesworth, have not answered my question."

He glowered. "Why should I not be here? Duncombe is a good friend of mine."

"It has nothing to do with your discontent with the Reform Club, then?"

"You are very impertinent."

"Deny that you were furious with Lord Palmerston earlier—I saw it. And that you would happily see the club fall into chaos!"

"I admit it, I was furious. I was deliberately slighted in the most direct manner. I founded the Reform—not that joke Ellice—and now I find myself endlessly forced to the side. I am supposed to be part of a union of progressive politicians, but Palmerston ignores and insults my friends and me. Why would I not be angry? But if you are suggesting I would go out of my way to bring down the club—and I presume you mean by murdering other members—you must be mad!"

"I would bring to your attention, sir, the *fact* that all the dead men were Whigs. And the *fact* that your friend Mr. Duncombe here was the only person who was present on all three evenings when the men died."

"The only person apart from the staff," said Molesworth.

"And Rowlands was my dear friend!" protested Duncombe.

"If you think Tommy could murder anyone—why, the very thought is absurd. He is the kindest man alive; he could not harm anyone."

"Except the tradesmen he puts out of business through not paying his debts," muttered Blake.

"What did your man say?"

"You would swear that you have no thought of cutting off from the Whigs and liberals and throwing your cards in with the Chartists?"

"What business is it of yours? You are a Tory. In any case, the Chartists are Tommy's particular interest, not mine."

"But you do not deny it."

"The radicals are being sidelined; we are outnumbered. What do we do? Accept it and endeavor to work within the party, hoping that, at some point, some of us might gain high office? At some stage, this Whig alliance will wrest power from the Tories. Or do we cut free, follow our true beliefs and possibly deny ourselves access to influence ever again? It is a question that has to be asked. Obviously, when I dreamed up the

Reform, I assumed the former was the best choice. But I would be dishonest, if not foolish, if I was not now to accept that the latter position has its points."

"So you will leave?"

"You do not know me, Captain Avery. I am a radical and an establishment man, just like Tommy. I feel the Reform Club is mine, in part at least, even if it is not quite the child I hoped it would be. I am proud that it is so much more progressive than the other clubs and that it admits Catholics and nonconformists and Jews, and that its table is the best in the land. I do not want to see it go down. On the other hand, I do not see why we should not cause a little mischief now and again to shake up those who consider it theirs."

"In the midst of a series of poisonings?"

"In the midst of the ostrichlike reactions and denials of men like Ellice."

"And what exactly do you mean by 'mischief'?"

Duncombe handed me a copy of a magazine entitled *The Satirist*.

"I assumed you must have seen it," Duncombe said. "It is hardly *The Times*, but something of the Reform's troubles have been leaked, and Molesworth and I were the sources. The other night at the Reform when you saw us, we told our fellow radicals about Rowlands. I know I promised you discretion, and I am sorry for it. That was the reason for my 'confession.'"

"I see. I apologize if I was unmannerly. I can only say it was based on a misunderstanding on my part."

He smiled hollowly. "Perhaps one day I shall laugh about it."

"GIVE IT HERE," SAID BLAKE, once we were outside, and took the magazine from me. "It's one of those London scandal sheets full of rumor and innuendo. They send a damaging story to the party concerned to see if they'll pay to suppress it. Sometimes they print it anyway." He scanned the page that Duncombe had marked. "I'd say this is a teaser." He held it out for me.

A certain gentleman's club not a million miles from St. James's has suddenly closed its doors mere days before it was to hold a famous banquet to celebrate a certain eastern potentate. Could it be that the infamous shadow of scandal can have penetrated its blameless doors and is stalking its marble halls? Or that the self-styled "greatest chef in London" no longer casts quite the spell he did? Whispers have come to our ears that certain members are dying to take their leave.

Blake said, "At least they have been careful."

"Careful?"

"It might have been worse."

"Worse? How could it have been worse?"

"It could have said, 'Soyer kills three with arsenic and strychnine.'"

OUR LABORS, it seemed to me, had produced nothing substantial. I had mishandled our encounter with Molesworth and Duncombe, and there were barely twenty-four hours until the banquet. I did not complain aloud, for I was increasingly sensible of Blake's sacrifice in remaining with me. But I was discouraged, and so we walked in silence.

"You weren't as bad as you imagined," he said at last.

"I lost my temper, I utterly misunderstood Duncombe and I humiliated myself. What if Molesworth goes to Lord Marcus and denounces me?"

"You know that he informed the press. I shouldn't imagine he wants

Lord Marcus to hear about that. It is not how I would have done it, but you were sincere, which inclined them to answer you honestly. Your anger was honest anger, not feigned to provoke. Duncombe admitted the radicals are angry, and you caused Molesworth to explain himself. I'd bet he never talks so freely at the Reform."

"You are becoming alarmingly charitable in your old age, Blake," I said. "And we are no nearer finding our quarry."

I returned to my wife, he to the kitchen to "observe." We agreed that we would make a late visit to the Provence Hotel after dinner, and that we would go to Smithfield in the morning before first light, when the livestock market was at its height and Hastings Bland the butcher would be at his labors.

WHEN I ENTERED HER ROOMS, Helen was scrutinizing herself in a long glass. I thought I recognized the dress but was not sure.

"Very pretty," I said uncertainly.

She shook her head. "It is years old. I was measured for a new gown this afternoon, but it will not be ready for several days, so Sarah will add lace to the collar of this one, and sleeves and some beads to the bodice, and that will be something."

She was at least delighted with the lodgings provided by Lord Marcus. The rooms were furnished in silks and velvets, and the address—King Street, St. James's—was the most fashionable she could have wished for.

"Lord Marcus has most generously supplied us with a cook. He may be a liberal, but he is really a very charming man. So attentive. But I suppose you are not going to be present for meals."

"I am—"

"—very busy, I know."

"May I explain what we are doing?" I tried to tell her, but when the matter of poison came up I could tell she was reluctant to hear.

"Another of your wild-goose-chase adventures with Mr. Blake, I suppose?" she said.

At the appointed hour, I escorted her to Lady Falkland's. Lord Falkland had been a senior figure in the Indian government and had lately returned to England. Helen had been a favorite of his wife's in Simla during the war with Afghanistan. She looked charming and was made a great fuss of. I answered questions about the quality of the shooting in Devon and my role in solving the Holywell Street murders. I fended off inquiries about "the enigmatic Mr. Blake"—former Company men were always curious about him—and more regarding my possible candidacy as a future Tory member of Parliament. We were declared "the picture of a charming young couple," by Lady Falkland, and Helen came away with a clutch of invitations. I think she was happy. And I? The day's events clung to me: the looming threat of the banquet, the picture in my head of Matty in her cell, the smell of the Marshalsea.

We returned home by carriage: Lord Marcus had lent us his clarence for the evening. Outside, a figure slipped from the muddy gloaming and materialized under a gaslight. Helen stiffened and clutched my arm.

"Mrs. Avery," said Blake, "you know me." He removed his spectacles and his hat.

She peered at him. "Is that you, Mr. Blake? Or whatever William is calling you now. It has been four years, I think."

"Yes, madam. I am going for the moment under the name Maguire."

"I suppose you want my husband?"

"If you are both agreeable."

"You must promise you will not take him into danger."

"No danger, madam. Not tonight."

"Then I will bid you good night."

The footman ushered her into the house.

We set off at a brisk pace, the gaslights providing pools of light in the darkness.

"Where have you been?"

"Went into a couple of taverns round Crown Passage. There's a deal of gossip about a man dying horribly in the dining room of one of the clubs. More bloody with each retelling. Innards on the Turkey carpets, all that. What about your wife?"

"She does not know you are a wanted man."

Chapter Nineteen

We were neither of us much in the mood for carousing, but the guests at the Provence very much were. Frenchmen crowded the tables, drinking and gossiping. Francobaldi himself was in the thick of the drinking, red-faced and laughing; I pointed him out discreetly to Blake. At a table on his own, Morel watched his fellow cooks, his expression morose.

"No cards tonight, Monsieur Morel?" I said.

"I have made my wagers for today. And I am not in the mood for crowds." As if to confirm this, one of the carousers looked over and met his eye, nodded respectfully and turned back to his friends. "By all means, sit down. Have you news of Mathilde?"

I sat down. "Maguire," I said, "bring us a bottle of claret and buy something for yourself."

"Very good, sir," said Blake. Morel looked at Blake just a little longer than necessary then turned his attention to the party. We watched silently for a while.

"Might I pour Monsewer Morel a fresh glass, sir?" Blake said, when he returned with a bottle.

Morel flinched but nodded. My glass filled, I raised it. "Your health, sir." Morel nodded. "It has been a hard day," I said.

He nodded again, heavily. "One must try to make the best of things, I suppose." He smiled ironically.

"Monsieur Morel, you know that Monsieur Soyer has asked me to help him. May I ask for your advice?"

"Of course," he said reluctantly.

"It seems to me there is some rivalry among your community of chefs."

He looked at me warily.

"I wondered, seeing you there alone, whether you might be asking yourself which of your fellow chefs you would entirely trust."

"I must tell you that I was not. There *is* rivalry, of course. But if you are considering that one of these men might be responsible for the deaths at the Reform, I should say that was impossible."

"And why is that?"

"They may strive to exceed each other, but they do not truly wish each other ill. There may be rivalry, but there is also admiration. Monsieur, there are so few of us who understand what we strive for, we are precious to each other. And to poison our dishes? It would be like a doctor breaking his oath. It is impossible. Also, how does a chef from another kitchen effect such a thing? You ask my advice? I will tell you." He looked me full in the face, his expression pained. "I wish it were not true, I know that Alexis cannot bear for it to be true, but if someone poisons our diners deliberately, how can it be anyone other than someone within the Reform itself?"

"In the kitchen?"

"Where else?"

"You have an idea of whom?"

"If I did, I would tell you. Believe me, until a few days ago I thought our kitchen was a perfect engine, all the parts working toward the same end." Now he seemed bitter. "But I think it would be impossible to carry out such things from outside, unless one had aid from someone within."

"Then let me ask a different question," I said. "Is there anyone else here I should speak to who might be able to throw any light on this matter?"

Morel seemed irritated. "I can think of no one."

"Could one of Soyer's rivals"—I groped for an example and thought of the boy whom Benoît had almost stabbed with a knife—"tempt someone dissatisfied with their progress, or short of money, or beaten too many times, with the promise of money and promotion? Something is added to a sauce and Soyer's reputation is destroyed?"

Morel sat up, almost agitated. "I would say it is not possible."

"Monsieur Morel, it was you who told me that Francobaldi had no self-control and would do anything to best Soyer. And you who said that the man I saw him strike here, Monsieur Comte, was little better."

"I have no love for Francobaldi, believe me." The words emerged jerkily. "His desire to triumph in all things is tedious. His resort to violence is childish. On occasion, I have thought he must be mad. But if he wished to harm Soyer he would take a knife and stab him; he would not do it in this way. Besides, I cannot believe him a murderer."

I was startled by the effect my question had had upon him. "Someone else, then. Monsieur Comte, with whom he had the—ah, argument when I was here last?"

"He is very ambitious, but it is unthinkable."

"More unthinkable than one of your own cooks poisoning your dishes?"

He looked down and pursed his lips. Blake nudged me and shook his head.

"I am sorry to have disturbed you, Monsieur Morel. I have no wish to make your evening worse."

"Why did you pull me back?" I asked Blake.

"He wasn't going to tell you any more."

"You are sure of that, are you?" I said.

He nodded. "Besides, I've been watching him."

I looked at him hopefully. "I've nothing to say," he said. "Just notions."

"I wish you would share some of those notions with me."

On the other side of the room, Francobaldi stood up and sauntered toward the door, and I followed after him.

"Captain Avery! Captain Avery!" His breath was thick with brandy fumes, but the drink had loosened him rather than inebriated him. He tipped his hat. "So, you have put yourself at Alexis's service, eh? Tell you what, the bugger's going to need it. This your man?" He gave Blake a cursory glance. "I like you, Captain Avery. You are a soldier, a real man, who is not content to sit back and let the world have its way with you. You have fought for your life, and I salute that. Come and talk to me about Soyer. I'll tell you what you need to know. Come and see me. Tomorrow morning." He clapped me, too hard, on the back. "I know things. I'll be in the kitchen at the Union. You may learn something useful."

He stepped in front of me and pushed his way out into the dark.

"Where did you say he was from?" said Blake.

Returning to Lord Marcus's rooms, we found a message from Mr. Percy apologizing for the late hour but requesting my presence at the club as close to midnight or thereafter as could be managed. Gimbell would let me in, he said. I longed for my bed, but the possibility of news could not be ignored.

There were still a few at work when Blake and I arrived at the kitchen: a couple of Perrin's sauce-makers, with their accompanying soldiers, waiting for vast cauldrons of bones to boil, and two pastry cooks almost asleep over their whisks.

In the butler's room, Mr. Percy was still in his daytime suiting. "I am so sorry to call you from your slumbers," he said.

"You have discovered something about the poisoning?"

He looked guilty. "Oh lord, sir, I'm sorry if I gave that impression. It is something else I hoped you could help us with, for which your presence would be most welcome."

"You are very cryptic, Mr. Percy," I said.

"All will soon be revealed," he said, and smiled. He lit a candle and passed it to me.

"Lead on," I said, bemused.

We followed him up the servants' stairs to the ground floor, across the saloon, up again to the mezzanine floor and along a corridor into which I had not hitherto strayed. The fearsome housekeeper, Mrs. Quill, whom I remembered from the night Rowlands had died, was waiting for us, wrapped in a great quilted bedcoat, her nightcap tied under her chin, holding her own candle.

"Well," she said briskly, "do what you must, Mr. Percy."

Before us was a row of identical brown paneled doors. Percy rapped on the first. There was no reply. The incarnation of calm dignity, he gave two further knocks. The housekeeper pursed her lips and stared at the door as if it had itself committed a crime. A sense of unease began to rise within me. I had not even troubled to ask why my presence was so necessary. Beside me, Blake was very still.

Percy now inflicted upon the door a round of rapid knocks and called out, "Mr. Scott, are you there? We must speak. It is very important."

There came no answer. Percy smiled reassuringly and turned to the housekeeper.

"Will you do the honors, Mrs. Quill?"

She brought forth a ring heavy with keys and, passing me her candle for a moment, extracted one with thumb and forefinger and passed it to Mr. Percy. He took it, fitted it to the keyhole, turned it smoothly within the lock and opened the door.

It was very dark. I made out a curtained window visible only by its blue-lit edges. Percy and the housekeeper walked across the room, and Percy set his hand to another door and opened it. There was a scream and the oddly recognizable sound of sheets and coverlets being fumblingly arranged. Blake and I followed behind. Looking over Percy's shoulder, I saw Mr. Scott in the middle of the bed, a coverlet drawn up to his nose. On one side of him was a girl in some undress, quite horrified, whom I did not recognize. On the other was a prone figure covered by the sheet, making a vain attempt to hide. Strewn across the floor were various articles of clothing. Not wishing to make the scene any more awkward than it was, I remained in the shadow, with Blake behind me.

Percy looked resigned. Mrs. Quill, however, palpitated with outrage.

"Mr. Scott! How could you!"

"Now look here!" Scott said weakly, pulling the sheet more tightly about his neck. "What on earth is the time? How dare you march in here!"

"Netty!" said Mrs. Quill, in a voice that would have struck fear into a small military division. The girl, I saw, was very young and frightened. "And who's the other one?" she said. "There's no help in hiding. Come on, covers off." The figure remained prone. The housekeeper seized the sheet. There was a struggle, wax was spattered everywhere and the sheet flew back. Matty's nemesis, Margaret, lay in the bed, bristling with anger, clutching the ends of the sheet to hide her modesty.

The housekeeper shook her head. "You foolish, foolish girls. You have destroyed your character and thrown away your position. What will you do now?" Margaret lay in mutinous silence. The younger girl lowered her head and began to cry quietly into her hands. Scott made no attempt to comfort her.

"Begone!" he demanded. "What a gentleman does in his own time is of no concern to anyone else. They were quite willing."

"It makes me choke to hear you, Mr. Scott," said Mrs. Quill. "And we all know it's not the first time either. We shall turn our backs, and you two girls will pick up your linen and leave. Take yourselves off and pack your belongings. I want you both gone before breakfast."

The sobs of the younger girl, Netty, became noisier. We turned away. There was some awkward shuffling, a crack of palm on skin and a noisy protest from Scott.

"Get away, you witch!"

Margaret had slapped him. "Bastard!" she said.

"Out!" roared the housekeeper.

In a moment, Margaret had wrapped a blanket about herself and slid past Percy. She gave him a look, and he shook his head and took her arm. She struggled against him. "I'm going!" she said, then turned back to the bed, where Scott lay.

"You bastard! You promised me!" Without a word, Percy hustled her from the room.

Once the door was shut, Scott began to wheedle.

"She's no better than a whore, that one. Truly, she came to me. Always looking to advance herself—brought the other girl with her. And I am only flesh and blood, a man on my own. A saint's virtue would have been tried. And I fell, I succumbed to sin. I admit it. But I swear nothing like this will ever happen again. On my life."

I had heard such excuses before. What man hasn't? But never had they sounded quite so unappealingly self-serving.

"Enough of your blather. You have been the ruin of these two girls," said the housekeeper fiercely. "I do not know what you said to poor, silly little Netty. I suspect nothing but fear would have put her in your bed."

"Can we not come to some agreement?" Scott said to Percy, as if she had not spoken. "Surely we can. I swear that this will never happen again. I can make it worth both your whiles. Percy—cases of spirits, champagne, whatever you want. No more arguments about costs. I swear. Mrs. Quill—whatever you want for housekeeping, it's yours."

"Mr. Scott," said the housekeeper, "you are a poor excuse for a man."

"Please. I beg you."

"Captain Avery," said Percy, "you are witness to Mr. Scott in his embarrassed state, attempting to buy us off."

Scott peered past the flickering candles of Percy and the housekeeper and saw me for the first time. I had been reluctant to magnify the shame in the room, but now I came forward. Blake remained in the shadows.

"Captain Avery!" Scott almost wailed. "It really is not what it seems, I assure you. I have been tricked!"

I looked away.

"Mr. Scott," said Percy, rubbing his forehead wearily, "you will present yourself to the members of the committee after breakfast. I should have your belongings packed, if I were you. We will be watching your rooms in case you should take it into your head to make off with anything that is not yours. It is, you'll remember, no more than you allowed the butler, when he was let go."

Scott rounded on him like a cornered rat. "How dare you, you jumped-up footman! You think I cannot weather this? You'll see that I shall. And I'll have you, Percy, make no mistake. I'll tell them what you have been up to."

"Enough, Mr. Scott!" said Mrs. Quill. "We will hear none of your dirty little threats. You have already done more than enough. You should weep with shame."

"He hates me, Captain Avery. They all do, but he especially. They want me gone so they can continue with their dirty scams and dishonesties, which I—I honestly exposed. I suppose you think that with me gone you shall snake your way into my shoes, Percy? Well, let me tell you, you'll never rise to my level. You are a servant born, and a servant you'll stay."

"Mr. Scott, I do not believe there is a single member of staff who will mourn your departure," said Percy. "And that is because you are lazy and incompetent and would not know a set of accounts if it lay down before you and recited its contents. Mrs. Quill, Captain Avery, shall we?"

We turned as one, and left Mr. Scott to contemplate his fate.

Mr. Scott never had his audience with Lord Marcus and the committee. Sometime before eight, he managed to disappear from the club, with several sets of silver cutlery and a sheaf of banknotes that were not his, to the order of a hundred pounds.

Margaret and little Netty, who was a housemaid, had also both left by the time I returned to the club. I had pointed out that there was good reason to believe that at least one of them may well have been coerced by Mr. Scott, and that, now that Matty was being detained, the kitchen could ill afford the loss of more of its staff. Mrs. Quill said it was regrettable, but that they had to be made an example of. Since the club was a keen employer of females, its conduct and the conduct of the females within it must be above reproach.

• • •

I ROSE AT FOUR in order to reach Smithfield before light.

The banquet was to begin at seven in the evening.

Blake appeared with a rough black coat, a worn topper and his sack of possessions. He was too thin, his shoulder blades visible through his shirt—I should have liked to have sat him down to a decent meal, or three.

"You're a sight too smart," he said. "Where are your country clothes and boots?"

"In the country."

And that top hat . . ." He shook his head.

"But I cannot go out hatless!"

"On your head be it, then."

"Good lord, a bad joke from Mr. Blake." I was touched; he was trying to cheer me. He opened the wardrobe and flicked through my togs.

"Here—you need something you won't mind not wearing again," he said. He took out my traveling get-up and my second-best boots.

"But I shall be wanting them to go home in," I protested.

"Where's the dandy I first knew? I miss him."

We took a cab as far as Clerkenwell, then walked through the odorous mire stirred up by a hundred carts, feet and hooves. The roads about were so absurdly narrow and so clogged with carts and wagons packed with livestock there was no other way. The scale and the press were extraordinary: wagons, livestock, hard-faced drovers, whooping boys and excitable dogs all surged toward the one destination. I lost Blake almost at once. I should have worried, but I became quickly caught up in the ghastly spectacle. The squares stretched out into a sea of pens in which livestock—cattle, sheep and pigs—were packed impossibly tightly. Around the sides of the squares were rows of slaughterhouses, tallow makers, butchers and sausage makers, from which a frothing stream of blood and warm effluvium issued, clogging the gutters and feeding the mud.

The air was alive with bellows and bleating. The drovers screamed and swore and beat the animals with cudgels, twisting tails and spearing the tender parts of hooves in order to force them into ever tighter spaces. In the half-light, one could see steam rising from the reeking bodies of the cattle, penned nose to nose and haunch to haunch. Bullocks were tethered so tightly their tongues hung swollen from their mouths, and cows were pierced with prongs and goads until their sides ran. Everywhere was a smell of violence and pain.

As a countryman, I was well familiar with animal husbandry and cattle markets. But I had never seen anything on this scale, and the crushing conditions and casual cruelty it produced were hateful. The animals were frightened, and the place seemed to bring the worst out in the men, who argued and bellowed as loudly as the beasts.

Eventually, Blake hove into sight. Such was my horror of the place, I forgot to chide him for disappearing.

"This is no way to treat livestock," I said.

"The city has grown out of all passing," said Blake. "It needs more meat. The City Corporation makes more and more each year from the sellers' fees and is in no hurry to see its little gold mine move beyond its boundaries. So, three times a week, the streets become impassable and run with blood and guts."

He reached into his shirt and pulled out a greasy piece of paper.

"Seen this?"

It was a handbill entitled "The Double-dealing of Alexis Soyer, the 'Famous' French Chef." Underneath was a rough sketch of Soyer, making much of his askew cap and his voluminous jackets, and below this the following words:

Many are familiar with the ridiculous figure of Frenchman Alexis Soyer, self-styled "great chef" and "genius," with his absurd dress and his boastful excesses, which have brought him great attention. In truth, he is nothing more than a common charlatan, a cheat and a fraudster, hungry only to enrich himself at the world's expense. He claims to be the high priest of French cooking, and to serve only the best. He fills the bellies of his rich customers with poor dishes and bad meat purchased from the paunch cookers, gut spinners and bone boilers of Smithfield. We should not be surprised to discover he has poisoned at least one or two in his haste to enrich himself at his customers' expense.

"Someone else who really dislikes him. Where did you find it?" I said.

"Over there." He pointed to a wall plastered with bills. "There are a few posted round the market."

"It mentions poisoning."

"If you were going to slander a chef, that is what you would say."

"Any notion of where it came from?"

"None. I asked about it."

We walked on in search of Hastings Bland's premises, which was one of the larger slaughterhouses. "Butcher and Slaughterer" read its sign, in white and red. Within the shop, the air was thick, warm and rank.

At the farthest end a broad, swarthy man with curling whiskers, an apron and bloodied arms like great hams was dispensing orders to his subordinates. We approached a young boy and told him we wanted to speak to Bland. The boy went and muttered in the man's ear. He looked up and nodded: a dismissal.

"He will see you in a minute if you'll wait outside," said the boy.

"What will I say?" I asked Blake, having no idea how we might broach the matter.

"We'll ask him straight out about it, I reckon," said Blake. "I'll do it."

Hastings Bland emerged a few moments later. He was in his shirt-sleeves, his cuffs rolled to his elbows. He wore an old top hat and fisherman's boots which came up to his thighs, and was rubbing the blood off his hands onto his already bloody apron.

He addressed me. "I am Bland, and I sell the best beef in England. 'Tis market day, and I do a deal of the slaughtering myself and must keep my boys up to the mark, so you'll appreciate we aren't accustomed to receiving gentlemen like yourself at this hour of the morning. What may I do for you?"

The words were courteous enough, but the manner in which they were spoken was abrupt.

"You supply Soyer and the Reform with a good deal of meat?" said Blake.

"Who wants to know?"

"I am Maguire, and this is my master, Captain Avery."

"That tells me nothing. But yes, we supply the Reform, and plenty of reputable establishments, too."

"You don't consider the Reform reputable?"

"I'll be honest—doan like 'em, doan trust 'em. Go round like they're kings, jumped-up buggers—begging your pardon, sir." He looked at me as if begging my pardon was the last thing he'd ever do. "As I say, we're not used to gentlemen here at this time of the morning. But them at the Reform might not be so high and mighty for much longer."

"Why's that, then?" said Blake. Hastings Bland looked at Blake as if he were trying to catch him out. "I thought Soyer was venerated all over town."

"'Venerated'?" choked Bland. "'Venerated'? Not from what I hear."

"And what do you hear?"

"Poisoning club members, that's what. Killing them off dead. Frenchie's in trouble."

"Surely not!" I said. And then, "If it is true, what is causing it?"

Hastings Bland shrugged. "Who cares? Maybe that Frenchie can't keep his kitchen in order. Dirty furrin habits." Which was quite something to say in the midst of the stench and carcasses of Smithfield. "I'll tell you what, he doan pay his bills on time. And he buys bad meat cheap."

"Why d'you say that, Mr. Bland?" said Blake.

"I've me reasons."

"Who's he buying it from?"

"Who wants to know?"

"If you know, why not tell us?"

Bland tilted his head as if to gesture the whole of Smithfield.

"Mr. Bland, you can do better than that," said Blake.

"Any bloody hole in the wall you like. They ain't fussed."

Blake stared at him. "Seen this?" He brought out the crumpled handbill. Bland glanced at it.

"No." He smiled. "Seems to me it proves my point, though."

"I think mayhap you're the one who started these stories. Slander's a crime, you know. Could take you to prison." Blake came up close to Bland and stared directly into his eyes. Hastings Bland was taller and a good deal broader. "Is it because they sent your meat back? Because your meat wasn't good enough? Because they're buying from Robinson's instead now? I know every printer in the city—wouldn't be hard to discover who'd had them made."

Hastings Bland looked from side to side. A few men had stopped and were now idly watching the altercation. I believe that if we had been alone he would have come at Blake with his fists.

"Who are you? Rozzers?" he said. "Call your man off, Captain Whatever-your-name-is, or I'll have to teach him a lesson about behaving hisself."

He took one of his hands and wiped it on Blake's lapel. Blake smiled his infuriating smile and stepped back, making a little bow.

"I tell you," Hastings Bland said between gritted teeth, "the Reform kitchen owes me money, and not just a few pennies here or there. I know what I know. Now, you'll waste no more of my time." He stamped his booted foot and kicked a lump of mud in my direction. Some of it landed on my hat, which I had been holding out of courtesy. Satisfied, he turned and marched back into his bloody domain.

We returned to St. James's on foot: no cab would have carried us. My boots were encrusted in a noxious stew of mud, blood, dung and detritus, and my trousers were sodden to my knees. I smelled appalling. Blake's jacket was soiled. We took the back streets to avoid being noticed.

"Well, he was easy to dislike," I said at last.

"Yes," said Blake, and offered no more.

"Do you think he may be our man? He hates Soyer and the Reform enough."

"I wouldn't rule it out. He's not supplying meat for tonight, so we have time to consider." We walked on in silence. From time to time, Blake gave a nasty, rattling cough. At length, we came to a small, insalubrious market where butchers' meat sat next to tripe, cat's meat and shriveled vegetables.

"What is this place?"

"Clare Market," he said. "We're hard by St. Giles Rookery. There were six slaughterhouses up there." He pointed to a dank, narrow lane. "Along with a tallow melter and a tripe boiler."

"You were here as a child." I was always avid for details of his past, as keen as he was to avoid revealing them.

"On Saturdays, the blood from the slaughterhouses gathered in pools in the road. Didn't seem wrong to us. We were used to the stench. We used to collect dead rats. Threw them at costermongers or sold them to the cat's-meat men."

"You must know someone who could discover if the Reform is purchasing meat from less respectable suppliers."

"I could if I were Jeremiah Blake and free to go about as I pleased."

We could not avoid the great thoroughfares in the end and, halfway down the Strand, among the early morning coffee sellers, we came upon a hawker selling a very particular broadside.

"Poisonings in Pall Mall! Foul Murders in Club!" The title was writ large, and there was a sketch of men in frock coats slumped around a dining table, their eyes staring. I purchased all thirty copies for a penny each. The sheet described in lurid detail a series of poisonings "at a Certain Grand Club for Gentlemen in the Heart of Pall Mall," and the deaths that had resulted from them:

> *Writhing in anguish, his face now a ghostly, bluish hue and forced into a ghastly, mirthless grin, the blood gushing freely from his mouth, he begged the Almighty for mercy, cried for his children, and then, with a final ragged breath, expired.*

The details bore little relation to the facts as I knew them, and the Reform was not named.

"A bit of gossip in a flash journal, a bill and a broadside, all in the last twelve hours," I said. "Good reasons to be alarmed, wouldn't you say?"

"Three dead, the place closed, police on the door—it was hardly to remain a secret forever," said Blake.

"You are not staying for breakfast?" said Helen. I had washed away the ordure of Smithfield and was preparing to set off for Francobaldi's kitchen.

"I haven't the time. Forgive me, Helen, I cannot stay very long."

"What a surprise."

"I am sorry, but I have so very much to get done by this evening, my dear. If you had let me tell you about it, you would understand."

"Don't chastise me, William."

"I apologize. I will stay and take coffee with you."

"That is three apologies in so many sentences."

We sat, I endeavoring to hide my impatience, she naturally aware of it, and drank our coffee in silence. Helen, it seemed to me, had turned herself to glass. Those about her—myself most of all—had come to avoid saying anything difficult or unpleasant, or too close to the nub of things, for fear that she would break. I could not blame her. India had taken so much from her, but now a mountain of unsaid things had grown up between us.

And so the unspoken thoughts arose in me again, as they had for months: *Is this how we are to spend the rest of our lives together? Will we never speak of your feelings about our child?*

"My dear," I said, "let me explain why I must go, please. Besides the poisoner we are looking for, the banquet that was to have been canceled is now taking place—this evening. It will require all our attention. But I assure you, when it is over . . ."

"If you will be attending the banquet, am I not invited?"

"I shall not be attending, Helen, I shall be in the kitchens watching the food, and there will be no ladies; it is for gentlemen only, politicians and the like. But afterward, I know Monsieur Soyer will be delighted to entertain you."

"In the kitchen, like a servant?"

There were some leaves of paper on the occasional table by the mirror. I picked them up. "You have a letter," I said, smiling. "Any news of Fred?"

An exasperated grimace crossed her face, so swiftly that anyone who did not know her as well as I would not have seen it. It made my heart clench in my chest. She picked the pages up and handed them to me.

"It's from your sister," she said briskly. "He is healthy. Your father is complaining about your absence. He seems in a fine old mood. I do wonder what he would say about your residency at the Reform."

"If you are so determined to tell him, please feel free," I snapped. I regretted the words at once. "I'm—"

She flinched. "Do not apologize. I joke," she said, "I joke. As for today, I have a number of calls to make, and I do not require your company. Do you not wish to know the arrangements?"

"If you would like to tell me."

"This afternoon, I have invitations to call on several East India Company ladies, and Lord Marcus's wife has asked me to call, too, tomorrow," she said. "I am told she is very elegant. Lady Catherine Grealey has invited us to dinner tonight. I had assumed that you might be detained. It just so happens that Henry Darrow is going and has offered to escort me—I told you he came up with us, didn't I? I do not need your approval to accept him, do I?"

Some would say a married woman should not be escorted to dinner by a man neither her husband nor a relative, nor one who, though some twenty years her senior, clearly admired her.

"Of course not."

"There is something else you can do for me. I shall want a carriage."

"No one has a carriage in London."

"Except Lord Marcus."

"My dear, he is one of the richest men in the city."

"How am I to travel, then? On foot? In an omnibus?"

"No, of course not. I will arrange to have a hackney cab placed at your disposal for the afternoon."

"I suppose that will have to do."

Chapter Twenty

Blake said the news of Scott's departure had been received with satisfaction in the kitchen—though with less than twelve hours to go to the banquet, no one had much time to crow. Word had begun to circulate that it was Scott who had put Margaret up to informing against Matty. It was said she had spurned his advances and he had wanted this revenge. Few, however, spoke of her innocence, since that would mean admitting aloud that the poisoner was still at large.

Francobaldi's kitchen was at the Union Club, which occupied a mansion from the previous century on Piccadilly, overlooking Green Park. It was nothing on the scale of the Reform Club, but it was a well-maintained, handsome stone building, and through its tall windows one could glimpse great, twinkling chandeliers.

The kitchen was far smaller than the Reform's, but not unimpressive. Long tables were laid with fresh vegetables, fruit and game. There was a wall of copper pans, a large, polished iron range upon which various cauldrons bubbled, and two tall, thin fireplaces with the coals built up high to create a larger area for roasting blasted out enormous heat. This was a novelty I remembered from Soyer's kitchen. Where the cooks prepared their dishes, however, was excessively crowded. They jostled each other, perspiration streaming from their faces, with a type of soldierly sullenness that I knew from the army. Indeed, there was an air of simmering anger throughout the kitchen that was almost unpleasant.

"What is it about this place?" I murmured to Blake.

"It's like Hobbes's vision of the world," he said.

"What?"

"Can you not smell it? Rivalry, competition. Some thrive and others are crushed."

I had no time to consider this observation, as Francobaldi came up behind me and clapped me on the back—a great blow, even for me—and I was winded for a moment.

"Captain Avery! You came! You like my kitchen? It's not quite the Reform Club, but . . ."

"It seems remarkably productive." It was the first thing that came into my head. He seemed to like it well enough.

"Let me give you the tour."

Having come to know Soyer's kitchen, the various areas and arrangements of Francobaldi's made more sense to me: the sauce cooks, the soup cooks, the meat cooks, the fish cooks, the vegetable cooks and the *pâtissiers*, and their various helpers and apprentices, kitchen boys and potboys. There were no women.

I commented upon the tall and narrow fireplaces, what a fine idea they were, and how I had also noticed them at the Reform.

"They are not Alexis's creation," Francobaldi said curtly. "They were the invention of the sublime Carême, who cooked for His Majesty King George IV."

He pushed his way between his cooks, dipping a finger in a sauce and declaring it inedibly salty or picking up a salad frond and dangling it into his mouth before announcing the dressing was good—leaving the maker either utterly crushed or puffed with pride. He picked up a pastry and thrust it into Blake's palm.

"Your man looks like he needs a few good meals. Are you starving him, Captain? Eat up!" He waited expectantly.

Blake took a bite, and nodded. "Very good, sir."

Next he picked up a plate on which a piece of beef had been artfully placed, and sliced into it, his expression growing ever darker. In a sudden movement he tipped it onto the floor.

"This cannot be served!" he cried. "It is like the sole of a fucking Wellington boot! The diner would loose all his teeth if he attempted this!" He seemed furious, then suddenly burst out laughing. The cooks laughed, too, with relief. Francobaldi looked about and they all stiffened again.

"We must be better!" he said. "Who made this? Who made this?" He pointed at the splattered mess on the floor. After a pause, a pale, ginger-featured young man stepped forward.

"Marius, Marius, what were you thinking? What persuades you that this is acceptable, when it is in reality a fucking abomination?"

"*Je ne sais pas, Chef,*" said Marius, in a small voice.

"*En anglais! En anglais!* I'm concerned for you, Marius!" Francobaldi said, putting his arm round the boy's neck as if he might break it. "How can I count on you if you cannot tell the difference between a piece of meat and a piece of India rubber? It is a disgrace, Marius! That an animal died to give us this and you have tortured it in such a way!" He let go of the boy and pushed him backward.

"Yes, Chef," said Marius. His hands shook.

This seemed to inflame Francobaldi. "I'm thinking, perhaps, Marius, that I cannot count on you? Can I count on you, Marius?"

"*Oui, Chef*—yes, Chef," said the poor creature miserably, and his face flushed puce. The kitchen seemed to become yet more charged. Marius's fellow chefs drew away from him, and he was left standing on his own.

"Let me see you prove it, Marius. Sauté me a cutlet. In a pan. Now." There was a plate of them on the long table. His hands shaking, Marius took a small copper frying pan, put a knob of butter in it and placed it upon one of the shining black ranges.

"Stop your shaking, Marius!" Francobaldi shouted. "Control yourself!" Strangely, Marius could not stop shaking. He did, however, manage to pick up the cutlet and place it in the pan.

"No! It is too soon, you caw-handed jack! The pan isn't hot enough. You'll spoil it!"

The young man swallowed, squeezed his eyes to slits and tilted the pan, spooning melted butter over the cutlet, but he was hardly able to keep the butter from shaking out of the spoon. Francobaldi began to seethe with impatience, his face and body growing tauter and tauter until, eventually, he could bear it no longer, and he pushed Marius aside and took hold of the pan himself.

"Do I employ a room of idlers?" he barked. Immediately, all but the meat cooks withdrew to their stations.

"This is how you do it, you fucking sapskull," he said, scooping the butter gracefully over the cutlet and letting it burst in small, shining bubbles over the browning meat. Marius stood by dumbly.

"Now, pass me a turning knife." The young man reached for a long, flat utensil with holes in it, but it slipped from his fingers and fell in a clatter at Francobaldi's feet. He knelt down to retrieve it. A fresh rage possessed the chef as he watched his minion grubbing around before him.

"What are you doing?" he shouted, and dealt the boy a great blow on the head. The young man fell back, stunned. Francobaldi kicked him.

I had learned painfully that it was better not to intervene in a disciplinary matter involving another man's troops.

"Out of my sight! That's right, No-brains, I cannot look at you!" Francobaldi shouted. And the boy, almost gratefully, ran out of the kitchen, his colleagues covertly watching him flee.

Francobaldi leaned against the range, finishing the cutlet, moving his copper pan this way and that. The task seemed to calm him. He called for a plate and then scooped the meat out onto it, without marring the plate with a speck of fat. By the time he turned to Blake and me, he seemed to have entirely forgotten the whole business with Marius.

"Taste this," he said, and before I knew it, he pulled a piece of it off the bone, and his greasy fingers were forcing it into my mouth. "Good?" I nodded, trying not to gag. "Now, Captain, let us go and talk."

We passed two cooks assembling a plate of fish, a perfect square of milky white flesh atop a pale mousse flecked with green.

"Good," he said, and they stood to attention, pleased with themselves.

"Come, here is *mia cameretta*, my snug," said Francobaldi. "Not as large as Soyer's, of course, but comfortable enough. May I offer you refreshment, Captain Avery? A small glass of brandy? Some porter for your man?"

We declined.

The room had a small desk with a leather bureau chair, two deep armchairs and a fire in the grate. One wall was hung with pictures, just as Soyer's was. The armchairs looked almost identical to those in Soyer's room.

"It is most generous of you to give your time to me, Mr. Francobaldi," I said, taking a seat. Blake stood behind me, holding his cap.

"I like soldierliness, Captain Avery—and I can see it in every inch of you. We chefs are not so very different from you. A well-run kitchen is like an army troop: obedience is everything. And I thought perhaps it might be of benefit to you to hear from someone who knows Soyer but is not of the Reform."

I nodded. Blake and I had discussed what I would do. Let him talk.

Do not give too much away. "Is there something particular you would like to tell us—me?"

He shifted in his chair. "I thought you'd ask me questions."

I sat back in my chair.

"Do you know much about Monsieur Soyer's troubles, Mr. Francobaldi?"

"I cannot pretend I have not heard about the young dandy's death. And"—he sighed, brought his arms up and folded them behind his head in an oddly casual manner—"I know about the two gentlemen from three nights ago. Soyer is in trouble. *E nella merda.*"

Plainly, he had not heard about Matty. "So, tell me," I said, "what do those 'not of the Reform' say about it?"

Francobaldi licked his lips. "That he has overstretched himself. That the Reform cannot pay. They are short as it is. They overspent on the building and are arguing with the architect over his fee. There will be a court case."

I nodded.

"Alexis is very generous, very—extravagant? He always wants the best, and lives upon a grand scale. He is not perhaps so careful with his accounts. The bills mount up. The club is late to pay them. Can the club afford him? And for how long? That is what people say."

"Anything else?"

He tilted his head to one side, as if considering.

"This is a competitive business. We chefs find companionship with each other but we are also great rivals. The suppliers want to impress and at the same time to cheat us. Our employees and masters demand the best but are not willing to pay for it. It is a grand battle for survival." He grinned. "It is life itself."

"And Monsieur Soyer is at the top of the pile, sir," Blake said.

"I think you met my manservant, Maguire, last night. He was with me in India; we have long worked together. As a matter of fact, he speaks rather good Italian."

"Oh no, sir, just a little to be getting by on. I do apologize for interrupting, sir," said Blake. "You were saying that it is a competitive business, sir, that it is a grand battle."

"Yes." Francobaldi was put off his stride. "One must live hard, and it is not always possible to play entirely by the rules. Especially if one is not sure how long one will remain, as your man says, 'at the top of the pile.'"

There was a pause. Blake poked me sharply in the back.

I leaned forward, trying to compose my features into an expression both sincere and manly. I had no idea if I was succeeding.

"Mr. Francobaldi, we are both men of the world. I should very much like to know your honest opinion of Monsieur Soyer."

"I admire him. But I make no secret of the fact that I'd like to best him. We don't all have the resources of the Reform Club's kitchens, however. I wonder, too, if all is truly well with him. He smiles and smiles, and never sleeps, and never frowns, never seems to tire. Do you see that?"

"I had not thought about it," I said.

"We successful chefs, we all work hard and strive for the best. But Alexis . . . perhaps he has made a pact with the devil." He laughed.

"What exactly do you mean?" I hoped I looked confiding and reassuring.

He did not need asking twice.

"Soyer has 'arrangements.'"

"'Arrangements'?"

"You know. Deals. Financial interests."

"I saw his inventions—does the Reform frown on his other interests?"

"Some say they keep him from the kitchen. But no, I mean that that kitchen has a reputation. Presents received in return for orders. Bills padded and the extra divided between the kitchen and the supplier. His apprentices' fees in his pocket. Of course, many kitchens do this. The luxuries we deal in are a temptation. Just last week I had to dismiss a butler. He was ordering cases in and then selling every sixth bottle for his own profit. He will never work in a grand house again. I shall see to that.

"To be frank, the Reform's kitchen accounts aren't what they should be . . . I thought you should know this. Others wouldn't be so straight with you."

"You are saying that Soyer is dishonest," I said.

"Not I, but people . . ." He licked his lips again.

"How far do you think Soyer would go?" said Blake. "Would he poison someone?"

Francobaldi was taken aback. He laughed uneasily. "Your servant is very direct. I couldn't . . . I cannot see what the advantage would be, but then, where men start to doubt each other, and money is at stake, things happen."

"So you do suspect him?" said Blake.

At that he retreated, half laughing. "How can I say? But you might wonder about his staff. They've laid down their knives in protest on occasion. Maybe they don't love him quite as he would like them to."

"Might I ask another question, sir?" said Blake. The courtesy seemed belated. I braced myself.

"Are there any members of Soyer's staff whom you would advise us to watch closely?"

Francobaldi scratched his chin; it was clear he did not like being pressed.

"For example, what do you make of Mr. Morel, sir?" said Blake.

Francobaldi stirred uneasily. "He is a decent enough lieutenant, not an artist, and there are younger and more talented men in the kitchen who snap at his heels, and he knows this."

"Mr. Perrin?"

Francobaldi shrugged. "Him and others. I do not rate them especially highly."

"What about the suppliers? Could one of them be so angry as to wish to harm the Reform kitchen?"

Francobaldi laughed. "It's possible, I suppose. Not all of them are as respectable as they seem, and there's certainly falling-out over deliveries and payment."

"It seems such a fine business, cooking and that," said Blake. "I was wondering, sir, have you come across much actual ill-doing in kitchens and such?"

"You must forgive Maguire," I said. "He is a great reader of blood and thunders. He loves a good murder."

Francobaldi smiled. "The culinary world is not without its dramas. We are a passionate band. Some years ago, a French chef who cooked for the Duchess of Leinster murdered a rival whom he suspected of trying to oust him. I, too, have had my own trials. When I was working for the Marquess of Oldham in the north some years ago, I heard another chef wanted my position and was willing to do almost anything to get it. I will not elaborate on the details of our relationship. I had to make a trip to London. When I returned the next day, one of the potboys had disappeared, and my recipe book with him. Such a book is everything to a training chef. It had all I had collected over the years—all my best dishes, all my ideas for new ones. This chef wanted to make me nothing less than unable to cook. Later, it was made known to me that the boy had been seen at the local coaching inn talking to a stranger. I knew my rival had taken the book, or had arranged to have it taken."

"What did you do?"

"I went to the marquess and explained my situation, that my precious book had gone and that I suspected this man, though I could not prove it. Thankfully, I have a good memory, and some of my recipes I had committed to paper elsewhere. I am glad to say my master's table did not suffer and his faith in me was renewed. But I tell this story to show that people will go far to get what they want in this business."

"And your rival?" asked Blake.

"He is a chef for an old lady who entertains very little. Skilled, but not inspired. His star is on the wane." He sat back, smiling widely, pleased with himself.

"May I ask you another question, Mr. Francobaldi?" asked Blake.

"Your manservant is most inquisitive," said Francobaldi. "Whatever you like. I may not answer it, however."

"Do you always play according to the rules?"

He smiled again. "Most of the time."

"How far would you go to best a rival?"

He began to laugh, covering his mouth with his hand.

"It is a good question. Actually, I must tell you that I hatched the whole thing. I knew my rival wanted my position, so I scotched him. I said my book had been stolen, but I hid it. In going to my employer myself, I made him look dishonest and conniving, then I demonstrated my skills in cooking for him without my book."

"Though you had it all the time. And what of the potboy?" said Blake.

"I gave him a little money . . . I think he went to London. He knew he could not come back."

"How much further would you go?" My anger began to get the better of me.

"What do you mean, Captain Avery?"

"I was shown a copy of your menu three days ago. The pastry castle, it seemed to me, was extraordinarily like the pastry crown with the stuffed chickens and skewers of truffle and crayfish that we had at Monsieur Soyer's dinner. In fact, the description made it sound identical."

Francobaldi sat up. "Do you accuse me of stealing Soyer's dish?" he said with a half smile. I smiled back. I did not find his menaces daunting. "Are you accusing me—"

"How much further would you go, Francobaldi? What would you do to best Alexis Soyer? Would you kill a man?"

Francobaldi leaped to his feet. "How dare you!"

Blake, somehow, had got between us. "Captain, might I respectfully remind you that we are late for the Reform."

"I would *never* poison a man! Never! It is a coward's way! A woman's method. As a chef, I should be ashamed to do such a thing!"

"Like stealing a man's inventions and not admitting to it?"

"Get out of my fucking kitchen! I swear, if you spread that dirty lie, I'll—"

"You will what? You do not alarm me. I know your sort."

Blake began to bustle about me, nudging me out of the snug in such a way that neither Francobaldi nor I could get at each other.

"I hope you do not mind me saying, Mr. Francobaldi," he said, "but might I ask where you are from?

The question seemed to throw Francobaldi. "I am Italian. From Modena. I was trained in France, as the best chefs are—what of it?"

"Your English is excellent, sir," said Blake. "Fluent. You might be a native."

WE STRODE AS FAST AS we could up Piccadilly, Blake wheezing so violently I feared he might choke.

"You saw him," I said. "The man has no self-control. When he is angry, he will do anything . . . Wait, you are *laughing*."

Blake's face was twisted, I realized, in mirth.

"What is so amusing?" Blake waved the question away. "What did you make of him then, seriously?" I said, trying a different tack.

"I'd be surprised if he was our man."

"Why not? I reckon he is capable of anything. I cannot bear the thought of Matty languishing in that cell and he at large and so pleased with himself."

"Listen to me. He's jealous of Soyer, all right. But it's not him. Don't let your anger cloud your judgment."

"How do you know?"

"He's easy to read."

"Blake!" I said, grinding my teeth. "Then explain it to me—how you read him." I expected no answer but, after some minutes, he said, to my surprise, "Francobaldi is jealous of Soyer—so much so that he almost hates him."

"Well, I can see that."

"But I see what people do and don't know they are doing it. So, just before Francobaldi said Soyer's name, his face screwed into a scowl. Just for a half second. I'd wager fifty pounds he had no idea he was doing it. Then, each time Soyer's name came up, his eyes would bulge and his jaw jut, just for the briefest of moments. His passion is almost uncontrollable."

"Which makes him a perfect suspect."

"But at the same time, he felt he had nothing to hide. It was visible in all of him, even in the way he stood, his legs widely planted; and how he sat, his legs splayed; his elbows sticking out at all angles—so at his ease, so confident. He's not the author of Soyer's misfortunes, but he's enjoying them and thinks to benefit by them. *That* he could not hide, nor how good it tasted to him, speaking ill of Soyer—I've rarely seen such lip-smacking and lip-licking."

"Maybe he was merely flaunting his confidence?"

"I'd say not. I'd say this manner, this confidence, was a yardstick.

Against it, we compare what took place after we began to question him: the moments when he didn't tell the full story, when he did lie, when he protested his innocence."

"And what were they?"

"First, he tells the story about the stolen recipe book. As he finishes, he takes a short breath, closes his mouth tight and smiles. To me, that said he knew more about the story than he was telling, something that pleased him, something he was bursting to say. And so I ask a small question, and his plan to best his rival comes tumbling out. Second, I ask him where he comes from, and he says he's from Italy, and as he says it he opens his eyes wide and he doesn't blink. People do that when they want to seem truthful; he would have had no notion he was doing it. But he could not keep it up, this wide-open, unblinking look, and so in his guilt he looked away, then rubbed his hands across his face as if to hide himself from us—as good as admitting he's lying. Third, you suggest he might be responsible for the poisoning. The response is quite different: he knows we know he has it in for Soyer, he knows he hasn't done this, he is outraged, furious and alarmed."

"But he was sneaking enough to dispose of his rival, and he lied about stealing Soyer's recipe," I said, unconvinced.

"He didn't deny stealing it; he tried to force you to withdraw the accusation."

"There you see it, his anger: he is violent and unpredictable. Someone who regards life as a fight for supremacy and would do anything to win."

"I don't deny he's a bruiser, just that he is not our man."

"Wait. Are you saying he is not Italian?"

Blake grinned again. "Giovanni Francobaldi, my arse. His parents might be Italian, but that accent was made in Clerkenwell. Did you not hear? It all but disappeared when he lost his temper? 'Caw-handed jack'? 'Sapskull'? Who says those things but a Londoner born and bred?"

"You mean he is pretending to be a foreigner? Why on earth would an Englishman do that?"

"Avery, you country joskin. Who would take an English chef seriously?"

"What about what he said about all not being well in the Reform kitchen and that Soyer is responsible? Whatever we may think of Francobaldi, he is not the first to say it."

Blake sobered at once. His eyes narrowed. "We'll have to ask Soyer."

Chapter Twenty-one

The kitchen. A frantic air prevailed. Every cook had a soldier in attendance. It was more crowded than I would have believed possible. More guards stood before the meat larders and cold kitchens and in the butler's pantry.

"We must speak, Monsieur Soyer," I said quietly.

Soyer would have protested, I think, but one look at Blake persuaded him, and we followed him into his office.

"You have found something?" he said hopefully.

"Vides tes poches."

"Please, Blake, I have no time for this."

"Vides tes poches."

Bemused, Soyer reached into the pockets of his trousers and drew out a laundered handkerchief and several torn pieces of paper.

"Et les autres," said Blake.

Soyer reached into the various pockets of his frock coat, drawing out a pocketbook, more crumpled notes, a number of small coins and two small enamel boxes. These Blake pounced on. One he placed in his pocket; the other he gazed at and began to turn over and over in his hand.

"Pretty little thing," he said. "So, is the Reform paying its debts?"

"What is this, Blake?"

"My question."

Soyer shook his head. "What have you heard?"

"That the club is in debt, and that the kitchen has a reputation for dishonesty, for demanding bribes, padding bills and not paying its suppliers."

"This is nonsense! The club is in dispute with Barry over his fee, but that is due to extravagance on both their parts, and because neither will own to it. Besides, Lord Marcus and a number of other rich members would never allow it. It is nothing to do with the kitchen."

Blake shrugged.

"You've not answered my question."

Soyer stood up, then sat down again, his eyes on the box. "We pay our bills. Sometimes there are delays, but this is a common practice. All large kitchens such as ours take time to pay their accounts."

"And what about the stealing, the padding, the bribes?"

"I have a banquet to prepare. I have no time . . ."

"You do," said Blake, leaning over the table and fixing him with a fearsome look. "Tell me what happened when the committee discovered what was going on."

"But this is nonsense! These are rumors spread by rivals. Was this Francobaldi? He cannot help himself."

"Tell me, Soyer, or by God I'll walk from this room and out of this place, and I'll take this with me." He held the small enamel box.

Soyer stood up.

"Sit down!" said Blake, as furious as I had ever heard him. "I have not finished with you."

Soyer put his face in his hands. "You friend is gone quite mad, Avery."

The enamel box sat on Blake's palm. With his right hand, he prized it open.

"*Non*, Blake!" Soyer pleaded.

Blake pressed his right forefinger into the tiny white grains and lifted it slowly to his lips.

"*Non!*"

Blake dabbed the grains onto his tongue and closed his mouth.

Soyer stood up and tried to rush around the table. "*Crache-le!*" he cried. "Please! Spit it out!"

There was a jug of water upon the sideboard. Blake took it up and swigged from it, then spat it out onto the floor.

Soyer stood stock-still, for once wordless.

"Arsenic," said Blake, wiping his mouth.

With his right hand, he took the other enamel box from his pocket, opened it and sniffed.

"Strychnine," he said, holding it up.

He stared at Soyer.

"Truly, it is nothing. It is a misunderstanding, nothing more."

"Nothing?" said Blake.

Soyer tried to muster his dignity. "They are nothing. Return them to me."

Blake put the boxes in his pocket.

Soyer balled his hands into fists, his shoulders hunched. "You will return them to me. They are no one's business but my own." He turned to me to appeal. "Captain Avery?"

"Three men dead of arsenic or strychnine poisoning," I said. "I should hardly say they are nothing."

Blake watched him, inscrutable, appraising. There was a long silence. Then Soyer cleared his throat.

"You say I never sleep. It is true, I barely do. With all there is to do—the life of a chef, the things I wish to achieve—I cannot doze off before the fire and, besides, it is not in my nature. I must work, I must be Soyer, I must give every last shred of my strength, of my *vitalité*, to it. Coffee is not enough. These revive me: one grain of arsenic once or twice a day. And after a while, when I have been taking it for some time, a grain or two of nux vomica instead. In very small doses they prime a man, they give him strength and appetite for the day."

I said, "Mr. Thackeray said that in certain fashionable London sets men are using small amounts of arsenic as a pick-me-up. I think that is what Rowlands was doing."

"And the strychnine?" said Blake.

"It is used in many tonics. My apothecary simply suggested I take the thing itself, in very small doses. It keeps me alert, ensures I give of my best, and that I do not fail."

Blake turned away. "And you did not think to tell this either to Avery or to me after Rowlands's death."

"Naturally, at first I had no idea it was of any relevance, and then, when the Captain told me of Rowlands, I intended to tell him, but the moment passed. The next day came the other death. I knew I had done nothing wrong, but I admit that I feared that you would not believe me, since I was in possession of both. I thought that you would—"

"—that we would think you had deliberately poisoned these men yourself?"

"I would never! I swear it on my life."

Silence.

"I am sorry. But what I say is true," said Soyer. "Perhaps I am foolish to take these, but I find they help me. But I did not—could not—contaminate my own food. My *métier*, my vocation, is to feed and give pleasure. And I am ambitious; foolishly so, some say. I have great plans for the future, and I have Emma and, when it is born, our baby to take care of. Why would I do this? I should have to be mad."

"Madness can be found in the least likely places."

"I implore you."

Blake would not look at him, and answered coldly, "Avery owed you nothing but took on this work out of a sense of duty, and you told him nothing. You know what I risk being here, and you told me nothing."

"I regret it, I do, with all my heart."

Blake turned to the door. "And you know what we think about this banquet, and that we are here because we are forced to be."

"Blake, do not abandon me." He spoke in a low voice.

"We will have it all out—all of it—now."

"*Oui!* I tell you whatever you want to know. The accounts, the money, whatever it is. I will show you that I am, truly, an honest man." Soyer went back to his chair, sat down and began to rub his chin as if puzzling out how to begin.

Blake stood by the door, as if he might depart at any moment. I really thought he might.

"It is true, there may have been—there have been—some questions regarding the kitchen's accounts. You must understand, it is the largest kitchen of its kind in London; we must order a great deal, expensive items sometimes, and this certain members of the club have complained of, ever since we first opened. They complain for nothing."

Blake put his hand on the door handle.

"And," Soyer said hurriedly, "it is also true that some items in the past have been ordered and paid for and then never found their way to the members, while some others never—"

"—never existed," said Blake.

"Yes. And some wines and spirits were on occasion made use of by members of the staff." He shrugged. "*Ça arrive.*"

"And the committee discovered it."

"Almost by accident. Scott—good riddance to him—thought his role was to give orders and fawn over the members, but he barely understood a balance sheet. He was supposed to manage the accounts for the whole club and, I admit, this may have been exploited."

"By you."

"By the kitchen. But his office was chaos, and he was the chief reason that bills were late or lost, or not paid. At least at first. Complaints were made. We came to him and demanded explanations. He was—what is the phrase?—out of his depth, utterly. He knew that if his mismanagement was discovered, he would be dismissed on the spot. But somehow he realized that some of our bills did not concur with actual provisions. And when the committee began to ask questions, Scott gave them our bills. There were some inconsistencies.

"I was called up to answer for them before the committee. It was humiliating. Let me swear to you, I myself have no need to do such things. I am the best-paid chef in London now; I have my own business interests. But my *équipe* are loyal to me, and I am loyal to them, and so I answered for them and took responsibility for these things. My enemies on the committee, and those who have little experience of the widespread nature of these matters, tabled my resignation. Instead, I was reprimanded, and my standing with the committee has been harmed. They are quicker to think ill of me now. However, I like to think it was not all for the worse. I banned those practices in my kitchen. No more gifts, no more skimming or padding. I told my staff that I would not tolerate them at the Reform. And now the kitchen produces its own accounts, separate from the rest of the club's. We must be beyond reproach, and now we are, and we are independent of Scott, whose incompetence and bad morals have at last caught up with him."

"So the kitchen is honest now."

"Yes. Though I had to make examples. Some weeks after this, our butler was caught stealing spirits and once again demanding payments from certain wine merchants. It was not the first time. I dismissed him on the spot. I have not yet replaced him, but Percy admirably covers his duties."

"Who are your enemies on the committee, and why are they enemies?"

"You know them—Beare and his friends. For lack of anything else, they now complain about the cost of ingredients."

"What about Molesworth?"

"Molesworth? A courteous man of taste."

"He argued for your dismissal."

"He did?" Soyer looked most put out.

"Who else were you protecting?"

"I am sorry?"

"Who was skimming and taking bribes?"

"I would rather not say. It is not relevant to your *recherche*."

Blake scratched his head and turned the door handle.

"The butler," Soyer said heavily. "Several of the kitchen clerks—it is easy if you are ordering supplies and making the accounts. Two of them left." He cleared his throat. "Gimbell was selling kitchen leftovers when they should have been made use of in the kitchen or distributed to the staff. There was a sprinkling of other things about the kitchen, fairly minor. A pastry cook who was taking flour and selling it, some *commis* who stole the small beer, a few such things. The butcher."

There was a silence. Blake came back into the room and stood over Soyer's desk.

"The butcher. Is that why Hastings Bland hates you so much?" he said.

"Who? Oh, the meat supplier. A most uncouth, argumentative, boastful fellow."

"He said he was owed money. And he accuses you of buying bad meat cheaply."

"This is nonsense! We purchase only the best. We have on several occasions returned meat to him because it was not to our standard. He does not take kindly to criticism."

"Take care, Alexis, I must have the truth. Who orders and buys the meat?"

"After Benoît, Morel and I have decided upon dishes, the butcher. And Percy."

Blake shot his hand out, grabbed Soyer's shoulder and shook him.

"The truth, for God's sake!"

"*Eh bien!*" Soyer said, looking for a moment quite terrified. "When money was short some months ago, the butcher and Percy acquired meat from someone I should not have patronized, had I known. It was a mistake, but they were attempting to help me. Bland somehow discovered and trumpeted this. It is possible Percy has been making matters difficult for him; it seems to me he deserves it."

"Not paying him and turning his orders away."

"It is possible."

"And Percy, since he oversees all the ordering and accounts, I suppose he was engaged in this stealing, too?"

Soyer bowed his head. "You do not understand; in large kitchens, it is almost expected. And he is exceptional at his job."

"I want to speak to him."

"Now?"

Blake nodded.

"We have a banquet to prepare for, you know," said Soyer.

I went out and told a potboy to summon Percy.

"So, Francobaldi—why do you tolerate him?" asked Blake.

Soyer sighed again. His eyes strayed wistfully to the papers on his desk. "I pity him. He is a competent chef, good enough. But he will never be me. It pains him. I suppose he is spreading rumors?"

"He says the kitchen is famed for its dishonesty. He suggested that you personally had dishonest financial arrangements."

Soyer smiled ruefully. "So, he does not accuse me of poisoning, at least."

"Would you think it of him?"

"Of poisoning—*non*. He may strike out in sudden anger. But to make a plan slow and deadly? *Non*. I do not think so."

Blake nodded. "How bad are the club's finances?"

"I am but the chef; they would hardly inform me."

Blake waited.

"The rumors about bankruptcy? I think they are started by those who do not wish the club well. There are in this club some of the richest men in the land. They are good for the money."

Percy came in. He looked at us quizzically.

Blake made no attempt to play the manservant. "Mr. Percy, we've heard you have been padding and skimming the accounts."

Percy looked at Soyer, who gave a small nod. He rubbed his chin, and when he spoke he was brisk and cool and quite unabashed.

"It is true. I did, but I do not anymore."

"So you admit you cheated your employer," I said.

"I did. I do not seek absolution for it; it was wrong."

"You felt no guilt?" I said.

"Such things are not unusual in our business," he said. "I know that is not an excuse, but I will try to explain it. It is not hard to be tempted when one works for men and institutions with incomes so much greater than anything one could ever hope to earn. I had worked long hours and very hard since I was a lad, and have done an excellent job for all my employers. One assumed they hardly noticed, if one added a few pennies here and there and, mostly, they did not. I do not proffer this as an excuse; it is simply the way it often is. Until the Reform, I did not believe I did much harm, when I saw what sums my employers were willing to lavish upon themselves in comparison to what they paid me."

"But you stopped," said Blake.

"Yes, for Chef's sake, and because our kitchen is a special place. My actions brought opprobrium upon Monsieur Soyer, which I deeply regret. He took the reprimands himself and ensured we kept our jobs. It has weakened his hand with the committee. I should add that, in my opinion, Mr. Scott, who brought it all to the committee's attention, was himself far from above reproach, quite apart from his ineptitude and bad morals."

He looked again at Soyer. "Might I get on? There is a great deal to do . . . Perrin needs various recipes."

"I think perhaps Morel has them. Do you have any more questions, gentlemen?" said Soyer.

I silently inquired of Blake. He closed his palm.

"No, indeed, and thank you for your time, Mr. Percy—and Monsieur Soyer."

"Forgive me," I said to Blake when we were out in the kitchen, "but I cannot see that we learned anything that gets us closer to our goal."

"I had to ask him," said Blake. "What else can we do but examine every possibility?"

Morel rushed past, seeming, if possible, more harassed than ever. Blake hailed him.

"Monsewer Morel," said Blake, "Mr. Percy is looking for you."

"I do not have time."

"Mr. Perrin needs some recipes."

"I do not have them!" Morel said, louder and more passionately than necessary. "And I have better things to do than to act as secretary to all the world. Matty copied them out; they are no doubt in Chef's office, or with kitchen clerks. Perrin knows this!"

"I know that you, Monsewer Morel, do not need recipes, as you know all the dishes by heart."

Morel seemed to relent a little. "It is a consequence of working so long in this trade: you commit all to memory. But you must excuse me."

Blake looked after him.

"Are you any closer?" I pressed

"Notions, notions, that's all, Avery," he said irritably, his eyes darting around the kitchen.

Something caught his eye. A boy: a stolid, knowing creature with the obligatory smear of dark smut across his forehead and short, dark hair that stuck up at the back. He was on his way to the servants' door. He carried a cloth messenger bag over his chest, and under this a sagging canvas coat and a gray muffler that had seen a deal of use. He looked like any of the hordes of ownerless boys in the capital, though more warmly dressed than many. The kitchen evidently knew him, as one of the pastry chefs had given him an apple, which he clutched appreciatively. Blake began to move. He did not take his eyes off him.

"What?"

"I'm following that boy."

"Here, little monkey," called Perrin. The boy dodged the cooks and soldiers, and returned to the sauce chef, who took the boy's chin in his hand and laughed, and pressed a new-baked bread roll into his palm. The boy grinned and thrust it deep in his pocket and went on his way, though not before casting an appraising, even envious, glance at the kitchen itself.

"Who is he? Do you know him?" I said.

Blake shrugged. "Delivery boy. Brought some jars of something for the kitchen. And collected something. See, his bag is tented. There's something in it that wasn't before."

"And?"

"Let's see," he muttered, then "Sir," more loudly.

I let him help me into my coat and out we went, up the steps and left into Pall Mall toward the Carlton and St. James's Palace.

"There he is," said Blake. The boy was walking jauntily some thirty yards ahead of us, feasting on his apple.

"Blake, what is this? We have barely ten hours," I pleaded. The boy waited for the crossing sweeper then ran across Pall Mall and turned off into the streets about St. James's Square and my new lodgings. We followed him across King Street and up Duke Street—nipping at his apple until it was little more than a string of seeds and fibers, whereupon he flicked it into the gutter and pulled out the roll, from which he derived, if his swaggering back and bobbing head were any indication, a good deal of enjoyment—and emerged onto Piccadilly. Blake nodded at the boy and raised his brows.

Past Burlington House, past Albemarle Street, where Ude lived, he went, then Dover Street, until he stood facing the Union Club. We looked at each other. The boy crossed the road and darted round the side of the club into the alley into which the club's kitchens issued.

"I'll go," I said.

"I'll go," said Blake. "You'll shine out like a virgin in a brothel. I'll meet you down Piccadilly, by Fortnum's." Before I could protest, he had dug his head into his muffler and his hands into his pockets and was deep into the alley. I did as I was told and walked up to Fortnum & Mason grocers, taut with anticipation and at the same time worried that every moment we spent here might be better used elsewhere.

"Spare a penny for a girl as has lost her good name? Captain?" It was the girl Margaret. She looked out from a lane that ran off Piccadilly, wrapped in a thin coat, a small bag resting by her feet.

"And who was only too quick to destroy the good name of another, quite innocent girl."

"I was put up to it, I swear it. I'll tell you everything. But you'll have to pay me." She paused.

"So you admit it."

"I'm frightened."

I felt only revulsion. "Of Scott? Save your breath. I'm in a hurry." I set off back down Piccadilly toward the Union Club. Blake stepped out in front of me.

"Well? What did you discover?"

"Not here."

Where does a master converse with his manservant except in the privacy of his rooms? We stepped into Green Park, avoiding the unfortunate women who crowded the place with their importuning.

"He went into the Union's kitchen. They let him in, knew him. He came out again after a good ten minutes, eating a tart—at least he's not going hungry. Whatever was in the bag was gone."

"How could you tell?"

"Edges were different, hung different."

"He might have moved it about."

"I know the lineaments of a bag. I was trained to it years ago. Package was gone."

"And then?"

"He went to the end of Dover Street and then east toward Regent

Street. I reckon he runs errands for one of the fancy spice shops. I ran up to him, looking out of puff, and asked him if he was the boy who had taken the papers from the Reform kitchen. He said he was. I said I'd been sent by Morel. He'd made a mistake and needed his papers back."

"Morel? That was a risk surely?"

"Boy looked discomfited. He said he'd been told not to speak of such things. He stuttered. I said, 'It's all right, I know all about them. Can you give them back to me?' He shook his head. I said, 'You handed them into the Union kitchens?' He nodded. I told him, 'Never mind,' just to continue as before and not to speak of it. He asked if they'd be cross with him. I said Mr. Morel wouldn't because it was his mistake. He looked pretty down in the mouth, so I said I would square things with Mr. Francobaldi—which cheered him up tremendously."

"Morel? What are you saying?"

"Morel is giving Soyer's recipes to Francobaldi."

"That is preposterous. They hate each other."

"Do you remember when we began to interview the staff? Morel dropped his papers—notes on recipes, he said. Now he says he never uses recipes, and everyone in the kitchen knows it. Why else would he be copying out such things if not for someone else?"

"Why would he betray Soyer, to whom he owes everything?"

"Money."

I shook my head.

"Or because he thinks Perrin will oust him. He certainly fears it."

"I will not believe it."

"Not everyone is as loyal as you, Avery. Morel is passing recipes to Francobaldi, and Francobaldi pays well for them, because he wants to be Soyer, but he hasn't the talent."

"Do you believe they may be behind the poisonings after all?"

"It is possible." He looked blank. "The boy will meet us here in a few minutes, after he's run his last errand. I told him I'd pay him for his trouble. Then we'll return to the Reform and have it out with Morel."

THE KITCHEN was in disorder. Nay, I should have called it uproar. Preparation and cooking seemed to have ceased entirely. Soldiers and cooks had retired into their own groups and were talking intently and excitedly among themselves. We pushed our way through the melee until I found myself opposite Mrs. Relph. For once, she was not angry with me.

"Bless me, Captain Avery, what a time you have come at! The whole place is at sixes and sevens," she said.

"What news, Mrs. Relph?"

"Our Matty has been released! Mr. Percy sent the news about Mr. Scott leaving and Margaret's dismissal to the sergeant who questioned her, and he agreed that there is nothing he can charge her with, though she is not all free of suspicion. We could do with her, but Chef says it may be best not to have her in the kitchen, just in case . . ."

"That is capital news!" I said.

"It is, sir, but then, not five minutes since, young Perrin was discovered putting something in the sauce. They say it's arsenic."

"I cannot believe it!"

"Describe it to us," said Blake brusquely.

She fixed him with an affronted look, but told us anyway.

It transpired that Perrin had been at his station laboring over some final version of a grand sauce for the evening. He had in his hand a small pot from which he spooned a little white powder. He beckoned one of the junior cooks to come and taste it. The boy took a mouthful, swallowed it. After a moment, he told one of his colleagues that it had tasted odd, bitter and that his mouth felt strange.

Perrin was standing at the sauce counter. Before him was a line of bowls full of broths, gravies and sauces ranging in color from gamey brown to the palest milk. The soldier shadowing Perrin took the little pot from him. Perrin was startled. He said he had just picked it up from the table; it was arrowroot, for thickening the sauce. He held it up to the light, close to his eyes. Another cook pointed out that the arrowroot was still on the table. The soldier took hold of Perrin, who began to protest. The vermin boy was called to look at the pot's contents. He said he thought it was arsenic.

Thus, all activity in the kitchen had ceased, and everyone had gathered around the principal kitchen to observe and murmur.

"We are waiting for Chef," said Mrs. Relph.

We pushed our way to the front of the gathered. Perrin looked utterly bewildered and was saying over and over again, *"Je ne comprends pas. Qu'est-ce qui se passe?"* (I don't understand. What is happening?) On either side of him was a soldier.

Soyer appeared, unsmiling and breathing heavily. He took the offending little pot and examined it. Then, before a wondering audience, he carefully put a tiny amount on his tongue, then spat it swiftly into a handkerchief—at this Blake grunted—and declared it to be arsenic.

There was a collective gasp, then the kitchen exploded with voices. Perrin started to say that he could not remember how he had come to be holding the cruet, but he swore he had been certain it was arrowroot. Soyer had turned the color of plaster. The soldiers took hold of Perrin's arms.

"Pourquoi je fais ça?" Perrin kept saying. "Why would I do this? Chef, *c'est une erreur. C'est fou!"* Soyer looked as if he might cry and, for once short of words, muttered briefly to the soldiers, then turned away. The soldiers pulled Perrin, who was still denying his guilt, out of the kitchen and up the stairs. The young cook who had swallowed the spoonful was given an emetic and taken to lie down.

The hubbub had risen to almost deafening proportions. Like some mindless automaton, Soyer stood upon a chair and began to shout.

"There is no excuse for leaving your stations. This is a great blow, but it will be weathered. We must continue as we began. We have a dinner to prepare, and we have no time to lose. I demand that we carry on. Chefs, take your places. Soldiers, return to your positions."

"But, Chef, if Perrin—"

"Back to your stations! You will continue with your work as if nothing has happened. And let us remember that another of our own, Mathilde, has already been released by the police."

The kitchen went quiet at once. The throng disbanded; the staff returned to their work.

Soyer descended from his chair. Morel was next to him. Soyer picked up Perrin's sauce, threw it into a basin and turned on the faucet. Blake strode across to the basin and would have pushed him out of the way, then remembered himself. Before he could scoop any up, it was halfway down the drain.

Soyer did not notice; he had gathered the *sauciers*. "What dishes did Monsieur Perrin attend to? What sauces?"

Perrin's second-in-command consulted with the other cooks. "We believe there must be a mistake, we do not believe he can be the culprit. It must be a mistake."

"Answer my question," said Soyer shortly.

"He oversaw everything, as usual."

"The question is: must everything be thrown away? Is anything safe? I must determine what I have to remake, and if I have time to do so."

"We saw him season the bowl you discarded with the arsenic, but none of us can recall him using it for anything else."

"Have you tasted everything?"

"Everything that has been so far completed."

"Then we will throw all these on the counter away, and we will start again."

"You cannot throw them away," said Blake, "They must be tested."

The other cooks looked at Blake.

Soyer nodded dully. "Take a small amount of each and put it into a jar. We will have them delivered to Mr. Wakley. Though the results—"

"Will not return until after the banquet. But at least you will know if they were poisoned."

"But some of these sauces—" said one of the *sauciers*.

"No questions. We must start again. Bring me my apron. Bring me the list. I must have three gallons of veal stock, butter, onions, carrots, flour, milk, cream. Will we need to make more consommé?"

The other cooks set off to gather the ingredients for the new sauces, leaving Soyer and Morel. I studied the latter, I could not tell if he was glad at his rival's fall; he simply seemed shocked.

"What do you make of this?" said Soyer.

"It's not him," said Blake, quietly but firmly.

"Ah, I cannot hear this! We saw him with the arsenic in his hand."

"If he had been administering it so lavishly in the past, do you not think someone would have noticed it before? And do you really believe him capable of it?"

Two cooks brought a great cauldron filled with clear brown liquid and set it on one of the great gas ranges. Soyer glared at Blake to indicate he should be silent. Then he took a long phosphorus match out of a drawer and turned a knob on the range, whereupon the gas flue under the cauldron began to emit a small whistle. He struck his match on a rough block and placed it by the gas flue. A crown of flame shot out.

"It is not a matter of what we believe, it is what we saw," Soyer said, as quietly as he could.

"I disagree," said Blake.

Morel said, "Captain Avery, your manservant is impertinent."

"And yet I would advise you to listen to Mr. Maguire," I said, as much to remind Blake of his disguise as to answer Morel.

"Not now," said Soyer. "I have too much to do. Thank the Lord that Mathilde is free. The committee asked—insisted—she not return to the kitchen for the moment, so I shall send her to help with the soup kitchen, if she is willing. A feminine touch. It is a perfect solution, *non?*"

"It's a fine solution," said Blake. "Now, please, let me explain."

Reluctantly, Soyer and Morel moved closer and we all clustered by the range so we might not be heard.

Blake pushed his glasses up his nose. "Perrin has no interest in politics or position, he simply wants to cook. And I think it would have been very easy for him to pick up something left near him, thinking it to be arrowroot."

"What do you mean?" said Morel.

"Mr. Perrin is shortsighted. If I may say so, sirs, I know something about bad sight." He tapped his spectacles (which, of course, were clear glass). "He does much to hide it, but he is so shortsighted he can barely make out anything unless it is very close to him. No doubt this is why the kitchen maids think his eyes are so 'soft,' and why he in turn can barely recognize them unless he stands very close.

"When he works, he bends very close over his bowl, and reaches out for things without looking for them. I'd say he had memorized where he expects to find his salt and seasonings and picked the arsenic pot up by mistake."

Morel said, "Does arsenic feel like arrowroot?"

"It can. It depends upon the size and texture of the grains," said Soyer.

Morel stared at him.

"Someone deliberately placed the arsenic pot so that he would pick it up. Someone wanted him caught," I said.

"Yes, or to distract attention, or to throw the kitchen into more confusion."

"Who?" said Soyer.

I looked at Morel. He did not look at me.

Blake said nothing.

"I am certain it is not Perrin. We will speak to the boy who tasted the sauce, and the cook who accused him, the soldier who took him," I said.

"But how should I proceed?" said Soyer.

"Just as you said: go on as before, sir," said Blake. "Do not lift your guard. Proceed as if the poisoner is still at large: soldiers watching cooks, cooks tasting everything."

Soyer was now leaning over his vast stew pan. "I shall barely have time to remake the sauces. I—we, have a great deal to do."

Blake nudged me.

"With your permission, Monsieur Soyer, we have one small matter to discuss with Monsieur Morel."

"Gentlemen, please."

"It will not take long. And it is very important."

Soyer turned away from us. He did not want to hear any more.

"André," he said to Morel, "they will not stop until they have had their way. Take my office."

Morel said he must wash his hands. Blake stiffened: he thought he might run.

"Are you sure of this?" I said quietly. "We may end up depriving Soyer of his right hand just after having lost Perrin. And if you are wrong—"

"No alternative," said Blake, as Morel returned to us and we went to Soyer's office.

There was an awkward silence. I examined one of Soyer's relish jars with great attention.

Morel said, "You think it was I—"

"You who what?" said Blake.

"It was well known I did not like him, but—"

"I wanted to ask about the boy who runs errands, the one who likes his food," said Blake.

Morel looked enormously relieved, but confused. "I know him. He's a good boy. Quick at his tasks; we give him leftovers. How he loves them!"

Blake watched him almost sadly.

"He has made himself an errand boy for a number of the fine shops about Piccadilly," I said.

"Yes, he brings us spices and herbs and special ingredients. Chef and I have discussed offering him a position one day."

Blake nodded. "A fine opportunity for such a boy. He's made himself a daily route. I see he does errands for Francobaldi as well."

"Does he? Well, as you know, Mr. Francobaldi cannot resist following where we lead."

I had no idea how to continue. I looked at Blake pleadingly.

He said, "Mr. Morel, we know you are passing recipes to Francobaldi. We know that this boy takes them for you and goes to the Union Club, where he gives the envelopes to Mr. Francobaldi."

"That is absurd."

"Please, Mr. Morel," I said. "I do not know why you have done it; I can only imagine that you must have felt forced to it somehow. Perhaps you feel—mistakenly, I am sure—that in some way your position here is at risk? I am certain it is not."

"I assure you, Captain Avery," Morel said coldly, "I feel no such thing, and I must assume that this is some foolish attempt at a joke on your part. If not, I am deeply insulted that you should say such a thing."

I said, "Monsieur Morel, I am deeply sorry, but I know it to be the truth."

"I ask you not to persist with this nonsense, or I must have nothing more to say to you." He gave me a look of anger and disappointment mixed, and walked away.

"Mr. Morel." It was Blake. "You must understand why Captain Avery raises this."

Morel continued to the door. Then he turned. "That you could think . . ." he said furiously.

"Mr. Morel, we know." Blake brought out of his pocket a sheaf of papers written upon in a neat, measured hand. "*Croustades* and *filet de bœuf à la Jeanne d'Arc.* Crayfish in champagne, Soyer's lobsters with plover's eggs."

"Let me see those!" Morel snatched a few pages from Blake's hand.

"Ha!" he said triumphantly. "What is this? These make no sense. Just a line of letters in no language I have ever seen."

"We know they are in code, Mr. Morel. Captain Avery and I were in Signals in India." (This, in fact, was patently untrue on my account, but I knew Blake was well versed in such matters.) "You have just substituted one letter for another—it is not a hard code to crack—and the recipes are in French. And it will not be hard to prove that the writing is yours."

"Your manservant is quite a prodigy," said Morel bitterly. "What else does he do, aside from deciphering codes and speaking French?"

"He has Italian and a number of Hindoostanee dialects, Mr. Morel. I should add, we have these from Francobaldi's office. We showed them to the boy. He knew they were the pages you gave to him because, once before, he had looked at them, out of curiosity. He is learning to read and hadn't been able to make anything of them. He was most concerned that you would be cross with him for having let them into the hands of anyone else. Mr. Maguire persuaded him that we were acting under your instructions."

"How very considerate of you, Mr. Maguire." He held himself straight, with the dignity of the condemned man.

"I do not claim to know or understand your relations with Mr. Francobaldi," I said, "but since you have chosen to act in such a manner, which, you must agree, is contrary to Monsieur Soyer's interests, we have a duty to look into it and to see if anything connects it to the poisonings. Is there anything you can tell us about them?"

He shook his head. "I should say, how could you think such a thing of me? But I see in your eyes I am quite traduced. I cannot believe that any chef would deliberately poison the food he cooks. That, I swear. If I had any idea where this could be issuing from . . ." He turned away, overcome, and we both averted our gaze. "Even so, this dinner is a stupid, stupid risk; I do not understand why Alexis is taking it. I think it may destroy him. As for the recipes, I felt I had no other course."

"Perhaps Francobaldi brought some impossible pressure to bear?" I said hopefully.

He shook his head. "I did it willingly. Perrin will supersede me in a few months' time. It is plain to see. And I have debts. I have worked hard for years, but I have little talent with money."

My own recent occupation of the Marshalsea came suddenly and horribly vivid before my eyes. It seemed absurd that such a place should be the fate of anyone who worked as industriously as Morel.

"If you were in trouble, could you not have asked Soyer rather than betraying him? Surely he would have helped you?"

"I told you, he sees Perrin as the future. I knew I must do something for myself. Francobaldi offered me a good deal of money. He believes the recipes will open up some avenue of opportunity from which he has hitherto been barred. He does not understand that he will never be of the first class. He is a copyist, and that is what he will always be."

He inspected his fingernails. "Shall we proceed to Alexis?"

I would have nodded, but Blake said, "No."

We both gaped at him.

"You will finish the preparations and remain his *sous-chef,* Morel, at least until after the banquet. He cannot afford to lose you now."

"And yet you accuse and shame me now?"

"If you are willing to sell his secrets, what more would you be willing to do to harm him? We had to consider you a likely suspect for the poisonings."

"But now you do not?"

"No."

Morel rubbed his face again. "I am glad to hear that. May I ask why?"

Blake stared at him, boring into his eyes in that way he had. "It's many things. But I am certain you are not the poisoner. And, given that, I think you should stay and see Soyer through this."

"If there are casualties from the dinner, I am doubly damned—for betraying him, and for preparing the dishes. I would never work again."

"Call it atonement for your sins. You owe it to him, and I believe you will feel worse if you leave now."

"And if I refuse?"

"You won't get far. Soyer will be informed, and the police will come for you. There may not be a particular charge, but the fact that you have been betraying your chief will not dispose them well toward you. I would rather you saw this matter as a choice rather than an obligation."

"And if I stay?"

"You get to make your peace with Soyer yourself."

Morel stared at Blake. "You are no manservant. Who are you?"

Blake merely shrugged.

Mrs. Quill permitted us to visit Matty—with a housemaid in attendance—in her housekeeper's room on the first floor. The maid knitted quietly in a corner while Matty sat in a chair, curled up tight into a kind of ball and wrapped in a blanket. Her ordeal had left her strangely distracted but, as she talked, a powerful anger awoke in her as she spoke of Scott's departure.

"I'm glad he's gone. I'll thank Percy when I see him. Shake his hand. I always hated Scott," she said. "Not two months gone he got a housemaid I knew, Esther, in the family way"—she paused and glanced at me—"with child, I mean. He promised her he'd see her all right. But the moment it showed, she was dismissed by Mrs. Quill, and not a word from Scott. Bundled her out at daybreak, before I was even up. Nobody's seen her since. He'd try it with any girl who'd oblige. He promised them treats and dinner, or a new scarf or bonnet, or to put in a word with Mr. Soyer, and if he thought he'd get away with it, he'd tell them they'd see no promotions if they didn't. I bet that's what he said to Netty."

"Did he try this with you, Matty?" I said, much troubled.

"Me? Wouldn't dare," she said fiercely. "He knew I'd cut off his tallywags if he came near me."

"Matty!"

The housemaid bent closer over her knitting.

"He did try it once, when I first arrived and he thought I was green and easy, but I told him where to go. Then I was Soyer's girl."

"Soyer's girl?"

"Oh, don't you start. I mean, he showed me favor. I was sharp and hard-working and I could write and I was on the up. Well, that was then."

She looked at her hands. There was a small bruise along the side of her narrow wrist and the mark of a healing burn on the side of her right forefinger.

"And will be again," I said.

"We'll see. They've let me out, but they won't let me back in the kitchen."

"And Soyer has placed you in charge of the Spitalfields kitchen. Over all those cooks. He shows his confidence in you."

"Not in charge. They wouldn't listen to me. Not now."

She was silent for a moment, then she said, "Someone said Scott used to be a major domo in a claphouse for posh toffer."

"Matty!" I said. "We cannot talk about such things! You cannot know such things!"

"Damn, Captain, I spent five years on Holywell Street! What do you think I didn't see? You know what gets me? Everyone knew what he was up to; no one spoke of it. What I minded was that, at least on the street, you knew what to expect; it was honest in its way. Here, the kitchen maids and the housemaids are told to preserve their virtue and not have their heads turned, but nothing was said when he preyed on them." She turned from me. "Tell me, Blake, am I wrong? Is there something I don't understand? Men lie and misbehave and get away with it. I knew what it was like in Holywell Street, but I always thought that somewhere like this would be different. And now I wonder if there's anything but hypocrisy anywhere."

"But Scott is gone," I said.

Blake took her hand but said nothing.

AT THREE O'CLOCK of the afternoon, four hours before the banquet, I presented myself at Soyer's office. Lord Marcus and Molesworth—the first time I had seen either in the kitchens—along with Soyer and Percy, had come to hear my conclusions, such as they were. Morel was missing.

"I cannot imagine what has happened to him," Soyer said anxiously. "I have sent two messages to his lodgings. He is not there. He is always so reliable."

"The girl has been released, and I am told you are convinced Perrin is not the poisoner, even though he was caught red-handed," said Lord Marcus heavily. Molesworth said nothing but regarded me balefully. I admit I was not happy to see him.

"For the following reasons," I said, and repeated Blake's arguments.

"Perhaps Mr. Morel is the culprit, then?"

"I do not think it is he, and I am sure he will be back," I said. I hoped he would.

"Where is he, then?" asked Soyer tightly.

"Captain, I appreciate your efforts, I do. But are you not making difficulties where none exist?" said Lord Marcus.

"Believe me, sir, I do not believe it is Morel. And I am deeply sorry, sir, that I do not have another name. We have looked at everything we could think of. We have questioned everyone we could."

"I hear you have mortally offended Mr. Molesworth," Lord Marcus observed.

"He is entitled to his opinion," said Molesworth coldly. "He was simply wrong. About a good deal, it appears."

"We have tested deliveries," I went on, "and had no positive results. My manservant, Maguire, has observed the kitchen from every angle. We cannot be certain how the poison was administered, simply that it was. As for Russians, Collinson told me to leave the embassy to him and, otherwise, we have found no evidence of any connection to them."

"So, by your own lights, you have failed," said Molesworth.

"Yes, sir. But I do have one more suggestion, though it is somewhat rash," I said.

Blake sighed and rubbed his ear.

"Tell us," said Soyer.

"We—I—will be the last line of defense. I will eat something of all that is to be served. Whatever is made in advance, I will eat early, so we can have as good a chance as possible for any effects to be seen. Whatever must be done for the guests at the table, we will taste as it goes. It is perhaps not the best idea, I know. Someone could simply sprinkle some arsenic over something as the food goes out. One *entremet* could be poisoned and all the rest perfectly good. But I want to stop this horror as much as any man, and this is all I can suggest."

"Captain Avery, I am deeply touched," said Soyer. "I am not sure I can allow it."

"You will allow the diners to eat your food, but not me?" I said.

"With the express reason to see if it poisons? There is something terrible about that. But you are right. I cannot serve my own food without being willing to partake of it, myself. I, too, will taste," said Soyer.

"No, sir," said Percy. "You will be making final preparations and serving, Monsieur Soyer. You will not be able to taste everything."

"I will do my best."

"I should like to volunteer myself," said Percy.

"You will not have time," said Soyer. "You will be upstairs, overseeing the waiters and then here with the wine, but the offer is noted."

"I have arranged everything, sir. To the last detail. The footmen and the underbutlers know their work. I could certainly stay for a while, sir. Please, I should like to."

"For a while, then."

"I am moved by your persistence, Captain Avery," said Lord Marcus. "Personally, it seems to me that Perrin is clearly guilty. But, as chairman, I have a duty to the club, and I should like to accompany you in the early tasting. After that, I will have to absent myself to greet the arrivals."

"I will taste, too," said Molesworth drily. "If only to show—though I should not have to—that I am no less committed to this club than you, Marcus. Also I should like to observe the captain, who has such faith in me."

I swallowed. Blake grunted and looked resigned. "I'll do it. It's rash and unscientific, of course, but it's something."

"Is your servant always given to speaking his mind so bluntly?" said Molesworth.

"I would have thought you, as a radical, would appreciate honesty in a working man," said Blake.

For once, Molesworth was without an answer. Lord Marcus smirked.

"So," I said, "we will taste and continue to have as much of the food's preparation as we can manage supervised by the soldiers. When dishes go out to the diners, the soldiers will accompany the waiters. The under-butlers and footmen will be watched by the soldiers as they open and pour the bottles of wine. Gentlemen," I said, not quite believing what I was saying, "we have a quorum."

Chapter Twenty-two

It was three hours until the banquet. The food that had already been prepared was under guard by the Scots Fusiliers. They had orders not to touch anything, on pain of court-martial. The cooks were nearing their limit. Tempers were fraying, and every cook had a burn or a knife wound, to the extent that Percy was now patrolling the kitchen, administering salves and binding cuts.

We sat in Soyer's study at the large table: Blake and myself, Lord Marcus and Molesworth, the two latter wrapped in kitchen whites so as not to sully their evening clothes—and Percy, once he had completed his medical duties; as unlikely dinner companions as I could imagine.

"The rules, gentlemen," I said. "Each item is to be tried by one diner. Notes to be kept of who ate what. Two to three spoons each, then five minutes until the next dish. If you detect any tastes that seem alien to you, or any unusual reaction—pain, tingling in your mouth, throat or even in your extremities, however small, you mention it at once. I cannot say how effective this will be."

I had not been sure how I should feel about eating my way through the dishes in order to discover if they were fatal; I suppose I had thought that the apprehension of danger would dull my appetite. I was surprised to find that the opposite was true. The sense that every mouthful might be one's last added a kind of zest to the occasion, and I sat down with a peculiar sense of anticipation. I was reminded of the battlefield in the moment before a skirmish.

Of my fellow diners, Blake showed nothing in his expression, Lord Marcus did his best but was clearly frightened, Molesworth was characteristically nonchalant, Percy utterly correct—though his nerves were apparent in his habit of continually shooting his cuffs. Soyer overlaid his anxiety with light chatter.

We began with the soups. For me, *potage à la* Victoria, a pale golden, thickened veal broth garnished with parsley and cockscomb seeds. My spoon trembled slightly as I brought it to my lips. I grinned and took it. It seemed to me the acme of warmth and meaty fragrance; made the more so, I suspected, by the lingering sense of danger. I took another mouthful.

"No need to overdo it," said Blake.

Molesworth looked up from his *Comte de Paris*, a dark-hued consommé in which delicate ribbons of macaroni and tiny balls of chicken mousse floated. He raised an eyebrow.

Blake, meanwhile, tasted *potage à la* Colbert, a vegetable soup with tiny dice of Jerusalem artichokes, all cut perfectly identical to the size of peas. Percy tried a *potage à la* Louis Philippe, named after the current, undeserving incumbent of the French throne, a soup flavored with stock and turnip, to be finished with cream and the first impossibly thin asparagus just before serving. Soyer took sips of everything. We waited a few minutes. No strange tastes, we agreed.

The fish would have to be tried much closer to its serving, as would most of the meat dishes. Waiters, each accompanied by a soldier, brought in the various sauces for the fish: I had a sauce Mazarin, a creamy concoction of the soft, coral roe of a lobster, destined for a poached turbot, while Lord Marcus tried a fragrant sherry sauce that would dress a salmon trout, and Percy the *crème gratin* for a dish of Severn salmon that was due to arrive at any moment. Soyer returned to the kitchen.

We passed on to the garnishes and braises: miraculous veal quenelles for me, a frothy asparagus purée, a stuffing of truffles and mushrooms for capons, braised ox tongues, poached crayfish and fish quenelles for the others.

We went on to those of the twelve entrées that were ready. I took the tiny spring chickens and ham braised in a shiny Madeira sauce. I recall Lord Marcus, blinking and mopping his brow after every bite, tasting tender cubes of hare in a blood sauce, and Percy, with splendid calm, trying little balls of warm quail pâté. Blake took a small, flaky pastry cup of mackerel roe and little molded meat jellies of rice and lambs' tails.

One of the kitchen clerks came in, asking for Percy. He left us, and when he returned he asked our pardon but he was needed elsewhere. We wished him well and continued.

Molesworth suddenly started from his veal sweetbreads and puréed cucumbers and began to cough. We looked up from our plates. He turned very white and waved his hand up and down before his face.

"Monsieur?" said Soyer.

"Gentlemen, I think perhaps there is something bitter in these." Molesworth began to shake.

Soyer passed him water and a concoction of milk and egg white, which, he had explained, should help mitigate the effects of any arsenic. Molesworth tossed it back immediately.

"May I?" said Blake.

Molesworth nodded. Blake helped himself. "No. I'd say it is clear. Soyer?"

Soyer took a bite. He shook his head. "A false alarm, I think, sir," he said.

Molesworth sat down. He took several deep breaths and tried to recapture his composure. "So you are both familiar with the taste of arsenic," he said at last. "Monsieur Soyer and Mr.—Maguire, is it?—or is it Mr. Blake?"

I felt myself go cold. Blake stared determinedly at the table.

"I'm not a bloody fool," said Molesworth. "Who else should you be? Rude, ill-tempered, leading the captain by the nose. I mean, has not everyone realized?"

Lord Marcus looked astonished. Soyer suddenly became very preoccupied by his tendon separators.

"Oh, I have no reason to expose you, Mr. Blake. I want this mess arranged as much as anyone." He looked pointedly at Lord Marcus.

"As do we all," said Lord Marcus.

"Besides," said Molesworth, "you may be dead by the end of this."

Blake took off his gloves and his spectacles. "I may."

"Ah," said Molesworth, staring at Blake's hands, "so it was two missing fingers. Shall we continue?"

No more was said. Of the *entremets,* I essayed curried lobster balls, but we were forced to leave most of the vegetables, for they would not be cooked until the last minute, and went on to the first of the prepared desserts. I had brandy-soaked cherries in little, round, hard toffee cases, elaborately domed meringues, charmingly shaped fruit jellies to be served on beds of whipped cream, small, crisp apricot tarts and little squares of sugared pineapple jelly bonbons.

From time to time, one of us would own to uncertainty about a taste, another would try it, and it would be judged not obviously dangerous. Blake noted all this down on a series of papers. Molesworth and Lord Marcus seemed to have accepted Blake's unmasking, though it occurred to me that perhaps the endless stream of dishes and the thought that every bite might be their last were making such claims on their attention that it was hard to think of anything else.

Next came the various constituent parts of Soyer's giant dessert assemblages, his *pièces montées*. They were to be put together at the last minute, for they could only hold together for so long before collapsing into a puddle of cream, sponge and soggy fruit. In the midst of this, the footman—it was Jeffers, with whom I had first discovered Rowlands as he sickened—came to announce that Lord Marcus and Molesworth were needed upstairs.

There was an hour and a half until the dinner.

"I bid you adieu, gentlemen," said Molesworth. "I think I have emphatically scotched any suspicions anyone could possibly harbor of me. If one of us is to die, let us hope it takes place before the first course."

Lord Marcus stood up, tremendously relieved to be finished, and came and pressed my hand. He nodded at Blake. "We will speak later," he mumbled. Then, more loudly, "Your efforts will not be overlooked."

I gave Blake a hopeful look, anyway, as if to say, *There, you see?*

He shook his head.

In the kitchen, a cheer went up. Moments later, Soyer, wreathed in smiles, dragged Morel into the study.

"He is here! We are saved," he said, embracing his *sous-chef*. Over his shoulder, Morel gazed at us. Blake shook his head. We had kept his secret.

JUST AFTER SIX, one began to hear the sound of carriages arriving outside the club. Now Blake and I were alone—though Soyer came in when he could. We had tried the constituent parts of the grand desserts (though we would have to return to more entrées and savories once the dinner began). The least ambitious of these was a concoction of meringues assembled into the shape of a Chinese pagoda, with early strawberries and Soyer's elaborate joke of lamb cutlets that revealed themselves, on closer inspection, to be cake, cream, frangipane and icing. There were two further large assemblages. One, Soyer called the *gâteau britannique à l'amiral*, the British admiral's cake: a pale sponge had been carved into the shape of a man-of-war and iced with rice-paper versions of the Egyptian and English flags. Within it would be placed chilled, sliced fruits and iced peach mousse. The last was the *crème d'Égypte à l'*Ibrahim Pasha, a dessert in the shape of a pyramid in which light meringue cakes had been carved into the shape of the great square stones of the pyramid, mortared with a pineapple cream and faced with thin, transparent sheets of spun sugar. On top of this would be placed a portrait of Mehmet Ali Pasha, also in spun sugar, and underneath it, etched upon jelly and framed with gold leaf, a portrait of Ibrahim Pasha himself.

We tasted the constituent parts of the ship, but the pyramid, wheeled in by Morel, was now complete.

"How can we ensure this is safe?" Morel said. "Of all the things in the banquet, this surely will be the one the pasha will find most arresting. Were I a poisoner, this is what I would choose to dose."

"It is the *pièce de résistance*," said Soyer. "Lord Palmerston particularly requested it."

"No one must eat it," said Blake. "You will have to make sure of that."

Soyer sighed.

We had done everything we could for the moment and would have now to wait for dishes prepared closer to their serving. Feeling none the worse, save rather full, I went to look at Pall Mall. It was nose-to-tail full of vehicles, and on each side people had gathered to see the arrival of the Egyptian prince. The newspapers had promised a description of the dinner itself in the following day's editions.

There was a footman's jacket on a hook. I put it on, took the servants' stairs to the ground floor and peeped through the half-open door to the saloon. The club was as full as I had ever seen it, with gentlemen in formal evening dress.

The company fell back as Lord Palmerston stepped into the room. Next to him was a short, stout man wearing one of those red felt hats known as a fez and with a lavish salt-and-pepper beard and deep, sunken, tired eyes. His black velvet jacket was embroidered about the edges with gold braid. Pinned to its lapels were a dozen golden rosettes, and about his neck he wore ropes of gold chains. Ibrahim Pasha, for it was he, was followed by three more somberly dressed, mustachioed men, all wearing fezzes. The crowd applauded, and the small, tired man, the famous general of the Egyptian army, waved graciously. Lord Marcus, Ellice, Molesworth and Beare came forward, bowed and were introduced. Lord Marcus was still stiff with nerves, while a strained little smile played on Molesworth's lips. Other worthies were presented, until at last Soyer came forward, in a black velvet suit and with his red velvet cap at its ridiculous angle. He made a deep bow before the prince, who smiled and began to applaud. The rest began to clap, too, though, to my eyes, the gentlemen appeared somewhat strained. I wondered how many of them had had sight of the cheaper papers. Then Palmerston steered the prince into one of the smaller reception rooms, and Soyer, Lord Marcus and the inner committee followed.

The banquet would begin soon.

IN THE KITCHENS, the heat had never seemed so great, and the presence of the soldiers had become truly irksome to the cooks. Morel clapped and shouted, to apparently little effect. They had, of course, all been working almost without ceasing for two days, and though most of them seemed to think that Perrin probably was the poisoner, the air of threat and fear still lingered.

It was not such a surprise when, just as we had sat down to start tasting again, a cry went up in the kitchen. Two of the junior cooks from the roasts station were shouting.

"It's him, it's him! Bloody *Deutsch*!"

The whole kitchen stopped. No one dared leave their post, but everyone was attending. Matty's accuser, Albert, was surrounded.

One of the two junior cooks, a Scotsman, said, "He tried to get round the soldiers who were guarding the meat braises. He's been at it all day, making a thing of it, boasting that he could, on and on. He's always been a bad 'un. It's him. He's the one."

"It was a joke," Albert protested, grinning too broadly. "That is all, just a joke."

Silently, the ill feeling in the kitchen rose up and fixed itself upon him. No one had liked him much, and plenty had detested him.

"I mean it," Albert said. He tucked a straggling lock of greasy hair under his cap. The gesture was oddly childlike. "I meant no harm. It was just a joke."

"He's a German, sir," said the Scottish junior cook. "We heard you was looking at the Germans."

One of the kitchen maids howled and launched herself at Albert, almost knocking him down.

"Bastard!" she screamed. I dashed forward, took hold of her and pulled her off. It seemed to me she had the weight of the kitchen behind her. I had no idea what the next moments might bring.

Soyer appeared then, and clapped his hands. "Back to work! All of you! *Mes amis!* Captain Avery will take care of this! We have work to do. *Maintenant!*"

I thought they would ignore him. But the moment passed and they moved grudgingly back to their places.

The junior cooks described what they had seen. The account was garbled but, apparently, Albert had boasted that he could get at various dishes under guard, and had pestered the soldiers and tried to get into the warming cupboards, until his peers had long since stopped even pretending to be amused. Eventually, the two junior cooks had lost patience and denounced him.

"Can you do without him?" said Blake. Soyer nodded. "Lock him in a room until after the banquet. He'll pay the price of having wasted our time. Or," he added as an afterthought, "I suppose he may end up in Newgate Jail."

"You hear that? Newgate and the noose for you, if there's a trace of anything noxious," I said. "Confess now, and we may be able to help you. It's more than your Russian friends will do for you."

"I do not know any Russians," he said sulkily. Disappointingly, I believed him.

"We'll try any *relevés* and meat dishes he may have worked on," I said.

Blake and I returned to Soyer's room to start upon the next courses.

A footman was waiting for us.

"Jeffers!" I said.

He nodded. "Upstairs says to say, sir, that he is eating!" The banquet had begun.

"Who? Ibrahim Pasha?"

"Yes, sir."

"But he has a taster. And he doesn't eat."

"This time he does, sir."

"Can they not stop him?"

"How, sir? He insisted he must try Chef's works for himself. He loves the soup. The taster barely had time to swallow before he started in. The rest of the guests are hardly eating."

"They've heard the rumors."

Blake leaned back. "How is your stomach?" he said.

You knew there would be more. And there will be, the second note Soyer received had said. "None the worse." I felt a strong desire to laugh. "And you?"

"Never better."

"Bring us the rest," I called.

It was the *relevés* and roasts—great haunches of mutton from the South Downs; more of lamb, and a vast baron of roast beef on an almighty platter—which threatened to finish me. When I was faced with these meaty leviathans, the whole endeavor suddenly seemed impossible. I felt myself lose heart.

"Chef asked if you might take a little off the bottom," said Jeffers, wrestling with the beef, which, it must be said, was so large it seemed impossible that one man could do anything much with it.

"Let me help," said Blake. "I'll hold it down."

"If you please, sir," Jeffers said. "I'll do my best, but I'm nothing compared to Mr. Percy. He's a master when it comes to carving."

"Yes, I've seen him do it. He is an artist," I said politely, as the poor man struggled to take a little meat off the side.

"What can we really do with these great pieces?" I said. "What if one end was contaminated and not . . ."

"An artist?" Blake said, interrupting.

"Oh, yes, sir," said Jeffers. "How he wields the knife! Like he was born to it."

"How would you learn such skills?" Blake said.

"Long service?" I said.

"As a butcher maybe. Or a surgeon?" said Blake, standing up. "He said, do you recall, that going into service was not what he had planned? But he had to because his father lost his business. Do you know"—he turned on Jeffers and stared intently at him—"what Percy did before he went into service? Doctoring, surgery?"

Jeffers looked flustered. "Can't say I do, Mr. Maguire."

"Is he always the one with the salves and the bandages when someone's injured in the kitchen?"

"I have seen him binding cuts—there's a lot of them in a kitchen. Did I say something wrong?"

Blake had left the room. I followed him. The kitchen now seemed oddly bare of familiar faces. No Perrin, no Matty, Morel just there in person, all but gone in spirit. Scott dismissed. No Percy.

Blake was conferring with Soyer.

"Is Percy returned?"

Soyer was distracted. "We had a message from the soup kitchen," he said. "Mathilde asked that Percy might come and help. The cooks have been unruly; they need a guiding hand. For all our troubles here, we are at least well ordered. I sent him at once. I am sorry, Blake, I have no time, we have three hundred soups to serve."

"Does he always treat wounds and burns?"

"Often, but Blake, I cannot—"

"Does he have a set of knives?" Blake said.

"He keeps them in the butler's room. He is very proud of them."

"I must see them."

The room was locked. Soyer called for Morel, who came, but not before Blake had almost broken down the door.

"Where would he keep them?" Morel pointed to two long, well-worn leather boxes on the highest of a series of shelves, lined with silver-plated teapots and dishes.

I stretched up and brought them down. Inside the first, upon old but beautiful watered silk, were two knives with fine bone handles and long, thin, well-polished blades, sharp on the side and blunt at the tip.

"They are unusual," said Morel.

"These are surgeon's knives," said Blake. He opened the other box. Inside there was a hacksaw with several spare blades. "We must go."

"What?"

"To the soup kitchen."

I shook my head. "What about the banquet?"

"It's not the banquet. All is well with the banquet. Don't worry about the banquet. Alexis, tell Lord Marcus the guests can eat anything they choose."

I expected jubilation. Instead, Soyer looked ashen. "It is too late. It was to start at seven," he said.

"We'll see," said Blake. "Come, William."

He pushed his way out of the kitchen, and I followed him along Pall Mall, as he fought his way through the still-milling spectators toward Trafalgar Square.

"What—" I ventured as I drew level with him.

"We must get to Spitalfields. We need a cab. It's just short of an hour by foot."

There were two hansom cabs by the water troughs in the square, both about to be taken. Blake reached the first, thrust the gentleman climbing into it out of the way, and climbed in. I tried to apologize as I followed him. The driver complained, but Blake pushed a note into his palm and he set off, still grumbling.

"Explain this to me," I said.

Blake was wheezing from his exertion. I felt a pang of concern about his health as I waited for him to recover.

"It's not the banquet. It was always the soup kitchen. The club is not the mark, Soyer is."

"He feeds the poor poisoned soup on the night he feeds the rich on lobster tails," I said.

"A party of ragged schoolchildren are to eat first. It's all arranged."

"Oh, good God!" I saw a line of hungry children, holding bowls. "From seven, Soyer said. It must be near half past."

"I know."

"And Matty is there."

"I know."

We both sat, hunched in silence. I would have jumped out and run, but I did not know the way. I put my head out of the cab window.

"Can you not go faster?" I shouted at the driver. "I'll pay double." The horse leaped forward as the whip struck its sides.

My watch said twenty-five after seven. I felt breathless with apprehension.

"So it's Percy," I said. He nodded. "I cannot believe it." But in my heart, I feared it was true.

"He'd know about pharmacology and poisons and dosage. As steward, he has authority to order anything, and he confessed he'd been false with the accounts."

"But surely he could not buy enough to poison the soup for the whole kitchen—he'd need so much. It would surely come to light?"

"Arsenic and strychnine are cheap, and he is the steward of a large club with many rooms and the biggest kitchen in London. A large bag of arsenic to take care of the vermin? Two? Of course, sir."

"But he works so hard, and he is devoted to Soyer."

"Is he? I always thought him a cold fish. Too correct. And last night, when Margaret cursed Scott, she said, 'You promised.' I reckon now that she was talking to Percy."

I saw the scene in my head. It seemed to me quite possible.

"Damn me, but she was there, on Piccadilly, this morning, when I was waiting for you. She asked for money, but I sent her on her way. She said she had something to tell me, and that she was frightened. I thought she meant Scott. I clean forgot."

Blake rubbed his brows.

"I should have listened to her," I said. He raised his hand to silence me.

We did not speak for some time.

"I reckon Percy set her to accuse Matty," he said eventually. "And that Percy put the arsenic out for Perrin to pick up. He arranged Scott's dismissal. He has stripped the Reform of Soyer's closest supporters and his own rivals."

"Do you think he knew about Morel?" I said. "Whenever Morel protested about recipes, not needing them or not having them, Percy gave me the most pointed look. The note said, 'All shall be taken from you.' But for what? Money? Position? What does he want?"

"Revenge. To be the only man left when Soyer falls." He put his head in his hands.

Fear rose in me. "Where are we?"

"Finsbury Square."

I dug coins out of my pockets. "Would we be swifter on foot?"

He sighed. "Not me."

I tried not to look at my watch, but I could not stop myself. Twenty minutes to eight o'clock. I could not bear to think of the scene unfolding at the soup kitchen; I could not stop myself from imagining it.

The cab swung into a wide thoroughfare.

"Norton Folgate. Stop here." We stumbled out of the cab, I dropped coins in the driver's glove, and Blake began to run. He turned down one street and then another. He was already gasping; I knew he should slow soon. He pointed forward, and I set off without him. Ahead of us, a crowd and what looked to be a large, gray tent, and next to it a steam engine, all illuminated by a dozen gaslight moons getting brighter by the moment as darkness closed in.

"Stop!" I cried.

Chapter Twenty-three

Stop! Stop!" Faces turned, startled. Close to, the crowd was a collection of wretched men and women, excited, expectant, but many and restless. Small children were sitting on the cobbles. Many of them looked dismally thin and underfed. The luxury and quantity of the food we had consumed at the Reform seemed suddenly distasteful by comparison.

"Stop!"

The steam engine billowed smoke into the evening. A long line snaked into the tent, carrying bowls. Two young cooks I recognized were handing out bread. A number of police stood about the square.

I barged into the tent. "Matty!" I shouted. "Matty!"

I wrestled my way through the lines. Some jostled me; all stared resentfully. There were rows of long tables at which children were sitting, a bowl and spoon before each one. Round the sides mounted on high shelves were barrels marked "Pure Water." And at the far end, on a platform, below a portrait of Her Majesty the Queen, there was a great drum on wheels some thirteen feet high, with what looked like a slender chimney emerging upward from it. It was being stirred by two cooks standing on chairs, with great iron ladles. Other cooks were bustling about, some counting out spoons and dishes, another cutting bread. Two stood over two great stew pans. Next to them, Matty was issuing orders. Despite her slightness, she seemed admirably capable. To one side were several well-dressed ladies and gentlemen observing, local alderman or charity workers and their ladies. They were attended by two police constables. Percy, I could not see.

"Matty!"

She smiled, then frowned. "Captain? Should you—"

I reached her. Now I was gasping. "Where is the soup? You cannot serve it."

"Everything took longer than we planned. The drum would not heat. The soup would not cook. The crowd is getting restless. We are only now ready. What do you mean, stop?"

"Thank God! Have you tried the soup?"

"Not yet."

I do not know where he came from, but Percy appeared, accompanied by two men, one a curate in a loose black coat and white cravat, the other a man of modest means, plainly in his Sunday best. He was perfectly composed.

"Matty, are we ready? Captain Avery, what brings you here? Not bad news, I hope?"

I turned away from him. "You cannot eat it," I said to Matty.

One of the cooks had raised a small bowl to his lips. I dashed it from his hands, then overturned the two stew pans. The contents, thick and grainy green, spattered over the cobbles.

Matty exclaimed. One of the constables came forward and tried to take my arm. I pushed him off.

"Hi!" A furious shout came from the crowd in the tent. It swelled. Percy's companions looked indignant.

"Captain! Are you feeling quite well?" Percy looked appalled.

"As if you did not know."

"Is he mad?" said the man in his Sunday best.

"Matty, the soup is poisoned. We are sure of it. It's him." I looked at Percy.

"Have you gone mad?" she said. "Look." She turned to the crowd. "They've been waiting for hours."

"Who is this man?" said Percy's priestly companion.

"It is poisoned, I tell you. Why would I lie, Matty?" I said.

She hesitated.

"Who would do such a thing as poison a soup kitchen?" said one of the grand ladies.

"Someone who wants to make chaos," said Blake, who had come up behind me.

"I think you must have eaten something that has not agreed with you, gentlemen," said Percy. "Come, Matty, we must begin."

"Matty," said Blake, "did you send to the kitchen to ask for Percy?"

"Soyer sent him. Didn't trust me in the end. But I'm doing all right, aren't I, Mr. Percy?"

"Very well indeed. Your mistake, Mr. Maguire: Monsieur Soyer sent me."

"That's not what Soyer said," said Blake. "In fact, he said the opposite."

Percy look mildly surprised. "He must have been distracted."

"Has he done anything? Has he put anything in the soup?" said Blake.

"He seasoned it, stirred it."

I turned to the muttering crowd. "The soup is not good! You cannot eat it!" I shouted. "There is no food here that is fit to eat. You must go home!"

"Looks all right to us. We was promised food!" someone cried. Some of the children started crying.

"I know, but it will make you ill. It has arsenic in it. You cannot eat it."

"We was promised!" someone else shouted. "We will have soup!" Another took up the chorus: "We're hungry. We will have soup!"

Blake said to Percy, "You eat it."

"I would be happy to."

"Get a bowl."

"These people need food—they are hungry. Would you deny them?" said Percy.

A bowl was brought, and a cheap tin spoon. The tent fell silent. I do not think the crowd could quite hear what had taken place, but they knew something significant was in the offing.

Percy smiled. He did nothing.

"Go on."

He looked at the soup. He smiled again and took up the spoon. Dipped it into the bowl.

"Why wait? Eat it."

Slowly, he brought the spoon to his lips. He smiled. He gazed at Blake.

He put the spoon down.

Shouts began at once. Then, suddenly, children and men were working their way round the tables, even climbing over them toward us.

"You from the station in Wood Street?" said Blake to the bemused constables. "One of you had better fetch your friends. The other can watch them." He pointed at the alarmed aldermen and grand ladies. "We'll do our best to keep them away from the boilers till you're back." Both wavered, then one began to push his way out.

"You're a churchman," he said to the vicar, or curate, or whatever he was. "Talk to them, calm them."

The churchman and his companion, plainly a local man, began appealing to the crowd for calm.

"We must wait to discover the truth of this," said the churchman.

"Patience is a virtue." Some of those at the front listened; others remained determined to get at the soup. People further back were intent on displaying their anger and disappointment. A table was knocked onto its side.

The children and many at the front shrank back to the side of the tent, looking terrified. One of the grand ladies began to cry piteously that they must escape. Blake's expression darkened. From inside his black coat, he drew out a knife that looked like an Indian dagger, and made a great slash in the back of the tent.

"This way, your majesties," he said. The constable held the rip open as the gentlemen and ladies climbed through, all dignity quite deserting them. After them, Blake beckoned a troop of scared children and those who were cowering away from the chaos.

"Get to the station," Blake said to the constable, and he nodded and made off into the evening as fast as he could.

Blake called to Matty; she shook her head.

"I'll watch him," she said. Percy had not moved. He stood just where he had been when he had put the spoon down.

Some of the constables from outside had pushed into the tent and were shouting for the crowd to disperse. Some began to leave, but others had more mischief in mind. Another table went over, and its benches. Some men seized the barrels of water; one was launched at a constable. Someone threw a glass at a gaslight and it splintered onto the crowd. Someone screamed. A group of people surged toward us.

One man shouted, "Poison us, would you?" Others were still calling, "We will have soup!"

For a few minutes, it was all we could do to keep ourselves standing. I found myself next to Blake. He smiled grimly.

"Perhaps we should sing the *Marseillaise*," he said.

Half the crowd were desperate to escape; others were knocking over tables and benches in rage. A group tried to slip round the side to reach the boiler. Blake and I ranged ourselves so these were directly behind us, but they were many and we were two.

"There's nothing for it. You'll have to upend it."

"But it is twice the size of me!"

"Use those iron ladles as a lever!" Blake said. He took out his knife and brandished it.

"So who wants some!" he roared, in primest cockney. That slowed them. Then, "Listen to me. The soup is poisoned. It will kill you. There'll be food—good food—tomorrow, I swear it."

To be honest, I had little hope of being able to dislodge the great boiler. It was made of iron and heavy with soup. I picked out the most robust tool I could see, a pair of double tongs half as long as me, and tried to wedge them under the drum.

"Here! Let me help!" Matty was next to me. There was a little space between the boiler's wheels and the ground. Together, we managed to insert the tongs in here. I pushed with all my might on the other end.

It rocked a little.

Blake was repeating again and again, "The soup is poisoned."

I pushed down again. It tipped a little, but not enough.

"Come on," said Matty. "Both of us, together." I cannot think of any other time when I should have asked such a thing of a woman, but we were desperate. Seeing us, however, a roar went up from our assailants and, as one, they swarmed past Blake, knocking him backward. There was nothing he could do to stop them.

"You cannot!" I shouted. But they pushed past me, too, toward the boiler. Instead of drinking from it, however, they lent their weight to overturning it. Like a tree being felled, the boiler was tipped sufficiently to begin to topple, then was brought down by its own weight. It went over with a heavy, gong-like sound. The liquid gushed onto the cobbles. Within moments, we were wading through its contents.

Then the gaslights went out. I scrabbled about, feeling the soup on my fingers. I called out for Matty. The sudden dark gave pause to the crowd, and the act of overturning the boiler seemed to have assuaged some of their anger. People turned to leave the tent. From the whistles and shouts and the gleam of a few lanterns, I assumed the constables were gaining the day. Near us, at the front, however, those who remained had now fixed upon Percy as the author of their troubles, though he was barely visible—just a dark outline in precisely the same place as he had been since the start.

"There he is! He's the one!" the cry went up. The vicar and his friend, the local worthy who had arrived at the tent so hopefully with Percy, were told to stand aside. To their credit, both refused and tried to reason with the protesters. Through the gloom I saw a man step onto the platform and push the vicar. He held his ground.

"Let us have him. He would have murdered us."

"We do not know what the truth is, lad," the local man in his Sunday best was saying. "Come now, I know you all. Would you judge a man without all the facts? We must wait. Let the police determine the truth."

I thought they would rush the platform.

"Matty!" Blake called.

"Here!" she cried. She was back with Percy. We could just make out their two figures. There was a large tent pole in the midst of the platform, and we were able to clamber around this without being noticed.

"We'll take Percy out through where I cut the tent," said Blake. Percy, who had said not a word, did as he was told, and we bundled him and Matty toward the hole that Blake had cut. The men were still in heated argument with the vicar, but a couple of them saw what we were up to.

"They are taking him!"

"He must not get away!"

Matty climbed through, then Percy and Blake. I was the last, standing before the hole. I raised my fists. In the darkness, I could not tell how many there were.

"Don't tempt me, boys. I like a good ruckus."

"Get out of our way."

"You go home. The police will have him. They will make sure he pays."

Someone came up close to me. "Ain't he the one who started all this? You were the one what said the soup was bad. You kept us hungry."

"Would you rather be hungry or dead?"

In hindsight, I see this might not have been the most judicious of answers.

I felt the air whisper as a fist passed my jaw by a hair. I shot back, a blow to the stomach and one to the face. There was a groan. Then someone jabbed me in the stomach and I doubled over. There was a hard boot in my chest—several boots, in fact—and I went over. Then more boots.

There were whistles and light. Shouts and more whistles. Voices calling for quiet. Buzzing round my ears.

Bluebottles, I thought.

Chapter Twenty-four

I raised myself onto my knees, carefully, then slowly tried to stand, not without difficulty. The tent was dimly illuminated by lanterns. It was enough, however, to see that the hungry had disappeared back to their rooms and that almost everything which could have been had been overturned, and many of the gaslights were broken. One side of the tent had collapsed. It had begun to rain, and around the upturned boiler the thick, scummy residue of the barley soup was driven into the ground by the drops.

I felt myself over gingerly. Bruised ribs—I hoped no worse—and a bloodied nose.

"It's him, sir. He was the one that started it." It was one of the two constables whom Blake had sent for help. "He said the soup was poisoned."

"Seems you have caused a riot, sir. I'll thank you to accompany us to the station."

. . .

SPITALFIELDS POLICE STATION was a former watch house on the corner of a churchyard, more like a cottage than a lock-up. But cells there were, and they leaked.

I endeavored to convince the sergeant that I was neither madman, nor roysterer, nor rascal, but the vicar and the grand ladies and gentlemen who had taken shelter in the station, as well as several rioters who were locked up in the other cell, were all more than happy to identify me as the man who had cried out that the soup was poisoned. Blake, Matty and Percy were nowhere to be seen.

"If you'll pardon me, sir," said the sergeant, who had a ponderous manner and a West Country accent, "since the offending item is now spread across the cobbles of Spitalfields Market, you have nothing with which to prove the poisonousness or otherwise of the comestible."

At last, one of the club's young cooks was brought in. He had been hiding in a back street, afeared for his life. He confirmed who I was and, with a great show of reluctance, the sergeant sent a message to the Reform. It was perhaps eleven by then. It seemed quite possible that no one would come till morning. I settled in for my second night in prison in three days. I wrapped myself up in my damp coat, closed my eyes and did my best to avoid the drops.

They came in the early hours: Blake and Soyer. The former silent, but finally divested of his mustache; the latter still resplendent in velvet, chattering, gesturing, smiling. The sergeant and the constables on duty were quite dazzled. They had known about the soup kitchen, of course, but to actually meet the famous Mr. Soyer! He set about explaining, extravagantly and at some length, that I had uncovered a terrible conspiracy concerning the poisoning of the soup kitchen and must be freed immediately.

The sergeant, charmed but not persuaded, said that I had incited a riot and could not simply be released, even to someone as august as Mr. Soyer.

At this, Blake, who had thus far said not a word, produced a letter signed by Sergeant Loin of the new Detecting branch of the Metropolitan Police. It said that my presence was required as soon as possible at the Reform Club, in connection with investigations into crimes committed there and with which the evening's events in Spitalfields were intimately entwined. In the process of these, it should come to light whether I had either caused an unjustified panic or had saved several hundred souls from a ghastly death. It invited the sergeant to send a constable to escort me.

With a great show of reluctance, the sergeant agreed. A cab was summoned from Bishopsgate, the constable climbed on top with the driver, and we set off.

"DOES MY WIFE KNOW where I was?" I asked.

Blake shook his head. "I told her you were required all night. Lord Palmerston's orders."

"You have Percy?" I said.

"He's at the club."

"Has he confessed?"

Blake laughed his mirthless laugh. "He won't speak. That is, he said two things: 'I would not taste the soup because Captain Avery was so certain it was poisoned,' and 'Morel is selling Soyer's recipes to Francobaldi.' Then nothing more. Loin says he can't hold him much longer."

"But the soup?"

"Did you take a sample?"

I shook my head.

"Nor I. We went back to the market, but the rain had washed it all away. We have no way of proving it was poisoned. Percy has admitted nothing. His rooms held nothing. His refusal to eat the soup means nothing."

"But Matty saw him season the soup."

"Nothing wrong with seasoning the soup."

"And Morel?"

Soyer spoke. "He has confessed to what he did." And he began to weep. "*Mes amis,* I am undone. Forgive me."

We rode for a while with no sound but the cab's rattling wheels and Soyer's sobs. I felt too all-in to do more than listen.

"I am torn in two," he said at last. "Tonight was a triumph, the dinner a *triomphe*! Even Lord Palmerston was delighted. Tonight, I lost both my trusted lieutenants. Two men I thought I could trust above anyone. Tonight, you saved many lives and the soup kitchen was—*un désastre*. But I know it can work. And what will the newspapers say? Am I destroyed?"

"There's a good chance Avery will be proved to be a mad troublemaker. In which case, you will be the innocent victim of his insanity," said Blake drily.

"You told me it was poison!" I said.

"And you always do what I tell you."

Soyer dried his eyes and laughed.

"Why don't you send all that's left from the banquet to the soup kitchen?" said Blake.

"That is an excellent notion!" said Soyer excitedly. "There is a great deal of food. The guests were—how shall I say?—a little cautious in their appetites. We will make amends for last night! It will be remarkable! I myself will supervise it."

"How did you manage the letter from Loin? I assume it is a forgery," I said.

"I went to see him, explained things," said Blake.

"You mean you revealed yourself to him?"

"He has given me a few hours to see what I can gather about Percy. I return to the Marshalsea tomorrow."

"So we shall both be going to prison."

I COULD HAPPILY have never passed through the Reform's elegant doors again.

Percy sat in the kitchen at the twelve-sided table. With him were Loin, a couple of constables and Lord Marcus, who dozed at the far end. Percy sat quite still, sometimes looking ahead and sometimes down at the table. It was almost as if he was somewhere else. He seemed not to hear the exchanges around him.

"Has he spoken?" said Blake.

"Not a word," said Loin.

"Have you the soup?" said Loin.

Blake shook his head. "There was nothing left."

Percy permitted himself a smile. Loin looked as if the air had been squeezed out of him.

"Sergeant Loin? May I?" said Blake. He sat down next to Percy. Their knees touched. "Such a grand plan, on such a grand scale, Percy." There was a long pause. "Such care over so many months, and executed so stealthily. Concealed so cleverly." Again, he paused. He had never been discomfited by silence, but we, the listeners, all strained for an answer. "Do you not want to explain it? Do you not want people to understand how sharp you were? You must burst to."

Percy did not answer, but he did move his knees. Blake waited. Finally, Percy allowed himself to look at Blake.

"I am honored to think that you consider me worthy of attention, Mr. Blake," he said. Then, almost pityingly, "But I have nothing to explain. I do not need to be *understood*. I did not poison anyone. You cannot prove I did."

"But you hate him—Soyer—don't you? A few hours since, you were licking his boots as if your life depended upon it. Now, you will not even look at him."

Percy looked away.

"How cleverly you have deprived him of those he relied on: Morel, and Perrin, and yourself. You probably helped Soyer's secretaries on their way, too? And I thought you liked Matty. You knew where she'd come from, what she'd come through. But you had Margaret inform against her and made her a suspect, all the same. Used her handwriting for the notes to Soyer—so easy to find the recipes she'd written. Then you put that pot of arsenic just where Perrin could not see it but would reach for it. You are an observant man. Perrin works hard to conceal his short sight. And you knew all about Morel's collusion with Francobaldi, but refrained from telling Soyer until he was at his lowest point."

"I have done nothing that is against the law," said Percy mildly.

"You've half broken this kitchen with suspicion and fear. Destroyed the suppliers' trust in Soyer and the kitchen. Almost brought down this club. And tried to poison hundreds of hungry men, women and children. It must truly be a mighty hatred."

Percy met his gaze but said nothing.

"When did it start? Soyer said you asked him to take you on. Did you admire him then, or did you always hate him? Or did it change when he stopped letting you pad your pockets? Or is it that you cannot see why you are not the master here? You should have been a doctor, a respected man of independent means, if your father had not lost his business."

"Oh, *spare* me," said Percy.

It came to me that Blake did not expect Percy to confess but was making the case to Loin.

"And the poison. I thought at first that you were testing your dosages. Now I think you were quite decided on your methods: a slow, drawn-out stirring up of fear and confusion. Then strychnine, as well as arsenic, just to show them it was no accident. Poison is the worst of deaths, don't you think? Takes all a man's dignity and gives him unendurable pain. And, of all poisons, strychnine—it's a monstrous death. Most who use it don't know how cruel it is. But you knew, didn't you?"

Percy gave him a strange look. It reminded me of nothing so much as a benevolent uncle indulging a young nephew. It was infuriating.

"How did you do it, Percy? My bet is you put it in the wine. Tipping in a few grains before you poured a glass. Tell me, Percy, I know you want to, I know you do."

Percy lowered his eyes.

"When did you decide that it would be the soup kitchen and not the banquet? Was that always your plan? And how many did you expect to harm? A hundred, two hundred? Only, say, fifty? Likely more, because the Spitalfields poor are ill-fed and their bodies have little to fight the poison with."

"Not necessarily," said Percy.

"Not necessarily?" Blake said.

"Not necessarily. A healthy body will succumb to poison just as a sick one will. It simply takes a little longer." There was a silence. "As you say, I had some doctoring training."

"And all to discredit one man." Blake sat back, and the room was quite still. "Sometimes I find myself wishing I still believed in hell."

"I poisoned no one, Mr. Blake. You have no evidence for it, only your own suppositions."

"You must admit, Percy, that your current manner is strange enough to raise suspicion," I said.

Percy paid me no heed. "Why are you here, Mr. Blake?" he said, almost kindly. "Are you not due back in prison in only an hour or two?"

Blake stood up. "Last chance."

Percy did not answer.

"I'm off," Blake said.

The policeman nodded. "Make the most of your freedom, Mr. Blake. You have a few hours before morning."

I followed him to the door.

"Stay here," said Blake. "Tell Loin your story."

"Is Matty safe?" I said.

"She's abed. Wake her after dawn. She can give an account of seeing Percy adding something to the soup—it's something."

"So there is nothing to keep him?"

"Not nothing, but not enough."

"And what will you do? I mean, I would understand if you chose to go. To take that ship. You cannot live in Collinson's pocket. Maybe now is the time."

He touched me gently on the arm. I watched him walk away.

I gave my account of the soup kitchen and the riot to Loin.

"Come, Mr. Percy, don't you have something to say about this?" said Loin, rubbing his eyes when I had finished.

Percy inhaled, examined his cuffs and gave a vague smile.

Loin scowled. He began to question Percy, to cajole and shout and thump the table. Not once did Percy speak, nor even look at him.

Soyer sat down by him. "Please, Percy," he said, his voice thick with emotion, "if you ever held me in esteem, speak. What have I done to so offend you?"

Percy looked straight ahead as if Soyer were not there.

"I thought we understood each other. Have I not treated you well? Say something. Exonerate yourself. Anything. Explain. But please, I cannot lose you and Morel and Perrin."

Percy turned away from him.

I fell in and out of sleep, my head resting on the table. Loin continued to ask questions, which Percy continued to ignore. The hours passed. Lord Marcus eventually took himself upstairs to find a bed. One of the constables asked Loin in a low voice why they did not simply take Percy to the cells, even if they could not arrest him. Loin muttered that they must wait for Mr. Blake. Soyer went to sleep in his office.

Would Blake return? A part of me wished him on that ship to America, away from Collinson's sinister influence. But then Percy would likely go free and I would be back in jail, charged with incitement to riot. Loin disappeared to sleep. The constables continued to watch Percy, who sat upright, apparently oblivious to us all, eyes open, no sign of fatigue. Loin reappeared. It was dawn.

I WENT TO RAISE MATTY. I found her asleep on the top step of the servants' stairs, her head on the bare boards, her body on the stone step, a shawl wrapped about her. My footfall roused her.

"You are safe," she said, stretching. "They sent me to bed. But I thought I might be needed. Has he confessed?"

"No. He will not speak." I sat down next to her. "You would not happen to have a bowl of the soup about you? We have no proof that it was poisoned, you see. I was arrested for causing a riot. I think my defense may very well rest on it."

"Oh no, I've nothing. What became of the rest?"

"It spilled over the cobbles of Spitalfields Market."

"And Mr. Loin says Blake is going back to prison."

"But you'll say what you saw? That you saw him add something and stir it?"

"It looked like salt. He stirred it into the soup and, now I think of it, he did not taste it after."

"I am sure what you have to say will be of use."

"I thought he was my friend," she said. "I trusted him. When we came back here he was so cold."

I took her hand and squeezed it gently. "There are still people you can trust. Soyer. Mrs. Relph, Blake, me. After all this, Matty, you must stay here. You cannot give up."

"I don't know . . ."

"Soyer will need you. He has lost Morel, and Percy. Maybe Perrin. And you have come so far."

"I don't know if it's for me. There are people here who hate me. Maybe my place is on the street."

"Everyone knows you were sinned against, and they were glad when you were freed. Your place was never on the street. The world is full of faithless, weak people, but you are not weak and you should have faith in yourself."

"You'll be going soon, won't you?" she said.

I nodded. I could not bring myself to tell her about Helen.

We sat quietly for some time.

WHEN WE RETURNED to the kitchen so Matty could give her account, there was still no sign of Blake but the scullery and kitchen maids had begun the daily round of scrubbing and washing. Percy had been taken to the butler's pantry, where he sat, unchangingly silent and blank, occasionally smiling to himself, his mind apparently somewhere else. He could not be kept at the Reform much longer.

Loin took me aside. "I will take Percy up to Scotland Yard for questioning, but I will not be able to keep him long."

"Blake will come," I said. "I assure you."

"I am not sure your assurances are worth much when it comes to Mr. Blake," said Loin.

"Just a few more minutes."

"He will not come," said Loin, drumming his fingers. He did not.

Loin sighed and decided they must leave. The constables hauled Percy roughly to his feet and pushed him out into the corridor. Blake was there, waiting and whistling nonchalantly.

"I thought you'd be an hour or two," said Loin crossly. "We've waited all night."

"Give me a moment." Blake returned a few moments later, holding Margaret by the arm. She looked sallow, and her cheeks were sunken, as if she had been wrung out.

When she saw Percy she turned to flee, but Blake caught her. We returned to the butler's pantry: me, Loin, Matty, Percy and the three constables. Blake walked Margaret into the room. I realized she was leaning upon him.

"Sergeant Loin, this is Margaret. She needs something to eat and drink, something simple. Until two days ago, she worked at the Reform as a kitchen maid. She was dismissed the night before last, at Percy's behest. Tell him what you saw, Margaret."

"I was waiting in his rooms the morning before I was dismissed, that's to say, the day before yesterday." She was breathless. "I—I had a look about. Under his bed I found three big bags of white powder. I knew what it was, because it was the same as the bags that I seen locked in the poisons cupboard."

"What was it, Margaret?"

"It was white arsenic, sir." There was a dead silence in the room.

"And what happened next?"

"I don't know how it happened, but I knocked over one of the bags and the powder went everywhere." She shivered at the recollection. "I did my best to scoop it up and put it back in the bag. I was so frightened of what he'd do if he came back and found me there with it. It got all over my fingers, so I ran from the room to wash them. I didn't know what to do."

"Why didn't you tell anyone, Margaret?" said Blake.

"I was going to, honest, but then the banquet was happening again. I thought if I said anything, they'd think I was in on it. So I went to talk to him. I was frightened, but I didn't know what else to do. I said I'd seen what was under the bed. I wouldn't tell anyone, but he had to get rid of it. I offered to help. He wasn't angry like I expected; he said it wasn't what I thought, and we'd get rid of it that night. But I needed to do something for him first. I shouldn't have believed him, but I wanted to."

"May I ask," said Loin disapprovingly, "what the girl was doing in Mr. Percy's room in the first place?"

"Margaret?"

In a small voice, she said, "I was Mr. Percy's mistress. He said he loved me, and that he'd see I was made first kitchen maid. He bought me presents: a brooch, a hat, a shawl—I can show you them. I was in his room that morning because the kitchen was shut and I had no duties. We'd gone there together, but then he was called away. He had to leave me there; no one could see me come out—I'd be dismissed. I'd never been in his room alone before, so I had a look about."

"Why, she's nothing more than a fallen woman spurned!" said Loin angrily.

Percy looked her at her with mild distaste.

"Life is muddy and untidy, Loin, you know that," said Blake. "Let her speak. Tell us what it was that he wanted you to do before you disposed of the arsenic."

She hesitated, and brushed a hair from her eyes with a shaking hand. "He asked me to accept Mr. Scott's attentions."

"Had this happened before?" said Blake.

"Yes," she said dully. "I loved him. You do anything for the man you love, don't you?" She looked about at us, entreatingly, but always avoiding Percy. "It meant he had something over Scott. We all hated Mr. Scott, I reckoned it was a good thing."

"Was there a reason Mr. Percy wanted something on Scott?"

"He told the committee what Mr. Percy was up to with the skimming and all to save his own skin. He told me he'd have Scott, but he promised I'd be kept out of it. I see I was stupid to believe him now. He brought Mrs. Quill and the captain"—she nodded at me—"to Scott's rooms that night when I was there. He never said he was coming."

"What happened?" said Blake.

"I had my bag and I was leaving when he found me and asked me to come to his room to talk. I hoped he would explain, or give me a bit of money. He said he was sorry; Mrs. Quill had found out about Scott and there was nothing he could do. I didn't believe him. He poured me a glass of brandy. He said it was for old times' sake. I knew then he wanted rid of me, and what the arsenic was for. He told me to drink. I didn't want to"—she became breathless again—"but he was watching me. So I took a sip and pretended to swallow it, and smiled. He turned away, and I spat it back into the glass and held my hand over it so he couldn't see. I didn't mention the arsenic at all; I said I needed money. He told me to have another sip. I was frightened and so I did. I spat it out into my handkerchief, but then he made me have a third and, that time, I had to swallow it. Then I asked him for money. He turned nasty on me, said I must leave and that if he ever saw me again he would kill me. I ran. I thought I was going to die. I had nowhere to go. I found a doorway in Crown Passage and sat down in it. Later—I don't know how long afterward—I was very sick." She said, in a quieter voice, more shamed I thought by this than by her previous confession, "It was like my innards were burning."

It explained her pallor and wretched look.

"You believe he poisoned you?"

"I'd swear to it. But it didn't kill me, I didn't drink that much. In the morning—yesterday—I got myself up to Piccadilly. I saw the captain; I wanted to tell him about Mr. Percy. But he wouldn't talk to me. Don't blame him. But I was too sick and frightened to come back here. I crawled back to Crown Passage and lay there until Mr. Maguire—Mr. Blake—came and found me."

"Were there other things Percy asked you to do before you were dismissed?"

"Yes. He said Chef was so vain he couldn't see things under his own nose and deserved a bit of mischief in his kitchen. With me, he used to make fun of Soyer. He told me once that, when he came to work for Soyer, he thought he was a god, a genius, but now he knew he was the Napoleon of fools. That is what he called him. It started with Chef's secretaries. Throwing away their papers, putting powders in their drinks so they'd oversleep. Little things, here and there, 'cept they did all end up leaving."

"And Hastings Bland?"

"Percy took his meat and never paid for it. He told Chef he sent it back because it was bad. I swore the meat was bad. I said I was there when he got rid of it. He sold it off himself after. He was proud of it. Bought me a brooch. When Bland complained, he swore Bland was sending bad meat. Why would anyone disbelieve him? He was loyal Mr. Percy. There was another week when he said he didn't have enough in the accounts to pay for prime meat. Soyer was somewhere—with some duke or something—

Morel was elsewhere. He persuaded the butcher to take some meat that was no good from another supplier. He laughed about it later. He kept the money. I think it happened with other orders, too."

"Anything else?"

"He told me to say I suspected Matty of the poisonings." She ducked her head. Matty gave a small gasp. Margaret did not look at her. "I had sway with some of the girls and cooks, convinced them, too. I was surprised when he told me, but I didn't like her, so I can't say I was that unwilling. I thought maybe he was doing it for me—I was supposed to have that kitchen maid's job, and she just walked in, played up to Soyer, and they all fell for it. Well, she's won that one now."

"He never told you what he wanted out of this?"

She shook her head. "I didn't ask. He didn't like me to. He'd get angry. He could be so cold. Struck me now and then. But that's men for you. Once, he said he should have been a doctor and a surgeon, but it was taken from him. He said his father lost everything and he was forced into servitude. He said, one day, we would escape to the higher station we deserved. He only said it once, but I remembered it, because I thought it meant he'd take me with him."

"And what has prompted this sudden confession?" said Loin.

"Mr. Maguire—Mr. Blake—found me." She looked up at Blake. "He'd sort of guessed it all. He told me I couldn't hang for what I'd done, I was just Mr. Percy's pawn. He said, if I told, Soyer might give me my character back. And"—she brought her now tear-stained face up and gave us all a look of implausibly girlish contrition—"I wanted to tell the truth."

"Have you anything to say, Percy?" said Loin.

Percy looked away.

"Tell them, Margaret," said Blake.

"When I left his room, I took the glass with me. I hid it in the linen cupboard just down from his room. It should still be there with what's left in it. The cupboard's rarely used." She drew something from her pocket and put it on the table. "This is the handkerchief I spat the brandy into. Mr. Blake said it would be useful."

I could have kissed her.

"Mr. Wakley can test the contents for arsenic," said Blake. "And I'd have him look under Percy's bed."

For the first time since he had arrived, Loin's scowl disappeared. He stood up and shook Blake's hand. "Well done, sir," he said, and sent a constable to retrieve the glass.

A snort came from the hitherto silent Percy. "This proves nothing. The girl is just revenging herself on me because I let her go. That handkerchief could have come from anywhere."

Margaret looked at him.

"How can you say that? See his true face? Cold and cruel." She fell back into her chair, exhausted, and Blake gave her some water. She took a sip.

Percy stared at the wall.

"After I found Margaret," Blake said, "I went to see if I could find where the arsenic had come from. I knew it wasn't on the Reform's books, because all their orders were accounted for, and I had visited all the druggists the club ordered from, and anyone besides within two miles. But there's a wholesaler in hard goods near Spitalfields. I went back there, got them to open up. Over the last four months, they have had three orders for a large bag of arsenic for the Reform Club. All ordered by post or messenger boy. I've each of them here. One was signed by Morel, one by Scott and one by Mrs. Quill. I'd swear Percy was responsible for all of them; if he was falsifying accounts, I'd bet he can manage a little forgery."

The constable returned with the glass in which there was still almost half an inch of brandy left.

"Will you come make a statement, girl? And you, Matty?" said Loin.

Margaret nodded.

They hauled Percy to his feet. Loin announced he was arresting him. Percy did not respond.

We trooped out into the morning. There was a chill, but the sky was clear. We stood on Pall Mall, Blake and I, Loin, his constables, Margaret, Matty and Percy.

Loin took Blake aside. "I imagine you have a good deal to be getting on with," he muttered. "I see no reason to keep you. I'll have Perrin released and see what I can manage about the charges against the captain. If Collinson wants you, he can find you. Not that I said that. I'll deny it if I'm asked."

Blake blinked—the only indication that he was surprised; that he understood that, for the moment, he was free. He said to Percy, "Was it the wine?" The question was posed almost carelessly.

Percy smiled. "I did nothing, Mr. Blake."

Loin turned on his heel, and his entourage followed him. We watched them snake up Pall Mall.

"Why?" I said. "All this destruction for what?"

"He was jealous of Soyer. Didn't Ude tell you that envy is the guiding sin of the kitchen?"

"But Percy said he loved Soyer at first."

"I reckon his admiration was always tempered by envy. He felt he should not have been in service at all. When the club became such a success and Soyer more famous than anyone could have expected, his admiration curdled. And when Soyer told him he must stop skimming and then forced on him the indignity of saving him, I reckon he truly hated him. He designed a plan to destroy Soyer's reputation and exploit his rivals' weaknesses so that, when all was done, he would be the only man left: calm, capable Percy."

I felt the horror of the week slip, just a little, from my shoulders. There was a hawker on the street selling the *Morning Chronicle*. The headline on the front page ran: "Ibrahim Pasha Royally Entertained at the Reform Club. Soyer Triumphant Again."

Blake bestirred himself. I tried to think of something to distract him.

"When did you know it was Percy?" I said. "How did you read him?"

"There was something about him. Too correct, too solicitous—I don't know. But I had no proof, and I'm not always right. I can't say exactly how it works. I just watch people: the smallest gestures—a twitch, a yawn, a blink. How they hold their hands. Where they put their feet."

"Where did it come from? From when you were in India? Before?"

He knew what I was getting at, but he spoke anyway.

"For the two summers before I was sent to Calcutta, my pa sent me off with a man called Big Ned to work the summer fairs. I was one less mouth to feed. They started me out picking pockets. There was a woman, a great, fat dame who called herself 'Madam Cagliostro, handmaid of the fates.' She wore an old red turban stuck with paste rubies, and told fortunes. Sometimes I'd steal something from her customers and, if she felt like it, she'd give it back at the end—magic! They didn't even know it had gone. They'd leave full of wonder. Then I began to drum up custom. The old madam, she saw something in me. Said I had the gab, the eye and the memory. I'd walk the fair to bring her customers. Sometimes she'd give me a little bag of humbugs or licorice. I'd watch people and ask them questions in such a way that they didn't see what they were giving me. Then I'd tell her what I'd observed, all they'd said, but she'd also say, 'What did their mouth look like when they said that? How much did they scratch? What did they do with their hands?' She used everything, and made such good use of it. She'd tell them about themselves and they'd be amazed at what she knew. And I was amazed, too. I watched her whenever I could. When I was taken up in India by the Secret Department, they discovered I could do this, but they started me looking for lies, for what was not being said. It became second nature."

"When I was a boy, I dreamed of running off to the fair," I said wistfully.

"I would have been the one who took your sixpence and knocked you into the mud. On a good day, I might have taken your boots."

We stood and looked at each other.

"Well," I said, "What's it to be? America? The Marshalsea? Groveling to Collinson? Sleeping for a hundred hours?"

"Breakfast," he said.

Historical Afterword

Alexis Soyer (1810–1858) deserves to be far better known than he is. The second of the three great French chefs who came to Britain in the nineteenth century and became giants in the history of food (the other two were Marie-Antoine Carême and Auguste Escoffier), Soyer is perhaps the least well known, but he is, I think, the most fun, the most modern and, arguably, the most influential beyond the confines of the grand kitchen.

He was the first real celebrity chef, a brilliant, inventive cook and a shameless self-publicist. In style, one might describe him as part Heston Blumenthal, part Jamie Oliver. He had a line in crazy (and, to our palates, probably slightly disgusting) fantasy dishes (for example, desserts made to look like roast lamb with all the trimmings) and, at the same time, a genuine mission to educate the British—the British poor, in particular—to eat better and more nutritiously. From his early thirties, he was in London and involved in improving the food in hospitals and workhouses. He published a series of best-selling cookery books, from impossibly complicated recipes for other professionals (*The Gastronomic Regulator*, from which many of the dishes in this book come) through a household-management manual for middle-class women that predated Mrs. Beeton by twelve years (*The Modern Housewife*), to his highly influential *A Shilling Cookery for the People*.

He was a champion of seasonal and simple dishes: the energetically sociable writer W. M. Thackeray would cancel prior arrangements in order to eat his bacon and beans. (Thackeray also endlessly ribbed him in the pages of *Punch* magazine and portrayed him in his novel *Pendennis* in the guise of the ridiculous Frenchman Mirobolant.) Soyer was also, for his time, unusually generous to female cooks. He said he liked having them in his kitchen; they were better tempered and less dramatic than men. We know that he credited one of the Reform's kitchen maids with helping him turn his ideas into recipes that ordinary people could use, and he admired a cook at the Russian Embassy called Miss Frederick, who helped him with big catering jobs on several occasions.

He comes over as an irrepressible, joyous, sometimes ridiculous figure, manically energetic, dreadfully sycophantic to the rich and titled (who were often unpleasantly snooty in return), appallingly pretentious (he called the gas stove he invented the Phidomageireion—apparently, Greek for "thrifty kitchen") and barely literate—in English, at least, relying on a series of secretaries to transcribe his words. He seems to have been terrible with money.

He was also a brilliant logistician, inventor and innovator on a grand scale. In 1855, he went out to the Crimean War at his own expense to overhaul the desperate state of army catering, and ended up completely reorganizing the entire provisioning of the British Army. In the course of this, he invented a portable army stove that used a tenth of the fuel of the army's previous arrangements, and which it continued to use until the 1950s. It is, perhaps, not surprising that he died aged only forty-eight, in 1858.

. . .

Although this book is entirely fictional, many of the events described did actually take place, though I have played about with the dates. For example, the Reform Club did hold a fabulously grand and complicated banquet for Ibrahim Pasha, conqueror of Syria and son of the elderly ruler of Egypt, Mehmet Pasha (who was regarded by the British as a dangerous troublemaker), but it took place in 1846, not 1842. The menu included the dishes I describe, and the papers went mad for it, the *Globe* writing, "The impression grows on us that the man of his age is neither Sir Robert Peel . . . nor even Ibrahim Pasha, but Alexis Soyer."

Soyer did reinvent the soup kitchen, but in 1847. He came up with a thirteen-foot, three-hundred-gallon soup boiler on wheels, and a steam bread oven that could bake nine thousand four-pound loaves in twelve hours, both of which could be heated by one fire. He set up a prototype in Spitalfields for the local silk weavers made destitute by cheap, mass-produced silk, then took it to Ireland during the famine, where it served nine thousand meals a day. In 1850, he prepared the Royal Agricultural Society's annual banquet, feeding a thousand hungry farmers in Exeter. There was so much food left over that Soyer arranged a second dinner the next day for the town's poor.

The Reform Club, with which Soyer's reputation was so deeply intertwined (he spent thirteen years there), was set up in 1837 by a group of radical MPs, including William Molesworth, very much as described in this book. The radicals had by now combined with the more conservative Whigs and were informally known as the liberal party, but they were outnumbered and outgunned by the Whigs, who kept control of the party for another twenty years. Although some of the radicals strained against their collaboration with the Whigs, nothing as dramatic as the events recounted in this book ever took place. Molesworth remained a radical all his life and was the only one to serve in the liberal government of 1853.

When the Reform Club's grand new building opened in Pall Mall in 1841, its kitchens were quickly dubbed "the Eighth Wonder of the World," the most modern, the most advanced of their kind, and thousands turned up to take tours of them. They were full of practical, ingenious ideas invented and designed by Soyer himself, and were the first large kitchens to use gas ovens in which the temperature could be adjusted. Soyer was a great advocate of gas, which was far cleaner, safer and cheaper than wood and charcoal, and predicted that, one day, the whole world would cook with it. The Reform soon became better known for its delicious dinners than its politics.

Throughout his time at the Reform Club, Soyer had a stormy relationship with its committee. He was censured for insolence and, in 1844, for financial dishonesty, when he was accused, along with the butler and the kitchen clerk, of having falsified the butcher's account. Some accounts suggest that he was covering for his staff. A vote to sack him was defeated by seven votes to six, and he resigned in outrage. It was only through the careful management of Lord Marcus Hill, the club chairman, that he got his job back. The matter left a permanent bitterness in his relations with the club.

Incidentally, the club's first secretary was called Walter Scott, and he was sacked within months of taking the job, for incompetence and for "entertaining" housemaids in his rooms.

Even for the Victorians, poisoning was the quintessential Victorian crime, although it's likely that poisonings were just as prevalent during the decades before Victoria came to the throne. Arsenic (the doyen of domestic poisons) and strychnine had been cheap and easily available—used largely for killing vermin—for decades. What changed in the Victorian era was that chemists began to come up with tests which proved the presence of poison. English chemist James Marsh devised the first test to reliably prove the presence of arsenic in 1836.

Trials involving poisoners reached their height in the 1840s, when there were ninety-eight poisoning trials in Britain; virtually all were domestic crimes. Many of the defendants—though by no means all—were women, and poor working-class women at that. In 1843, Elizabeth Eccles and Sarah Dazley were both executed for poisoning: Eccles killed five of her children and a stepson (though she was also suspected of having poisoned at least five other, earlier children); Dazley poisoned her first and second husbands, and her son. Poisoning might be used as a means to collect on that marvelous new invention, life insurance (which one could take out on a family member without them knowing), to knock off a difficult spouse or get rid of expensive extra mouths to feed.

I have to confess that I have found no cases of deliberate mass poisonings such as the book describes but, in 1858 in Bradford, two hundred people were poisoned, of whom twenty-one died, after eating sweets accidentally made with arsenic. The confectioner had intended to bulk out his sweets with plaster of Paris but mistakenly bought arsenic.

Food contamination, food adulteration and food scares are subjects which return again and again, as the 2013 horse-meat scandal reminds us. Food adulteration was a massive issue in Victorian Britain, where food was unregulated and frequently mixed with all kinds of horrible things in order to make it cheaper, or go further, or look more attractive. Bee Wilson, in her history of food scares and adulteration, *Swindled*, gives a terrific account of this. The first great public health and anti-adulteration food campaigner was Thomas Wakley, founding editor of

The Lancet, still one of the world's leading medical journals. Week after week, he exposed evidence of food swindling. Legislation didn't arrive until 1860. For years, his stories were received with apathy, and often opposition; plenty of free traders reckoned that a bit of harmless adulteration was OK, it was simply a profitable form of competition.

In the early 1850s, incidentally, Wakley and his researcher Arthur Hassall discovered that Crosse & Blackwell were putting "a very considerable amount of COPPER" in their bottled gooseberries and pickled gherkins, and lead oxide in their tinned anchovies, to turn them red.

In 1851, a Swiss doctor called Johann Jakob von Tschudi published a scientific paper about a group of peasants of the Lower Austrian Alps who had been taking normally lethal doses of arsenic for generations because they claimed it gave women a rosy complexion and men more energy, that it helped digestion, prevented disease and increased sexual potency. When they stopped taking it, they experienced withdrawal symptoms. There had been rumors about these Styrian peasants for decades, but now the story became a sensation around the world, and for a while there was a fad among fashionable Londoners for consuming neat arsenic.

Acknowledgments

I'd like to acknowledge—and recommend—a few of the books I consulted and read during the writing of this book, and from which I have stolen brazenly. There are a number of biographies of Alexis Soyer. In my opinion, the best and most enjoyable by far is Ruth Cowen's *Relish*. For Victorian food scares, I plundered *Swindled: The Dark History of Food Fraud*, by the excellent food writer Bee Wilson. Rather to my surprise, there really are a lot of good books about poison! I'd recommend John Emsley's *The Elements of Murder: A History of Poison* and, even more highly, Gail Bell's terrific *The Poison Principle*, a book that takes in family memoir, the history of poisons and her own career as a chemist. For the Reform Club, I relied on George Woodbridge's *The Reform Club, 1836–1978*, and *Reformed Characters: The Reform Club in History and Literature*, edited by Russell Burlingham and Roger Billis.

I'd like to say a big thank-you to the people who have so helped me on this book over a difficult time: my long-serving (and probably long-suffering)

U.K. editor, Juliet Annan; assistant editor Anna Steadman; and my U.S. editor, Sara Minnich—all three completely invaluable. Thanks also to my excellent copyeditors Sarah Day and Dorian Hastings, the always indefatigable Caroline Pretty, and my U.K. and U.S. publicists, the lovely Sara D'Arcy and Katie McKee. And, of course, my agent of twenty-two years, Bill Hamilton. Finally, thanks to John Lanchester. He knows what for.